# Born in the BRIAR PATCH

Bev Clarke

ISBN: 1-4392-3247-4
EAN13: 9781439232477

Visit www.booksurge.com to order additional copies.

The fiery evening sun was setting as the group of barefooted plantation workers struggled home from a hard day in the fields. With fatigue etched across their faces and the hoes and forks across their shoulders moving to the rhythm of their bodies, rest was the only thing on their minds. The men, walking at a faster pace led the group with the older women following closely behind. Bringing up the rear was a mixed group of young men and women, who in spite of a tiresome day were still enjoying each other's company.

Sarah Bottomsley was observing all this from her upstairs window. They passed beside the concrete wall which separated the Great House from the alley way which led to their huts. She noticed that some of the women were in the family way. Still staring at them she ran her hand over her bulging belly. It would be her second child. The first was stillborn. How she envied these women who seemed to have no problems with their pregnancies. They toiled all day in the fields, but brought healthy and robust babies into the world. Miss Una who had learned the midwifery skills from her mother was usually called upon to assist with their deliveries. Their carefree spirit saddened her. Here she was, mistress of Bottomsley plantation envying those people whose standard of living could in no way possibly compare with hers.

Born into a well-to-do family, she had been squired away to live on the Caribbean island of Barbados by the handsome and rugged plantation owner John Bottomsley. He was not a terribly well-educated man nor was he affluent, but he had a good head on his shoulders and knew he could make it in the colonies. Love triumphed and Sarah found herself by his side, trying to cope with the hot sticky weather. She could never get used to the heat and it was all compounded by her parents' hatred of the colonial world. John Bottomsley on the other hand loved the island life. He could be seen on his favourite horse riding around the plantation inspecting his crops, which afforded them a very comfortable lifestyle. From sunrise to sunset, he would oversee the running of the plantation. He watched as the workers carefully planted the sugar cane suckers which would eventually bring him the bulk of his fortune.

The closest Sarah Bottomsley came to sugar was having it placed on the table for her cup of sweet tea. She knew nothing of the hardship of planting, caring for nor the reaping of sugar cane. Nothing mattered to her except those fields of long blades which looked like grass kept her in the lifestyle to which she was accustomed. Since she had become pregnant, he had moved to another bedroom. She missed him but was comfortable being alone, especially during the hot and sticky summer nights. She also knew that after dinner, when she had retired for the evening, he would slip out of the house. She never questioned him perhaps because the truth might have been too painful. She pictured her husband with one of the daughters of another plantation owner who was only too eager to jump in and fill her position. There were very few eligible white men on the island and many of these young girls found themselves going to England to find suitable husbands, and still for others a married man was not a problem. Sarah knew her husband loved her, but she could not be a wife to him now, especially in the way he needed a wife, so she closed her eyes to his many indiscretions.

She was still at the window when the smut lamps were lit outside the workers' huts; an empty bottle filled with kerosene and rags for the wick was all they could afford. This did not detract from their happiness as they assembled outside and sat and laughed together. She could see their shiny black faces from the glow of the lamps which they placed in a hollow on the bare earth. With the help of the wind, the black smoke and the smell of kerosene worked their way up to her nostrils. Each Friday evening after receiving their wages, they would line up outside the small grocery store which Mr. Polgreen ran on behalf of their employer. There they would purchase their week's supply of kerosene, corn meal, flour, sugar, rice and other farm produce which the owner grew for their sustenance.

Mr. Polgreen was not a friendly man. He thought he was there just to weigh their produce, accept their money and have them out the door as soon as possible. Each one of them secretly hated him because of his indifference towards them. Should one of his friends or countrymen enter the shop, it was understood that the workers would step back and wait until he had happily chatted with and looked after them; then grudgingly he would continue to serve the field hands. He considered himself of a higher class although he was never seen as a guest at the Bottomsley dinner table. If he felt generous, he would sell them the rice bags for one shilling. Emblazoned across these sacks were the words 'Demerara, B.G.' The poorest of poor used these bags to make clothing for themselves and their children. For these unfortunate ones, there was no end to their being teased.

Sarah's thoughts were disturbed when Nellie her housemaid entered the room.

"What is it Nellie?" she asked in an impatient manner.

"You waiting on the master for dinner Miss Sarah?" she asked in pidgin English.

"That's a stupid question. You know we always eat together in the evening."

"Today is Friday ma'am and he always come home late on Fridays."

"Oh yes. It *is* Friday. I forgot about that. Then I'll eat alone," she replied without turning her head.

"Yes ma'am," said Nellie quickly leaving the room.

The laughter from below caught her attention again. She listened closely but couldn't hear everything that was being said, but she knew they were telling stories which had been passed down from generation to generation. The older children gazed into the story teller's face while the younger ones played a version of hide and seek. The Grandmas sat on their wooden stools and bounced the younger children on their knees. She had heard the words time and time again.

Trouble tree don't bear no blossom.
Trouble tree don't bear no blossom.
Trouble tree don't bear no blossom,
Come along here let me kick you in your bottom.

Nellie and Miss Ella the cook were now even more urgent in their meal preparation since they did not want to incur Sarah Bottomsley's wrath.

"You know Miss Ella," said Nellie, "one day I going to be just like the mistress."

"What kind of nonsense is that?" Miss Ella asked hands akimbo.

"You know how Miss Sarah does dress up in those long dresses and does always smell real good?"

"Nellie, don't look at the nice clothes. You look in the mistress face? Miss Sarah ain't a happy woman."

"Why you think that Miss Ella?"

"Child, you ever see Miss Sarah smiling? She longing to be a mother, but it just ain't happening, and the master eyes seem to be straying. We don't have the fancy clothes and pretty house, but we happy. When I go to church on Sunday, I always pray to be happy. Although we got to sit down behind them in all their fancy clothes, the good Lord still looking down on us with the same two eyes. But Nellie, I want you to know that you are a real pretty girl. With that nice skin and good hair, you look just like your Daddy."

"You know who my Daddy is Miss Ella?"

"Your Daddy? Girl you confusing me. All this talk about pretty clothes is confusing my head," she said trying to change the subject.

"You hiding something from me Miss Ella. You remind me of my sister Nora. She ain't interested in nothing. When I try to talk to her about things like this, she tell me that I am foolish. I want to talk just like the mistress, real fancy and sweet; and to wear makeup and nice clothes too."

"Stop talking gibberish and get the mistress dinner on the table before she take a turn in you; and Nellie, my mahmee used to say that clothes hide the character."

"What is that supposed to mean?"

"You are a bright girl Nellie. Think about it."

"I don't understand what it mean Miss Ella."

"Your sister Nora got sense. She know that the good Lord make it so. We are to serve Miss Sarah and she is to be our mistress."

"Sometimes I don't understand you and the way you think Miss Ella."

"Then tell me this, why you think that we doing all the cooking, and putting the food on the table and she is just coming in to eat; and all we are saying is yes Miss Sarah and no Miss Sarah?"

"When my Mahmee was living, she tell me we used to be Kings and Queens back in Africa. That was before we come here to work on the plantations."

"Well I don't know where your Mahmee get her information, but we surely ain't kings and queens now, so you had better hurry and put that food on the table before she take away some of your pay again."

"I don't understand Miss Sarah. I was never late and only because of this one time, she take a shilling out of my pay, but I tell the Master and he give it back to me."

"You real hard ears Nellie. In all the years I was serving the Master and the Mistress, I was never, ever late."

"When you get your menses, you don't feel sick Miss Ella?"

The older woman cackled like a setting hen.

"Girl, I can't remember the last day I see those things. I am too old for that, thank God!"

"You real lucky Miss Ella. I hate them and I can't wait to be just like you. No menses!"

"Don't say that child. You young and you need your menses so that you could have children."

"But Miss Ella, why you never had no children?" asked the young woman.

"I don't know. Only the good Lord can answer that."

"But you look happy without children. I want about five or six."

"I don't see you and that boy Cudjoe together no more."

"I don't want him to be no father for my children. He ain't too bright and another thing I want to ask you Miss Ella is why Nora can't work in the house with me and you?"

"We can't have Nora in the kitchen Nellie."

"But why not Miss Ella?" she asked.

"The Mistress would not approve. Your sister skin ain't nice and pretty like yours. We cannot have Nora serving the Mistress."

"She is my sister and I look after Miss Sarah."

"You just ain't getting it Nellie. Nora is only good to work in the cane fields, not in the household with the family. She too black! Now hurry Nellie before we end up in trouble. Don't keep the Mistress waiting."

Before any more words could be said, the quiet tinkling of a bell was heard. The Mistress was ready and seated, waiting to have her dinner served. Nellie placed the dish with the white boiled potatoes next to the platter with the chicken breast which was equally as white. This was Sarah's favorite meal which Miss Ella regularly prepared, but could never understand how anyone could eat such unpalatable food. On the other hand, cooking for John Bottomsley was another thing. He loved Miss Ella's cooking and the local spices which she used.

Nellie placed her dinner on the white porcelain plate and she proceeded to dine while Nellie waited on the side, in case there was anything she needed. She ate in silence.

She then gently dabbed the corners of her mouth with the napkin and waited for Nellie to remove her plate. Nellie was tall and slender and as she leaned over to remove the dishes, their eyes met, and she quickly looked away, but Sarah for the first time realized what a pretty young woman she was. Her white turban was skillfully tied around her head and her long white dress, covered by an apron of equal length made her seem even taller.

"Tell Ella it was delicious," Sarah finally said.

"Yes ma'am," said Nellie humbly. "You want anything else Miss Sarah?"

She did not answer and with the wave of her hand, Nellie was dismissed and her employer returned to the window. The silence was deafening. The children and their parents had all gone to bed.

* * *

# 2

It was an unusually hot day and Sarah sat on the verandah reading a book. In the other hand was a fan, which she occasionally moved from side to side when there wasn't any breeze. Nellie came out with a tray which held a pitcher of lemonade and a glass. She poured some of the refreshing drink for Sarah Bottomsley and left. The woman hardly raised her head, but stretched out her hand, lifted the glass and drank. How she hated the heat! But she could see the beautiful ocean dancing on the horizon and kept on gazing at it as she quenched her thirst.

She felt uncomfortable. She was heavily with child and shifted her weight from one side to the other. Her discomfort was growing worse by the minute and she stumbled to her room and stretched out across the bed, leaving her fan and her book outside.

Seeing the book open and the leaves fluttering in the wind, Nellie knocked gently on her door, and then opened it. Sarah was having labour pains.

"Miss Ella, we have trouble," said Nellie frantically.

"Calm yourself and tell me what is wrong."

"It look like if Miss Sarah is going to have the baby."

"Send one of the boys who can run fast to get Dr. Sims."

"Lord, have mercy," proclaimed Nellie.

In a flash she was out of the house and down the alley way. She spoke to a young boy in a pair of ragged pants who then flew past her like a bolt of lightning and was soon out of sight. When Nellie returned, Miss Ella was nowhere to be seen, but she soon found her in Sarah Bottomsley's room.

"Young Joseph is on the way to get the doctor," said Nellie.

Sarah could only groan for she was suffering.

"I will put the kettle on the stove," Nellie continued. "Dr. Sims will want hot water."

She had seen Miss Una the midwife boil water each time there was a delivery, and felt it was the right thing to do."

"We should let the Master know Miss Sarah," said the older woman.

"I don't know where he is right now. I think he went to the Barkers," she said between gasps.

"I am going to send somebody to get him," replied Miss Ella.

She went to the kitchen and spoke to Nellie.

"You know where Master Bottomsley is?" she asked the young woman.

"I don't know Miss Ella."

"I older than you child and I ain't blind. He waiting inside your hut?"

"I don't what you talking about Miss Ella."

"I see the way he look at you and I know where you going when you sneak out and leave me with all the work. Find him girl!"

Nellie returned without Mr. Bottomsley. He was nowhere to be found. Perhaps he *was* over at the next plantation. Dr. Sims arrived and the poor young boy, who had been sent to fetch him, was now headed for the next plantation at the same speed. Unfortunately by the time John Bottomsley arrived, his wife had miscarried and was resting.

"She needs a lot of rest for the body and the spirit," said the doctor. Perhaps a couple weeks away from here would help her."

"Do you mean I should send her away?"

"Just to recuperate," said the doctor.

"I can't go away now. It's almost time for the harvest."

"You said she hadn't seen her parents for a long time. Why don't you send her off to see them?"

"I didn't think of that, but I guess it would do her the world of good, and it would take her mind off things."

And so Miss Ella and Nellie were put to work packing Sarah Bottomsley's trunks for the long voyage. Nellie felt a bit of relief because she knew she wouldn't be running after her mistress for the next couple of months, and she would have John Bottomsley all to herself.

One month had passed since she had lost the baby and things were slowly getting back to normal. Occasionally she could be seen staring out the window at the little children down below. It seemed like a bitter pill to swallow. She who had so much to offer could not bring a child of her own into the world. Since she was going on a long vacation, her husband made it a point to be home early each evening so they could dine together.

"Play something for me," he said as she sat at the piano.

"What would you like to hear?"

"Anything!" he replied.

The aromatic smell of his tobacco wafted through the air, as she tinkled the keys and played a classical melody for him.

"Did you like it?" she asked.

"I did. Play something else," he said.

Nellie and Miss Ella listened to the music coming from the drawing room while they cleaned up the kitchen and stored the pots and pans away.

"I think Miss Sarah feeling better," said Miss Ella.

"I think so too, but I hope she still going away."

"You know Miss Sarah leaving on Saturday. Why you think she would change her mind?"

"Because she and the master getting along real good," said the naïve young woman.

"You and the master got something going on. I know that Nellie, but don't get your head all confused girl. Remember what I say; we all got our place in life."

"But he like me Miss Ella. I know that."

"Of course he like you Nellie. You give him something that make him feel good. I don't think Miss Sarah make him feel that way, but be careful. What sweeten the goat mouth, does burn his backside."

"I don't understand all these things you keep telling me. What sweeten the goat mouth Miss Ella?"

"Never mind Nellie," said Miss Ella. "One day you will remember my words."

"Listen Miss Ella, it real quiet now. Miss Sarah finish playing."

"Then go and see if they want anything!" said an impatient Miss Ella.

She returned with a long face.

"Something wrong Nellie?"

"They gone to bed," she replied.

"Miss Sarah must be tired."

"I don't think so," said Nellie with downcast eyes. "They in the mistress bedroom."

"I think you lost your senses. That is his wife. You only there for him to play with when he feel like it. Anyway Nellie, listen to me. You only going to get your soup according to the way you hold your bowl."

With those words ringing in her ears, Nellie ran through the back door and all the way to her hut. There she cried her eyes out. An uneducated black kitchen hand and the master of a prosperous sugar cane plantation! What did she expect? She knew what Miss Ella had said was probably the truth, but she couldn't help her feelings. She thought he cared for her because after each sexual encounter he always rewarded her with a length of calico to make a dress or to do with as she pleased. She would normally share the cloth with her sister and on occasion with Miss Ella or Miss Una; and sometimes he would put two shillings extra in her pay packet. She never did spend much of her pay because she always ate in the kitchen and didn't need too many clothes. Her spare time was spent with the rest of the plantation workers because there was nowhere else to go, or waiting patiently to please the man she thought loved her. Occasionally some of them would go to the other workers' huts on other plantations, but more often than not, they were just too tired to make the long trek on foot.

Nellie deposited her pay in one of John Bottomsley's old socks which she had found in the rubbish bin. After carefully mending it, she now had a repository for her hard-earned money. This she kept hidden in the straw inside her mattress and not even her sister Nora was privy to this information.

She remembered the first time that John Bottomsley had given her two shillings. She was only fourteen years old and he had surprised her when he entered her hut. She was naïve and had no idea what he wanted, but remembered how much it had hurt when he penetrated her. It was a bit of a disappointment because it was not as wonderful as others had described it; in addition the sight of blood after he had finished just made her want to wash and keep washing. Things had changed. She now looked forward to his visits, not only for the calico and the money, but for the pleasure she derived from his touch.

John Bottomsley lay in bed beside his wife. It had been a long time since the two had any kind of intimacy. He felt a little awkward as he clumsily turned to kiss her. She was love-starved and responded eagerly to his touch which made him relax. He pulled the pins from her blonde hair and her tresses flowed across the pillow like a river. He gently played with her face and then with her hair. She kissed him and he kissed her back.

"I don't want to leave you," she said.

"Time will fly and you'll soon be back here with me where you belong. Besides you haven't seen your parents for a long time and you know they're eagerly waiting to see you."

"You're right dearest," she said cupping his face with her hands. "I want you to know that I will give you a child. I know you want that more than anything else in this world."

"I would love you to have our child, but if it doesn't happen I will be happy with just you Sarah."

"I love you John," she said as she drew closer and passionately kissed him.

He returned her kiss and desire rose in both of them. He hurriedly disrobed as she lay waiting for him. He found her breasts under the flimsy negligee and she moaned as his lips encircled her taut nipples. It had been a long time and they were now both ready to explore each others' bodies. After what seemed liked an eternity of kissing and touching, the two bodies were now ready to explode. She gasped and her body rose to meet his. She was close to ecstasy when everything came to a screeching halt.

"I'm sorry my love," he said. "It has been such a long time since we've been together like this."

"That's alright," she said smothering him with kisses.

"I promise it will be better the next time."

They lay in each other's arms and soon their passion was renewed. This time there was nothing to apologize for, and so they slept until the bright sunshine streamed into the room.

"I'm sorry Miss Sarah," said Nellie as she saw John Bottomsley's naked body.

"That's alright Nellie. I must be up anyway. We'll be ready for breakfast in about an hour."

"Yes ma'am," said Nellie eyeing John Bottomsley's dead instrument which she too shared from time to time.

* * *

## 3

Bottomsley Great House was now unusually quiet. One could hear a pin drop. Sarah was on a ship sailing towards the north east and there wasn't a lot to be done, especially since Mr. Bottomsley spent his lunch hours with the other plantation owners. Sometimes at night he would also have dinner with them, leaving Nellie alone and frustrated. She thought that in his wife's absence he would've spent more time with her.

"Why you don't go and visit Cudjoe?" her sister asked.

"He got somebody else," she said. "He spending all his time with Ermy."

"You didn't have any time for the poor boy. You can't expect him to sit around and wait on you. He is a man and a man need to be with a woman. He would go mad if he keep waiting on you."

"You just like Miss Ella. Because I don't go to sleep with him, that don't mean that he will go mad. That is foolishness."

"It ain't foolishness. You don't know that when a man got needs and can't get rid o' them, he does go off in the head?"

"You trying to tell me that all these men around here doing it often?"

"You're right! Even Master Bottomsley doing it."

"What you know about the Master?" Nellie asked defensively.

"His head ain't going to blow off as long as I am here."

Suddenly there was a lot of scampering going on outside.

"I leaving," said Nora. "I can smell tobacco."

Nellie rushed to the basin of water she had in the corner and quickly washed herself. No sooner was she finished, than the door to her hut opened and John Bottomsley stood in the doorway.

"Evening sir," she said to him.

He threw himself on the straw mattress and was soon fast asleep. She moved the smut lamp to the far corner of the hut to keep the kerosene odour away from his nostrils. As quickly as he had fallen asleep, he was again awake and his hands roughly grabbed her breasts. She pulled her arms out of her dress to give him easy access to her mounds of flesh. While his hands groped, he kept his eyes closed until his instrument fought to free itself from his riding pants. He pushed her against the mud wall of her hut and his lovemaking began. He was snorting like a horse and groaning like a pig that was ready for slaughter. She too was enjoying herself but concentrated more on his pleasure than on hers. He rode her like a horse and she bucked all the way to the finish line. There was no gentility in their lovemaking. It was hot and steamy in the wattle hut and the sweat just poured from both their bodies. He pushed her towards the bed and threw his lifeless weight on top of her, almost to the point of suffocation. She did not complain. The roughness of the hard mud had grated against her forehead and the clamminess between her legs did not help her situation. He finally got up, reached down and pulled his trousers from around his ankles and went to the door. There was more scampering going on outside as the door opened. Some of the villagers had obviously been trying to peep through the cracks in the mud wall.

"Nellie," he said turning around, "wait for me in the house tomorrow evening."

"Yes sir," she answered without hesitation.

Why did he want her to wait in the house? He had not given her anything, and would perhaps give it to her then. She knew she was special to him. It didn't matter what Miss Ella said.

The two women tried to keep themselves in the Great House by scrubbing and dusting. Everything was washed and ironed and the house sparkled from every corner. Dinner had been cooked and awaiting Mr. Bottomsley's arrival and Nellie greeted him as he entered and headed for his favorite place, the plantation chair.

"Would you help me with my boots Nellie?" he asked. "I am exhausted this evening."

"Yes sir."

Placing her back to him, she stepped over his leg and grabbed one boot. With his other foot firmly planted in her lower back, she pulled off the first one. She now did the same thing with the other boot and then offered to put his dinner on the table.

"Tell Ella I would like to see her right away," he said to her.

The older woman was beside herself with worry. She had never before been summoned by Mr. Bottomsley. Nellie listened behind the kitchen door, because she too was curious.

"Yes sir?" she asked standing before him.

"Ella," he began, "since my wife is not here and there isn't much to be done in the house, I was wondering if you would like to come out to the fields to help out? We've got to clear the trash and plant young suckers for next year's crop and I need all the hands I can get."

"Yes sir," she said, "and how much money you going to pay me?"

"Did you study law Ella?"

"No sir, I didn't have a chance to study nothing. I just got a good head on the old shoulders."

"Alright Ella, how about an extra two shillings?" he asked.

"Every week sir?"

"Two extra shillings per week Ella," he replied.

"I can live with that sir."

"What's left to be done around the house, Nellie can look after. Actually I can do with both of you out there, but I think someone should remain in the house."

"Yes sir," she replied. "If that is all, Nellie will bring in your dinner."

"I'm not quite ready for dinner Ella. You can go. Nellie can serve my dinner when I am ready."

He shook his head and smiled as she made her way back to the kitchen. He liked Ella. She was a gutsy woman.

"Thank you sir," she said disappearing behind the kitchen door.

Nellie was feeling a little smug. She had heard the entire conversation and was happy she didn't have to go out to the fields.

"I sorry to hear about that Miss Ella. You know that as soon as Miss Sarah come back, you will be back in here with me."

"Don't worry about me Nellie. You look after yourself and don't forget all the things I tell you. Right now you is only a substitute and you should not expect more than that."

"I think you wrong Miss Ella. I know he like me."

"Of course he like you. He like everybody. Look after yourself Nellie," she said as she stood at the kitchen door.

"G' night Miss Ella. Tomorrow I coming by to see you."

Nellie was left alone in the kitchen as Ella made her way to her hut. She was not happy with the decision her employer had made, but she was a clever woman and understood why he had done it that way. Miss Ella was forty four years old and had worked in the fields when she was a young girl. She and her friend Una had worked side by side until the wife of another plantation owner plucked her from the fields to work in the house. After they returned to their mother country, Ella moved to Bottomsley plantation along with many of the other workers. She and

Una were inseparable since then. Now in the mid morning of her years she was once again thrown into the mire of the sugar cane fields. Even if it were only for a short while until Sarah Bottomsley returned, it was still a disappointment. Did she think she was too good for the fields? It was common knowledge that the household staff felt themselves a notch above the others; but at least she would be side by side with her good friend Una.

"Una," she called out as she stood in front of her hut.

"You early this evening. The Master eating out tonight?"

"Come out and catch some fresh air and let me tell you the whole story."

Una brought a bench just big enough for the two of them to sit on.

"Ella I know when something bothering you. Tell your old friend what it is."

"I going back in the fields with you tomorrow morning."

"What you telling me girl? You mean that his wife is still on the high seas and he throwing you back into the cane fields already?"

"It is only until Miss Sarah come back."

"How could he take a woman of your age and put her out in the fields? Your body ain't used to the hot sun."

"But Una, you know I ain't no fretty-fretty girl. My body is used to hard work and if I got to do it again for three months, it certainly ain't going to kill me."

It suddenly became dark and there was a sudden clap of thunder followed closely by lightning which lit up the evening sky. The two women ran into Miss Una's hut for cover as the sky yawned and wretched, sending torrents of water crashing down on the galvanized roofs.

"I like to hear that rain beating down on the roof," said Miss Una jumping up from the bed.

The rain water was pouring through an opening in the corner of the house where she had hung her Sunday-go-to-meeting clothes. In the nick of time they were saved, but it was too late for her broad rimmed white hat. By the light of the smut lamp, she dried it gently with a piece of cloth before it had a chance to be bent out of shape.

"Una, you mind if I spend the night here? I really don't feel like going to out in this bad weather."

"Ella we were friends for a long time and you know you can sleep here if you want. I got a new nightgown that Nellie give me, so you can use it tonight."

In the darkness and between claps of thunder, the two women talked and comforted each other until they fell asleep.

* * *

# 4

Nellie waited impatiently while John Bottomsley still seated in his plantation chair with half a glass of rum in hand, snored in chorus with the chirping of the crickets. Exhaustion, heat and the alcohol he had consumed seemed to have taken its toll on him. Time and time again, she arranged the utensils on the tray and looked to see if he was awake. A cool breeze wormed its way through the window which had been left open the day after Sarah left on her trip. She usually kept every window closed at night for fear of being attacked by mosquitoes. The kitchen was fitted with a heavy door to keep food odours from penetrating into the living areas. Ella kept the window open in order that the heat from the cooking pot would not stew her brain. Even with the little window open to let the fresh air in, they were sometimes still soaked to the bone from the perspiration which oozed from their pores. Ella would lift her pinafore and wipe her face to prevent the sweat from dripping into the cooking pot, but sometimes it would still happen and she would laugh.

"What don't kill does fatten," she used to say.

John Bottomsley stirred and opened his eyes.

"Nellie," he shouted, "Is my dinner ready?"

She rushed around like a banshee in heat trying to get his dinner on the table as quickly as possible, while he picked up the daily newspaper and looked at the front page. There was nothing of interest there, so he laid it on his lap and his eyes followed her everywhere.

"Do you know how to read Nellie?"

"No sir."

"Would you like to learn to read?" he asked as she continued to fuss around.

"I don't know sir."

"Yes or no is the answer Nellie."

"I think so sir."

He sat at the table and ate in silence while she waited behind him. She watched as he chewed each mouthful and dashed to refill his plate when it was empty. He finally wiped his mouth and reclined in the chair.

"So you would like to learn to read and write Nellie."

"Yes sir."

"I'll see what I can do about it," he said standing up.

She never did realize how tall he really was, since he always had to slouch when he came to her hut. Standing in the light she thought him a very handsome man, although she did not like the colour of his hair. It looked like yellow straw. When Sarah was at home, it always seemed to look different.

"Thank you sir," she said.

"Come into my room when you are through cleaning up," he said.

"Yes sir."

With the speed of lightning, she had everything done, then she ran to the outdoor toilet which she and Miss Ella used and hastily washed herself. She knew why she had been invited to his room and wanted to be clean.

"Come in," he said as she gently knocked on the door.

She had entered the room before only to clean it, and felt a little odd on entering and seeing him lying half naked on the bed.

"Come in. Don't just stand there," he said.

She stood beside the bed and looked out the window. There was just too much light. She was not used to seeing his naked body with the light shining on it.

"What is it Nellie. Would you prefer to go to your hut?"

"No sir, it just too bright in here,"she replied.

"Well, we'll see what we can do about that. Is that better now?" he asked blowing the light out.

"Yes sir."

If a little light made such a difference, he would only be too willing to accommodate her. After what seemed like an eternity of heaving, shoving and heavy breathing, he slumped on top of her and was soon fast asleep. Afraid to disturb him, she too fell asleep under his heavy weight, only to be awakened by the crowing of the roosters coming from the direction of the village huts. She tried to ease her body away from under his, but he awoke and again he sought satisfaction. She was happy there was no one else in the house that might discover them, because as far as she was concerned, this kind of thing went on only at night, and definitely not in the morning.

His performance did not equal that of the night before, but he seemed satisfied. He jumped out of bed, grabbed his trousers and put them on. She wondered if he wasn't going to take a shower. He didn't.

"You can sleep here until my wife returns," he said to her.

Those words were music to her ears. Nellie the housemaid would be sleeping between soft white sheets next to her master. After making himself a quick breakfast, he left without a word, and she looked out just in time to see Miss Ella and Miss Una with hoes on their shoulders and enamel food carriers in their hands. She felt a little sad. She had a good relationship with Miss Ella and looked to her for advice, and now there was no-one, but she was inside the master's domain, taking the place of his absent wife.

Night after night it was the same procedure. John Bottomsley was first and foremost in her thoughts and all others came second.

She spent her time thinking of every possible way to please him; not that he recognized her efforts, but at the end of each week, she found three shillings more in her pay packet. In addition she no longer paid rent for the steamy hut she occupied.

Hurrying home each Friday night, she deposited her weekly wages into the sock which she kept inside her mattress. She would also get a change of clothes for the week ahead, and since John Bottomsley was showing more interest in her, she made bloomers from the calico which he had provided. They were not nice and silky like Miss Sarah's, but they were clean and white, and she made sure there was a clean fresh one for every night of the week.

All alone after the workers had left for the fields, she walked to the back of the house and looked up at the bedroom window where she and John Bottomsley had their nightly trysts. She wondered if the villagers stood there at night, just as she was now doing and what could they hear? She rested under a breadfruit tree which hung heavily with small unripe fruit. These trees had been planted by the previous owner for his enjoyment and also to feed the plantation hands. Not only had he planted breadfruits, but soursop, sugar apples, ackees, bananas, golden apples, avocadoes, a variety of mango and an assortment of plum trees. There were mostly fruit trees and after the workers had picked the fruit, they were expected to take the best of the crop to their employer's kitchen. As delicate as Sarah Bottomsley was, she had a definite liking for the small sweet bananas they called figs, turpentine mangoes, and a sweet plum they called a bird plum. The latter were bright yellow when ripe and attracted a multitude of birds.

Nellie walked in and out of the trees looking at each branch. She had a longing for golden apples, but it was not yet golden apple season. It seemed rather strange because never before had she such a desire. She knew that Sarah Bottomsley had such yearnings when she was with child, but she hoped it wasn't so in her case.

It was midday when John Bottomsley returned home accompanied by a young girl whom Nellie had never seen before. She had straw-like yellow hair, just like his and her skin was red as if she had spent too much time in the sun. She was not pretty but spoke very well.

"Nellie, set the lunch table for two," he said.

The young woman ignored her presence and chatted away happily with him. They seemed awfully familiar with each other and he referred to her as Ginger.

"What makes you think you would make a good teacher?" he asked.

"Why do I have to be a good teacher?"

"I want you to teach the children of the plantation workers."

"Do they need an education to work in the fields?"

"The work is too much for me, so I want to train the workers. I need people who can weigh the sugar cane and tell me how much they weigh. I need workers to help make the rum and they must be able to read measurements."

"I know someone who can help you with the daily operation of the plantation."

"And who would that be?"

"My brother Thomas," she replied. "He is planning to move here and I know he will need some kind of employment."

"Alright, please have him contact me when he arrives. He can be my assistant if he fits the bill. So what about you, are you ready to take the job?"

"I think you are wasting your time," she said.

"The position is still open. The weekly wages are good. If you're not interested, then I will find someone else."

"Don't be so hasty Johnny boy," she said smiling at him from across the table.

It was obvious she knew him well.

"Does that mean you will take the job?"

"When do I start?"

"As soon as possible," he said. "Instead of playing around the hedgerows and distracting their parents, they should be in school learning how to read and write."

"I admire you John Bottomsley. You are a good man. They aren't many men like you on this island."

"Does that mean you're still interested?"

"Yes."

"Then I'll have to get you some supplies. You'll need slates, pencils, text books, and a blackboard and easel."

"And how do you plan on getting these wayward children into a classroom?"

"How long have you been on the island and what makes you think they are wayward?"

"Coming from uneducated parents who aren't in the least bit civilized, what am I to expect?"

"You will be surprised Ginger. They are the most obedient and polite children I have ever seen, such as you will not find back home."

After their lunch was over, Nellie cleared the dishes. She now thought Ginger was going to be her teacher. She could hear their voices as she went about her chores in the kitchen. There was much laughter and then it was suddenly quiet. They had both disappeared. She crept down the hallway to his bedroom where she noticed the door was slightly ajar. He was sitting on the bed and Ginger was on her knees before him. Nellie had no idea what was going on. Whatever it was, he was enjoying it immensely.

*"What is she doing?" she wondered. "Why she eating it?"*

She continued to watch them. He writhed and groaned while she continued to administer to him, but the look on his face told Nellie he was in pain. Suddenly his whole body shook and trembled and he grabbed her straw-like hair. It was all over and she left the house just as she had entered; looking like a lady.

Hatred swelled in Nellie's breast, and she felt low. Lower than a slug under a rock! She thought she had meant something special to him, but then she had never done such a thing to him and maybe this was what these people did to each other to make them happy. She had never seen anything like it before and wondered if this was the reason that Sarah Bottomsley was not able to bring a living child into the world.

* * *

# 5

Shortly after Ginger's visit, boxes and cartons arrived at the plantation and a reconstructed shed was opened as the Bottomsley School. His peers derided him for an act which they deemed stupid, but he was determined to follow his mind. Ginger Hurley was a good teacher, but she was not a kind person. The children were punished for the slightest infraction and made to stand with their faces in the corner. In spite of this they had made great strides in reading and writing. She too was proud and surprised by their achievements, since she had been convinced they were much too uncivilized to grasp any kind of knowledge. Her employer was also very pleased, but her constant presence on the premises did nothing to allay Nellie's fears. She needed to talk to someone she thought would understand, and after a long day in the fields, Miss Ella found her sitting on her doorstep.

"Howdy Miss Ella," she said.

"What bring you here girl?" the older woman asked. "I thought you did forget your friends and family."

"You alright Miss Ella? I think about you all the time out there in that hot sun, but the mistress coming back soon and we will be together again."

"You ain't come here to tell me that you miss me Nellie. What's on your mind?"

"Well you know how the Master feel about me," she started.

"Tell me what is on your mind," said Miss Ella impatiently.

"I think I am in the family way."

"Why you think so?" the older woman asked.

"I longing to eat golden apples and it ain't golden apple season."

"But that that don't mean a thing child."

"Every morning I got to run outside and throw up."

"That don't sound too good. You still having your menses?"

"I ain't had them for over two months Miss Ella. What am I going to do?"

"He know?" asked Miss Ella throwing her head in the direction of the Great House.

"I don't know."

"What you mean, you don't know?"

"I didn't tell him nothing."

"It ain't going to make one bit of difference. I always used to tell you that the cockroach ain't had no right at the hen party, but you didn't listen to me."

"I know Miss Ella, but I thought I was special."

"Child we all special in the eyes of the Lord," the woman said. Don't put too much faith in man. Man will always disappoint you."

"How you know so much about life Miss Ella?"

"I used to be young once. I wasn't born at this age Nellie."

"And another thing Miss Ella, I don't understand why he spending so much time with Ginger."

"He spending time with ginger? I didn't know he was growing ginger."

"I talking about the school teacher," said Nellie, now laughing loudly and forgetting her problems.

"You must explain yourself properly. I didn't know her name was Ginger. What kind of a name is that?"

"I don't know, but she is a nasty girl," said Nellie.

She bent over and whispered in Miss Ella's ear as if there was someone else around to hear.

"We ain't used to those things. Those white people do some real funny things."

"But I think he did like it Miss Ella."

"That way, she would never be in the family way."

"What am I going to do Miss Ella?"

"You ain't happy you carrying the Master child?"

"Yes but I don't know if he is going to be happy."

"If you change your mind, we could always send Mr. Fitz to pick some bush. You know he is a master at what he do. He learn it from his great, great grandfather who come all the way from Africa."

"I ain't want to do that Miss Ella."

They were interrupted by Miss Una and two more elderly women who came by to chat and pass the time away.

"Well God bless my eyesight," said Miss Una looking scornfully at Nellie. "We ain't seen you since you become the mistress of the plantation. Wa law! Wa law!" she said laughing out loudly.

"Una give the child a chance," said Miss Ella. "She in a lot of trouble."

"What kind of trouble?" asked Miss Una. "She break the mistress china bowl?"

"We going to have some more pickneys around here."

"You with child?" asked Miss Una. "Have mercy Lord. The Master know?"

"How you know it belongs to the Master?" asked Miss Ella.

"Who else?" asked Una. "She forget all about us and was spending all the time underneath the Master."

"Leave Nellie alone," said Miss Ella. "She ain't in the frame of mind for any kind of teasing. Think Nellie, that child you carrying is going to be white like you or whiter."

"Why you saying that Miss Ella?"

"Between you, your father and you know who, it got to be a real white child."

"But you say you didn't know who my father was."

"I say that?" asked Miss Ella pretending to be innocent.

"Tell Nellie who her father is," said Miss Una. "She got a right to know."

"I hate putting my mouth in other people business, but Nellie, your father is the overseer at Henley plantation. Your mother Hilda was a real pretty little thing and he take a shine to her and you is the result."

Nellie said goodnight, turned around and left. She had heard too much for one evening and her head was in a muddle.

"You alright girl?" shouted Miss Ella.

"I alright," she replied.

"You can always come to me when you need help Nellie. Don't let pride stand in your way."

"Thanks Miss Ella."

Nellie could hear her employer's voice as she entered the kitchen. She did not recognize the man sitting across from him, but they spoke about the plantation and it seemed as if the young man would soon be working there. Mr. Bottomsley got up and refreshed their drinks. The man had a beautiful accent, and spoke like someone who had a lot of education. As a matter of fact, he spoke like the teacher Ginger Hurley and his face was beet red just like hers. Maybe he had spent too much time in the sun, like they all did.

"Have you had dinner yet?" John Bottomsley asked.

"No, but I promised my sister I would dine with her tonight."

"A bright girl she is," her employer said. "In just a few short weeks the children can read and write."

"That's my Ginger. She was always the brighter of the two of us."

Nellie now knew who he was. No wonder he spoke like her and had the same skin colouring.

"So you won't be returning home. I want to be sure that if you do take the position, you will be staying around for a while. It is hard work especially in the harvest season, which you've just missed. It's now time to brew this lovely drink which we have here," he said holding up his glass.

"Are you saying you also make rum?"

"Every single drop," he said. "Now you understand why I need help and lots of it. I'm trying to teach the young boys how to read and write. At least they can help with the weighing and the measuring. Some of them are quick learners."

"Well thank you sir. I must be going. Ginger must be waiting for me."

"Oh I almost forgot. I've got something for you."

He pulled a letter from his pocket and handed it to Mr. Bottomsley.

"From your sister?" he asked.

"No, it's from your wife."

"Where did you see my wife?"

"I didn't see her. A friend of mine knows her family quite well and he asked if I would oblige Mrs. Bottomsley and deliver this letter."

"That was very kind of you. I do hope you stick around."

Thomas Hurley left and he sat down to read the letter, just as Nellie was coming into the room to find out if he was ready for dinner.

"Not yet," he said. "I will let you know."

London

My beloved John,

Time is quickly flying by and soon I'll be home again with you. You can't imagine how much I've missed you and Bottomsley. Although it is the beginning of summer, the weather is absolutely wretched. I had forgotten how miserable it can be here. It must be wonderful back there with the beautiful sunshine and chirping birds and the laughter of the children coming from below. I hope Ella and Nellie are taking good care of you, or has Mother Bottomsley moved in take over the running of the house? Papa has gout and Mama is still running after him although she hasn't the strength to do so. I invited them to visit and even the doctor said that the sunshine would be good for both of them, but they are stubborn and will absolutely not travel to an uncivilized country. Sometimes I pity their archaic way of thinking, but there is nothing I can do.

I have not been very well and thought I was having a bout of influenza, but mama's doctor told me I had nothing to worry about because I am once again in the family way. He has prescribed different medicines for me which I must take on a daily basis. They would provide the needed nutrients for the baby. So you understand my beloved why I am so anxious to be there with you. The ship will be sailing very early for the return journey, so I will be going down to Southampton to spend one week by the seaside and to visit a school friend there.

I look forward to seeing you soon again, so until we see each other again, I am sending all my love.

Your darling wife,

Sarah

John Bottomsley was elated and had worked up an appetite. He summoned Nellie and had his dinner brought in and while she was doing so, he read and re-read the letter. He had not realized how much he had missed her and thought of all kinds of surprises for her return.

After dinner, he retired and immediately fell asleep leaving Nellie to bring everything in order, but she was curious as to the contents of the letter. She stared at the words on the page and was totally frustrated, because she couldn't read. She thought of asking Clytie to read it to her, because her son who was now attending the Bottomsley School, was teaching her everything Ginger Hurley was teaching him. She however crawled into bed next to him and slept peacefully. The next morning the letter was still there. It was not necessary to put it away because he knew she was illiterate.

At midday a wagon used for transporting sugar cane arrived at the Great House with two cows and a coop full of chickens. Mr. Fitz who was now too old to work in the fields, and attended the gardens, appeared on the scene. His woolly grey hair, peeping out from under his cloth cap which covered most of his forehead, made his beady little eyes even smaller.

"Hey you," shouted the scruffy white driver. "I have a delivery here for Mr. Bottomsley."

"He ain't here right now," answered Mr. Fitz.

"Well you can take them and put them in the back until he comes home."

Mr. Fitz helped the man to carry the coop with the chickens and placed it under a mango tree; then he tied the cows to another nearby tree. No sooner had the driver left than Nellie appeared on the scene to find out where the animals came from.

When Mr. Bottomsley arrived home, he went straight to the back of the house, where Nellie and Mr. Fitz were still discussing the additions to Bottomsley plantation.

"I see my animals have arrived," he said.

"You come home for lunch sir?" Nellie asked.

"No."

"What you going to do with all these the cows and chickens?" she asked.

"Fresh milk and fresh eggs," he said. "My wife is coming home soon and I want to surprise her. Tell the boys I want two of them to remain here on Saturday morning because we have to build a stall for the animals. And Fitz, make sure you put some manure to the roses; I want everything to be perfect when my wife comes home."

Mr. Fitz's mouth hung open as he stared at the two big-eyed animals and then at Nellie, who couldn't have been more jealous. He had slept with her almost every night since his wife left and still he didn't seem to care too much for her. More and more, his actions were proving Miss Ella right.

* * *

# 6

The same scruffy old man who had delivered the animals one day earlier was there again. This time his cart was overflowing with lumber.

"Anybody here to help take this lumber to the back?" he shouted.

"I can help you," said Mr. Fitz who was attending the gardens at the front.

"Then let's make a start. I have another delivery before the day is over."

In silence the two men carried the lumber to the back and placed it where the sheds were to be constructed.

It was Friday evening and the workers had all been paid. It was late when John Bottomsley arrived home and he was tired. He stretched himself out on the plantation chair after having made arrangements for the building project for the next morning. As usual Nellie was there at his beck and call and was very eager to please him. His favorite drink beside him, he sipped it slowly and stared out the window. He had not slept with her all that week and could now feel the passion rising within him.

"I'm going to bed right after dinner," he said. "I am tired."

She knew that meant his performance would be at best poor, but pleasing him was foremost in her mind. She had to make him care deeply for her. She remembered what Ginger had done to him and decided that may just be the thing to gain his affection. Proving her love for him *must* strengthen their relationship. As he lay waiting, she entered the room and knelt in front of him and proceeded to give him pleasure he had not expected. He sat up and positioned himself for the exhilarating experience.

"Where did you learn to do this?" he asked.

Thankfully before she could answer, someone was knocking impatiently on the entrance door. He did not want to answer, because the sensation was heavenly, but the visitor was persistent, so he had no choice but to see who it was.

"Who's there?" he asked through the closed door.

"It's your mother," Millie Bottomsley said.

"Just a moment Mother," he said bundling Nellie out the kitchen door and hiding his nakedness under a pair of trousers.

"What took you so long?" she asked.

"Did you want me to appear naked at the door? And what are you doing here at this time of the night anyway?"

"Really son, why don't you sleep in pajamas?"

"On warm nights like this I don't need pajamas Mother."

"I must say, sometimes you have a tendency to behave just like your father."

"The berry never falls far from the tree Mother."

Anyway, I understand Sarah will be back soon and I want to make sure everything is in tip top shape for her return."

"Where is Father?" he asked. "And why couldn't this have waited until tomorrow?"

"Your father is playing cards with his friends. He brought me here and didn't even wait until I got into the house before taking off. Sometimes son, I wonder about him."

"So are you going to tell me what brought you here at this ungodly hour? And don't tell me it has anything to do with my wife."

"I have to make preparations for Sunday lunch. You know Reverend Allamby is coming over after Sunday service. I also took the liberty of inviting that nice young lady Ginger and her brother Thomas."

"Without my permission Mother?" he asked.

"I didn't think you would mind. Aren't you going to invite me in?"

"Of course, come on in. Are you staying the night?"

"If it's alright with you," she said.

"Nellie has already left for the evening, so you will have to sleep in Sarah's room."

"What time does she normally start in the morning?"

"Around six thirty!" her son replied. "Why do you ask?"

"I need her help with the preparations for Sunday lunch. I thought we should bake a lemon cake or something like that for dessert."

"Then you should get Ella to help you and you should also pay her a little extra if you want her to work on the weekend."

"But she always works on Saturdays, doesn't she? Why should we pay her extra?"

"Because Mother, since Sarah left I didn't see the need for two persons in the house, so I asked Ella to help us out in the fields."

"That shouldn't matter," said Millie Bottomsley.

"Mother!" he said with irritation ringing in the word.

"Alright son, if that's what you want, then so be it."

"Thank you Mother."

The next morning, there was a lot of hammering and a commotion was going on outside. Millie Bottomsley stared out the window to see her son in the midst of a mountain of lumber and a sea of black faces.

"He could've waited until I was up," she fretted. "And where are those two who are supposed to help me today? I guess I will have to make my own breakfast."

Just as she was about to put the kettle on, Nellie opened the kitchen door.

"Morning ma'am," she said.

"What time do you start in the morning Nellie?"

"About half past six ma'am, but the Master say I can start later because Miss Sarah ain't here."

"Never mind, make me some breakfast."

"What you want ma'am?"

"A couple of those delicious muffins with some guava jam and a pot of fresh tea! I would also like two poached eggs. Make a fresh pot of tea. I don't want that old tea that my son made for himself. It has been sitting around much too long. And Nellie, you must have turpentine mangoes somewhere."

"Yes ma'am."

"Then I'll have some fresh fruit too, and you can tell Ella I would like her to help with the preparations for Sunday lunch."

"Yes ma'am," said Nellie to the list of orders Millie was handing out.

Nellie was not fond of the woman, and more so since she had interrupted her the night before and killed any chances she might have had in strengthening John Bottomsley's affections towards her.

"Is that a hambone in there?" Millie asked stepping back and peeping into the larder.

"There is still some meat on it ma'am."

"Then remove the ham and make some hambone soup today. My husband loves Ella's hambone soup."

"Yes ma'am," said Nellie now more upset than ever, because she too had been patiently waiting on the hambone.

When Miss Ella opened the kitchen door, she started to relate the sad story of the hambone.

"Well I can only hope she pay me extra. Since the Master send me out to the fields, I don't work on Saturdays or Sundays. Beside that, Sunday mornings I go to praise my Lord," said Miss Ella as she opened the larder and inspected the hambone for any scraps of meat that were still clinging to it.

"I don't know Miss Ella. You will have to ask the Master about the pay."

"I don't want him to think that I greedy, but I ain't no fool," she replied as she pulled a piece of meat from the bone. "Nellie I think there got ants in the larder. You younger than me. Crawl under there and see if the larder feet still in water."

Nellie did as she was told and found the containers to be indeed empty, which she then re-filled. This was the method used to prevent insects from climbing into the larder and invading the foodstuff.

"You don't have anytime to keep this house in order. You spend all your time underneath the Master."

"That ain't true Miss Ella," she said jumping to her own defence.

"Then tell me how the ants get into the larder. If you did doing your work properly, that wouldn't happen."

Nellie didn't have a chance to respond. The brakes of a car screeched outside and John Bottomsley's father, who was also called John, stumbled out and made his way to the entrance.

"Shame on you John," said his wife Millie. "Why must you always embarrass me?'

"Shut up woman and get me a drink," he replied.

"Don't you think you've had enough? Ella is making you your favourite. Hambone soup!"

"Nice, nice," he replied. "In the meantime I need a drink."

Miss Ella and Nellie were giggling at the performance going on in the drawing room, when the younger John Bottomsley entered the kitchen. He was sweating profusely from labouring on his cow stalls and chicken coops. The two women pretended to be busy but carried on eavesdropping when he was out of sight.

"How long were you here Father?"

"Long enough to have had a drink," the man replied.

"Tell him he can't have another drink," his wife said. "He's already intoxicated."

"Mother's right," the younger Bottomsley said. "Ella has made lunch. Have something to eat and then we can have a drink together."

"You're a good son," he replied. "You are nothing like your mother."

Mother Bottomsley rang the dinner bell and Nellie hurried in with the soup tureen which she placed on the sideboard and then served each of the family members.

"Where is the hambone?" growled the older Bottomsley.

Nellie hurried back to the kitchen to fetch the bone when she saw Miss Ella already sitting at the kitchen table with the bone to her mouth and enjoying the scraps of meat which were still attached to it. She snatched the bone from her, apologized, then placed it on a plate and hurried back to the older Bottomsley, who did the same thing Miss Ella had been doing.

"Really John," said his wife.

"Know what your problem is Millie?"

"Thank you Nellie," said the younger Bottomsley before his father had a chance to continue and embarrass his mother in front of the servants.

Nellie pretended she wasn't listening, but the younger Bottomsley knew she was. She retreated to the kitchen where Miss Ella also seemed to be enjoying the entertainment.

"Is he enjoying the hambone?" she asked.

"I think so."

"Those two don't have any class at all," said Miss Ella shaking her head.

"But they are funny and we always get a good laugh when they come around," said Nellie peeping into the dining room.

"Nellie, tell me something. How you feeling?"

"I alright Miss Ella."

"You should get some of those rose hips from Mr. Fitz. Miss Sarah roses full of rose hips, and they good for the blood and keeping you cool at night. He say anything about the baby?"

"Who?" she asked. "Mr. Fitz?"

"What Mr. Fitz know about your baby? I talking about the Master."

"No he did not say nothing."

"You know that the Mistress coming home soon."

"Yes."

"And you hear that she is expecting another baby?"

"No Miss Ella. How you find out?"

"Keep your eyes open, your mouth closed and your ears to the ground. Then and only then will you know everything."

"Now I know why he was so happy the other night. The Hurley fellow give him a letter and he read it again and again. I was going to ask Clytie to read it for me, but then it disappear. Now I know why he bring home the chickens and the cows. We will get fresh milk and fresh eggs every day."

"That's what it look like Nellie. You make sure you get some too. You have to have a strong constitution to bring that child into the world. But Nellie you cannot take up the Master letters and show them to Clytie. It ain't right. It just ain't right."

* * *

# 7

Reverend Allamby's sermon was all about love and caring for each other, because they were all God's children.

"Amen," whispered Miss Una to her friend, who only shook her head as if she was trying to absorb every word the reverend was saying.

The colonials sitting in the front pews just kept fanning themselves with their elegant little fans similar to those Queen Victoria might have used. As a matter of fact, they thought they were all queens in their funny little hats. Some had broad rims with roses stuck in the hatbands, others had them cocked over one eye which led one to wonder how they were ever able to follow the words in the Bible or in the hymn books. They hardly batted an eyelash when the reverend stressed the point of loving thy brother as thyself. Of course in their minds, this did not pertain to their household servants who washed, cooked, cleaned and looked after their children.

Millie Bottomsley was like a pepper fly barking orders at Nellie and Miss Ella. She wanted things done her way and not the way they were used to doing them.

"What she think?" asked Miss Ella. "I was doing this job before she know what good living was."

"Don't worry about the Master mother," replied Nellie. "She only want to see that everything run smoothly."

"What you trying to tell me Nellie, that after all these years I don't know what I doing?"

"No Miss Ella, I didn't mean it like that."

"Go in there and tell the old fowl cock that lunch is ready."

Nellie did as she was told but before she had a chance to relay the message to Mrs. Bottomsley, Reverend Allamby spoke to her.

"Did you enjoy the sermon this morning Nellie?"

"I didn't have a chance to go to church this morning sir."

"What is it Nellie?" Millie Bottomsley asked, interrupting their conversation.

"Miss Ella want you to know that lunch ready."

"Let's finish our drinks and then sit down for lunch," Millie said.

As soon as Nellie was out of sight, she continued to speak.

"It always amazes me that they are always with child."

"What are you talking about Mother? Who's with child?"

"Are you blind son? Can't you see that Nellie is in the family way?"

"I never noticed and speaking of the family way, I want to announce to all here present that Sarah is expecting our child."

"Congratulations," said Reverend Allamby.

The others joined in to wish him and his wife well.

"Maybe I should move in to take care of her until the baby arrives," said Mother Bottomsley.

"If I were you, I wouldn't allow it," said the older John Bottomsley to his son.

Everyone laughed and imagined him to be teasing, but he knew his wife well and knew it wasn't a good idea.

"That would have to be Sarah's decision," replied his son as he watched Nellie put the lunch dishes on the buffet.

He looked at her from every angle but could see nothing and she could've been a fly on the wall for all they cared. They ate heartily and carried on their conversation as if she wasn't there. Only John Bottomsley looked at her, and even then it was only at her stomach. He wondered if the child was his.

*"It must be my child," he thought as his mind wandered. "My God, I've got two women expecting children from me at the same time."*

"Isn't that true son?" his mother asked.

"What? I'm sorry. I was just thinking of Sarah."

"She will soon be back and everything will be just as before," said the reverend.

"I can't wait for the little one to come along," said the older John Bottomsley.

"Tell me Ginger," said the reverend, "how are things at the school? Are the children learning well and do you like the role of teacher?"

"Amazingly Father, they are quite fast learners and eager for new things. I must admit I too have learned lots from them."

"Like what? Pray tell," said Millie Bottomsley.

"Did you know that there is a system of underground caves stretching almost the complete length of the island?"

"I've never heard that," said the older Bottomsley.

"I wonder where they heard such a preposterous thing," Millie said.

"From their grandparents," she replied. "Apparently during the days of slavery, the slaves would escape and hide in them for years at a time."

"I've heard that myself, but never really had a chance to research it," said the younger John Bottomsley.

Nellie walked in just as Ginger was inviting her employer to go on a fact finding excursion with her.

"Perhaps if you would like, we can try to find them next Saturday. Of course that's your day off and if there is anything urgent, your new overseer would be more than happy to step in for you, right Thomas?"

"Of course Sis," he replied.

"That's not a bad idea," the younger Bottomsley replied. "We can pack a picnic basket and make a day of it. I've been working way too hard."

"It doesn't look good for the two of you to be going off alone. After all John is a married man and we don't want those tongues wagging. His father and I will accompany you. I too am curious about these caves."

"What wagging tongues Millie?" asked her husband. "The only tongue wagging would be yours. I have plans for next Saturday, so you will just have to go without me."

"Saturday is family day; that's when families do things together, isn't that right Ginger?"

"That's a family matter Mrs. Bottomsley. You'll have to sort that out between you. I give advice only when it concerns the children."

"You should see how she throwing herself at the Master."

"Who?" asked Miss Ella.

"The school teacher,"said Nellie. "She want to take him to see the underground caves."

"That is what you call throwing herself at him?"

"Yes Miss Ella. She want to get close to him even though he is married."

"But the Master ain't interested Nellie. He looking forward to Miss Sarah return."

"He is going with her next Saturday Miss Ella."

"And what the others say?"

Miss Bottomsley fixed her real good. She say it wasn't proper for a young girl like Ginger to be going off with a married man."

"That is the truth, but the Master ain't a child and can make his own decisions."

"Which side you on Miss Ella?"

"I ain't on any side. I am just telling the facts as I see them."

Miss Ella could only shake her head, since Nellie did not seem to realize what she was saying. She didn't think she was doing the same thing she was accusing Ginger of doing.

* * *

# 8

"Are you expecting a baby Nellie?" asked John Bottomsley as she stood before him in his bedroom.

"Yes sir."

"Why didn't you tell me? Is it my baby Nellie?"

"Yes sir."

"How can you be so sure that I am the father?"

"Because I don't sleep with nobody else sir."

"I will look after the child, but you must not tell anyone else about it."

"Yes sir."

"How many people have you told?"

"Only Miss Ella and Miss Una," she replied.

"We must make sure no one else finds out; and tell Una and Ella they must not spread it across the plantation."

"I will do that sir."

John Bottomsley's mind was now in a whirl. He thought of Sarah and what she might do if she found about it. He thought of his mother. Good Lord! Millie Bottomsley! She would bring fire and brimstone down upon Nellie because she would be convinced it was her fault. With his mind still rolling like a tornado, he stretched out on his bed to think. All Nellie could think of at that moment was making him happy, so she knelt in front of him and finished what she had not able to do the previous Friday night. He closed his eyes tightly and groaned. His heart was saying no because he felt guilty, but his body was saying yes, yes. After what seemed like ages, he could no longer control himself and his body broke into spasms. She thought of the Snowball man who made his rounds on Sunday afternoons with his colorful dyes and his block of ice which he shaved and portioned out. Everyone listened for the tinkling of the bell which heralded his arrival. She thought of the cool feeling of the ice shavings on her lips and the sugary taste of the dye which flowed down the sides, like lava erupting from a volcano; but this was not to her liking. She was doing it all for John Bottomsley, the man she loved, and the man who would always put her on the back burner. Nevertheless she then crawled into bed beside him and slept.

Early the next morning, he got out of bed and stared out the window. It was a beautiful morning but he didn't seem to notice. His mind was now on the problem he had created. The plantation hands were stirring, but he had no desire to go to the fields. Looking at Nellie who was still fast asleep brought out his gentle side. She looked so innocent as indeed she was before he had deflowered her. Unlike Sarah, she had no one to care for her and she was just as far along in her pregnancy as his wife was. A smile seemed to linger on her lips. Her brown skin against the white bed sheets brought out the beauty he had never before noticed.

*"If things were only different," he thought. "I cannot abandon her."*

If John Bottomsley loved Nellie Peterkin, it was difficult to tell, but he knew she loved him. How he must have hurt her time and time again. He felt guilty about the position she was in and his selfishness in putting her there. He did not care what the others might say, but Sarah would be humiliated and so would his parents. He couldn't possibly put his wife in such a position. However something had to be done for the unfortunate young woman. Would the child look like him? Nellie was very light skinned and having his child meant she could bring a child just as white as he was into the world. His heart started to beat faster. Would anyone be suspicious of him when they saw the child?

There was nothing he could do but try to find a way out for all parties concerned. He made himself a cup of tea and left the house before she was awake. Hearing the voices of the children coming from the school below, and the bright sun coming through the open window, she jumped out of bed. It was too late. John Bottomsley had already left and she had not prepared his breakfast. She went to the window and looked down. She couldn't hear Ginger Hurley's voice, but the children were obviously repeating what she had told them.

A is for apple

B is for bat

C is for cat

And so it continued until they had reached the end of the alphabet. She too wanted to be able to read and write. Her employer had promised to teach her but had done nothing about it. Perhaps he had forgotten or it wasn't important to him. In the meantime her friend Clytie had learned enough, that she could read passages from the newspapers which John Bottomsley had discarded. Her son was still teaching her everything that Ginger Hurley taught him. No one except her best friend and Miss Ella knew and they intended keeping it that way.

"Don't hang all your clothes on the line," Miss Una had said to her.

And so Clytie had kept the secret close to her heart.

Nellie's load was lifted since she had told John Bottomsley about her pregnancy and now she had gathered up enough courage to speak to him again regarding his promise to teach her to read and write.

"Sorry Nellie," he said. "With everything that has been going on, I completely forgot about it. I cannot send you to Ginger Hurley because more than likely, it would raise her suspicions."

"What suspicions sir?"

"She might find it strange my wanting servants to read and write."

"So who is going to teach me?"

"I will Nellie, but you've got to be patient."

"On Thursday afternoon, would you and Ella make something nice for a late lunch? Sarah will be back then."

"Miss Ella is still working in the field sir."

"Wednesday will be her last day. I said it would only be until my wife returned."

"Alright sir, I will talk to Miss Ella and we will fix something nice."

"Thank you Nellie," he said as he watched her disappear into the kitchen.

***

# 9

Nellie spent the early part of the evenings with Clytie and her son Jonas learning to read and write. She was surprised to see how well her friend was doing and hoped she would soon catch up. Her days were spent cleaning and polishing since Sarah Bottomsley was on her way back, and the evenings of course were reserved for John Bottomsley.

The day had finally arrived and not a speck of dust was visible on the mahogany furniture. On the dining room table was a magnificent floral bouquet and the eight cane-bottomed chairs were standing neatly side by side like the soldiers in a row. The chair covers in the drawing room were all washed and ironed and the plantation chair where John Bottomsley sat each evening looked as though no one had ever sat upon it. It had been quite a while since Nellie had seen so many flowers in the house. On each of the occasional tables sat a vase with a single rose from Mr. Fitz's well-tended gardens.

Freshly cut roses sat on Sarah's bedside table and a pitcher of cold water stood beside the wash basin on the wash stand. Nellie sprinkled her towels with Rose Water and put them neatly beside the pitcher. Her negligee lay at the bottom of the bed just waiting to be worn and one of her cotton dresses was hanging behind the door so there would be something cool for her to put on when she arrived.

"One day I am going to have a good life just like Miss Sarah," said Nellie as she examined her handiwork.

"That could happen if you listen to me and take my advice," said her employer.

"I didn't know you was home sir," she said feeling a little ashamed he had heard her.

"You know you can no longer sleep in the house now that my wife is back," he said to her.

"I know that sir."

"But I will still come by and visit you in the hut," he said. "Nellie," he said after a moment, "would you like to move away from here?"

"I don't have nowhere to go sir."

"You can live somewhere in the north of the island, in a house of your own!"

"I don't have enough money to buy a house sir."

"We can talk about it another time. Right now I must pick up my parents because they also want to be there to meet Sarah."

"Yes sir."

"Make sure everything is done by the time we return."

She closed the windows in the bedroom to keep the room cool and after a quick look, was satisfied that everything was in order, so she closed the door.

The smell of freshly baked cakes permeated throughout the house in spite of the kitchen door being closed. Nellie and Miss Ella were now cooking Sarah's favorite meal; poached chicken breast with boiled potatoes. They thought of ways to make it as delicious as possible since Sarah had no love for aromatic spices.

"What you smiling at Nellie?" asked Miss Ella as Nellie was looking out the window with a smile pasted across her lips.

"You have to promise me that you ain't going to tell nobody what I am going to tell you," she said.

"I don't know what I am promising, but I ain't going to say a word, so tell me child."

"The Master ask me this forenoon if I want to move away from the plantation. If I want to move, he would get a house for me in St. Lucy."

"Girl, the Good Lord don't come, but he send. I real happy for you Nellie. God know you need a break in this life. I glad he is going to be looking out for you. Not like your no-good father who left you and your mother almost destitute. Listen to an old woman and take heed Nellie. When you see a man in the gutter and the dog is licking his mouth, don't you feel sorry for him! Somewhere along the way, he do a lot of wrong things to a woman. I don't want to spoil your happiness; I just want you to understand about life."

"But if I leave Miss Ella, I will miss you."

"Take your time child. Right now we still have a lot to do and the time is short.

Miss Sarah boat must be there already."

"I don't have nothing else to do. The table ready and the bedroom ready and all she got to do is come home. I glad you are back here Miss Ella. Sometimes it was real lonely here."

"Don't tell an old woman lies. You was living like the mistress of the manor."

"And I was enjoying it too Miss Ella, so it going to be real hard to move back into my little hut."

"How many places you set on the table Nellie?"

"Four. The Master's parents coming too."

"Lord have mercy. We got to put up with them already?"

"Just think about the hambone," said Nellie, "and it would bring a smile to your face."

The black Vauxhall wended its way down the long driveway which led to the Bottomsley Great House. John Bottomsley was at the wheel with his wife beside him. It was a beautiful day; warm, but not overly so with a light breeze working its way across the estate. This was the type of weather Sarah liked and it showed by the expression on her face. His parents sat in the back and quizzed her about life and the goings on back in the home country.

"Sometimes I have a yearning to go home again."

"What will you do there Millie? There won't be anyone for you to order around."

"You will be there."

"Forget it Millie. I will leave this island only when they stretch me out in a box, and not even then. Much too cold under the earth," he said with a shudder.

"I never thought I would have missed it as much as I did. I missed the sunshine, the flowers, the fruit, the children and most of all I missed you John."

"Speaking of children," said Millie, "did my son tell you that he opened a school for the plantation children? I don't know what they will do with all that education."

Before her husband could answer, his father spoke to Millie.

"Millie I am always reminding you that it is none of your business. It is our son's money and he can do with it as he pleases."

"Mother you forgot to tell Sarah that I also bought two cows and some chickens."

Millie became offended.

"I'm glad you are back here Sarah. Do you see what I had to contend with alone? Neither of them listens to me."

"Because you interfere in everyone's business Millie," said her husband.

Sarah asked her husband to stop and she got out of the car, followed closely by Millie Bottomsley. Sarah could see Mr. Fitz still working in the garden and she had forgotten about the rich, pinkish creamy color in which they had repainted the house. Against the backdrop of the garden, the house reminded her of the colonial homes she had seen in the southern states of North America. Mr. Fitz had even planted flowers in the window boxes outside her bedroom window and also outside the guest room.

The columns were now draped in bougainvillea with tendrils reaching almost to the roof. She stopped and smelled each flower. Everything looked just perfect!

"What did you do to the roses Fitz? They are lovely."

"It is nice to have you home Miss Sarah. I used the manure from the cow pen and from the horse pen."

"From now on, it will be your responsibility Fitz. You do a much better job than me."

"And did Miss Sarah have a safe journey?" he asked beaming because of the compliments she had paid him.

"Yes thank you."

"Sarah I want you to know that Nellie is expecting a baby," said Millie.

"Nellie's expecting?" asked a surprised Sarah. "That means I'll have to find someone to replace her. That makes me sad because she is so dependable."

"How dependable can she be if she never gave a thought about you before she did such a stupid thing?"

"Miss Sarah," shouted Miss Ella. "It is nice to see you again."

"Yes we really missed you," said Nellie.

* * *

# 10

"Now Nellie," said Sarah Bottomsley, "I want you to tell me everything that has been going on."

"Not a lot Miss Sarah. The Master buy chickens and cows because you going to need fresh milk and the chickens will lay eggs everyday. We got a school too. Miss Ginger is the school teacher and she showing the children how to read and write."

"Who is Ginger?" asked Sarah.

"I don't know Miss Sarah, but she talk real pretty; even some of the children now talking just like Miss Ginger."

"I guess I'll meet her before the week is over."

"Miss Ella did not work in the house with me. The Master wanted more help in the fields, so Miss Ella work out there when you was away. We have an overseer now. Oh I almost forget Miss Sarah. He is Ginger brother. Thomas Hurley is his name and it look like he doing a good job."

"Why do you say that Nellie?"

"The Master never trust nobody, but he left him in charge when he went down to the docks. I wish the Master would find somebody else to run the food shop too."

"Don't tell me you don't like Polgreen."

"He ain't very nice. He make us stand out in the hot sun while he doing this and doing that. He don't let us into the shop together. I know it belong to the Master, but we wish we had somewhere else to buy food. Sometimes he try to steal our money."

"How does he do that Nellie?"

"He charge more than the food cost. Last week I pick up a little lamp there and he charge me too much."

Sarah Bottomsley could only smile. Nellie had told her that nothing much had happened during her absence, but yet she narrated story after story.

"How far along are you Nellie?" she asked.

"How far long?" she asked with a quizzical look on her face.

"I mean the baby Nellie."

"Oh that! He is about three months."

"Why do you say he? Would you like to have a son?"

"It don't matter Miss Sarah."

Sarah smiled again. She had had short conversations with Nellie before, but now realized there was more to her housemaid than met the eye. Nellie was also in her third month just as she was, and sadly she would have to find a replacement when she left.

"I'm a little tired now Nellie. Wake me when lunch is ready. And by the way Nellie, did Ginger also come by for lunch?"

"Just one time and she was with the Master parents, Reverend Allamby and Thomas Hurley."

"Alright Nellie, I think I'll take that nap now."

"Miss Ella," said Nellie, "something strange just happen."

"What happen child?"

"The Mistress ask me if Miss Ginger ever come by for lunch."

"And what you say?"

"I say only one time, with a few more people."

"And what she say?"

"Nothing. She went in to take a nap."

"Don't get mix up in their business. They would be like two peas in a pod and you would be out in the road, so keep your mouth shut."

"Alright Miss Ella," the young woman replied.

Around three o'clock a racket could be heard coming from outside. School was over and the children left the classroom with much jubilation. They were laughing and reciting what they had learned earlier that day.

*Mary had a little lamb*

*Its fleece was white as snow.*

*And everywhere that Mary went.......*

The child who had been reciting the poem had obviously forgotten the rest of it. Others tried to help but they too had forgotten. Ginger Hurley came out and she was smiling.

"Come on Toby," she said. "I know you haven't forgotten."

He grinned and looked around at his class mates.

*And everywhere that Mary went,*

*The lamb was sure to go.*

"I will teach you the second verse tomorrow. Don't forget to tell your parents you need proper, clean clothes for school. I will see all you tomorrow bright and early."

"Alright Miss Ginger," they said in unison.

Sarah looked down from her window at the goings-on. She saw Ginger Hurley with the children and guessed she was the school teacher Nellie had spoken about. She thought her name very appropriate. Her hair was reddish blonde. It was more like the color of turmeric than it was of ginger. She seemed like a nice person and it looked as though she got along well with the children, and her mother in law's comment flashed into her mind.

*"What would these children do with an education?"*

She thought of her husband and how kind he was to offer free education to these hapless youngsters, but her return did nothing to diminish the passion in her husband's trousers. Every evening he found himself in Nellie's hut for his dose of satisfaction and she patiently waited for him and administered it.

"You still building the house for me in St. Lucy?" she asked one night.

"Of course Nellie, but not right now," he said. "I have a lot of things to do before I can go up to there."

"Yes sir," she said her heart full of disappointment.

"Will you still be able to work?" he asked.

"The baby only three months old, just like Miss Sarah baby."

Without a word, he got up and left.

"I didn't say nothing wrong," she said to him.

Outside the children were still playing. They were chasing and trying to catch the fireflies as they danced between the trees. John Bottomsley had taken a longer route in order to avoid the prying eyes of the likes of Miss Ella and Miss Una. He knew that they knew what was going on, but now that his wife was back and in the family way, he tried his hardest to be discreet.

"You see what I see Ella?" asked Una.

"No, what you see?"

"The Master trying to hide. I can see him walking between the trees."

"You right Una. That is the Master. He can't stay away from Nellie. If I was a little younger, I would try my luck too."

"Don't make me laugh Ella. An old fowl cock like you thinking of getting Master Bottomsley between the straw?"

"You ain't listening to me Una. I said if I was younger, I would try. Look how happy Nellie is!"

"Why she so happy? Because she carrying the Master child?" Una asked. "That ain't nothing to be proud of. Now if he was going to do something good for Nellie, I would understand, but what she going to do with a little pickney under that galvanize roof?"

"You talking too much Una. If you would keep quiet for just a minute, I would tell you a secret."

"Well out with it Ella."

Miss Ella looked around to see if there was anyone within earshot.

"Just between you and me Una, the Master promise Nellie to build a house for her in St. Lucy."

"What you telling me Una? Nellie must be real sweet, but I am happy for her. I hope that something good happen for Clytie too. Gone are the days when we take our youth and use it to scrub and clean for these people. Clytie is just as pretty as Nellie. This kind of work is just for people like you and me Ella."

"Tell me something Una. What you think about this school that they open for the children? I just wondering what they going to do with all that learning."

"They could get better jobs with more money."

"Where they going to find those jobs Una? The only jobs we will ever get is working in the fields or in a hot kitchen."

"I don't like it when you talk like that Ella. We come a long way; just the other day, we used to be slaves. Now we free and can do what we want."

"This is what you call free Una? Look at the way we living. Look at this little hot place we have here with the sun scorching us to death. Running and jumping every time they call our name. What kind of freedom is that Una?"

"We might suffer now Ella, but our children and our grandchildren will have it a lot better than we had it; so I'm glad the Master is providing the young ones with some learning. I think our time is gone Ella, but a bright star shining for the young ones. Look at Clytie! In no time she learn to read and write, and it is only what my little grandson is showing her."

"I still say that we hardly any better off than in the times of slavery."

"I don't know too much about slavery Ella, but from what I gather, they used to beat slaves when they feel like it. They work every day and never get a penny for their hard labour. Don't tell me that what we got now ain't better."

"I just know that we all got our place in this world, and ours is to serve."

"Ella I going in my bed because you annoying me by the way you talking."

"Alright Una, I going to see you tomorrow, and by then you would understand that what I saying is true."

"Ella there is nothing you can say that could bring me around to your way of thinking."

* * *

## 11

"Now children," said Ginger Hurley, "you must write the same thing on your slate that I am writing on the blackboard."

They fidgeted a bit before getting their slates and pencils in front of them.

"And no spitting on the slates to clean them," she said. "I have a wet cloth here. You may come to me one at a time and I will give it to you."

She turned her back to the class and continued writing when she heard them scrambling to stand. She turned around and looked at the female standing in the doorway.

"May I help you?"

"No just carry on," said the lady.

"If you are looking for the entrance to the Bottomsley home, you have missed it. Go through the path again, turn to the left and there you will find the entrance."

The children were still standing although Ginger Hurley had beckoned them to sit.

"My name is Sarah Bottomsley."

"I'm sorry," said Ginger. "I never expected to see you here."

"I wanted to see the school and see how the children were getting along. You may sit," she said to them, "and please continue Miss Hurley."

She watched as Ginger took the children through their paces. She was impressed with her teaching ability and also wanted to have a close look at her because she suspected Ginger was her husband's lover. Not pretty but rather bright. As she sat lost in her thoughts another visitor entered the classroom, but stepped back when he saw Sarah Bottomsley.

"Sorry ma'am," he said. "I didn't know you were here. I came by to see my sister."

"Then you must be Thomas Hurley."

"Yes ma'am."

"Sarah Bottomsley," she said extending her hand.

"Pleased to meet you ma'am," he replied.

"Go out and play. I will come and get you in five minutes," Ginger said to the children.

That was music to their ears. Some of them would rather have played with the little mongooses they had caught and tied up outside or run around with their home-made toys. Their ingenuity was unimaginable. But then the toys which were available in Polgreen's store were much too expensive and toys were not a priority to their mothers or fathers. Ginger Hurley discreetly rubbed her hand on the back of her skirt to take away the whiteness of the chalk before she extended it to her employer's wife.

"Pleased to meet you ma'am," she said. "I've heard lots about you."

"Have you?" asked Sarah.

"Yes. Your husband told me you were at home on holiday. He said you would soon return but I didn't realize you were already here."

"Yes, I arrived two days ago."

The three discussed pleasantries about the trip and life in England. Sarah was curious and questioned her further.

"And how long have you been on the island?" she asked Ginger.

"About eighteen months."

"And where did you meet my husband?"

"At the Applegate plantation," she replied. "Philippa Applegate, the Applegate's daughter is a good friend of mine."

"I see. I must be getting back," she said to them. "It was nice meeting you both. You should come around sometime for drinks. I would like that."

"Thank you ma'am," they both replied.

Sarah realized that Nellie was having problems with her daily chores. Firstly she could see it and secondly she was in the same position and knew how she felt. She had difficulty bending and would tire easily. She thought it must be tough for someone doing manual labor in a hot kitchen, so she spoke with Miss Ella about finding a replacement for her.

"And why you didn't ask Miss Sarah if Nora could work for me until I had the baby?"

"How many times I have to tell you that Nora ain't suitable for house work?" Miss Ella asked.

"Miss Ella, I know Miss Una would not think the same way you thinking. You just like the other plantation owners who think we good for nothing."

"Girl!" exclaimed Miss Ella. "You have to show respect to older people."

"I respect you Miss Ella but you don't think like Miss Una."

"What you know about how Una think?"

"Because when I ain't happy, I go to Miss Una and she give me good advice."

"But I thought you always come to me for advice Nellie," said Ella now feeling a little left out.

"Yes, but you always put me down and I know that I good for more than cleaning and cooking," she replied.

"Don't let Una fill your head with nonsense."

"It ain't nonsense. Why you don't go and ask Miss Sarah about Nora?"

"Because I know what she is going to say. Nora too black to work in the house."

It was no use arguing with Miss Ella and she couldn't ask Sarah Bottomsley either, so she settled for Miss Ella's choice. She had chosen Miss Una's daughter Clytie. She was as fair-skinned as Nellie, in spite of the fact that her mother was blacker than black. No one asked and no one was informed of this strange phenomenon. They all knew Nellie's father worked as a plantation overseer, but Clytie's remained a mystery.

Sarah discussed the replacement with her husband who thought that under Ella's guidance, Clytie would do a good job. They also discussed Ginger Hurley and her brother Thomas, but came to a slight hitch when Sarah said she had invited them over for drinks. He seemed a little afraid to have his lover in such close proximity to his wife. Sarah was tired and decided to go to bed leaving her husband in his favorite chair.

Half an hour later John Bottomsley was sitting on Nellie's bed waiting for his evening dose of satisfaction. When it was all over, he stretched himself on the bed and puffed on his pipe.

"So Clytie will soon be replacing you," he said.

"She going to do a good job sir."

"Remember that house we spoke about in St. Lucy?" he asked.

"Yes sir."

"I will give it to you soon. I also want you to know that I will be a good father to the child."

"Yes sir."

"Nellie you know that my wife has problems and has never been able to give me a child."

"I know that sir."

"The plantation will one day belong to our child if anything happens to me or to my wife."

"You really mean that sir?"

"I do Nellie. She will go to the best schools and will have all the things you didn't have. Do you understand what I mean Nellie?"

"Yes sir."

"So if Sarah's baby dies, will you allow us to bring up your child as our own?"

"But you could have another child by Miss Sarah sir," she said now fully understanding what he was saying.

His last statement threw her into a panic.

"You say that you going to build a house in St. Lucy for me and Emily."

"Then she wouldn't be close to good schools and I wouldn't be able to name her as the next plantation owner."

"Don't do that to me sir," she pleaded. "I don't want to give away my Emily."

"Think about it Nellie. I will still build you the house as I promised and we can carry on just as we're doing now. You won't have to worry about anything or anybody, nor will you have to work as hard as you're working now. I can set you up in some kind of business. Whatever you like Nellie. Maybe we could have another Emily. Think about it and think of Emily's future."

* * *

# 12

She was called Millie and rightly so, for in the middle of the night she struck the island with a vengeance. Winds of over one hundred and twenty miles an hour swirled through the trees and uprooted them. Galvanize sheets flew around like kites caught up in the wind and the low lying areas were all flooded. John Bottomsley turned on his radio to the BBC, but there was nothing. Through the flickering light he could see objects flying around and he could also hear the voices of the workers as they tried to salvage what was left of their belongings. After looking in on his wife who was still sleeping soundly, he put on his boots and hurried through the back door.

"Sir," a young boy said, "what we going to do with the cows and the horses?"

"See to the horses first. Make sure they are tied up properly and keep the barn door closed. I'll be there in a minute."

He went to Nellie's hut and banged on the door. She looked as if she had seen a ghost. The howling of the wind along with the thunder and lightning had scared her tremendously.

"Get dressed," he said. "I'll be back in a minute."

He went to Ella's hut and found her already dressed and praying to her Lord to save her from destruction.

"Come on Ella. You and Nellie go over to the house. If Sarah needs anything, please look after her. I'll be there soon."

Everyone else went to the school building since it was a new and secure structure. Crying children, weeping mothers and the men from the village all hoarded together to wait out the storm. After two hours the winds abated and dawn was creeping up on the horizon. Millie's destruction was visible everywhere they looked. Mr. Bottomsley told them there would be no work, but they would be paid. Eagerly they set about repairing the damage which Millie had left behind. Some of the huts had disintegrated under the force of the winds, uprooted trees lay across the pathways and fallen fruit was everywhere. The damage to the Great House was minimal and Nellie's hut, sheltered by three other huts was virtually unscathed. Hanging on to Miss Ella, she made her way back to her little home and the first thing she did was to search for her money. She pulled it out and counted it. Every cent was there so she stretched herself out on the bed and was soon fast asleep. Miss Ella did not fare as well. The water had seeped in and all her possessions were soaked in muddy water.

"They pick the right name for that devil," she said to Una as she surveyed the damage.

"Count your blessings Ella. Some of us a lot worse off."

"What happen to yours?" she asked Ella.

"Not much. In just a little time, I'll have it all back to normal."

"We still alive, praise God," said Ella. "Let me look in on Nellie. It almost time for her to deliver."

Miss Ella pushed the door and there was Nellie on the bed in agony.

"Come quick Una," she shouted. "I think the baby coming."

"How long you did like this Nellie?" Miss Una asked.

"About half hour Miss Una," she replied.

Nellie let out an ear piercing scream and grabbed onto the straw mattress.

"I think it is time to get some hot water Ella."

"I going to send Clytie up to the house to help out and I will get have to get the water from there because we can't light a fire outside. It too wet."

Nellie lay panting and puffing. Three hours went by and there was still no baby in sight.

"I can't take the pain no more. Please help me Miss Una," she said.

"Hold on Nellie. I coming back in a minute."

She was back with a small vial and a spoon, and proceeded to feed Nellie with the contents.

"Castor oil Miss Una?" she asked making a frightful face.

"It will help you. The pain will soon be gone Nellie."

Miss Ella opened the door to inquire if the baby was born.

"Not yet, but it will happen soon. I just give her a dose of castor oil."

"I got to go back to the house, but I coming back soon. I got to keep an eye on Clytie. She ain't know what she doing yet."

"You tell the Master about the baby?"

"Yes and he say he will come down as soon as it is born."

"Alright Nellie," said Miss Una, "you have to help yourself. You have to push out the baby."

"Alright," she said clutching Miss Una's hand.

Thirty minutes after the castor oil was administered, Nellie gave birth to a healthy baby girl.

"She real pretty Miss Una."

"That's right Nellie. She is a pretty baby. You buy anything to put on her?"

Miss Una did her job just as well as Dr. Sims did his, although she had no practical training. She had watched her mother and had stepped into her shoes after her death. Miss Una left and Nellie and the baby slept peacefully.

Later in the afternoon, Miss Una returned to see how they were doing when John Bottomsley appeared on the scene.

"I'm here to see Nellie and the baby," he said.

"Yes sir," said Miss Una taking her cue and leaving.

"Remember I said I was going to have a baby girl? Emily is pretty," she said to him.

"She is," he replied looking at the child who was so white that it could have passed for his and Sarah's child.

"Have you enough to eat Nellie?"

"We can't cook nothing because it too wet outside."

"I'll have Clytie bring you some lunch and dinner and each morning you'll receive two pints of milk."

"Thank you sir."

"You should keep the window open so that the fresh air can pass through and keep it cool."

"I don't want Emily to catch a cold. She still very delicate."

"Then you should sit outside. I'll send one of the boys to clean up and make outside comfortable. Here is some money to buy some things for Emily."

She held out her hand and clutched the money until he had left and then she looked to see what he had given her. She gasped. Ten shillings! She had to hide it before anyone saw it. She placed a pillow next to the sleeping child, deposited her money into the sock and then hid it where no one could ever find it. Before she had a chance to return to bed, Miss Ella knocked on the door and came in. She wanted to see the baby and to inform Nellie that Sarah Bottomsley seemed to be on the verge of giving birth. The two women were discussing Nellie's future and the future of her child when Nellie suddenly burst into tears.

"Miss Ella, the Master tell me that if Miss Sarah child die, he would like to take Emily so that he and Miss Sarah could bring her up as their own child. That way she will get the plantation. He say he still going to build the house in St. Lucy for me, but I don't know what to do Miss Ella."

"We can only pray that Miss Sarah child will live, but I don't think he can take away Emily just like that. For as long as you can, tell him you never will give up Emily, and when you see that you don't have a choice, then you pretend that you change your mind. He wouldn't want nobody to know that he was sleeping with the servant. You know how that would look? And when Miss Sarah find out, I wouldn't want to be in his shoes at all."

"But Miss Ella I want Emily to have all the things I never had. I don't want her to work the way I had to work; scrubbing pots and working in a hot kitchen like me and you."

"Nellie there ain't nothing wrong with honest work."

"You understand me Miss Ella. I want the best for my child."

"It look like if the father want the same thing too, so think about it girl, especially if you going to get a brand new house up in St. Lucy."

Emily woke up and started to cry.

"Hurry and give her the bubby. I think she hungry," said Miss Ella.

Nellie followed her instructions. She opened her calico blouse and the child suckled greedily.

* * *

# 13

Life was getting back to normal at the plantation. Millie was forgotten and the reaping of ground provisions had begun. Nellie's meals were still being sent down and she was enjoying the cow's milk which John Bottomsley had ordered for her. Whenever it was possible, she would be seen sitting outside her hut with the beautiful little child.

However in the Great house the storm clouds were on the horizon. Sarah Bottomsley took an instant dislike to Clytie and pretended she didn't exist. When she did acknowledge her presence, it was disdain and hatred.

"Ella," she shouted one day.

Miss Ella who was now suffering from rheumatism moved as fast as she could to her employer.

"Yes Miss Sarah?"

"You recommended her to me, didn't you?"

"I don't understand Miss Sarah."

"I am talking about Clytie," she said shifting her weight from one side to the other.

"Is something wrong?"

"She stole my diamond ring Ella."

"She won't do a thing like that Miss Sarah."

"Are you accusing me of lying?" she shouted.

"No ma'am, but I know Clytie since she was a little girl. Una didn't bring her up like that."

"Well if she didn't steal it, you did."

"You can't mean that Miss Sarah. I was working in this house for longer than I can remember and you never missed notthing."

"Well Ella, I will leave it up to you to try and find that ring. If it is not found, I will call the constable and you will both have to leave, and I don't mean just working here in the house, but you will both have to leave Bottomsley forever."

"Alright Miss Sarah, I will talk to Clytie."

Miss Ella returned to the kitchen to find Clytie sitting at the table reading the newspaper from the previous day.

"You ain't frighten she catch you reading?"

"No," she replied.

"Child you don't have to hang all your clothes out at once. You should have secrets when you around these people."

"You want to know what it say here on the front page?"

"Yes," said Miss Ella peering over her shoulder.

"It say that we have a shortage of educated people here on the island and they are encouraging more people from the home country to come here to live. If there were more people like Mr. Bottomsley, we wouldn't have this problem. He is helping us a lot more than they do on the other plantations. I understand that some of the workers on the other plantations want to send their children here to Miss Ginger."

"Where you hear that?"

"I hear everything. They want their children to be educated just like the children here at Bottomsley."

"I have to ask you something Clytie."

"You look very serious Miss Ella. What is wrong?"

"Tell me the truth Clytie. You teef (steal) Miss Sarah diamond ring?"

"You know me better than that Miss Ella. I can't even get close to that woman. She don't like me so I keep out of her way. You know that I don't go into that bedroom."

"I believe you child, but she tell me that if I don't find it, she will call the constable and we will have to leave the plantation."

"God is my witness Miss Ella. I didn't touch any ring."

"The baby probably got her behaving like that. I will try to talk to her again. She must be missing Nellie."

"She is a fool. She is so blind that she can't see that Nellie is carrying on with her husband and I won't be surprised if that child isn't his."

"Clytie!" shouted Miss Ella, "don't let me hear you say anything like that again. The song say, it does take two to tango. If that is so, it ain't all Nellie fault."

"But it is the truth Miss Ella."

"Don't worry Clytie. Don't make anymore trouble around here. You don't know what the Master would do if he find out that you talking that way."

"I don't know anything about no ring, so you tell her that."

After struggling home from a day in the hot kitchen, Miss Ella stopped by Nellie's and told her the story about Sarah's indifference towards Clytie and the disappearance of the ring. Nellie explained that Sarah Bottomsley always threw her diamond in a vase by the window and had perhaps forgotten. Of course Nellie also contributed Sarah's behaviour to her pregnancy. A few minutes after Miss Ella left, Clytie also came by and related the sad story to Nellie, and was relieved when Nellie told her the same thing she had told Miss Ella.

Although Emily was small and fragile, Nellie would bundle her up and take her over to Clytie's where Jonas continued to teach her to read and write. She could now read the newspaper and she could write, but still had a little way to go. John Bottomsley as usual, still came by to see how his daughter was coming along.

He went by Nellie's that evening to tell her that the house he was building for her in St. Lucy was almost finished, which was music to her ears. She then told him the story of Clytie and the ring and he offered to take it from the vase and show his wife. He was leaving when he ran into Clytie who seemed terribly distraught.

"Mr. Bottomsley, you should come home. I think the Mistress is going to have the baby."

He first went to see his wife and then drove off to get Doctor Sims.

"Clytie will stay with you while I get the doctor."

"No bring Ella instead."

"She is looking for Miss Una. She knows about these things."

Clytie stood at the foot of the bed and waited. Sarah Bottomsley was unusually quiet in spite of the fact that she had had so much pain before.

"How you feeling ma'am?" Clytie asked.

"I'm having a baby. What do you think?" she snapped.

"I was only wondering if you was having any pain."

"No."

"But you had a lot of pain before."

"Well I don't have any now," Sarah replied.

Clytie left the room after Miss Ella returned accompanied by Miss Una.

"The doctor is on the way Miss Sarah," Miss Ella said.

"I know. My husband went to get him."

"You having any pain Miss Sarah," asked Miss Una.

"None at all," she replied. "I was having pains about an hour ago, but they have all disappeared."

Miss Una left the room and went to the kitchen and told Clytie she should put the kettle on because the doctor would need a lot of hot water.

"You think something is wrong Ma?"

"I don't know, but then again I ain't no doctor. She should be having some kind o' pain. It is only natural."

"You think the baby dead Ma?"

"We have to wait for the doctor Clytie."

* * *

# 14

"Clear the room," commanded Dr. Sims.

The two women and Mr. Bottomsley hastily retreated. Miss Ella and Miss Una joined Clytie in the kitchen while Mr. Bottomsley took a seat in his favorite chair. He stood up and looked out the window, then went back to his chair. He was nervous and felt totally out of control. After about an hour, he heard a loud scream and rushed to the bedroom door.

"How is she?" he asked.

"Send in a kettle of hot water," the doctor ordered.

Clytie rushed to the door with the kettle, put it down and was about to leave when the doctor opened the door. He was no longer wearing his jacket and his sleeves were rolled up to his elbows.

"Not so fast," he said. "Come in."

She was afraid. She had seen her mother deliver a couple of babies before but then it was not Sarah Bottomsley's child and Dr. Sims was never present.

"I need your help and you must do exactly as I say."

"Yes sir, but if you want good help, my mother deliver all the babies on the plantation. She could help you. She waiting in the kitchen."

"Then get her. Tell her to wash her face and hands. I need her right now."

"Is she alright?" asked Mr. Bottomsley as she rushed past him.

"She alright."

Miss Una opened the door and went into the room. There was much moaning but no cries from a baby. After what seemed like an eternity, Dr. Sims opened the door followed closely by Miss Una.

"Sorry John. There wasn't much I could do. You'll have to bury the little one."

"Thank you Doctor," he said as he found the closest chair. "Wait here Una. Sit for a minute while I see the doctor out."

"And John, I've left some tablets for her. She should be given one every six hours. They will help her to rest and keep her comfortable."

"Thank you. I'll see to it that she rests."

"One more thing John, she shouldn't have anymore children."

"Yes Dr. Sims," was his reply.

Miss Una squirmed uncomfortably in the chair and waited.

"Una, I know you must be wondering why I asked you to wait."

"Yes sir."

"I want the death of Sarah's baby to remain a secret. I don't want you to discuss what went on here tonight with anyone. Not even with Ella or Clytie. Do you understand what I'm saying Una?"

"Yes sir, but that is going to be hard to keep it from them. They right there in the kitchen."

"Whatever you have to do, just keep it a secret," he said. "Come by and see me tomorrow evening around seven."

"Yes sir."

"How the baby?" Miss Ella asked Miss Una as she passed through the kitchen on her way home.

"The little girl alright."

"That is good news," said Clytie.

"You have to be up early tomorrow morning Clytie. You should go home because Miss Sarah will have you running tomorrow," said her mother.

A chill ran down Miss Ella's spine. She knew her best friend and knew her well. She could tell that something was not right.

"Drink a cup of tea Una," she said. "It was a rough night."

They heard the door to the drawing room close and Miss Ella and Miss Una peeped out to see what was going on. They saw John Bottomsley with a parcel in his arms and he was heading for the entrance to the village.

"I wonder where he going at this ungodly hour?" Miss Ella asked.

"To Nellie," said Miss Una as she wiped the tears from her eyes.

"Why he going to Nellie at this time of the night?"

"What you think happen tonight Ella?"

"Don't tell me that Una," she said as she too started to cry.

"Listen to me Ella. I ain't supposed to tell you that the baby gone. He beg me not to tell you or Clytie."

They waited at the window to see if he would return but he didn't. A short while later as the women were about to leave, the door opened again and he entered still carrying a bundle in his arms. He opened the door to his wife's room and went in.

"Time to go," said Miss Ella.

They both hurried to Nellie's hut. She was sitting on the straw mattress just staring into space. Miss Ella sat next to her and held her. Words were not necessary. They knew how much she was suffering. Next to the lamp was a bundle. Realizing what it was, Miss Una picked it up and left the hut.

"Bury it before it start to get bright," whispered Miss Ella.

Fifteen minutes later she was back and sat on the floor, while Miss Ella tried to calm Nellie.

"I don't think she alright. We got to get some nerve tea from Mr. Fitz. She ain't saying a word."

"She hurting Una. She really hurting. I say time and time again that there ain't much difference between what we are now and what we used to be. We still get treated like slaves."

"Shhhhh Ella. This ain't the time to talk about such things. I think she gone to sleep."

Miss Ella shifted her body and allowed Nellie to lay comfortably on the bed.

"Ella the doctor left some pills for Miss Sarah. I want you to get a couple of them."

"You asking me to teef (steal) and I ain't no thief," said Miss Ella.

"They ain't for me. They for Nellie. The doctor say they will help Miss Sarah to rest and I'm sure they will do the same thing for Nellie."

"In that case, I will see what I can do."

John Bottomsley sat on the chair next to his wife's bed and dozed off. Suddenly the baby began to cry and Sarah awoke and looked at it. Then she held it close to her as it tried to find her breast.

"Our daughter is hungry," she said as she lovingly looked at the child, who was now screaming from hunger.

She put it to her breast and the baby suckled, while Sarah examined every finger and toe.

"Are you happy?" he asked his wife.

"I told you I would give you a baby and of course I'm happy. She is a perfect little baby."

After they both fell asleep again, he quietly left the room and poured himself a drink. He sat in his favorite chair and pondered his life. He thought of Nellie and knew he had to get her off the plantation. The sooner, the better! He did not want to prolong her suffering. He had a story! He would tell Sarah that Nellie's child died and because of her grief, she had decided she no longer wanted to stay on at Bottomsley. He intended to make her life comfortable, far away from Bottomsley and its painful memories.

Early the next morning Miss Ella took Sarah's breakfast to her.

"Good morning Miss Sarah. How you feeling this morning?"

"Isn't she perfect Ella?" she asked admiring the child.

"She pretty just like you ma'am."

"Thank you Ella."

"I make two soft boil eggs for you. They will help to bring back your strength."

"Did you see my husband Ella?"

"No Miss Sarah. I make his breakfast but it is still in the kitchen. Maybe he went to get his parents to show them the baby."

"Perhaps you're right."

Miss Ella's heart sank and she hurried out the room. She could not help but think of Nellie, and she hadn't been able to get the pills from the bedside table. She would try when she went back to clean up the room.

"Come on Nellie, don't be so sad," said John Bottomsley. "Think of the bright future our daughter will have. Think of the day when she will be the proud owner of this plantation."

"I know that sir, but I can't help it. My heart never hurt like this."

"I must take you away from here before the week is over. By then the house will be finished and I will then put the necessary things inside."

"What things?" she asked.

"A bed, table, chairs and a cool box; all the things which you will need," he said.

"I don't want to go and leave my Emily," she said.

"But Nellie, we had a deal. I will come up and spend some weekends with you and sometimes during the week too."

"How can you be a good father to my Emily when you want to spend most of your time in St. Lucy?" she asked.

He was shocked by the question and found himself scrambling for an answer.

"I care for you and I care for my daughter and I will share my time with both of you."

"I want to see Emily before I leave," she said.

"Do you think that's a good idea?"

"No but I can't leave here and not know if I will ever see her again."

"Alright, but get your things together and I will find someone to take you up to your new home."

"I can bring Miss Ella and Miss Una up for a visit?"

"Whatever you want Nellie, but why don't you ask your sister to move with you?"

"I don't know if she want to move that far. Nora just about married sir."

"Nellie?"

"Yes sir?"

"You'll have to stop calling me sir."

"What I going to call you then?"

"I don't know, but sir won't be appro......right."

"I got to think of something sir."

He smiled. Old habits were indeed hard to break.

There was much sadness among the villagers. Word had spread that Little Emily had died in the night. Mr. Fitz came by with a rose only to be told that the child was no longer with them, and he too was heartbroken.

"Take this Nellie," said Miss Ella as she greeted Mr. Fitz. "This forenoon you have to take another one. It will help you to forget."

"You have a minute Miss Ella?" Nellie asked.

"I can't stop now Nellie. It real busy in the house. Miss Sarah got everybody running around. I coming back tonight and we will have a long talk."

When Miss Una arrived that evening, Nellie's frame of mind was no better than before and the woman did her best to console her.

"Nellie," she said to her. "It hard now, but you got a bright future. I can see it Nellie. It so bright you will have to put your hands in front of your eyes to prevent you from going blind."

"You really think so Miss Una?"

"I don't think so, I know so Nellie."

* * *

# 15

In an ironic twist of fate, Sarah Bottomsley decided to name her child Emily Charlotte, after her two favorite authors. Little did Nellie know that her child would still carry the name she had chosen. Even John Bottomsley found it hard to believe when his wife made the announcement, but he was happy the child would still be called Emily, the same name her biological mother had given her. He longed to pass the news on to her which he thought would bring her some form of comfort. Emily's arrival also brought Millie and the elder John Bottomsley over to see their new offspring.

"She is a real Bottomsley," declared Millie. "She has that cute little Bottomsley nose and those long slender fingers."

"My beautiful little granddaughter," cooed her husband. "You see Sarah, you just have to be patient and everything will work out."

"Thank you Father Bottomsley," she said as she admired her daughter.

"I know it's a bit early Sarah," said Millie. "But have you given any thought to a nanny for her?"

"Everything went so quickly that I didn't have the time to think about such things."

"Well it's time you did. We can't have her growing up like a penniless child. She has to have a nanny."

"I'll speak to John and we can probably find someone from the village to fill the position."

"Sarah Bottomsley, I won't hear of it! My grandchild has to have a proper nanny. An educated and cultured person who would teach her the social graces," Millie said.

"Who was your nanny Millie?" asked her husband. "Who taught you the social graces?"

"Ignore him Sarah. Since he came to this island, he has forgotten what it means to be civilized."

"Alright Princess Millie, I will get myself a drink and go on the porch until my son comes home."

"You do that, but don't drink all of John's rum."

"You are much too hard on him Mother Bottomsley. He means well."

"Do you hear the way he speaks to me Sarah? John would never dream of speaking to you in that fashion."

Millie Bottomsley had forgotten her roots back in the home country. She had forgotten how wonderful life had become only after she had set foot on the island. She now had servants at her beck and call, and was enjoying the lifestyle she had so longed for back home.

"What about the nanny Sarah?" Millie continued.

"Let me speak to John. She is also his child."

"Nellie could look after her until a proper replacement is found. By the way, did she have her baby?"

"Poor unfortunate Nellie," said Sarah. "Her baby died a couple days after it was born."

"Well that's one less mouth to worry about feeding," Millie said.

"It's still sad. I know how it felt when I lost my babies. I thought I would lose my mind."

"You can't compare yourself to her Sarah. You can afford to have children. They keep producing and have no way or means of supporting them."

"Are you trying to say that my son doesn't pay his workers well?" asked her husband who was on his way to refill his glass.

"You shouldn't be eavesdropping John. We are having a private conversation."

"By the way, where is Nellie? I'm tired of fixing my own drinks," he said.

"Nellie is sick Father Bottomsley."

"She should've had that baby by now. What did she have?"

"A little girl, but it died."

"That's a shame! She's a nice little girl, that Nellie."

"Get your drink and go back to the porch," said his wife.

"That I will do when I am good and ready Millie," he said. "You know that was no mistake they made a couple weeks ago."

"What are you talking about?" asked his wife.

"They named that damned storm after you and they certainly knew what they were doing."

Sarah wanted to laugh but was afraid of offending her mother in law. She knew the woman was pompous and it took the likes of her father in law to keep her in line.

"Where is my son anyway?" she asked ignoring her husband.

"He had to go to St. Lucy. He has a new project he's handling up there, but he'll be home soon."

"How about a nice cup of tea Sarah?" Millie asked. "I could do with one too."

Sarah rang the bell and Clytie came in.

"Yes ma'am?"

"Could you bring us a pot of tea and some of Ella's biscuits?" she asked not calling her name.

"Yes ma'am."

"Who's that?" asked Millie.

"That's Clytie. She's not at all like Nellie."

"Why do you say that?"

"Nellie was sweet and caring. Besides this one is a thief."

"What did she steal?"

"My diamond ring which John gave me for our anniversary," replied Sarah.

"Did you call the police?"

"Why do we need the police?" asked the younger Bottomsley coming in with his father.

"Sarah told me that thing stole her diamond ring. Why on earth would she need a diamond anyway?"

John Bottomsley went into the bedroom and looked at his beautiful little daughter who was fast asleep. He bent over and kissed her on the forehead. She would now be with him every waking moment of the day. He turned to leave and remembered the reason why he had entered the room in the first place. He looked inside the vase but saw nothing. When he turned it over, the ring fell out.

"No need to call the police," he said. "I found the ring exactly where you put it Sarah."

"Where was it John?"

"In the vase where you always put it," he replied.

"My goodness!" she said. "I had completely forgotten that I put it there."

Clytie came in with the tea and biscuits and set them on a little table in the drawing room next to the two women.

"Who are you?" asked the older John Bottomsley. "You don't look a thing like Nellie."

"Nellie is sick and I taking her place," replied Clytie.

"So you're Clytie," said the older man.

"Yes sir."

"Thank you," said Sarah when she saw where the conversation was heading.

"I still say they're not to be trusted," said Millie.

"What have you got against the sweet little thing?" asked her husband. "She has never done you any harm."

"John!" she said in a chastising manner. "She's a servant."

"Millie, you seem to have forgotten that when I met you, you were a shop girl near Shepherds Bush, but that didn't stop me from marrying you."

"How dare you compare me to them?" she asked on the verge of tears.

"Them who?" he asked teasingly. "Clytie's almost as white as you are."

"Can I get you a drink Father?" his son asked.

"Yes son. I need it to put up with your mother."

"I've been telling Mother Bottomsley about the project you're working on in St. Lucy," said his wife.

"It's nothing terribly important Sarah. I'm starving. Could you get Ella or Clytie to fix me something to eat while I change?"

"Of course son," said his mother.

"He was talking to Sarah. When they need your help they will ask for it."

"It's alright Father Bottomsley," said Sarah.

Millie was elated to get Sarah's backing and dashed off to the the kitchen to order the servants around.

"She's got to be kept in line Sarah. Give her an inch and she'll run away with the whole foot."

"She doesn't mean to be like that Father Bottomsley."

"Yes she does. You don't know your mother in law."

* * *

"She always like that Miss Ella?"

"And more child. We don't like when she come around. She seem to think that this is her house and we are the slaves."

"I could never work for anybody like that," replied Clytie.

"We got ways of fixing people like Millie," said Miss Ella.

"What do you mean?"

"Ask Nellie about the hambone. When we finish here, you run over and see how she doing. And while you there, ask her about the hambone. It would help to cheer her up."

* * *

# 16

"Miss Sarah?" said Nellie knocking as softly as she could on the bedroom door.

"Yes?"

"It is me Nellie."

"Come in Nellie. How do you feel?"

"Much better Miss Sarah. I come by to see Little Emily. She is a pretty child," said Nellie drawing closer to look.

"She *is* pretty, isn't she Nellie. One day you too will have a little one. I know how you feel Nellie. I also lost two of my babies."

"But it was different with you Miss Sarah."

"Not much different Nellie. Your baby died just like my babies died."

"You don't understand Miss Sarah," she said as the tears started to flow.

"What don't I understand Nellie?"

"Nothing Miss Sarah," she replied.

"It will be alright. When do you think you can come back to work? I would love you to look after Emily."

Sarah's thoughtlessness threw Nellie into a panic and she flew out of the room. Sarah just shook her head and went back to her book. Nellie flew through the kitchen door with Miss Ella in hot pursuit.

"What happen child?" the older woman asked.

"I didn't realize it would be so hard Miss Ella. I just see my Emily and I just can't take it no more."

"Only time will help you child. It really don't make any sense if you stay here. You would end up in the mad house."

"You right Miss Ella. I would go mad if I had to see her every day and not be able to call her my child."

"So what you going to do Nellie?"

"I am leaving. The house in St. Lucy finish and I want to take Nora up there with me. That way she wouldn't have to work in the fields no more."

"I proud of you Nellie. You thinking of your sister even though you got so much on your mind. God will look after you. But how you getting up St. Lucy?"

"I don't know but I will ask the Master."

"Don't leave without saying goodbye Nellie."

"You know I wouldn't do a thing like that Miss Ella."

Miss Ella returned just in time to hear a commotion coming from the direction of the schoolhouse.

"What's going on Ella?" asked Sarah.

"I don't know."

They looked out the window to see a little boy jumping up and down while his mother whipped him around the legs with a thin tree branch.

"When I tell you to go to school, I mean to go to school," she said as she continued to flog him.

"I am going tomorrow please," said the screaming child.

"I beating you because you tell lies," she said.

And for each word she spoke, the child received a lash.

"Excuse me Miss Sarah," Miss Ella said, as she headed for the back door.

In a couple minutes, she appeared with the unfortunate child and his mother.

"You going to kill him?" Miss Ella asked.

"Why you don't mind your business and stay in the big house?" she asked. "He is my child and if I want to kill him, I will do that. He is wicked and stubborn."

"You upsetting Miss Sarah," said Miss Ella looking up at the window where Sarah Bottomsley was standing.

The little boy was relieved to see the two women arguing because he was no longer receiving the lashes with the tamarind rod which his mother had sent him to pick.

"Look at this child feet. You should be ashamed of yourself."

"I tell you he stubborn and he won't go to school. He tell a lot of lies. He tell me he went to school but I know different."

"Why you don't go to school child?" asked Miss Ella. "I wish I could read and write. You have a chance. Take it."

The unfortunate boy could not answer because he was still sobbing and snot was running down his nose which he cleaned on the sleeve of the crocus bag shirt. The mother grabbed him by an ear and dragged him off leaving Miss Ella's eyes to follow them.

"Don't beat him no more. I know that he learn his lesson," she said as the mother disappeared with him.

That was the way they chastised their children. Their parents and their grandparents had all been brought up that way. There was no discussion about the mistakes made; a brutal flogging was always the way to solve the problems with children.

An hour later, the children were all playing outside and among them, the unfortunate boy who seemed to have forgotten the beating which he had received earlier. He was leading the group in some sort of a game which mimicked the lives of the adults.

My children, my children?
Yes mama.
Where you been?

At Grandpapa.

What did he give you?

Two sugar apples.

Where did you put them?

On the shelf.

And so the game went on and on until it became dark and they retired to their huts.

"What I won't give to be a child again!" said Miss Ella.

"Why you want to do that?" asked Clytie.

"Because they don't have a care in the world," Miss Ella said.

"Come, let's go and see what Nellie doing."

All her possessions were sitting on the bed next to her. Her clothes she had stuffed in a white calico bag and a few more odds and ends were still on the bed beside her.

"Nellie, you leaving already?" asked Miss Ella.

"The Master tell me to get ready. He coming back in an hour to get me."

"And what about Nora?"

"She coming up later."

"I am going to miss you Nellie," said Miss Ella wiping her eyes.

"The Master say you could all come up and visit once I settle in."

"Take care of yourself Nellie and don't forget us."

"Miss Ella I want you to keep an eye on Emily. Make sure she is a happy child."

"You know you don't have to worry about Emily. She is going to be in good hands."

Clytie arrived on the scene, found out what was going on and she too started to sob; occasionally drying her eyes on her long white apron.

"Can I come to visit you too Nellie?"

"You know that go without asking Clytie."

Another knock on the door and Miss Una was there.

"It hot in here. What going on?" asked Miss Una. "I just come by to check up on Nellie."

"You just in time. Nellie is leaving us," said her friend.

"Where you going Nellie?"

"Up to St. Lucy."

"I happy for you Nellie. Look after yourself and there will be a lot more babies for you."

John Bottomsley kissed his wife and daughter goodbye. He would be gone for three days, and so he placed his case in the car and without the slightest glance behind him, he climbed in and drove off.

One of the village boys knocked on Nellie's door. He was accompanied by a man they had never seen.

"He looking for you Miss Nellie," said the boy.

"I here to get you," said the man.

He gathered her things and she hugged her friends. There was more wailing than at a funeral.

"Don't forget I coming up next week," said her sister.

She looked around the hut, stepped out the door, then paused and looked up at the Great House. She envisioned her daughter in Sarah Bottomsley's bedroom fast asleep.

"Let me help you Miss Nellie," said the young man whose name was Clarence.

The group gathered in front of the hut and watched as Nellie climbed into the car which was taking her out of their lives.

"Our Nellie gone," said Miss Una. "Gone, gone!"

* * *

# 17

Dr. Sims knew that Sarah Bottomsley would probably be in a depressed state, and decided to pay her a visit.

"Please tell Mrs. Bottomsley I'm here," he said as he removed his hat and handed it to Clytie.

Sarah was sitting in the drawing room reading a book.

"The doctor here to see you," said Clytie.

"Then send him in."

"How are you feeling?" he asked Sarah.

"Very well Doctor. I couldn't be better."

"You seem alright, but are you really alright?"

"Why shouldn't I be?" she asked him.

"I'm taking about the baby," said a rather confused Dr. Sims.

"She's asleep. She's such a beautiful baby. I knew that one day it would have worked out for me."

"What on earth are you talking about?" he asked.

"Maybe if you came into the bedroom with me to see Emily, you would understand how precious she is."

Dr. Sims followed her into the bedroom and looked at the sleeping child. He no longer seemed confused. He was indeed totally confused.

"She looks just like my husband, doesn't she?"

"She does, and where is your husband Mrs. Bottomsley?"

"He went up north for a couple days, but he'll be back on Thursday evening."

"Please tell him I want to see him as soon as possible."

He removed his hat from the hat rack and left the house in great haste. Miss Ella peered from the kitchen window and saw him at the wheel of the car. He sat there for about five minutes staring into space, then turned the engine on and drove away.

"What you looking at?" Clytie asked Miss Ella.

"Dr. Sims."

"What he doing?"

"Sit down Clytie. I don't know how much time I got left on this earth, so I am going to tell you something."

"This sound serious," said Clytie pulling up a chair.

"You see how Dr. Sims left in such a hurry? He left like that because he is confused."

"About what Miss Ella?"

They did not notice Sarah Bottomsley walk past the kitchen door which was now slightly ajar. It was left that way so that Clytie could hear when Emily woke up. Sarah was heading for the porch when she heard the voices and stopped to listen because they seemed to be intentionally whispering to each other.

"You remember that night when Emily was born?"

"Yes."

"Nothing didn't seem out of the ordinary to you?"

"No Miss Ella."

"Now you remember the following day we hear that Nellie Emily had pass away that night?"

Clytie stared at Miss Ella.

"You still don't understand Clytie?"

"No Miss Ella."

Miss Ella dropped her voice even lower to tell her the secret and a look of horror glued itself onto Clytie's face.

"You mean that……..?"

"Exactly," said Miss Ella nodding her head.

Sarah Bottomsley tried her hardest to understand what they were talking about. She knew something was amiss and she knew it had something to do with her. Unable to hear or understand, she dismissed it as servant gossip.

"That is why Nellie left in such a hurry?"

"Exactly," said Miss Ella.

"So that baby Miss Sarah say is hers really belong to Nellie?"

"That's right."

"Poor Nellie," said Clytie. "But what that got to do with Dr. Sims?"

"Sometimes I wonder about you Clytie. You can't put two and two together? Dr. Sims know that the Mistress baby dead. Now she showing him a baby and saying it is hers."

"Ohh-h-hh-h-h!" said Clytie with a furrowed brow. "Now I understand. What you think he is going to do?"

"That is the number one question. We got to wait until Master Bottomsley come back. It going to be cat piss and black pepper around here."

"But how could she hold on to Nellie child like that Miss Ella?"

"I don't think she know or she don't care to know. There is none so blind as he who will not see," said the older woman.

Emily awoke and started to scream. Sarah did not move, but Clytie flew into the room to pick her up. She looked down at the child who bore absolutely no resemblance to Nellie, except for the wiry hair, but she saw Mr. Bottomsley's upturned nose.

"Come Miss Emily," she said picking up the child. "You hungry, ain't you?"

The child stopped screaming and looked up at Clytie. She knew she had to do all she could for the little innocent child; the child of her best friend. She went to the kitchen where Miss Ella had already put the feeding bottle on the table for her.

"My little Nellie," she said looking at the child as it drank greedily. "Miss Ella and I will look after you."

"Don't call her little Nellie. You may forget and call her that in front of somebody."

"That is true. Alright Little Emily, your little belly full?"

With that she started to rub the child's back as its little head lay on her shoulder. Emily belched so loudly that they both were almost hysterical from laughter.

"Now you feel good Emily?" Miss Ella asked rubbing her little head. "Why life got to be so complicated?" she asked looking up to heaven.

"Think about it like this Miss Ella. She will have everything she want and she will certainly have a better life than you and me."

* * *

The journey to St. Lucy was indeed precarious. The young man Clarence hardly said a word as he concentrated on his driving. Nellie hung onto the door handle and wondered if she would make it to her destination in one piece. She saw gullies as they drove by and some trees she had never seen before. There was the giant windmill where the workers took the sugar cane to be pressed into juice. There were too many hills and the roads were narrow and during the whole journey, she saw only two other cars. Except for a couple workers on their way home, the countryside of Barbados seemed like a lonely place. She had not yet reached her home and already loneliness was setting in.

After about an hour, the car finally stopped in front of a bungalow with many steps leading up to the entrance. She stared up at the house and wondered if it was her new home. It had not yet been painted, but it was a handsome house. She could see the windows with the shutters, very similar to those at Bottomsley. Clarence took her belongings and placed them on the top step. She was still staring at the house when he called out to her.

"Miss Nellie, you home. The door open. Just turn the handle and go in."

She slowly climbed the steps and looked inside. She could see a lamp burning on a little table. John Bottomsley had furnished the house as he had promised. Pieces of mahogany furniture dotted the living and dining rooms. In the kitchen was an icebox and something which resembled a stove. It was different from the stove they had used at Bottomsley. It stood on four skinny legs and there was an upside down bottle on the side which was filled with liquid.

"That's the kerosene for the stove," a familiar voice said.

She jumped because she was unaware of another presence in the house.

"I'm sorry if I frightened you."

"What you doing here sir?"

"I thought we had agreed that you would no longer call me sir."

"I forget sir."

"Since you don't know what to call me, I decided you should say JB."

"Alright JB."

"Do you like it?" he asked.

"I like it."

"Let me show you around," he said. "Here is your bedroom, and here is your sister's bedroom. This door leads to the bathroom and this one to the back of the house. You have already seen the dining and drawing rooms. I hope it is big enough for you."

"It bigger than I expect sir. Can I buy food around here?"

"Don't worry about that. I will send your foodstuff up at the end of each week. Speaking of foodstuff, do you think you can do what Mr. Polgreen does?"

"You mean like selling goods and weighing flour and things like that?"

"Yes, you must find something to keep yourself busy, and since there are no other shops around here, I think that would be something for you to do."

"How much money you going to pay me?"

"All depends on you. I can provide the foodstuff. You will run the shop and then pay me fifty per cent of the money you bring in. After you have enough money saved, you will buy your own foodstuff and everything you make will be yours."

"You mean the shop will really be mine?"

"Yes, do you remember I promised to look after you?"

"I remember that."

"I'm very tired Nellie. I should be getting to bed."

"Yes, it real late and you have a long drive back to the plantation."

"I'm not going back to Bottomsley tonight."

"So where you going to sleep?"

He did not answer, but headed straight towards her bedroom. She felt hot and sticky and needed to wash herself, so she went to the bathroom. In spite of the fact that John Bottomsley had virtually stolen her child, she had a very special feeling in her heart for him. She removed her head tie and looked at the new woman in the mirror. She liked what she saw and she was pleased with the corn rows which her sister had woven into her hair. She undressed and cleaned her body but forgot that her clothing was still at the entrance door. She peeped out, then wrapping her apron around her naked body quietly went to get them.

"Where are you Nellie?" asked John Bottomsley.

"I coming JB," she said.

Just as she put her calico nightgown on, he appeared at the bathroom door.

"I've never seen you without a head tie Nellie. You should stop wearing it," he said admiring the corn rows in her silky hair.

"Don't look at me sir."

"Why not? You're prettier without it," he said. "Are you ready for bed?"

He guided her to the bedroom and made hot mad passionate love to her, until exhaustion forced them both into a comatose state. That was the first time he had made love to Nellie and it was beautiful. It was no longer a quick lustful moment in her wattle hut. The sun was coming up as she quietly got out of bed and went to the bathroom, but he was following closely on her heels, forcing her to try to cover herself with her nightgown.

"That's not necessary Nellie; I've already seen you completely naked."

"That was different," she said still trying to cover herself.

After a satisfying breakfast which he had provided, he left for the Henley plantation. He told her about the experiments they were doing to increase sugar cane production and promised he would be back to spend the night. She however had one request.

"I want one of those machines they use to make clothes," she said. "I see pictures of them in the newspaper."

"Where will you find the time to do so many things?" he asked.

"I used to do the same things at the plantation. I work all day long and then at night, I used to make my own clothes. I can pay for it myself if you tell me how much it cost."

"Alright Nellie, perhaps twenty shillings."

"If you get one for me I will give you the money JB."

He knew that Nellie was thrifty, but hadn't expected that she would be showing any signs of independence that quickly.

* * *

# 18

Nellie was still deeply depressed, so John Bottomsley decided he didn't want to leave her alone. During the day, he would go to the Henleys, and early evening found him parking his car in the treelined grove behind Nellie's house.

While he was spending most of his time with Nellie in St. Lucy, Sarah was busy making plans for Emily's christening. No expense would be spared for the upcoming event because she had waited much too long for this moment. It was to be one of the proudest days of her life, but sadly her parents would not be attending. Her husband's family on the other hand, couldn't have been more proud.

He arrived two days before the big event only to be told that Dr. Sims was there and needed to speak with him urgently. He knew what the doctor wanted and had no desire to meet with him, but found it prudent to visit him and get the matter settled once and for all.

"I want you to tell me what's going on," said the doctor. "I was a witness to the death of your child and now there is going to be a christening. Your wife seems to think that she gave birth to this little girl."

"You don't begrudge Sarah a bit of happiness, do you?"

"You know this has nothing to do with happiness."

"Then what is it about?" asked John Bottomsley.

"It is about the child your wife says is hers."

"It is her child."

"Let's not play games. Where did you get the child John?"

"She is my daughter."

"Are you trying to tell me she is your own flesh and blood? Where is the mother?"

"She gave me the child to bring up as my own."

"Then she must be a plantation worker. Don't tell me you bought the child from her."

"I never said that."

"Slavery has long been abolished John. You just can't go around buying and selling human beings."

"It's much too complicated for you to understand."

"Why don't you try explaining it to me?" asked Dr. Sims.

John Bottomsley swallowed his pride and told the story in detail. Before doing so, he made the doctor promise never to utter a word of the conversation.

"So this I gather is much more than a passing affair."

"I don't know. I'm rather confused. All I can say is now that I'm here, I really miss her."

"And what about when you're there?"

"I don't know what you mean."

"Do you miss Sarah?" asked the doctor.

"I do but not as much as I miss her."

"Is it because she was able to give you a child?"

"It could be, but the child is with my wife."

"Considering the circumstances, I don't think there was a whole lot you could do."

"Does that mean you understand?"

"No I don't understand and can't condone what you have done, but I understand the precarious situation you found yourself in."

"Ella," said Sarah Bottomsley, "will you go over and fetch Nellie for me."

"Nellie?" she asked being caught totally by surprise.

"I can't do that Miss Sarah."

"Why not?" she asked in an irritated manner.

"Nellie gone."

"What do you mean by Nellie gone. Gone where?"

"Yes, she gone Miss Sarah," said Clytie quickly. "We think that because she lost her baby, she couldn't be around other babies. Last night when we went to visit she was gone with all her belongings."

"Why didn't anyone tell me? Why did it have to happen just before Emily's christening? John will have to start searching for her when this is all over."

"Yes Miss Sarah," said Miss Ella.

"I was waiting for her to return to look after Emily."

"She ketch me off guard," said Miss Ella as her employer left the room.

"Sometimes I think she is such a selfish woman," said Clytie. "How she expect Nellie to look after her baby when she just lost hers?"

"They like that Clytie. I always used to tell Nellie that. Miss Sarah ain't a bad person, she is just very selfish."

Emily looked like a little angel in her christening gown. Everyone fussed over her especially her grandparents. Mrs. Henley and one of her daughters were chosen as godmothers and Thomas Hurley who had ingratiated himself into the family was chosen as godfather. When Reverend Allamby poured the water on her yellow curls, she yelped like a wounded puppy.

"She's got a good set of lungs," he commented.

Back at the plantation, extra help had to be brought in to help with the preparations, because it was just too much for Miss Ella and Clytie to handle alone.

"I should be the godmother," said Clytie.

"Wake up girl," said Miss Ella. "Sometimes you remind me of Nellie."

"Look at Nellie. She don't have to do this no more."

"Everything got it price Clytie," she said. "Everything!"

The plantation workers turned out in full force. They were all waiting by the roadside to get a glimpse of the little girl who had brought this celebration to Bottomsley. When her father opened the car door and Agatha Henley stepped out with the child, cries of jubilation went up. Mrs. Henley slowly climbed the steps with the precious cargo, followed closely by her daughter and Ginger Hurley. Miss Ella's cuisine reigned supreme, and totally out of character, she too found herself barking orders to the people working with her.

"Everything got to be just so," she said.

"You making me nervous Miss Ella. Everything going well. They enjoying all the nice little things you make. And don't talk about the Master father, he ain't move from the table since he come through the door," said Clytie.

"I happy to hear that."

Little Emily had fallen asleep. She had never seen so many faces all at once, and her proud grandmother didn't want to let her out of her sight. Finally Reverend Allamby congratulated the proud parents of such a beautiful little girl and asked all present to say a word of thanks to Dr. Sims, without whom the miracle would never have taken place. John Bottomsley squirmed and did not applaud along with the others. Ten minutes later, the doctor left the celebration, thanking the host as he went out the door.

"I know what you think of me," John Bottomsley began.

"This is neither the time nor the place; besides your wife seems like a happy woman."

"Thank you," he replied.

After it was over, he went to the kitchen and handed an extra two shillings to Clytie and Miss Ella.

"Sir I don't mean to be forward," said Miss Una who was called in to wash the dishes. "You say I was to come by two nights after Emily born. I come back and I wait but you never come."

"Just a moment Una," he said. "I had totally forgotten about that."

He returned with an envelope and handed it to her.

"This is for you. Thank you for helping Dr. Sims."

"Open it," said her daughter.

"Why you want me to open it now?" she asked. "It is mine. Look it say that on the envelope. Una not Clytie."

"That ain't what it say Ma."

"Never mind, whatever in here is all mine."

"Come Ma, open it and let us see what you get."

"Have mercy Lord! I thank you," she said as she saw what he had given her.

"That money is to keep your mouth shut," said Miss Ella.

"And I intend to do just that," she said as she twisted her mouth with her fingers. "I thank you Lord. This will come in handy when I go up to see Nellie."

"Shhhhhhhh!" said Clytie. "Miss Sarah think we don't know where Nellie is."

* * *

# 19

Under the watchful eyes of Clytie and Miss Ella, Emily was growing into a lovely little girl. Sarah Bottomsley loved her daughter but was so preoccupied with herself that the rearing of the child had fallen upon Clytie's shoulders.

Meanwhile Nellie's business was doing well and she was also busy sewing clothing for the families living in the area. This brought extra income and since she always spent her money wisely, the amount in the sock just grew and grew. Having Nora, Percy and their two children around was not an ideal situation. It was difficult for John to come and go as he pleased. It wasn't a secret about her sister's life, but it was better for him to be discreet. It was amazing how little Nora saw of him, and when he was around, he pretended it was all business. It would be better if they had a home of their own, so she carefully broached the subject with her sister, who readily agreed. They found a piece of land at a good price close to the beach, because no one else wanted it. It was considered swamp land and a haven for mosquitoes. In a very short time a house big enough to accommodate the family of four, stood on the land. Every evening Nora would pick branches from the Duppy Bush and hang them in the house. This was supposed to be a deterrent against mosquitoes, although they weren't that many of the pesky insects around. This was another of Mr. Fitz's wonder drugs which he had passed around the village huts.

Nellie was now in a position to entertain John Bottomsley, how and when she pleased. Sneaking in late at night and leaving in the early hours of the morning was now a thing of the past. He was now spending more time with Nellie but continued to be discreet. He parked his Vauxhall in the grove of trees where it was not visible from the street.

"I want to see how things are progressing," he told her. "Bring the books and let me have a look."

He scrutinized every ledger and provided her with business advice.

"Just as I showed you! I'm very proud of you," he said as he examined her handwriting.

"JB, "she said to him. "I want a telephone. I was hoping that one day I would have a chance to talk to Emily."

"That's not such a good idea Nellie."

"You think I'm going to call and ask to talk to her?"

"Then what do you plan to do?"

"I was hoping that when she was with Miss Ella and Clytie, I would have a chance to hear her voice."

"You don't intend telling her anything you shouldn't?" he asked.

"You should bring her up here sometime so that I can see what she look like," she said ignoring his question.

"Let me think about it Nellie."

"Don't think too long JB."

Sarah Bottomsley sat on the porch reading a book and twirling a lock of her blonde hair. Emily joined her with a story book and a slate and asked her to read her something.

"Why don't you ask Clytie?" her mother asked knowing full well that Clytie and Miss Ella were supposed to be illiterate.

"Clytie, would you read to me?" she asked.

"Ask your mother Emily."

"She's busy. She said I should ask you."

It was one of the books Clytie had seen her son reading. It was called Caribbean Readers.

"So what you want me to read Miss Emily?"

Emily turned the pages and pointed with her finger.

"This one," she said.

It was the story of Brer Rabbit and Brer Fox. The child listened eagerly as Clytie read her the story and as she was about to read the last two lines, the child interrupted her.

"I know what happened. Brer Rabbit said to Brer Fox, ha ha Brer Fox. I was born and bred in the briar patch."

"How you know that Emily?" Clytie asked.

"Papa read the story to me last night."

Emily then took the slate and started to draw. The picture she said was of Brer Rabbit and Brer Fox.

"Which one is Brer Rabbit?" asked Clytie.

"This one," she said pointing to one of the drawings.

"Then write his name," said Clytie.

"I don't know how to write," the child said. "Papa never showed me."

"I am going to show you then."

Emily sat on Clytie's lap as she guided the child's hand and wrote the letters 'RABBIT.'

"That's rabbit," Clytie told her.

"I'll show Mama," she shouted.

"Go ahead," said Clytie without thinking.

"Look Mama. That's Brer Rabbit."

Sarah Bottomsley cast a glance at her daughter and after seeing the letters on the slate, showed some interest.

"Who wrote that?"

"Clytie wrote it for me. She told me the story of Brer Rabbit and Brer Fox."

"Did she read it from the book Emily?"

"She read it, just like Papa."

Sarah was speechless. She was convinced the two women in the kitchen could neither read nor write. She was annoyed to think they would try to trick her and decided to set a trap for them.

"You won't believe this John," she said to her husband.

"What won't I believe?"

"Did you know that Clytie and Miss Ella could read and write?"

"Where did you get such an idea?"

She held the slate up to him.

"I think Clytie wrote this for Emily today."

"Are you sure?" he asked.

"You can ask Emily if you don't believe me."

"Why are you so worried anyway?"

"They led us to believe they were illiterate."

"Did they Sarah? You believed they were. Anyway I don't see anything wrong with it."

"We have been leaving documents all over the place. They aren't supposed to be intelligent. They are servants."

"I can't believe you said that Sarah."

"Whose side are you on?" she shouted.

"I'm on no one's side. I just don't understand why you are making a big to-do about nothing."

"It's your fault. You're the one who decided we needed a school. What are they going to do with an education anyway?"

"Papa's home," said Emily running into her father's arms. "I want to show you my picture."

"Then show it to me Curly," he said using the nickname he had given her.

"This is Brer Rabbit. I wrote it myself. Clytie showed me how to write."

"Papa is very proud of you."

She kissed her father on the cheek and his face glowed with pride.

"When are we going to see Grandma Millie and Grandpa John?"

"When would you like to go?" he asked.

"Saturdee," she said not being able to pronounce the word properly.

"Then I'll take you to see them on Saturdee," he teased her.

He had forgotten his promise to Nellie that he would visit her that Saturday, and now he would have to think of something.

"Would you like to go for a drive too?"

"Yes, with Grandpa and Grandma?"

"If they want to," he replied.

"Will you be coming with us?" he asked his wife.

"No, I have an appointment to have my hair done. It is so yellow," she said looking at her reflection in the mirror.

"Then I'll take Emily to see my parents and then for a drive in the country."

"That's nice John. She hardly sees you anymore."

* * *

# 20

Word had spread across Europe that Barbados was indeed a paradise and greatly in need of skilled and educated people, so an influx of fortune hunters descended upon the island. Jobs were now harder than ever to find since these new comers had brought with them their greatest asset. They were all white. This put them to the top of the list for whatever there was to be had. Those locals who thought their lighter skin colour their golden spoon, were now fighting for jobs which they had considered beneath them. No longer did they have top priority for the preferred jobs, but found themselves falling even lower down the chain. Those who worked in the stores measuring and cutting calico and other materials were now now working in homes, mainly looking after the children of the Europeans. At least they could call themselves nannies; that being one step above the cooks and the housemaids. And not only did those on the bottom rung of the ladder have to suffer the indignities of their white employers, but now also with their own who felt they were better than they were. They expected to be waited on hand and foot by the servants, but ironically had to join them in the kitchen for their meals.

During John Bottomsley's absences and there were many of them, Thomas Hurley was a regular visitor to the plantation house. First it was under the guise of plantation business, but when he realized Sarah liked his company, he started to visit her as often as time allowed. He seemed especially fond of Emily. They discussed books, talked about their lives back in the homeland and sometimes, not too often, took rides together on horseback.

"He spending a lot of time around here," said Clytie to Miss Ella.

"It ain't none of my business," she would always reply.

"Just as long as he don't forget he ain't Emily father," said Clytie.

"The Master wouldn't let that happen."

"You can't blame Miss Sarah. The Master spending a lot of time in St. Lucy with Nellie."

"You think Miss Sarah suspect anything?"

"That woman living in she own little world. She believe it every time he say he going up to St. Lucy on business."

"Nobody can't be that stupid," replied Miss Ella.

"Clytie," shouted Sarah Bottomsley. "Would you fix a drink for Mr. Hurley?"

"What you want sir?"

"Is there any rum in the house?"

"Yes. There are three kinds."

He specifically asked for a certain brand with a drop of bitters. The trap was set. She picked the correct bottle and made the drink he had requested. He pretended it was not what he wanted and Sarah Bottomsley joined in.

"Mr. Hurley say he want Brown Sugar rum and I make the drink with Brown Sugar rum."

"Are you sure Clytie?" asked Sarah Bottomsley.

"Yes I am sure."

"Show me the bottle," said Thomas Hurley.

She retrieved the bottle of Brown Sugar rum and showed it to him.

"How do you know that is Brown Sugar rum?" asked Sarah.

"Because it say so on the bottle."

"Clytie you have never told me that you can read," said Sarah.

"I can't read," she replied.

"So how on earth do you know it says Brown Sugar on the bottle?"

"I keep all the pictures in my head ma'am."

Sarah Bottomsley and Thomas Hurley looked at each other. They both knew she was lying,

"Those two in there trying to trick me," she said to Miss Ella.

"What you mean?"

"They trying to find out if I can read, but I was too smart for the two of them."

"What happen Clytie?"

She related the story and the two women were in tears from laughing so hard.

*'Recruits wanted for the police academy,'* Clytie said as she read the newspaper.

"Be careful girl, somebody may see you reading."

"Nobody ain't in there. Miss Sarah went out and the Master left a long time ago."

"Read it again then."

Clytie read the complete article to the older lady who just nodded and listened.

"I think some of our boys should go to see if they can get jobs with the police," Clytie said.

"I keep telling you that they will only put we boys in their place if they apply for jobs as policemen," said Miss Ella.

"Times changing Miss Ella. If they don't take we boys, who else will they get? That ain't no fantastic job, but it better than working in the fields in that hot sun."

"Mark my words Clytie, it ain't going to amount to nothing."

"Well I still going to pass the word around and see what happen."

"Where they going to find time to go to the police station?"

"Where there is a will, there is a way they say."

It was hysterical watching the young men who had never in their lives worn a pair of shoes, trying their best to walk in canvas pumps. Naturally they couldn't have shown up at the police academy barefooted. They had to polish up their reading and writing skills in order to be considered. A great task lay ahead in preparing these young men for a future in the police force that would look after the security of the citizens and some of the young men were quite persistent. After leaving the fields, they would study earnestly, seeking help wherever they could find it. Meanwhile the young men and women in Ginger Hurley's class saw that their lives could be better and so they set out to learn as much and as fast as they possibly could.

* * *

# 21

Hard work eventually paid off because four years later, six of the young men were accepted as police recruits much to the joy of the villagers. Things were beginning to look up for the great grandsons of former slaves and plantation hands. Those who were unsuccessful would apply again or prepare themselves for some other job. The priesthood and teaching were now two enticing alternatives which were allowing the not so fortunate into their ranks, but those accepted were expected to be top of the line applicants. Ginger Hurley had done her job well and now decided it was time to look elsewhere for a more suitable position to fit her standing. Clytie's son Jonas, who was as sharp as a tack, she recommended as her replacement. His mother bubbled over with joy. The idea of her son teaching the village children made her a very proud mother. Ginger's brother had also found his niche, for in addition to being the plantation overseer, it seemed as if he had set his sights on the lady of the manor. When John Bottomsley was not around, he spent every spare moment by his wife's side. There were whispers among their peers, but so far no one had accused John Bottomsley of any indiscretion although he was spending more and more time with Nellie.

She had purchased a vacant hotel much to John's displeasure and had built another grocery shop a couple miles away from her home. The first shop carried the name 'Nellie's Bar and Grocery and was very profitable.

Their relationship was growing stronger and stronger and Nellie was hoping that one day she would have him all to herself.

The closer he grew to Nellie, the farther away it was from his wife. He saw in Nellie a kind, gentle and caring person, not only to him but to the families in the village, especially the children and the older people. There was no pretentiousness about her and he liked that quality. She kept a ledger called 'The Trust Book' for those who couldn't afford to pay for their groceries on the spot. Those people she allowed to pay at the end of every week. All debts were written in the Trust Book which would be brought out every Friday afternoon after the villagers received their weekly wages. Then on Monday mornings, barrels of salted pigs' feet and tails would arrive by lorry. Also in the delivery would be salted fish, mackerel, red and salted herring, rice, flour, potatoes, peas, onions and other dry goods. Nellie would pay for these purchases with the money she received on Friday evening.

"You is Miss Nellie?" a young man asked her one day.

"Yes, what can I do for you?" she asked.

"Sign here then Miss Nellie."

"What I signing for?" she asked.

"The new fridge," he replied.

"But I didn't order no fridge," she said.

"If you is Miss Nellie, then this belong to you."

Two young men lifted the huge, white contraption along with another piece of equipment from the lorry and placed it in the street.

"Where you want to put it Miss Nellie?"

"Carry it to the house. I coming to show you where I want it."

She thought it was from John Bottomsley and that meant it was something personal which she would prefer to have inside her home. It was a struggle but they managed to get it up the steps and into the kitchen.

"What about the ice box?" one of them asked.

"Put it in the shop," she replied.

After completing their task, Nellie gave each of them a red Ju-c (juicy) for the hard work they had done. The Ju-c was a local, sweet, refreshing drink which the locals loved.

"Don't carry away my bottles," she called out as they started to leave. "Every single one of those bottles cost two cents."

And so they chatted with Nellie about everything they saw that was new on the market, drank their drinks and went on their way.

* * *

"Miss Emily playing that piano too sweet," said Clytie behaving like a proud mother. "That is one good thing Miss Sarah do for that child."

"She claim she is the mother. It only right that she do something for her."

"If only Nellie could see her now!"

"What time it is?" asked Miss Ella. "We better hurry and get something to eat before Miss Sarah come back."

"What about Emily? She must be starving. Let me find out if she want to eat."

Emily said she was indeed hungry but wanted to eat with Clytie and Miss Ella.

"Alright Miss Emily, you go and wash up and get ready for your lunch," said Clytie.

Emily ran back to the living room and Miss Ella stepped through the kitchen door, cupped her hands around her mouth and shouted.

"Janey! Janey!"

A little girl came running. She was no more than six or seven years old, and wore an old dress which had seen better days. Her feet and legs were white which meant she had had been playing in the dirt.

"Yes ma'am," said the frightened child.

"Lord you is such a mess," Miss Ella said. "That is the only dress you got?"

"I got another one Miss Ella, but it for Sundees when I go to church."

"Pass me the lard oil bottle Clytie. I can't let this child inside the house with such dirty feet," said Miss Ella.

"What you planning to do?" asked Clytie.

"We just getting somebody to play with Miss Emily."

"You know Miss Sarah ain't going to like that."

"Who will tell her?" asked Miss Ella. "That child need somebody her own age to play with."

"I still say you playing with fire," said Clytie.

"You must be hungry Janey," said Miss Ella ignoring her co-worker's anxiety.

"Yes ma'am," said the child still wondering what she had done to be summoned by Miss Ella.

Both children seemed shy at first, but in no time, they were playing and behaving like children. Miss Ella and Clytie served lunch and little Janey was stowed away on a stool in the corner with an enamel plate on her lap. This did not daunt her enthusiasm because she was enjoying the meal.

"Can't I eat with you all the time?" Emily asked. "I like eating with you and Janey. It's much more fun than eating with Mama. She always tells me, 'not like that Emily; don't eat with your fingers Emily!' Look how much fun we are having eating with our fingers. Just like Grandpa Bottomsley."

"You think we doing the right thing?" Miss Ella asked.

"It doesn't bother Mama if I eat here. She doesn't care."

While they ate, the women told the children stories they had learnt from their grandparents and they were enjoying themselves immensely. After lunch, Janey was moved to the table and the two children continued playing together. They were laughing and were sometimes a bit noisy; so noisy that the two women didn't hear the car stop outside. It was Grandma Bottomsley with her newly acquired chauffeur. She caught sight of Emily seated at the kitchen table with the servants and almost had a panic attack. She sat down and took her smelling salts from her handbag. When she had sufficiently revived, she flew into action.

"Where is your mother Emily? And why are you sitting at the kitchen table instead of your proper place?"

"Hello Grandma," she said hardly hearing a word of the scolding she was receiving.

"It's your fault," she said shouting at the two women.

"It's not their fault Grandma. I didn't want to eat alone, so they allowed me to sit with them."

"That's no excuse," she continued staring straight at the two who had discontinued their meal and tried to look busy.

"I'll have a word with your mother when she returns."

"Where is Grandpa?" asked Emily looking past the miserable Millie Bottomsley.

"He didn't come with me my child."

"Are you here to see Mama about something important?"

"No, I wanted to see my son."

"Papa's not here right now, but he will be back by six."

"Sarah Bottomsley," shouted Millie before she had a chance to put her hat down. "Why do you allow Emily to eat in the kitchen with the servants? Don't you think it was time she was learning the social graces? She's eight years old now. She must be taught good table manners and she certainly isn't going to learn it from those two. Anyway why isn't she in school today?"

"If you give me a chance Mother Bottomsley, I will explain it all to you."

Emily stood between them looking from face to face, and then suddenly burst into tears. No sooner had the tears started, than Clytie was summoned to look after her. She sat on her lap as Clytie consoled her.

"I like Grandpa, but I hate Grandma," she said as Clytie hugged her.

"She ain't a bad person. She is just really fussy."

"Grandpa doesn't like Grandma either."

"Don't say that Emily."

"It is true."

"You just a little child and you don't understand everything."

"I understand everything. Now she is quarrelling with Mama because I was eating with you and Miss Ella."

"Don't worry about your Mama. She can look after herself."

"Emily?" shouted Millie Bottomsley.

"I don't want to see her ever again," the child said as she ducked under the kitchen table.

"She coming Emily. It going to be worse if you don't come out. If you come out, I will go to Polgreen shop and get you some sweeties."

"Promise Clytie?"

"Promise Miss Emily."

"Come and kiss Grandma goodbye," Millie said.

The little girl made her way to the drawing room coaxed from behind by Clytie.

"Promise Grandma you will be a good girl."

"Yes," she said holding out her face for her grandmother's sticky kiss.

No sooner was Millie out the door, than Emily started to clean her face.

"Mama may I go back to the kitchen with Clytie?"

"Yes darling," replied her mother as she stretched out in her lounging chair.

"Can Janey come to play with me again?" asked Emily.

"You want Janey to come back?" asked Clytie.

"Yes please Clytie. Will you get her?"

"What going to happen if Miss Sarah find Janey in the house?" asked Clytie.

"Don't worry about Miss Sarah," said Miss Ella. "She resting and you know she don't come past that kitchen door."

"Alright, I will see if I can find Janey."

Clytie was back in five minutes with the child whose legs were now covered with a mixture of cooking oil and marl.

"How you get yourself like that in just a few minutes?" Miss Ella asked.

"I went in the grass to jobby and a Santapee bite me here," she said showing Miss Ella her leg.

"I ain't feel sorry for you. You had no right going in that long grass. Why you didn't use the WC? You wash your hands? It's a good thing I have this candle grease in my pocket. Come here girl."

"Somebody was in the WC and yes ma'am, I wash my hands."

Emily watched the goings on as Miss Ella applied the candle grease to Janey's leg.

"What happened to her leg?" asked Emily.

"A Santapee bite her. By tomorrow that will be bigger than your head Janey, but the candle grease should keep it from hurting too much."

"What is a Santapee?" asked Emily.

Clytie and Miss Ella were so busy with Janey that they didn't see John Bottomsley's standing in the doorway.

"What's this I hear about a centipede?" he asked.

The two women were suddenly afraid. John Bottomsley had seen Janey in the kitchen and they didn't know what his reaction would be.

"A Santapee bit Janey," said Emily.

"It is 'centipede' darling," said her father.

"You're home Papa," said the little girl with glee.

"Just for a short while my little Curly," he said lifting her and kissing her.

"Where's Mama?" he asked ignoring Janey and the two women who were obviously praying to their God in earnest.

"She's resting and I'm having a great time with Clytie."

"And what did you do today?" he asked.

"I played the piano. Then I ate with Clytie and Miss Ella. Then Grandma came and shouted at us. Then she shouted at Mama."

"What did Clytie, Mama and Miss Ella do?"

"They let me eat in the kitchen. That made Grandma really angry and I don't understand why Papa?"

"Are you feeling better now?" he asked.

"Yes Papa."

"Tell me Curly. You really didn't want to go to school today."

She shook her head and smiled at her father.

"That wasn't very nice Curly. Going to school is very important."

"But I didn't want to go Papa."

"That's alright, but don't tell that to Grandma."

"Tell her that just Grandpa can come here, but she should stay at home."

"I can't do that. She's my mother and would be hurt."

"Grandma can't hurt. She doesn't have feelings," said Emily.

Sarah heard her husband's voice and joined them.

"John, please speak to your mother. I am not happy about the way she spoke to me today. Emily is my child and she cannot tell me how to bring her up."

"It's alright Sarah. Emily has already told me the story, haven't you?" he asked pinching his daughter's cheek.

"Yes I have Papa."

* * *

# 22

"I save up most of my money Nellie," said her sister. "Now I want to get something for myself and my family."

"What you planning to do?" Nellie asked.

"I want to open one of those fancy hotels."

"But we don't get fancy visitors up here."

"I want to open it down in the town."

"You mean you leaving up here to go to Bridgetown?"

"Yes, I hear you could make a lot of money."

"You think that if there was so much money out there I wouldn't have a hotel down there too Nora?"

"I don't think you too happy for me Nellie."

"I would be happy if I know you wouldn't be throwing away your hard-earned money, but you really don't want to live down there, because JB says it like Sodom and Gomorrah. Not only that, but there got too many hotels down there already," Nellie said."

"I want to give it a try Nellie. You never know unless you try."

"What about your house? What you going to do with it?"

"The children staying up here with Percy."

"You mean to tell me that you leaving your husband and children and going down there? You don't have that kind of experience Nora."

"I want to give it a try Nellie."

"Well Nora, at least there is one sensible thing you're doing. I glad you not carrying the children down there."

After discussing the situation with JB, who convinced her that her sister was an adult, Nora left with her sister's blessing to set up her business in the city. The running of such hotels was carried out by women who looked just like Nellie, but were mostly fat and bombastic. These women would sit prostrate at the entrance to their hotels welcoming guests and collecting their money which they deposited in their buxom chests. Unlike Nora, these women knew how to handle themselves.

At first, everything seemed to be going well, but Nora was perceived as a threat and was harassed at every turn.

"Country bumpkin come to town," they shouted or "go back to the cane fields Blackie."

She took it all in stride, but the clientele was not what she had expected. She was not used to seeing white people behave in an undignified manner. Usually when a ship entered the harbour, she could expect her hotel rooms to be filled with sailors. Having spent such a long time at sea, these men longed for the opposite sex and would bring their female companions into the rooms. This did not bother Nora, but sometimes they became drunk, rowdy and boisterous. Fights would ensue and they would damage all the new furniture she had spent her savings on. Some would leave without paying their bills and offered indecent proposals if she insisted on having her money.

* * *

"Nora ain't too happy JB," said her sister.

"You advised her, but she didn't listen. I know what goes on down there. I have seen and experienced it."

"I hope she come to her senses and come home," said Nellie.

He was about to answer when he suddenly clutched his stomach.

"What is wrong JB?"

"I've just had such a sharp pain," he said.

"Show me where you hurting."

"It was such a strange pain right here in my stomach."

"It must be gas. Let me get a dry ginger to bring the air of your stomach."

John Bottomsley drank it and said he felt much better, but the next morning it was worse than the night before. He hurried home to see Dr. Sims who examined him but could find nothing wrong. The medicine he prescribed did nothing to relieve his discomfort. Not one to sit around the house, he felt out of sorts, but could do nothing because he felt too weak. Sarah Bottomsley, not used to having him around all day became irritated at his constant presence. He was happy when Emily returned home from school for she was his only solace. She kept him supplied with water and peppermints. She considered peppermints good for every ailment. She also had a great dislike for Thomas Hurley, who in her young mind, she saw taking the place of her beloved father. She was also growing less fond of her mother whom she thought encouraged him. Clytie and Miss Ella realised there was something wrong and were also becoming very concerned about John Bottomsley's health.

"He ain't looking too good," said Clytie. "He look whiter than the sheets hanging out there on the line."

"But the doctor can't find nothing wrong with him."

"Something ain't right. Why you don't you go and talk to him Miss Ella?"

"What I going to tell him?"

"Ask him if he want some of Mr Fitz bush teas. It would do him the world of good.

"I don't want him to think that I interfering."

"If Nellie was here she would give him some bush tea."

"Alright then," said Miss Ella. "You worse than a setting hen Clytie."

Miss Ella entered the drawing room where John Bottomsley was lying in his plantation chair covered up to his neck with a blanket.

"How you feeling sir? I can get you anything?"

"I'm alright Ella," he said barely opening his eyes.

"Excuse me sir. I know it ain't none o' my business, but you ain't looking so good. I was wondering if you want Mr. Fitz to make some medicine for you. It really don't taste so good, but it will help."

"Then Fitz must know what's wrong with me if he's making medicine for my ailment."

"Don't worry about Fitz. He learn all about medicine from his grandfather, who used to do the same thing. His grandfather bring it with him from Africa."

"Thanks Ella. If I don't feel any better, I will let you know."

"Thank you sir."

"What he say?" asked Clytie as Miss Ella returned to the kitchen.

"He say that if he don't feel better he will tell me."

"What about Nellie? She must be worrying too."

"After all these years, she still don't have a phone. I just don't understand that."

"I hear a car Miss Ella. It must be Millie."

Miss Ella looked out the window and saw a strange man standing beside a car and looking around.

"You know him Clytie?"

"It look like that man Clarence who run messages for Nellie."

"I wonder what he want?" she asked out loud.

Nellie had dispatched Clarence to the Bottomsley plantation with a note to Clytie. She took the note and read its contents. She then scribbled a note on the back and took it back to Clarence, who got into the car and drove off.

"It is about time she get a phone," said Miss Ella.

"I think she don't have one because the master worried she might call too often to talk to Emily."

"That is foolishness Clytie. Nellie got more sense than that. Now you see where selfishness got the two of them today? Now that she really need one, she don't have one."

One week had passed and John Bottomsley was not much better. Dr. Sims came to see him again and again, but still his medicine brought no relief

"Sir, you should try Mr. Fitz bush tea. I know it would help you," said Miss Ella.

"It can't make me any worse than I am Ella. I'll try it."

Clytie went in search of Mr. Fitz and eventually found him sitting on a wooden bench at the back of his hut. He was having his dinner of pulped eddoes and red herring while a three legged iron pot sat over a roaring fire.

"G'day Mr. Fitz," she said.

"What bring you back here Miss Clytie? Ya want some eddoes and red herring?"

"You got enough?"

The old man went into his hut and came back with a plate and handed it to Clytie. She wondered how he managed to chew the eddoes in spite of the fact that he had only three teeth left.

"What bring ya here Miss Clytie?"

"Miss Ella want you to get the master some strong bush tea. He was sick for nearly two weeks and he ain't getting no better."

"What ailment he got Miss Clytie?"

"I think it got something to do with his stomach."

"He puking up Miss Clytie?"

"I don't think so. I think he got a bad pain that ain't going away."

"Alright. I going to see what I can find."

"Don't take too long."

"Miss Clytie, you know that it does take nearly two days to boil my medicine."

"Well you had better start boiling it soon."

The next morning, Miss Ella entered the room with a gill glass with an almost black substance and handed it to Mr. Bottomsley.

"It don't taste good, but it got a lot of healing power," she stated.

John Bottomsley gagged when the mixture touched his tongue. He had never tasted anything like it before, but he followed Miss Ella's advice and drank it all, followed by a bit of water to take away the bad taste from his mouth.

"I coming back around six o' clock with another dose."

"If my ailment doesn't kill me, your concoction certainly will," he said. "What on earth does Fitz have in that mixture? I have never tasted anything so vile."

"It got Sursee (Cerasee), Senna, Christmas bush, Wonder World and a couple o" Mr. Fitz secret ingredients in it. It going to make you feel a whole lot better. Just wait and see."

John Bottomsley was still asleep in his favourite chair. Now and then Miss Ella would go to check on him. The colour had returned to his face and for the first time in two weeks he did look better. She smiled. Mr. Fitz's bush teas seemed to be doing the job. He seemed to be in a deep sleep when the telephone started to ring. She rushed to get it before it woke him up, but Clytie had already answered it.

"Clytie?" said the voice on the other end.

"That is you Nellie?" she asked.

"Yes. I begging for a phone call Clytie. I want to know how JB doing."

"He much better, but he sleeping right now."

"That is Nellie?" asked Miss Ella. "Let me have a word with her."

"Nellie how you? You must be in a real pickle."

"Clytie say he feeling better."

"Yes. He had some of Mr. Fitz bush tea and he feeling and looking much better."

"Thank the Lord," said Nellie through tears.

"Stop crying Nellie. You need your strength to help him later on."

"I want to talk to him Miss Ella."

"I don't want to wake him up."

Clytie peeked around the corner and saw that his eyes were open.

"Excuse me sir, somebody on the phone want to talk to you."

"Who is it Clytie?"

"I think it is Nellie."

"Help me up Clytie."

He was still weak, but was able to make it to the telephone. The two women stayed out of sight but within earshot. He listened without saying too much.

"Give me a couple of days," he finally said.

Instead of lying down again, he went to the window and looked out. He was regaining his strength and was happy to be able to look out onto his estate once more.

"What are you doing out of bed?" Sarah Bottomsley asked as she returned home from her shopping.

"I feel so much better today," he replied.

"Finally that medicine from Dr. Sims seems to be doing you some good."

"Yes. Didn't you pick Emily up from school?"

"Yes. You know how she is. She made a stop in the kitchen to see Ella and Clytie," she said disappearing into her bedroom.

"Papa, Papa," said Emily trying to walk as fast as possible while balancing a glass in her hand. "You are standing Papa. I have the medicine for you and Miss Ella said I must watch you drink it."

She watched her father as he swallowed the putrid-looking concoction and made a face which showed how disgusting the mixture was. She too unconciously contorted her facial muscles just as her father was doing.

"You're feeling better Papa. I know you are."

"Yes Curly. Come and sit with me and tell me about your day."

He held his daughter in arms and kissed her on the top of her head.

"I prayed for you every night Papa. Just like Miss Ella told me. I promised God I would be extremely good if he made my Papa well again."

"You are my little angel," he said. "And Ella is a very smart woman."

"Yes she is Papa. She is really my friend, although she is old like Grandma."

"Do you know how old Grandma is?"

"One hundred?" she asked squeezing up her nose.

* * *

# 23

Much to her delight, John Bottomsley made an application to the phone company and Nellie's home was finally equipped with a telephone. Not only did she receive a telephone, but Reddifusion was now installed in the the shop. This took the boredom out of the days and also kept them up-to-date with the goings-on on the island. Nellie was especially happy to have the telephone because she was now able to stay in touch with her two best friends, but more often than not, she would have to hang up because Sarah Bottomsley was on the line. However, most importantly, she could keep in touch with her lover and he with her.

Four months had elapsed and John Bottomsley was back to normal. He was now working harder than ever because it was time to harvest the sugar canes. This meant he could no longer spend so much time with Nellie. He would drive up on a Saturday afternoon and return on Sunday afternoon.

"Where is John?" Reverend Allamby would constantly ask his wife after Sunday service.

"He's got a project in St. Lucy and can do it only on the weekend."

"One should never be too busy for God," he would always remark.

Reverend Allamby had heard the rumours circulating around Sarah Bottomsley and Thomas Hurley, but never did let on what he had heard. If Sarah suspected anything regarding her husband, she too never let on. Her life and her child's were still wonderful. They lacked nothing. Besides she was kept busy by her husband's overseer Thomas Hurley, who always sat quite a distance away from her during church service. Millie Bottomsley also complained that her son was working way too hard and had no time for them or his immediate family.

Nellie's life was also dominated by work. She toiled from dawn to sundown. She was thrifty and saved every penny from her dressmaking and from the profits of the shops and the meagre takings from the hotel.

"Don't you think you are pushing yourself too hard?" John asked her. "You are forty one and have done more than most people do in a lifetime."

"You trying to tell me I should give up everything?"

"No, but some of it," she replied. "You should sell the hotel and also the shop that Percy is running."

"Then what Percy would do?"

"Come here Nellie," he said. "Percy is a grown man. He is not your responsibility."

"But Nora business ain't doing good at all and I feel responsible for her and the children."

"Why don't you sell the hotel to Nora and Percy?"

"She don't have enough money to buy it."

"Make a deal with her. She must have some money from the business in the town. She can buy the hotel from you and can pay you a monthly fee."

"You mean like what she would do at the bank?"

"Yes."

"I don't know JB."

"That's one way you can get her back here where she belongs."

"Let me think about it."

All over the island, the white arrows from the sugar cane could be seen wafting like feathers in the breeze, and cart loads of sugar cane could be seen making their way to the sugar factories. The drivers of the carts would cluck their tongues and crack their whips as the old mules or oxen quickened their steps before that cracking sound of the whip made contact with their tired bodies. Groups of little boys waited practically on every corner just to grab some of the juicy sugar cane from the back of the carts, bringing annoyance and unspeakable harsh words from the drivers.

"Clop! Clop! Clop!" went the hooves of the poor, tired unfortunate animals, which had perhaps been making the third or fourth trip to the sugar cane factory in one day.

It was the same scenario at Bottomsley plantation. The tired workers after a hard day of cutting and loading sugarcane, stretched themselves out in front of their huts and chatted with each other. The sweet smell of crack liquor and the smoke from the smut lamps blended together and permeated the entire village.

"Smell that liquor?" Miss Una asked Miss Ella.

"I ain't taste a spoonful of that yet and that sweet smell is sending me mad."

"I ain't taste none neither and you know how much I like my crack liquor with some water and a piece of ice."

"If Miss Sarah did like it we would have some in the house ever since, but she don't like nothing like that."

"The master drink it. He like it," Miss Una said.

"That might be true, but he never bring a drop in the house."

"We still have to wait until they take the best out for the rum."

"You don't find it give you a lot of wind Una?"

"Child, sometimes I so glad that I sleep by myself, because I don't know how the roof of my little shack ain't blow off yet."

The two women cackled and carried on discussing the pros and cons of drinking crack liquor.

"When we going up to see Nellie?" Miss Una asked.

"Some Saturday when Miss Sarah busy," Clytie replied.

"I thought that since she so busy with that Hurley fellow, you would have more time and we could go up and visit Nellie together."

"What a thing that is Una? Miss Sarah and the master living in the same house and they don't have nothing to do with one another."

"That seem to be the way those people operate."

"Thank God I never had to go through that," said Miss Ella.

"I had my share of that and I am done with that. I happy to have my Clytie, but if I had to do it again, no siree. We happy the way we is, ain't we Ella?"

"You right Una. We certainly ain't missing out on nothing."

"Men ain't a thing but trouble."

"You just say a mouthful Una. I never had time for any of them."

* * *

It was just after midnight when the telephone rang in Nellie's house. She wondered who it could be as she struggled to find her way in the dark. She thought it might be John Bottomsley so she hurried. She heard her sister's voice on the other end.

"You frighten me Nora. I thought something was wrong with JB."

"Nellie things bad," she said as she started to cry.

"What happen?" she asked her heart quickening.

"They burn down the hotel."

"What hotel? Who burn it down?"

"My hotel Nellie," she said. "There ain't a thing left."

"You alright?" Nellie asked gathering her wits.

"I barely get out by the skin of my teeth."

"You got money Nora?"

"A little bit."

"Then find somebody to bring you up here tonight. Get out that place."

"Alright Nellie, but don't tell Percy nothing. I want to do that myself."

Nellie paced back and forth awaiting the arrival of her sister. She was afraid something else would happen before she made it out of that mire they called downtown. Relief came when an old car finally came to a halt in front of her door. A lone figure stepped out and climbed the steps. Nora was back home with all the possessions she owned, carried in a brown paper bag under her arm.

"That is all you got left?" her sister asked.

"Everything burn up in the fire Nellie."

"Come in the kitchen. I will make some tea and you can tell me how it happen."

"I don't know how it happen Nellie. I was looking out the window when I smell something burning. I didn't pay it no mind because down there, there got all kinds of funny smells. Just then a little boy shout that there was a fire in the back of the hotel. I just had enough time to run with this bag to get out before the whole thing start to burn. The fire brigade come, but they couldn't find nothing at all. They say it must be a kersey-noil (kerosone oil) lamp that fall over."

"What about the people that staying in the hotel?"

"It was empty for nearly two weeks Nellie. They would rather go where they have more fun and could mash up everything."

"Everything happen for a good reason. I glad enough you come back. I got something to offer you and Percy."

"What Nellie?"

"I was thinking about selling the hotel and thought you and Percy might want to buy it."

"But I don't have that kind of money."

"You talk it over with Percy and give me a answer. Don't take too long because I can't handle all these things no more," she said sounding like the astute business woman.

"You was always a real bright girl Nellie. I wish I did listen when you beg me not to move into town."

"I don't want to say I tell you so, but remember what they say. Hard ears you don't hear, hard ears you will feel."

"You're right Nellie. You're right. I wish I did listen to you and Mr. Bottomsley."

* * *

# 24

Emily Bottomsley had reached the age of nine and was now attending St. Wingate's School for girls. The only children seen in the school were children who looked just like her. She was a good student and made many friends, but her father was not at all happy with the school his wife had chosen, but then he had more or less expected she would have made such a choice. He thought that as one of the children born and raised on the island, she should have all kinds of friends, not only those of the plantation owners. There were schools where she could have met and befriended children from all walks of life, but Sarah Bottomsley had done it her way.

The sugar cane season was over and the kegs of rum were now sitting in cellars going through the aging process. John had a lot of free time and was spending more of it in the countryside with Nellie. He knew there was more to the relationship between his overseer and his wife than met the eye, but he dared not be the first one to throw the stone, since he was just as guilty as she, and because of Emily, he decided to play the part of being the good family man.

"Sarah," he said to her one day. "I am not a fool. I know there is something going on between you and Thomas Hurley. All I ask is that you remember Emily is my daughter. Keep Thomas Hurley away from her and please be discreet in whatever you do."

"Really John," she replied, "you don't for one moment think I am stupid. Our relationship is no longer one of a husband and wife. You and you alone have pushed me into Thomas Hurley's arms. You have forsaken me for someone else. I know there is no project in St.Lucy. You use that as an excuse to be with your lover. Who is she John?"

"That's not important Sarah. We have not been happy for a long time, so I don't blame you for anything that might have happened. I just don't want the servants gossiping about us, nor Emily seeing anything that's inappropriate."

"Whatever do you mean?" she asked.

"Keep him out of the Bottomsley bedrooms."

And so the way was clear for each of them to do what they pleased without having to lie or to make excuses. Emily was now a good pianist and her mother hoped she would one day become someone great in the music world. Emily hardly spoke to Thomas Hurley or his sister Ginger who had also taken another teaching position at the school she attended. She was surly bordering on rude and there was nothing Ginger Hurley could do. Punishing her was out of the question because she was afraid of incurring Sarah or John Bottomsley's wrath.

"I'll talk Sarah into sending her off to school in Europe," Thomas Hurley said to his sister.

"What about her father? He would never allow that."

"You're right. I'll have to think of something else."

"I just don't understand why she hates me so. Your relationship with her mother has nothing to do with me."

"It's the fault of those two women in the kitchen. They have spoilt her rotten. If we can get rid of those two, things might get better," said Thomas.

"Those women have been with that family for ages and Sarah trusts them implicitly."

"We'll just have to think of something."

After calling and speaking to his daughter, John Bottomsley and Nellie set off on a schooner to visit a nearby island for the weekend. It was a Friday afternoon around four when they sailed out of the harbour in the little lighter boat which took them to the bigger boat. They sat apart and hardly spoke to each other during the entire journey. Sometimes their eyes met, but she kept her eyes glued to a book so that no one would treat her as an illiterate, but it did her no good at all. She was totally ignored. John Bottomsley could see her plight and would occasionally speak to her not as his equal, but as an accompanying servant. She wondered how long she could suffer such indignity.

Some of the other travellers would doff their hats when they met him for he was well known on the island. He was not ashamed of his lover, but as a married man, was afraid of the gossip that would spread. And so, not wanting to hurt his wife and daughter, he continued his game of charades.

Upon reaching the guest house, he checked in at the reception while Nellie waited in the background. The clerk fetched his key and handed it to him.

"What about her?" asked the clerk pushing his head in Nellie's direction.

"She will share my room," he answered.

"That's not allowed sir," said the clerk.

"What's not allowed?" asked John Bottomsley pulling himself up to seven feet tall.

"Having such a person in your room sir," was his reply.

"Are you trying to tell me I can't have my attendant with me?"

"If you put it that way sir, I guess it's alright."

And so Nellie trotted off behind John Bottomsley and they climbed the stairs to his room. He closed the door behind them and Nellie, who was so hurt and disappointed burst into tears.

"I'm sorry Nellie. There was nothing else I could do."

"You could stand up for me, you know" she said through tears. "Is this what life together is going to be like JB?"

"You know how these people think Nellie. I can't go up against everybody who is unkind."

"If you treat me better, then everybody else would do the same."

He sat next to her and held her in his arms.

"I'm sorry Nellie. I can understand your pain. I will have to make some changes in my life, but for the sake of Emily, could you please give me some time. You know I want to be with you, don't you?"

She nodded.

Being in the middle of the town wasn't the ideal place for them, so John Bottomsley rented a car and they drove out to see the sights of St. Lucia. They found themselves on a beautiful beach which was deserted. He parked the car and they walked hand in hand along the sandy shore. Then they came upon three houses side by side.

"This is where I would love to stay," he said to Nellie.

"But it so lonely here JB," she said.

"We wouldn't have to worry about other people out here."

"If you look at it that way, I think it is a good idea."

"I'll go to see if any one is there."

He climbed the stairs and knocked on the door. A woman, whom it seemed he had awakened, came to the door.

"Is this your house?" he asked.

"No," she replied. "She belongs to you?"

She caught him off guard and he had no idea what she was talking about.

"I work here. The owner give me this job when I was only sixteen years old."

"Where is the owner?" he asked.

"He live down the road."

"Do you know if he wants to sell it?"

"You will have to talk with him. I really don't know."

"Can you show me where he lives?" John asked.

The woman got her hat and walked down the stairs behind him. She did not look at Nellie, but climbed into the back seat and instructed him where to go. Upon reaching their destination, he saw two unwashed children, two little girls playing at the front of the house. They had stringy blonde hair and from the colour of their skins, it seemed as if they always spent all their time playing in the sun. Their clothing was in good condition, but looked as if they had been wearing them for several weeks.

"Who are they?" he asked the woman.

"Mr. Applewhite two children," she replied.

"Don't they go to school?"

"I don't think so."

The woman got out of the car and went to the house, followed closely by John and the two children. A man who looked just as scruffy as the two children came out onto the porch.

"What can I do for yer fellow?" he asked in an accent reminiscent of what he had heard in the south of London.

"I was wondering if you were thinking of selling your house by the beach."

"Teddy Applewhite's the name. It all depends good feller, it all depends."

"On what?" John asked.

"The price good feller!" the man replied.

"How much do you want?"

It was obvious he didn't want to discuss any financial transactions in front of the woman, so he beckoned John with his head into the living room. They bantered back and forth and finally reached a price.

"I think we should drink to that good feller," he said.

He offered John a drink and they both drank it down in one gulp.

"How soon will it be available?" John asked.

"The moment you give me the cheque my good man," the eccentric man replied.

He made up an agreement and handed it to John, who then scrutinised its every detail.

"Yer will find everything in order. I am a gentleman of my word."

"In two weeks I will be back with the cheque. Can you wait until then?"

"I am a man of my word. I will wait until then. House and furnishings will be waiting for yer."

He walked down the steps with John and saw Nellie sitting in the car.

"Brought the missis with yer?" he asked walking up to the car and shaking Nellie's hand. "Yer mister just brought yer a lovely little property."

Shock registered all over Nellie's face. He did not treat her like a speck of dust the way everyone else did.

"Yer will enjoy it here. Peaceful, fresh air, ocean breeze and not another soul in sight, except for me and the children and Meta of course."

For the first time, the woman managed a little smile.

"Well Meta, yer will have to give the house a first class cleaning fer Mr. Bottomsley and Mrs. Bottomsley."

The woman seemed confused but promised to do her job and have the house ready within the next two weeks.

"Put the beds out to catch some sun," he said to her as the car slowly drove away.

With the strange woman in the car, Nellie had to control her enthusiasm until she climbed out.

"He called me Mrs. Bottomsley," she said.

"And aren't you pleased?"

"Didn't he see I wasn't……..

"You weren't what? Wearing your glasses?"

"Don't make fun JB. You know what I mean."

"Maybe he's colour blind."

"What do you mean colour blind?"

"It means he doesn't give a damn what colour you are, just like I do!"

That night they decided to leave all their problems behind and enjoy each other's company; something they had been doing less and less of.

"I'm going to make you a real happy man tonight," she said.

"You always make me feel happy Nellie."

"True?" she asked.

"Yes, you always make me feel really happy; not only in bed, but you listen when I talk. I know I can come to you with any problem I have."

"My Nellie," he said. "My precious Nellie!"

They lay in each other's arms and talked and talked. Then there was silence. She wanted to say something but he stopped her.

"Something wrong?" she asked.

"Listen," he said.

"I don't hear nothing," she said.

"Can't you hear the ocean? Listen."

"You know I never hear that before. Yes, I hear it before but I didn't really hear it."

"When we take over our little house in the country, we will hear this every night."

She snuggled up to him and soon they were both fast asleep.

* * *

## 25

"I wish we could stay here for ever and ever," said Nellie.

"I would too but we must not forget Emily."

"I want to ask you something JB. It got to do with business. Suppose something happen to me, I have all this money and all this property and I want to make sure that my daughter will get it."

"What are you saying Nellie?"

"I want Emily to get everything."

"What about Nora's two children Nellie?"

"They will get something too, but most of everything must go to Emily, my only child."

"That's going to be difficult right now, making a will and naming Emily Bottomsley as inheritor."

"I ain't interested in how it look. I don't want to go to my maker and she don't get what belong to me. I hear something about confidential something or other."

"Confidentiality! That means that solicitors are not allowed to discuss what is told to them in confidence."

"Well that is what I want to do. We can do it here?"

"We could but you have none of the ownership papers with you. It's really not a bad idea to have everything legalised here where it will remain a secret. When we return in two weeks, we'll make sure it's all done."

"What about you?" she asked.

"My will has already been made Nellie. Everything will go to my wife, who in turn will look after it until Emily turns twenty one. My wife must see to it that my parents are looked after, and if they are still alive when Emily turns twenty one, she must care for her grandparents."

"Your parents!" said Nellie with a horrified look on her face. "What will happen when they find out that you and me ….?"

"There will be lots of anger, but don't forget without me they couldn't exist on the island."

"That is true, but they ain't going to be happy about it."

"They won't be able to change my mind and regarding my property, they also can do nothing about it. Besides I have made provisions for them to be looked after."

"What about Thomas Hurley?"

"What about him?"

"Suppose he steal all of Emily property?"

"He can't do that to Emily. My will is written so that my wife cannot give anything to anyone but my daughter and my parents."

"That take a load off my chest."

"I didn't get where I am today because I wasn't a good businessman. I know what I'm doing. Don't worry Nellie."

"One more thing JB, remember that piece of paper I had to sign so you could take away Emily?"

"Yes," he said his face turning pale.

"Where is it?"

"Safely locked away," he replied.

"You don't think you should burn it?"

"Why?"

"I ain't going to take Emily away from you now. She belong to me and to you. I don't want that piece of paper to get into the wrong hands."

"I am the only one who can get into the safe."

"You sure about that JB?"

* * *

Nora had taken control and everything was in order when Nellie returned. She counted her money, checked her Trust Book and was pleased with what her sister had done.

"You enjoy the little holiday?" she asked.her sister.

"That other island pretty, but not as pretty as this rock. The people over there just as foolish as the people here, but JB stand up for me. He didn't let nobody treat me bad."

"He is a good man. You are real lucky Nellie."

"I know that Nora. Know what else he do for me? I now got a little house by the beach for just the two of us. It is in my name Nora. When we go on vacation, we ain't going to no hotel. We can stay in our own little home," she said with pride hanging on her lips.

"You is a real lucky woman Nellie."

"Nora, I got something real important to discuss with you. You know you is the only family I have and we must stick together, right Nora?"

"This sounds real serious Nellie."

"It is real serious Nellie. You ain't to say one word to nobody about what I going to tell you."

"I promise Nellie. I ain't going to tell it to one soul."

"What I going to tell you now, only three other people know about it already and they never open their mouths to nobody and I want the same thing from you."

"Alright."

"Don't even tell Percy."

"This is real serious Nellie."

"You remember back twelve years when I tell everybody that when I get up one morning, my baby was dead?"

"Yes Nellie," said her sister with eyes bulging.

"Well she ain't dead."

"What you trying to tell me Nellie? If she ain't dead, what happen to her Nellie?"

"You know JB was her father," said Nellie waiting for confirmation.

"You wasn't sleeping with nobody else, so it could only be JB."

"You also know that Sarah never bring a living child into the world."

"What you trying to tell me Nellie? You trying to say that Miss Sarah Emily is your little Emily?"

Nellie did not answer. She just stared at her sister.

"Lord havis mercy! You mean that white, white child belong to you Nellie?"

"She belong to me and JB."

"Lord havis mercy! What I hearing?" asked Nora now in shock.

"Only Miss Ella, Miss Una and Clytie know about this, so you understand you must keep it in your heart."

"But how that happen? You telling me that JB take away your child and give it to his wife?"

"Yes Nora."

"How could you let him do that?"

"Well he promise me that Emily would get the plantation and would have all the things I couldn't give my beautiful daughter."

"And you give away that dear child?"

"Yes Nora, and JB is living up to the promise. Little Emily is living a good life. She can play the piano, she is learning good at school and she is a real bright girl."

"I am sorry Nellie, but this is just too much for me to take in all at one time. You mean I am her aunt?"

"I am sorry I didn't tell you before, but my heart was so heavy, I just could not think about telling it to nobody else."

"Why you telling me now Nellie?" her sister asked.

"Well you never know what is going to happen in this life. I am going to divide up what I own between you and Emily. You know that she is going to get more than you. So if anything ever happen to me, you will not be surprise about nothing."

"And what JB saying about this?"

"He agree with me. So week after next, when we go back to St. Lucia, we will draw up the papers over there. We can't trust the people about here to keep their mouths shut. Even though JB tell me that they can't talk about your business, I know everybody got a bosom friend and in this situation, they would only be too happy to start talking my business."

"You right Nellie. I still say I wish I was as bright as you. You didn't even go to Brumley, and you smarter than those who say they had good learning."

"Think about it Nora. One good day Emily will be a doctor or a solicitor or she will give piano concerts and play just like Miss Sarah."

"What about a teacher?"

"No Nora. Ginger Hurley is a teacher. I want something better for Emily."

The sweet smell of tobacco wafted through the air and Nora got up to make her exit.

"I am leaving Nellie, I can smell JB tobacco," she said as she was halfway through the door.

"You don't have to run when he come by Nora. Everything is kind of alright now. There ain't nobody around here to hide from."

"You think Miss Sarah know about you?"

Before she had a chance to answer, John Bottomsley came through the back door puffing away on his pipe.

"Howdy sir," said Nora.

"How are you Nora?" he asked.

"I am fine sir."

"I was just telling Nora about our little vacation and how nice it is in St. Lucia."

"You should take her to see it sometime," he replied.

"I have to go," said Nora feeling a little out of place. "The children home waiting for me."

"How is Emily?" Nellie asked as her sister left the house.

"She's a beautiful girl. I just can't tell you how much I love her."

"I bet she love you too."

"I know she does. She's no longer a little girl. She's going to be twelve on her next birthday."

"Time does fly, don't it JB?"

"It certainly does. Just a couple years ago, she was Daddy's little girl and now she's taller than you Nellie?"

"She so big JB? I really want to see my little girl," she said looking out at the sky.

"How are we going to do it?" he asked.

"We got to think about something."

"I have a bit of bad news though."

"Don't tell me something wrong with my little girl," she said with panic written all over her face.

"No. It's Ella. She's not doing too well and my wife has brought in someone else called Ursy to take her place."

"What wrong with Miss Ella?"

"I don't know, but when you speak to Clytie, she will tell you."

* * *

# 26

Nellie had a restless night. Her thoughts kept turning to Miss Ella, the woman who had helped her through the rough times of her life; the woman she had turned to whenever she was in need of advice and comfort and a woman she trusted with her secrets. Miss Ella had turned sixty seven on her last birthday, but she had always seemed older. It was a mixture of hard work and hardship. She worked in the Bottomsley kitchen from sunrise to sunset, hardly getting a free day. She had no relatives, just her close friend Una and Una's daughter Clytie.

"JB," she said shaking him from his sleep.

"What is it Nellie?"

"I was thinking that I ought to bring Miss Ella up here close to me. She like my own mother. She was the only friend I had when I went to work in the kitchen. If something happen to Miss Ella and she want help I want to help her."

John Bottomsley drew Nellie close to him and squeezed her. She had a big heart and he felt reassured she would never leave him in the lurch.

"You didn't answer me JB."

"I did answer. Sometimes it is not necessary to use words Nellie. You are one of the kindest people I know, and that's why I love you."

She did not reply. In the darkness her head started to spin. She knew he had feelings for her, but he had never once told her that he loved her. Did his squeezing her mean that words were sometimes not necessary?

"You didn't answer me JB," he said teasing her.

"You laughing at me JB."

"Nellie, I would never make fun of you. You are much too precious to me."

"I like those words JB," she said to him. "Why you telling me all these nice things tonight?"

"Because I should've told you a long time ago," he replied.

"That is true," she said laughing. "But you did not tell me what you think about my idea for Miss Ella."

"I think it is a great idea. She has helped you through your lifetime and now it is your turn to help her."

"I should fix up that house next to the shop."

"You have two bedrooms Nellie, why not let her stay here with you?"

"You don't mind JB?"

"Ella has been with me from the first day I bought Bottomsley. She has always been respectful and helpful. I remember how she fed me with Mr Fitz's awful bush tea which helped me back on my way to recovery."

"Miss Ella do that?" asked Nellie.

"When she didn't give it to me, she made Emily do it. Miss Ella said I must watch you drink it," he said imitating his daughter.

They both broke into fits of laughter.

"Tomorrow I'll call Bottomsley and get Clytie on the telephone. She can explain what's wrong with Ella."

"Can you do something for me JB?"

"What Nellie?"

"I know you are the master of Bottomsley plantation, but if Miss Ella come to live with me, can you call her Miss Ella and not Ella?"

"If it makes you happy, I will call her Miss Ella."

"They always say that we should never call older people by their names unless we say Miss Ella or Aunt Ella. It is respect they say."

"That's not a bad thing Nellie. I always wondered why you referred to them as Miss Ella and Miss Una. Now I understand!"

"You sure it isn't going to bother you to call her Miss Ella?"

"It won't bother me. She's like your family and almost like mine."

"I like it when you talk like that JB."

Nothing was the same in the Bottomsley household without Miss Ella. Ursy had taken her place but did not have the refined qualities of Miss Ella. She and Clytie were constantly at odds, and worse Sarah Bottomsley did not like her. But then that was always the case with Sarah Bottomsley. She had to get used to someone before she could ever think of liking them. Although Clytie was not particularly fond of Ursy, she too remembered when Sarah Bottomsley had tried to defame her character and also when she, Clytie had refused to enter her bedroom because of her dislike of the woman and also fearful she might once again try to accuse her of theft. Clytie remembered that she had never received an apology even after the ring was found. However the good sense and level-headedness of Miss Ella was all that had prevented her from leaving the employment of the Bottomsleys. How she missed Miss Ella. She could discuss things with her that she couldn't discuss with her mother and now there was a deep dark void. Miss Ella was stricken with rheumatism and had had a mild stroke which left her unsuitable to carry out her duties in the Bottomsley kitchen. Ursy was not as attentive as she should be and because she had gone to school for three years and was not illiterate like most of the women who had worked in the household, she found it difficult to be humble like her predecessors were.

"Don't make such a big thing about every little thing," said Clytie.

"What do you mean by big thing? She doesn't like me and expects me to say Miss Sarah. I will call her Mrs. Bottomsley. I am not showing any disrespect and if she doesn't like what I call her then she could find somebody else to wait on her."

"Shhhhhhh! Not so loud," said Clytie.

"She isn't listening. She doesn't care if we live or if we cock up and dead. That woman love herself and only herself."

"You must understand that Miss Sarah had people waiting on her hand and foot for a long, long time."

"That don't make any difference to me Clytie. The only person she like on this earth is that thief Hurley."

"She like Miss Emily too."

"If that child didn't have a father like Mr. Bottomsley and good people working in this house, she would be just like her mother, but she is a nice little girl. Thank God for that."

"Miss Sarah ain't that bad Ursy."

"What about Miss Ella? That poor woman spent her days working like a slave in this house. Does she ask you anything at all about Miss Ella since she left this kitchen? No Clytie. Open your eyes and stop defending that woman."

"I understand what you saying, but she don't have to do nothing for Miss Ella."

"You go to church every Sunday. What does Reverend Allamby keep saying? Blessed are the merciful. She doesn't know how to show mercy, because it isn't in her heart."

"Clytie," Sarah Bottomsley's voice called out. "I'm going out for a couple of hours. You and what's her name can make sure that lunch is ready by the time I return."

"Yes Miss Sarah," Clytie replied.

"Yes Miss Sarah," said Ursy mimicking her co-worker.

Just as she was about to reply to Ursy, the telephone rang and she picked it up.

"Yes sir," she said.

There was a pause and she spoke again.

"She is not too good, but Mr. Fitz is making sure she drinks a lot of bush tea."

Nellie was on the telephone and inquiring about Miss Ella. She was going to visit Bottomsley to take Miss Ella to her home where she could be looked after.

"Ma ain't going to be too happy about that."

"Miss Una could move up here with Miss Ella if she want to."

"I will tell her this evening and let you know what she say."

Clytie was careful not to use any names because she didn't know Ursy very well and neither did she trust her.

Nellie's thoughts were now back to the little house beside the shop. If Miss Una was also accompanying Miss Ella, there wouldn't be enough room in her house, but they would be close enough so she could keep an eye on them.

John Bottomsley had the carpenters and masons busy making the little house comfortable for the two elderly ladies. Two single beds filled with coconut fibre, chamber pots and enamel cups for their tea, and whatever else was needed was placed in the chattel house. Nellie made sure every little thing for their comfort would be there upon their arrival.

It was all settled. Miss Una was also moving to the countryside with her friend Miss Ella. Against John Bottomsley's wishes, Nellie decided she would drive down to Bottomsley plantation with Clarence to pick up the two women.

She got dressed in her best and within an hour had arrived at her destination. Sarah Bottomsley was sitting on the porch and saw the car go by but paid no attention. As she got closer to Miss Ella's hut, Nellie heard voices coming from inside.

"Miss Ella?" she called out.

"Come in," came the reply.

When Nellie entered, there was a little girl with blonde hair sitting on her bed talking to her and using a piece of card to fan her.

"Nellie? That is you? I glad enough to see you."

"Howdy Miss Ella. How you feeling?"

"She's much better," said the little girl.

"Miss Emily, this is Miss Nellie."

Nellie's legs almost gave way and she quickly sat on the bed beside the two of them.

"You are Miss Emily?" Nellie asked.

"Yes," the child answered. "Are you here to take Miss Ella away?"

"Yes, she need somebody to look after her and I am going to do just that. You are a pretty little girl," said Nellie.

"Papa thinks so too. He always says that I look just like my mother, but I don't think so."

Miss Ella and Nellie looked at each other.

"You staying here with Miss Ella Miss Emily? I going up to the kitchen to say hello to Clytie."

"Do you know Clytie?" she asked.

"Clytie is my best friend," she answered looking at the child who had no idea she was her mother.

"I like Clytie. She likes me too. Sometimes I think I would like her to be my mother."

The tears rolled down Nellie's cheeks as she stepped outside and hurried in the direction of the kitchen. Clytie fell on her neck and hugged her tightly.

"God bless my eyesight. I so glad to see you Nellie."

"So you are Nellie?" asked Ursy. "Miss Ella is always talking about Nellie."

"How things?" interrupted Clytie.

"I just come from Miss Ella and Miss Emily down there."

"I was wondering where she went."

"She is down there in Miss Ella hut."

"Do you see what I mean Clytie? That child takes after her father. She has a good heart. She is nothing like her selfish mother."

"She is going to hear you," said Clytie.

"Clytie, who's that in the kitchen with you?" asked Sarah Bottomsley. "I can hear strange voices," she said opening the door.

She stopped in her tracks. She looked older although she was only one year older than Nellie. She was obviously still spending her time indoors because her skin was still as white as a sheet.

"Nellie?"

"Yes Miss Sarah."

"You've come back Nellie. How I longed for this day! You left without saying goodbye to me. How could you have done such a thing? Come inside and sit down."

"You look good Miss Sarah."

"Thank you Nellie. Tell me what has been happening and why you made the decision to come back?"

"I ain't coming back Miss Sarah."

"Then why are you here?"

"I come to get Miss Ella and Miss Una."

"Poor Ella, she had a stroke you know. What do you mean you came to get Ella and Una?"

"I have a little house in the country Miss Sarah and I taking the two old ladies to live with me."

"It looks as if you've done well for yourself Nellie."

"I trying Miss Sarah. I trying."

"Well if you change your mind, your job will still be waiting for you."

"Thanks Miss Sarah," she answered as Emily came into the room.

"Miss Ella is ready. Are you leaving now?"

"Yes Miss Emily."

"May I come to your house and visit Miss Ella?"

"You will have to ask Miss Sarah."

"What do you say Mama?"

"Ask your Father. He will probably take you."

"Goodbye Miss Sarah."

"I'm going to say goodbye to Miss Ella Mama. I'm really going to miss her."

"You're a good woman," said Ursy to Nellie. "May the good Lord bless you."

"Thanks."

"Look after yourself and the two old ladies," said Clytie. "I coming down with you. I got to say goodbye to Ma. I ain't going to be seeing her for a little bit. Ursy keep your ears open in case Miss Sarah calls"

"Tschuuuuuuuuuuups," came the awful sound Ursy always made with her teeth. "She could look after herself for five minutes."

Ursy too joined the group and headed towards the hut. Miss Ella was standing at the door, all her belongings packed together in a crocus bag.

"I going to get Ma,"said Clytie.

She came back with Miss Una who seemed quite strong and in good shape for someone who had toiled all her life in the sugar cane fields.

"The good Lord don't come, but he does send," she said hugging Nellie.

Clarence packed all their belongings into the car and they climbed in.

"I coming up at the first chance," said Clytie.

"Can I come too?" whispered Ursy in Nellie's ear.

"You can come too," she answered.

"Don't make any promises to her," said Clytie softly. "I don't trust her at all. She might let the cat out of the bag."

"Do you have a cat Miss Nellie?" asked Emily overhearing the word cat.

"No, but I can get one for you."

"Good, I will ask Papa tonight if he will bring me to see you. Will you get the cat soon? I can't have a cat of my own because Mama says they make her sneeze."

"I real sorry to hear that Miss Emily. I am going to try to find one so that when you come to visit, you can play with it."

"Thank you Miss Nellie."

"Look after her," Nellie whispered to Clytie.

"You don't have to worry your head Nellie. I love Emily like if she was my own flesh and blood."

It was a very sad day. Tears rolled down their faces as they watched the car slowly make its way down the driveway. Emily was beside herself with sorrow. Sarah Bottomsley stood on her porch and watched as the occupants of the car waved goodbye to their family and friends.

* * *

# 27

The women watched in silence as Clarence sped through the countryside with its lush sugar cane fields and fruit trees. Mango trees, ripe with fruit hung onto the narrow streets, along with avocadoes, breadfruit, sugar apple, soursop, limes, golden apples and every kind of plum tree as far as the eye could see. There were also fields of cassava, yams, pumpkins, potatoes and okras.

"I never see so much food in all my born days," said Miss Una.

"You're right," said Miss Ella. "I thought we had a lot of fruits at Bottomsley, but I can't believe my eyes at the amount of things that growing around here. Who all this belong to Nellie?"

"Different people Miss Ella," said Nellie. "All this belong to different plantations. If you look through the trees, you might be able to see the big plantation houses."

"It real peaceful up here," Miss Una said as the car stopped in front of a chattel house. "This is our house Nellie?"

"It belong to both of you."

Miss Una was the first to slowly climb the five steps followed by Miss Ella. They were both in awe when Nellie opened the door and they saw their new home.

"You do all of this for me and Una?" Miss Ella asked.

"I want you to be happy in your old age."

Miss Ella started to cry.

"Forgive this old woman for all the doubts I put in your mind. I know you would make something of yourself Nellie but I didn't know that you would take in two old women too."

"Remember when Nora and me didn't have anybody to look after us and I would come to you Miss Ella. I didn't forget how kind you was to me and my sister."

"Come, come Ella. There isn't any need to cry. Look at all these nice things Nellie buy for us. A rocking chair and you got one too. We don't have to quarrel about who is going to get the rocking chair."

"Every night before I put down my head, I used to ask the good Lord to take care of our Nellie up there all by herself and I think he was listening," said Miss Ella.

"Thanks Miss Ella."

"Now where you live Nellie?" asked Miss Una.

"Next to the shop," she replied.

"You mean that big house we pass by? The pink house?"

"Yes, that is my house."

"I tell you Una, he was listening when I ask him to watch out for Nellie."

"You want to see it?" she asked.

The three women walked over to the house and since she was stronger, Miss Una was again the first to climb the steps. Nellie held onto Miss Ella and assisted her in the climb.

"This is just as pretty as Bottomsley," proclaimed Miss Una, as she moved from room to room.

"Tell me something Nellie," said Miss Ella. "How you feel?"

"I feel good. Why you asking?"

"I was just wondering now that you see Emily, what you thinking."

"She is a sweet child. She got a heart just like the father."

* * *

The two women had settled in and life was on the upward path. Nellie and John had purchased their holiday house on the neighbouring island and spent many a weekend there. Miss Ella and Miss Una were still enjoying their newfound happiness and Miss Una sat at the cashier's cage in Nellie's shop and handled the incoming and the outgoing of the money. After so many years of hard work, she would have felt useless just doing nothing. She always had the daily paper open in front of her and pretended to be reading. This was a guise for those who had any thoughts of pulling a fast one on her. Miss Ella on the other hand sat on her front porch and listened to the BBC or she would be taken to Nora's where she could sit on the sand with her feet in the salted water. Nothing was too good for the woman who had treated her and her sister like daughters. Nora's children had also taken to calling her Granny which pleased her greatly.

Because of its location, the hotel was not at all profitable and Nellie decided once and for all to sell it. After discussing it with John Bottomsley, who thought it also a good idea, the property was closed and put up for sale. However there were no buyers so it remained closed for the better part of one year in which time Nora worked alongside her husband in Nellie's shop. As much as they wanted to purchase the hotel from Nellie, it was just too much of an undertaking for Nora and Percy.

Life at the Bottomsley plantation was still wonderful for the ruling class. Emily was growing more and more beautiful and was still the apple of her father's eye. Clytie had become her confidant. Things which she didn't tell her mother were told to Clytie in the strictest confidence. Her mother still enamoured with Thomas Hurley and he with her, hardly found time to be with her daughter, thus bringing fire and brimstone on her head from Millie Bottomsley.

"Aren't you ashamed? A married woman cavorting with the plantation overseer?" she asked her daughter in law.

"I'm not doing anything that your son isn't doing," she replied.

"If he's doing anything, which I don't think he is, at least he's being discreet. Who's he having an affair with? You are making a fool of my son Sarah Bottomsley and I don't like it."

"Tell me Millie, where does he go every Saturday evening? Where does he spend his nights?"

"If you were the wife you should have been, he wouldn't have had a reason to go elsewhere. You've got everything you want from life because of my son. You've never had to work for a shilling, and yet you cannot try to be at least discreet with that Hurley fellow. What about Emily? What does she think of her mother's disgusting behaviour?"

"Leave Emily out of this," said Sarah. "She is a happy well-adjusted child."

"All because of my son," protested Millie Bottomsley.

"Your son is hardly ever here. I am here with her every day."

"I hate to say this, but she is well-adjusted because Clytie spends lots of time with her and shows her love. My grandchild goes to the servants instead of her own mother."

"Did she tell you that?"

"No she didn't, but I've only got to listen to the way she speaks about Clytie to understand where she gets her love and security."

* * *

"Flying fish, fifty for a bob," screamed the voice from the loud speaker. "Come and get yer flying fish."

All the workers rushed out with their enamel basins to purchase their fish and it was a free for all with everyone pushing themselves up against the car for fear of the fish all being sold before they could buy some. The kind-hearted fisherman would usually throw in a few extra fish for the elderly and mothers with children.

"How many you want?" he asked an elderly Ada Brathwaite.

"Just one," she replied.

"One fish?" he asked.

"Yes, just one," she repeated.

"You ain't afraid that that one flying fish fly way from you?" he asked.

His question brought peals of raucous laughter from the on-lookers and embarrassment to poor Ada Brathwaite.

"Here Ada, take these two extra fish."

"Thank you son," she said scurrying away to the security of her hut.

It was a night of labour for the workers. They had the task of cleaning the fish and frying them since they had no means of refrigeration. Clytie would nestle hers out of sight in her employer's ice chest since Sarah hardly ever set foot in the kitchen furthermore looking into the ice chest. On such a night, she missed Miss Ella and her mother. This was a job they all had done together, but she was happy they were having a better life especially in their later years. She thought of what her life would be like when she too reached that age. Her son Jonas was a great source of hope. Since he had taken over as the teacher at Bottomsley, there was another source of income and he was well-loved and respected by the pupils. However a new public school had sprung up a couple miles from the plantation and he had already lost some of the students. His methods and way of thinking were modern, but he had not forgotten the ways of the men and women of the village. Whenever they needed advice, they would seek out Mr. Jonas, which made his mother extremely proud. She knew that she too would one day be walking out of Sarah Bottomsley's kitchen, never to return. Her greatest hindrance in leaving was the thought of deserting Emily Bottomsley.

* * *

# 28

Just when everything seemed to be going according to plan, life threw Nellie a vicious curve. John Bottomsley decided he would go home to Bottomsley, because he was not feeling well. He was going to see the young Dr. Sims who had taken over his father's practice. Miss Ella had supplied him with some of Mr. Fitz's bush medicines in case he needed them. After careful examination the young doctor gave him the worst possible news of a life expectancy of only six months. He inquired whether or not he had had any symptoms before and what he had done about it. He told him about Mr Fitz's bush remedies which had brought him relief until then. He then advised him he should continue these remedies since it would be the only thing that would bring temporary relief. He also said if there was pain, he would prescribe something stronger to ease his discomfort. So day after day, twice per day as Miss Ella had said, John Bottomsley drank the putrid mixture and was feeling well again. He had not divulged his secret to anyone except his parents.

"There must be something they can do. We'll take you to England where there must be some new medicines on the market," said a tearful Millie Bottomsley.

"I don't think so Mother," he said. "Dr Sims said there was absolutely no hope."

"Let's go to another doctor then," said his father who was drowning his sorrow with his favourite rum

"Do you know of another doctor?" his son asked.

"I understand there is a good one up in St. Lucy. He left his practice in England a few years ago and settled up there. We should go up to see him."

"Alright, I will do that."

"I'm coming with you son."

"I'm coming also," said Millie.

"I would prefer if just Father and I went," said John.

And so without an appointment, the two men set off to visit the doctor for a second opinion. Unfortunately the news was no better than before, but Dr. Norton explained that had John Bottomsley visited him earlier, he would have been able to help him. This made him rather angry since he had put his life in the hands of the now retired Dr. Sims who had failed to make a proper diagnosis.

"Damn that Dr. Sims," said John Bottomsley. "How could he have done this to me? He probably did it out of spite."

"Why would he do that?" asked his father.

"Sorry Father, I'm just really angry," he said. "He said he just couldn't find anything wrong."

"Didn't his son also tell you that had you sought help earlier, they might have been able to help you?"

"No," John Bottomsley answered.

"He's just trying to save his father's backside," screamed the older Bottomsley. "I need a drink," he shouted.

"We should be home in half an hour," his son said.

The two men drove in silence and as they passed Nellie's Bar and Grocery, the older Bottomsley told his son to stop the car.

"I need that drink now son. I can't wait until we get home."

"You don't want to go in there Father," said his son.

"Why not?" asked his father. "Don't they sell rum? I see a liquor sign outside."

"Alright then, I'll wait here for you."

"I don't like to drink alone especially at a time like this. Come son, it will also help you to forget."

John Bottomsley climbed the steps to the shop and his father followed.

"What are you doing here JB?" Nellie shouted just as the younger Bottomsley appeared at the door.

"Wait a minute. Is that you Nellie?" asked the older Bottomsley.

"Yes sir," she said as she looked from one face to the other.

"We always wondered what happened to you. After you lost that baby you just disappeared. Give me a gill of the best and one for my son."

Nellie poured the rum into a shot glass and then into their glasses. The older Bottomsley threw his head back and in one gulp swallowed the warm grog, while his son stared at Nellie and she at him.

"Give me another Nellie," the older Bottomsley said still shaking his head from the effects of the first.

"Drink up son. It will help you to forget."

John Bottomsley sipped his drink in silence as his father consumed drink after drink which made his tongue looser and looser. He then started to cry and to tell Nellie he was losing his son.

"Master Bottomsley," she said, "everything is going to be alright. What make you think you going to lose your son?"

"It's the drink Nellie. Don't listen to my father."

"Didn't the doctor say you've got only six months to live John?"

Nellie just about lost her composure and started to question the old man.

"What you mean he only got six months to live? Master Bottomsley look healthy to me."

"I know I can trust you Nellie. You worked for my son for many years and I know he would want you to know. Tell her son."

"We don't want to bother Nellie with my troubles Father."

"I don't mind," Nellie replied.

"It's true," said John Bottomsley looking her in the eye.

Nellie disappeared. Miss Una came running from her place at the cashier's cage because she too had been listening to the old man.

"Where did she go?" he asked his son as Miss Una took the smelling salts from her pocket and passed it under Nellie's nose.

"What happen Miss Una?"

"You pass out Nellie."

"Is she alright?" asked John Bottomsley.

"She coming around," said Miss Una.

"Come father. Let's go."

"We haven't paid Nellie yet," he said.

"Don't worry," said Miss Una. "Nellie say it is free."

The two men left the shop and a minute later John Bottomsley returned.

"Is she alright Miss Una?" he asked as Nellie sat glassy-eyed on a stool.

"She going to be alright."

"I'll be back in an hour," he said.

The older John Bottomsley was now in a drunken stupour and cried most of the way home.

"I always had an eye for that Nellie," he said to his son. "She is such a pretty little thing, but then I had to think of Millie. You understand me son?"

"Yes Father," he answered.

"Son, why did she call you JB?"

"She did?" he asked pretending he hadn't heard.

"When we walked in, she called you JB."

John Bottomsley could not believe that his father in his drunken stupour had remembered it. He had hoped Nellie's greeting had escaped his father's ears, but it hadn't and he now had some explaining to do since his father was not about to forget it.

"You've been messing around with Nellie son? Not that I blame you because she is as pretty as a picture."

"Have a goodnight's sleep and we'll talk more about this tomorrow Father."

He dropped his father off at the gate, and as he drove off, he caught sight of his mother hurrying down the garden path, but he continued because he was not in the mood to converse with her.

"What did the doctor say?" she asked her husband.

"Same as Dr. Sims," he said reaching for solace in the bottle.

"You always think you will die and leave your children," she said staring at her husband.

"Yes Millie. That's right, but we got tricked Millie. Our boy will leave us behind."

"I am sure if we went to England, he could be helped."

"Dr. Norton arrived from England a couple years ago and I'm sure if there was anything new, he would know about it."

"What are we going to do John?"

"What can we do Millie? Stand by him and help him when he needs us," he said as he tumbled into the nearest chair.

The older John Bottomsley threw his back and swallowed another mouthful of rum which burned his throat on the way down. He shook his head violently and squeezed his eyes shut. He poured himself another, got up and walked over to the window and stared out at the blue sky which to him was no longer beautiful.

"Millie," he said, "we saw Nellie today."

"Who is Nellie?" she asked.

"Don't you remember Nellie who used to work at Bottomsley?"

"Yes. Where did you see her?"

"She has a shop close to the doctor's office and she seems to be doing really well."

"She ran away after her baby died, didn't she?"

"I think that was the story."

"What do you mean John?"

"Nothing Millie," her husband replied.

"I want to talk to John," she said. "Has he told Sarah yet?"

"We are the only ones he has told and I told it to Nellie."

"Why would you do such a thing? Confiding in servants?"

"Stop this nonsense Millie. Our son is dying and you are standing on ceremony?"

"I just wondered why you would have to tell Nellie."

"My God!" he shouted. "What about Emily? What about our granddaughter? This will tear her world apart. She dotes on her father."

* * *

# 29

All John Bottomsley could think of on the drive to St. Lucy was Nellie. Although he felt like a man with a death sentence hanging over his head, he was still worried about the way she had found out about his illness. He went first to the shop and she wasn't there but the look in Miss Una's eyes said it all. Nellie had taken to her bed and couldn't be comforted. He opened the bedroom door and saw Miss Ella sitting next to her on the bed.

"I leaving you two to talk," she said lifting her weight from the bed.

"Thank you Ella," he said touching the old woman's shoulder as she passed by.

He sat on the bed next to Nellie and put his arms around her.

"Why you didn't tell me JB?" she asked.

"I didn't want to tell you right away because I knew you would worry too much. I was waiting for the right moment to tell you."

"I can't believe that something so important, you didn't tell me JB."

"I'm sorry Nellie, but I knew I just had to wait."

"But what you have to wait for?" she asked.

"For the right time to tell you," he replied.

"You making this sound real easy JB and I feel like somebody tear my heart out."

"I'm sorry Nellie. I wish I could change things but I can't."

"You still drinking Mr. Fitz bush teas?"

"Yes. The doctor said it was the one thing which will keep me going."

"We will get some more so you don't run out. I don't believe that you are going to leave me in six months."

"I can't believe it either," he said with resignation.

"You sure there ain't nothing more that we can do?"

"According to the doctor, there is absolutely nothing."

She started to wail again and then suddenly pulled herself together.

"I sorry JB. You should be the one crying and I should be strong. I bringing Nora down to the shop with Miss Ella so that we could go to the vacation house and I am going to look after you and make sure you relax."

"I've got so many things to do Nellie that I don't know how much time I can spend there."

"Find somebody to do it," she commanded. "What about that Thomas Hurley? What you paying him for? Put him in charge and get another overseer."

"If I do that Nellie, then everyone will be wondering why."

"JB I want to spend as much time with you as I can and I am not going to bother about what other people goy to say."

"My Nellie," he said putting his head on her shoulder. "What about Emily? It's going to be the hardest thing to tell her."

"We should tell her together."

"That's not a good idea."

"But why not JB?" she asked.

After coming this far, we don't want to jeopardise her future, especially where the plantation is concerned."

"As usual, you are right JB," she said as tears streamed down her face. "Why you don't bring Emily up next week to see Miss Ella? You have got to start spending more time with her."

"You want to see her too, don't you?"

"Yes, you going to bring her?"

"It would make you happy and it would make Miss Ella happy too."

The arrangements were made to bring Emily to visit Miss Ella on the following weekend. Nothing was said about Nellie because Sarah Bottomsley knew her daughter loved the old lady.

"She say yes?" asked Nellie.

"Emily is coming to spend next Saturday with you and Miss Ella."

"You say anything to Miss Sarah yet?" she asked.

"No, not yet," he replied."

"When you going to tell her?"

"As soon as everything is in order. I have a few things which need to be done before I can say anything."

"Don't take too long JB. You have to tell Emily about your condition."

"How do you tell a child her father is going to die?" he asked her.

"As long as she don't find out the same way I find out," said Nellie. "Your father know and when he drink, he always talk a lot."

"I know Nellie. What am I going to tell her?"

"Tell her exactly what the doctor had to say."

"I dread having to tell her such bad news. She's only a child with Clytie looking after her.

"Damn! Damn!" he said getting up and looking out the window.

He lit his pipe and started to puff on it. The sweet smell of the pipe tobacco sailed across the room to her nostrils. She wanted to stop him from smoking but she knew it was something he loved and she just didn't have the heart to forbid him. There was considerable weight loss and it would have made no difference to his health anyway. She was determined that he should enjoy whatever brought him a bit of pleasure. Closing her eyes, she inhaled the sweet smell and her heart sank. She understood his leaving would create a great void in her life, but she had to be strong for him and so when she cried, she cried alone.

* * *

# 30

The meeting point for the old men of the village was on the steps of Polgreen's rum shop which also served as the grocery store for the villagers. He was not happy to have them using his establishment as their meeting point, but the more men gathered there, the more money they would spend. They fired grog after grog until their elbows were just about frozen in that position. Polgreen's helper Mildred also made flying fish and cod fish cutters. A cutter was a small loaf of bread with a fried flying fish or two cod fish fritters neatly placed between it, then topped off with a couple drops of hot sauce. It helped to absorb the alcohol which the old men consumed from morning until evening when Polgreen opened and closed his doors. Then in a drunken stupour they would sing out of key until they reached the village, where they would fall in front of their huts and sometimes remain there until the following morning. On better days, they trimmed each others' hair by placing a calabash on the head and then scraping away with a straight razor whatever hair was left protruding from under the calabash; which by the way also served as an eating utensil. Some of them learned to make shoes from old rubber tyres from the plantation vehicles and many of them still utilised the crocus bags for clothing. In their poverty, they remained still a contented lot. Such was the life of the old man in the village.

The women on the other hand, did not approve of the way the men squandered whatever money they made especially drinking Polgreen's rum. They tended their crops on small plots of land which they rented from John Bottomsley. Behind each hut, they now grew their peas, okras, corn and sweet potatoes, thus supplementing their income. With trays on their heads, they walked to the mill to have their corn ground which they made into Pap or their national meal, Cou Cou. The meal was mixed with cooked okras and served with cod fish or flying fish sauce. Sometimes a villager would slaughter a pig and then they would have pig's liver or heart or lungs with their Cou Cou. Each portion was put into an enamel bowl then turned out onto a plate thus taking the shape of the bowl. An indentation was then made in the middle of the Cou Cou and the sauce along with copious amounts of flesh would be ladled into the indentation and would flow down the sides like lava from an erupting volcano.

* * *

Miss Ella set the table while Nellie dashed around the kitchen making sure everything was just perfect for Emily's arrival. She sat next to her father as the car slowly backed out of the driveway and almost crashed into another car. It was Thomas Hurley on his way to visit his wife. Emily did not look in his direction, but the two men raised a hand to each other and continued on their way.

"Papa, would you stop by Mr. Polgreen?" she asked.

"What do you want to buy?" he asked.

"Miss Ella likes talcum powder and Papa what should I buy for Miss Nellie?"

"I don't know," he replied. "Perhaps a box of handkerchiefs; I'm sure she would like that. Every lady likes to have a hanky."

"Then that's what I'll buy."

"Don't forget about Miss Una."

"I don't know her Papa."

"You won't want her to feel left out."

"What shall I buy her then?"

"I don't know. Buy her some talcum powder too."

"But the talcum powder is for Miss Ella."

"Let's look to see what Mr. Polgreen has in the shop and then we can decide what to buy for Miss Una."

The only thing they could find was a white enamel cup decorated with red roses and that was Miss Una's gift. Polgreen was extremely charming and wrapped each article in brown paper and even wrote the names of the three women on each individual article.

Nellie's heart was filled with joy and with sadness at the same time. She stood on the porch with Miss Ella beside her waiting for them to arrive, and watched as her daughter stepped out of the car accompanied by the man she loved. Emily ran straight to Miss Ella and hugged her. Her father, loaded down with her parcels watched them from the bottom of the steps.

"Come up Master Bottomsley," said Nellie.

"This is going to be difficult," he whispered to her.

"Hello Miss Nellie," Emily said shaking Nellie's hand.

"I'm glad you come by to see Miss Ella," said Nellie.

"I brought presents for everyone," she said reaching to take them from her father.

For each present given, Emily received a hug except from Miss Una who was still seated in the shop at the cashier's cage. Nellie was so touched, she began to cry. Emily was unaccustomed to seeing anyone cry when they were happy and didn't understand what was wrong. John Bottomsley knew it was more than the present which had brought Nellie to tears.

"She's happy that you remembered her. She's happy. That's all Emily."

With the sadness forgotten, Emily chatted away about Clytie and Ursy. She said how much she missed Miss Ella and wished that one day she would return to Bottomsley where she would help to look after her.

"I am too old now Miss Emily. Miss Nellie is looking after me, but you can come anytime and visit me. I would like that."

"I would like that too Miss Ella."

"Before we eat lunch Miss Emily, I have something for you," said Nellie.

"A present Miss Nellie?" she asked.

"You can say so. Wait a minute. I am coming back soon."

She reappeared with a little cardboard box and set it in front of the child.

"Oh Miss Nellie," she said. "You didn't forget. My own little kitten!"

"You got her a kitten?" asked John Bottomsley smiling at Nellie.

"Miss Nellie promised me Papa, and she remembered. Miss Nellie, you're just like Clytie."

"You know your mother is allergic to cats," said her father. "Where will you keep it?"

"She can keep it here," said Nellie grabbing the opportunity for regular visits.

"Then I will come every week to see her."

"It is a he Miss Nellie. You have to give him a name."

After thinking for a moment, she said the most hilarious thing.

"I think I'll call him Hurley."

"Why Hurley?" asked her father.

"He has a face like Thomas Hurley, don't you think Papa?"

John Bottomsley pretended he hadn't heard and so did Nellie who scurried away.

"Lunch is ready," she said as she placed the last bowls of Cou Cou on the table. "Clytie say I should make cou cou for you. She say you like it."

"Not really. She makes me eat it all the time."

"I didn't know that Emily. I can make something else that you like a lot."

Her father whispered something to her and she said she didn't like Cou Cou but would eat it because she knew that Nellie had gone to a lot of trouble making it for her. Everyone sat down to lunch except Nellie who still fussed around pouring lemonade and bringing in more goodies.

"Thank you Miss Nellie," said Emily. "This was better than Clytie's. She would be hurt if she knew I said that about her Cou Cou."

Miss Ella found it impossible to keep her hands away from the child she had helped to raise.

"Such a nice child," she constantly said. "Such a nice child, isn't she Nellie?"

It was an exhausting afternoon and John Bottomsley and his daughter were ready to go back to the plantation and she promised she would visit Miss Ella and Nellie as often as her parents permitted.

"I have something else for you Miss Emily," said Nellie and handed her a package.

"May I open it now? Is it another kitten?" she asked.

"No but you can open it," Nellie replied.

"This is so beautiful," she said standing up and putting the dress next to her body. "Where did you buy it Miss Nellie?"

"I make it just for you."

"I've never had such a pretty dress. Thank you Miss Nellie. Isn't it pretty Papa?"

"Now you've got to find somewhere special to wear it."

"I'll think of something," she said examining it.

As they drove through the countryside, John Bottomsley asked his daughter what she thought of Nellie.

"I like her Papa. She is just like Clytie."

"You think so?"

"Yes. She is nice and I really, really like her."

If only his daughter knew the woman she really, really liked happened to be her mother, what would she say? What would she do? Would she abandon Sarah Bottomsley for her maternal mother? Or would she ignore Nellie and cling to the lifestyle she had? Tears welled up in his eyes because he thought he might never know the answers to all those lingering questions.

Thomas Hurley's car was still parked in the courtyard when they arrived, and it really dampened Emily's enthusiasm.

"Papa, can't he find another job and stay away from our home?"

"He is an excellent worker Emily and I need him more than ever right now."

"You don't need him Papa. There are so many other people who would be happy to work for you."

"Emily?"

"Yes Papa?"

"Would you like to have an ice cream with me?"

"Where are we going?"

"Somewhere close to the ocean. I like to hear the waves especially when it is quiet."

"Sure Papa. What do you want to discuss with me?"

"Why do you think I want to discuss anything with you?"

"Because whenever you invite me for an ice cream, I know it will be something important."

He reversed alongside Thomas Hurley's car and drove out of the plantation yard.

She chose vanilla ice cream and he chocolate.

"What would happen if you found out your parents were not your parents Emily?"

"That's a silly question Papa. You are my father and Mama is my mother."

"Let's pretend we weren't. What would you do?"

She stared at him as the white cream ran down the cone and trickled on to her arm.

"You are my child," he said reassuring her.

"I don't understand the questions Papa," she said once again licking her cone.

"Something has happened Emily and I don't know how to break it to you gently."

"I am twelve years old and I'm a big girl Papa. You can tell me anything. I think you and Mama are going to get a divorce."

"Did she say that?"

"No Papa."

"Then why did you say that?"

"Because I think that's what you want to tell me."

"If it were only that easy Emily; if it were only that easy."

"Papa, please tell me what it is."

Just as he was about the break the bad news, he heard a familiar voice; that of his mother.

"I have been searching for the two of you all day," she said.

"Is something wrong Mother?"

"In your condition, you should be at home resting."

"I'm fine Mother," he replied.

"No you're not. Ask your doctor."

"What does Grandma mean Papa?"

"You mean you haven't told Emily yet?"

"I would have if you hadn't intruded."

"How could you call your own mother an intruder?" she asked on the point of tears.

"Are you ill Papa?" asked Emily.

"You're going to lose your Papa," he said.

"Where are you going?" she asked as she started to sob.

"I'm not going anywhere. I'm dying Emily."

The ice cream fell from her hand and she rushed out of the seaside snack bar. John Bottomsley ran after her and held her.

"Thank you mother," he said.

"I'm sorry son. I thought you had told her," she said running after him.

"Tell me it is not true Papa. What will I do without you Papa?"

"I'm not going just yet Emily. The doctor said I would go in about six months."

"That means no one else will love me."

"That's not true Emily," said her grandmother. "There is Grandpa and me. There is Clytie and there is your mother."

"She doesn't love me," wailed the child.

"Mother you've done enough harm already. Please leave us alone," he said as his mother stroked Emily's hair.

"I'm sorry son. I didn't mean to cause you any trouble. I will call you in the morning and then Emily and I can talk."

He took his daughter in his arms and tried to comfort her.

"Listen to me Emily. When I am gone, this is what I would like you to do. I want you to keep in touch with Miss Ella and Miss Nellie. They both love you very much."

"Alright Papa, but tell me it is not true. Tell me you're not going to leave me."

"I wish I could stay with you forever Emily, but my body is growing weaker day by day,"

"Is that why you allowed Thomas Hurley to run the plantation? And is that why you keep drinking Mr Fitz's bush teas?"

"Did you realise all that was going on?"

"I'm only twelve Papa, but I see a lot of things."

"You know that Bottomsley plantation will all be yours when I'm gone. Your mother will look after it until you are twenty one."

"If there is anything left to look after," she said with tears still streaming down her cheeks.

"Does she know?"

"If you're speaking about your mother," he replied. "No she doesn't know."

"When are you going to tell her?"

"I don't know," said John Bottomsley still holding his daughter in his arms.

"What about Grandpa? Does he know?"

"Yes he knows Emily."

"Will you tell Mama tonight? She should hurt too the same way I'm hurting."

"Do you think she cares Emily?"

"I don't know Papa."

* * *

# 31

Before there was a chance to tell his wife the bad news, his mother tearfully broke it to her. Did she do it because she wanted to make her feel guilty or was it because she wanted her to fulfil her obligations as a wife and to take care of him? No-one knew what lay hidden in the mind of Millie Bottomsley and no one knew what her intentions were. Needless to say her son was not happy about the interference and threatened to leave Bottomsley to spend his last days in peace. That he had intended doing anyway and thought there was no need to mention anything to his wife. Now it was all out in the open. He knew that if Sarah knew about his illness and if he were forced to stay at Bottomsley, he would have no time at all to spend with Nellie. Sarah was totally absorbed with her life with Thomas Hurley and he didn't want her pity nor did he want her to be with him when she didn't have the desire to do so.

Sarah Bottomsley did not take the news very well; after all this was her husband of more than twenty years. That must at least count for something. She persuaded her husband to remain at Bottomsley where there was household help and where he could be in close proximity of Dr. Sims, but even the doctor's name made the idea less agreeable. A false diagnosis by the doctor's father had actually signed his death sentence.

"Emily will be heartbroken if you leave," she said.

"My daughter understands that I need no pity nor do I want to stand in your way Sarah."

"You won't be standing in my way. I care for you and I want you to be comfortable."

"I will be comfortable Sarah. You can carry on your life with Thomas."

"Please do not do this to me John. I want you to stay. I'm begging you for the sake of Emily and me to spend these last moments with us."

"Please leave Papa alone," shouted Emily.

"I didn't know you were here darling," said her mother.

"You have spent all your time with Thomas Hurley and now you know Papa is ill, you are trying to be nice to him. He doesn't need you Mama. Clytie and I will take care of Papa."

"Nobody understands," she shouted. "No one! Not even my own flesh and blood."

John Bottomsley was shocked. He said nothing as his wife and his daughter became embroiled in a war of words.

"Grandpa and Grandma will come to help too," she said as the tears fell. "I won't be going to school anymore. I want to stay here and take of you Papa."

"School is very important Emily. I'll still be here when you come home in the evening."

The decision was made. John Bottomsley was going to remain in his home when he was no longer able to help himself. He had to break the news to Nellie and he also had to spend as much time as possible with her before the end came. The older John Bottomsley accompanied his son each time he made a trip to the north to visit Doctor Norton. Each time he asked himself if it would be the last, but according to the doctor his son was still doing very well and there was no need to be worried, at least for the present. Each visit to the doctor meant a visit to Nellie's Bar and Grocery where the older Bottomsley would have a couple drinks at Nellie's expense.

"Nellie girl," he said one day. "I'm happy to see you've made a life for yourself."

"Thanks Mr. Bottomsley," she replied.

"Tell me something Nellie. You love my son, don't you?"

"What kind of a question is that?" she asked.

"Father, what are you asking Nellie?"

"I'm old, perhaps drunk, but I am not blind. I have seen the way you look at each other. Not only with love in your eyes, but as if you are both trying to hide something from me."

Nellie was afraid to open her mouth and he realised it.

"Cat got your tongue Nellie?" he asked.

"Father you should stop harassing Nellie with your suspicions."

"Alright son, then I will ask you. What's going on between you and Nellie and please don't lie to your father."

"Alright Father, since you are so hell-bent on hearing the truth, I will tell you the truth. Yes, Nellie and I have been together for many years."

"What do you mean together son? You are married."

Nellie's face was turning all colours of the rainbow and she was praying that John Bottomsley would not mention anything about her daughter.

"I mean together Father. Nellie has been my strength for longer than I can remember. She listens when I talk and she is a source of comfort to me."

"I am not judging you son. I only wanted to know if my suspicions were right."

"Now that you know Father, what are you going to do?"

"Nothing," said the old man. "You are my son and your happiness and health comes before anything else."

"Thank you Father."

"No need to thank me son," he said as he headed out the door.

He turned around and looked at Nellie who had already started to cringe with fear of what he might say.

"Thank you Nellie," he said. "Thank you."

Relief gave way to tears and she cried on Miss Una's shoulder as the old woman did her best to console her.

"It turn out better than you thought Nellie. Don't cry. The old man like you."

"Every day JB life is coming closer and closer to the end Miss Una. What am I going to do?"

"The good Lord don't put more on a man than he is able to bear child. He know what he is doing."

"Why he have to take JB away from me?"

* * *

"Is there anything else you would like to tell me son?" the older John Bottomsley asked.

"Like what Father?"

"Anything about your life with Nellie?" he asked.

"There is nothing else to tell Father. All I would ask is that you not repeat any of our conversation to Mother."

"Tell this to Millie? Then I might as well take it to the newspaper. I know you think I talk a lot, but I suspected that you and Nellie had something going on and that's why I broke down and told her about your illness."

"Why didn't you mention it to me before Father?"

"Because I thought you were just having a fling, but hearing her call you JB, I knew there was more to it than just a roll in the hay."

"Aren't you disappointed?"

"Why should I be? It's your life and I know you're not happy with Sarah. Forgive me for what I'm about to say, but you and Sarah have outgrown each other. We are no longer living in the home country, so we have to adjust to suit the times and the situation. Sarah has not tried to fit in. She is the only woman living on this rock who hasn't got a little bit of colour on her skin and she is not interested in anything you are interested in. I can understand why you had to look elsewhere. Not only that, she could not bring one single living child into this world."

"Have you forgotten Emily Father?"

"No," he replied. "My darling little grand daughter! She has all your qualities John. I love her, but I have always asked myself where she got that head of unruly curls. The colour is yours, but the texture is definitely not her mother's."

"What are you trying to say?"

"Nothing son."

That night John Bottomsley lay in his bed and his life paraded through his mind. He thought of his life back in England and the boys he had played cricket with. He thought of his first girlfriend and wondered what had become of her. His thoughts focussed in on the first time he had set foot on the rock and how much he had loved it from the very first day. Then he thought about his beloved Emily and what would become of her. Financially she would be alright, but what if something happened to mess up her secure little world. What his father had said to him that evening bothered him. Did he know something about Emily's birth? If he did, he certainly wouldn't want to destroy his grandchild's life, and how could he have found out? She was his grandchild. It didn't matter who the mother was, she was his grandchild and he loved her. So did Millie Bottomsley of course but she was highly emotional and he really hoped his mother was ignorant about the facts surrounding Emily's birth.

Emily quietly entered his room and whispered to him.

"I'm here with your bush medicine Papa."

"I'm so glad you came in to see me," he said.

"Is something wrong Papa?"

"No, I was just thinking about you."

"You shouldn't think so much. You should rest."

He drank the dark, vile, bitter mixture and then swallowed some water to take the taste from his mouth.

"What were you thinking about?" she asked.

"Of my life back in England and my reasons for coming here," he replied.

"Do you regret coming here Papa?"

"Never! I wouldn't trade this for anything," he said. "I love it here and I hope you will make it your home even after I'm gone."

"I love it here Papa. This is all I know. This is the only place I can call home."

"You make me very happy Emily, very happy."

Clytie was ready to leave and as usual, she stopped in to see John Bottomsley before she went home.

"Clytie," he said to her. "Is my wife out there?"

"No sir, I think she went out."

"I want you to do something for me."

"What sir?" she asked.

"Do you know why I'm drinking so much of Fitz's bush teas?"

"Because you not feeling too good sir," was her reply.

"I know that you know I'm going to die Clytie."

"Why you telling me this sir," she said feeling rather uncomfortable.

"I know Nellie trusts you and I know you love my daughter."

"I love Emily like if she was my own."

"Good. I want you to do something for me Clytie."

"What sir?"

"I know you can read and write Clytie. Don't deny it, because this is very important to Emily."

"Yes sir."

"I want you to write what I'm going to tell you."

"He handed her a piece of paper and she followed his instructions.

"36 left, 44 right, 23 left.

"What this mean sir?"

"That's the combination to the safe. Do not give this to anyone, not to Mrs Bottomsley and most of all do not allow it to fall into Thomas Hurley's hands. When you notice that I can no longer look after myself, I want you to go to the safe find the paper with Nellie's X on it and destroy it. It is at the very bottom of all my papers. Don't let me down Clytie."

"But why you don't destroy it now?" she asked.

"Because.....do you know what it's about?"

"I think so sir."

"Well you know how important it is, don't you?"

"Yes sir."

Clytie stuck the piece of paper into her bosom and once at home, she hid it carefully.

* * *

# 32

That night before he went to bed, John Bottomsley insisted on speaking to Nellie. She did not have a good feeling because she knew his health had deteriorated rapidly, and his breathing had become rather shallow. She knew within her heart she would never see or hear from him again. She needed to talk and so she visited the two elderly ladies and found them in their usual position, on the porch in their rocking chairs and conversing with each other.

"That is a real pretty moon tonight, ain't it Nellie?"

"Yes, but sometimes I don't like a full moon."

"Something happen to JB?" Miss Una asked.

"I don't think he going to live through the night Miss Una."

"Don't talk foolishness girl. The Lord ain't ready for him yet."

"His voice was real weak Miss Una."

"He must be tired Nellie," said Miss Ella.

"My grandmother always used to say that when the moon full and beautiful, like it is tonight, the Lord call home his chosen children."

"That is true Nellie," said Miss Ella. "If he was born by the moon, he will die by the moon."

Una reached out and kicked Ella.

"But JB ain't going nowhere. His time is not up yet."

"You mind if I sit down here for a little while?" Nellie asked.

"Get a chair and rest your body child."

The grim reaper called at three thirty three that morning. John Bottomsley was called home to rest, with his mother, his father and daughter at his bedside. Sarah Bottomsley's nerves were not strong enough to deal with death, so Clytie and Ursy were both disturbed from their beds to cater to the family.

Emily clung to her grandmother and could and would not be comforted. The elder John Bottomsley sat beside his son's bed and held his hand which grew colder and colder as the minutes passed.

"Can I make a phone call Miss Sarah?" asked Clytie.

"Why do you want to use the telephone?" asked Millie.

"Millie, stop asking questions at this time of the morning. Just let her use the telephone," said John Bottomsley.

"Thank you sir," she said as she scurried back to the kitchen.

The ringing of the telephone at that early hour seemed like a bad omen. Nellie stumbled out of bed fully knowing it would be Clytie on the other end and what she would say. She lifted the receiver and waited.

"Nels?"

"Yes Clytie. Something happen to JB?"

"He is gone Nellie."

There was no response. Nellie flew out the door in her nightgown and the light of the full moon led her to the house where the two women waited. Before she had a chance to knock, Miss Ella opened the door.

"Come in Nellie. It is a bitter pill to swallow, but you know it was going to happen."

"He is gone Miss Ella. JB is gone."

Miss Una came out with a bottle of Limacol and poured some on Nellie's head.

"This will help you. You just try to relax Nellie."

She moaned and cried while the two women rubbed her head and hummed one of their church songs to console her. They too were fond of John Bottomsley and were deep in sorrow because it seemed like such a cruel thing. Death at such an early age was indeed a shock. He was only fifty one years old and one could say in the prime of his life. He and Nellie had found each other and had decided to make a life together, but it was not to be. Nellie's family gathered around her and mourned with her, for her loss was also their loss.

The Bottomsley family with the exception of Emily gathered in the drawing room but no one spoke. Now and again someone would sniffle which meant they were trying to be brave under the circumstances. Emily locked herself away and would open the door only to Clytie or her grandmother. Try as they may, they could not convince her to leave the confines of her room. One of the people in the world who truly loved her had been snatched from her life.

Clytie moved in and out from the kitchen to the drawing room. As she moved around, she kept whispering to herself. Yes she was also grief-stricken, but she was rehearsing the numbers which John Bottomsley had dictated to her. She was afraid she might miss the chance to grab that very valuable document before someone else got their hands on it.

Her chance finally came when the parents of John Bottomsley decided they had to go home and Sarah retired to her room. She looked around to make sure the coast was clear and then quickly went to the safe which was in the corner of his room. His bed had been stripped of its linen and the breeze lifted the curtains into the room from the open window. She suddenly felt afraid. She had seen death before but this was different. Although the bed was empty, she thought she could still see his body stretched out on it. She must erase the fear from her mind and do what was necessary and important. She opened his wardrobe door and his smell emanated from the clothes hanging there. It was all so realistic. She rehearsed the numbers once more and began to carefully turn the knob on the safe. First to the left, then to the right and then to the left again. She heard a very low click and knew she had done it.

Before she had a chance to look inside, she heard footsteps coming in her direction. She lowered the light on the lamp and quietly waited. The footsteps were those of John Bottomsley. She had heard them so many times before when he entered the house in the evening after a hard day's work. Her knees started to tremble and she held the lamp with both hands for fear of it falling and burning the house down. The footsteps started again, but this time, they went in the opposite direction, towards the kitchen. She breathed a sigh of relief and opened the safe. There was so much there, she didn't know where to start when she remembered he had said the document lay at the very bottom of the safe. With the document hidden away in her bosom, she crept out of the room and entered the kitchen.

"What you doing here Miss Emily?" she asked.

"Did you hear him Clytie?"

"Who Miss Emily?"

"Didn't you hear Papa? He came to my room and then he left again."

"You sure about that Miss Emily?" asked Clytie her heart pounding. "I didn't hear a thing."

"I know Clytie. I know. He came back to say goodbye to me."

Clytie accompanied her back to her room and waited with her until she fell asleep. She knew the child had not been dreaming, because she too had heard the footsteps. She tipped out of the house and entered the hut. There she removed the piece of paper from her bosom and looked at it. The evidence lay there in black and white before her. John Bottomsley had taken Emily away from Nellie and she had signed the agreement with an X. She had to destroy it and soon. The longer she kept it, the greater the chance of someone finding it and jeopardizing Emily's future. That night, that document was used to light the fire under Clytie's cooking pot.

All the plantation owners turned out for the funeral of John Bottomsley. From near and far they came to pay their respects and Sarah Bottomsley played the part of the grieving widow, although Thomas Hurley was never too far away from her side. Sadness filled the air as the hearse slowly made its way onto the church grounds followed by the plantation workers who walked two by two behind their departed employer. Emily stuck by her grandmother and she did not shed a tear, because there were none left t. The older John Bottomsley stood stony faced as his only son's casket was about to be lowered into the earth.

No one had seen Nellie. She decided it was better to grieve privately and so she watched the procession from the back seat of Clarence's car. Miss Una and Miss Ella sat quietly with her as the earth was thrown onto the casket and the family members gently lay wreaths onto the fresh earth. Nellie could see the whiteness of Sarah Bottomsley's face through the black veil which was there to hide any pain or sorrow. She seemed so fragile. Nellie thought it was possible she was really grieving. When she saw Emily, she was overcome with sorrow. The child was so strong and and at the same time, so weak. She clung to her grandmother and the two walked away from the grave followed closely by the elder John Bottomsley.

As they passed the car where Nellie was seated, John Bottomsley looked in and saw her. He stopped for a moment, stared at her and then followed his wife and granddaughter. Clytie followed them closely, because she felt Emily was her responsibility and she intended to be there in case she needed her.

"Thank you Clytie," Nellie whispered as she passed by.

Her friend turned, looked at her and followed the Bottomsley family.

"You alright Nellie?" asked Miss Ella.

She nodded as the old lady wrapped her hand around hers and uttered words of consolation which Nellie didn't hear.

"It is hurting so much Miss Ella."

"Let it out," said Miss Una. "Cry Nellie. Cry. It will ease the pain."

"I can't cry no more Miss Una. I just can't."

"We should go home. Call Clarence so we could get Nellie in bed. I think she's going to have a nervous breakdown."

"I'm alright Miss Ella. I just don't believe JB is lying under that cold earth."

"Child, life is quite a journey. Sometimes it real pretty, sometimes it ain't pretty at all, but it still a beautiful journey all the same. God is going to ease your pain. Just wait and pray."

As the plantation workers filed by, some of the older ones caught a glimpse of the three ladies, and in no time the car was surrounded. They had not seen Nellie or the two older ladies for a long time and of course were curious about them and how their lives were going. They also expressed shock over the early death of the plantation owner and wondered what the future would be like for them.

"Things always work out for the best," said Miss Una. "Only the good Lord know why he call him home so early. Anyway look after one another and remember the three of us in your prayers."

After they had all left, Clarence climbed into the car and started the engine.

"Don't go yet," said Nellie. "I can't leave without saying goodbye to JB."

She stepped out of the car and slowly made her way towards the grave site. She looked at the mound of earth and the flowers that had been placed on it.

"JB, how you could go and leave me so? Just when everything was coming together and I thought we would be happy, you up and left me. How could you JB?"

Realising things were getting out of hand Miss Una climbed out of the car and waited while Clarence helped Nellie back to the waiting car. She was beside herself with grief. She no longer spoke. She just moaned all the way from the church back to her home.

* * *

# 33

Miss Una was sitting in her position at the cash desk listening to the music on Reddifusion when a man entered the shop and looked around.

"I'm looking for Nellie Peterkin," he said. .

"Nellie sick. You want to leave a message for her?" asked a suspicious Miss Una.

"Do you think she will be here tomorrow?"

"I don't know sir. Like I tell you, Nellie sick and I don't know when she coming back."

"Does she live next door?"

"What is your name sir, and why you asking so many questions about Nellie?"

"I'm an old friend and just wanted to say hello."

"I am a old friend too and I never see you. Tell me your name and I will tell Nellie you come by asking after her."

"Don't worry. I'll stop by sometime again next week."

"You live around here?" she asked.

"Never mind, I'll come by next week."

"Whatever you say!" said Miss Una.

Miss Una was a little confused by all the questions the man had asked. She knew he was too old to be a friend of Nellie's, and she knew the only white friend Nellie had was JB. But what did he want? Why did he come by just after John Bottomsley's death? And then, she thought his face looked rather familiar. Try as she might, she just couldn't remember who he was. She didn't want to give Nellie the news right away, because she knew she didn't have the strength to handle another catastrophe if indeed this was one. She felt in her heart of hearts, he was not a bearer of good news. That bit of news would have to wait until Nellie was feeling better.

A similar scenario was taking place at Bottomsley plantation. Emily hardly ever left her room, not even to go to school and when she did leave it was only to communicate with Clytie.

"You want to visit Miss Ella and Miss Nellie?" Clytie asked.

"I'm not sure if Mama would let me go."

"I am going to see Ma next weekend Miss Emily. You could come with me. It would make you feel better."

"I don't know Clytie. I really miss Papa."

"That is what I mean Miss Emily. If you go to a strange place, it would help you to forget."

"But I don't want to forget Papa."

"It will make you feel a little bit better."

"Will you ask Mama if I can go with you Clytie?"

"Yes. You want to sleep up there too?"

"Yes, then I wouldn't have to see his face."

"Who are you talking about Miss Emily?"

"Mama's lover," she said without batting an eyelash.

"Don't say that Miss Emily."

"It is true. Will you go and ask her?"

"Alright."

No sooner had Clytie left than the telephone started to ring.

"Hello Grandma," said Emily.

"I am coming to get you so you can spend a little time with me and your grandfather."

"I can't Grandma. Clytie's taking me away with her this weekend."

"So you prefer to go with Clytie than to come to your own grandmother?"

"No Grandma, but she asked me first."

"It doesn't matter if she asked you first. Where are you going anyway?"

"To visit Miss Ella and Miss Nellie?" she replied.

"To visit Ella and Nellie," Millie asked. "Where will you sleep?"

John Bottomsley interrupted his wife.

"Millie, the child needs love right now. Not an interrogation. You know how much Clytie loves her. Perhaps she wanted to give the child a change of scenery. Have you forgotten she has just lost her father?"

"Have a good time Emily," Millie Bottomsley said.

"So you're not angry with me anymore Grandma?"

"I was never angry with you Emily. You know I love you."

"Thank you Grandma. Do you miss Papa too?"

"Of course I miss him. He was my son."

Emily saw Thomas Hurley's car drive up, and she headed for the solitude of her bedroom. She had no desire to see him or her mother for that matter. Clytie was called upon to serve refreshments, which she did and then headed back to the kitchen.

"So where is Emily?" Thomas Hurley asked.

"In her room," replied Sarah.

"Don't you think she spends too much time alone Sarah?"

"She'd rather be there than around me," she answered.

"Let's take her somewhere, perhaps a picnic or something like that."

"Sorry, but my daughter prefers to be with Clytie. They are going away together this weekend."

"Emily's going away with a servant?"

"Yes."

"Where on earth are they going?"

"To visit Ella and Nellie," she replied.

"Why do you allow your child to mix with those people? She should be mixing with her own kind."

"What do you propose I do? Tie her to the bed?"

"No, but you can forbid it."

"Normally I would Thomas, but Emily is grieving. Have you forgotten she has just lost her father?"

"That's true, but it just can't go on like this. You should think of sending her away to school where she can grow up among her peers."

"I just can't send her away like that Thomas."

"She needs a firm hand. You have no control over her so it would be advisable to send her somewhere, where she can be tutored properly and be brought up with some kind of discipline instead of hanging around with a bunch of servants in the kitchen. Even Ginger says she is a very difficult child. No matter what happens, she always seems to have her way in the end."

"It would be difficult handling her without having John's help and support. Perhaps I should send her to a boarding school. It would do her good."

"I'm glad you understand. I'm not trying to put distance between you and Emily, but she does need discipline."

While Emily was trying to forget about the loss of her father, plans were being made in her absence to ship her away from the island. No one would have believed a mother could be so cruel, but she had always been a weak person and Thomas Hurley's persuasiveness took precedence over her daughter's well-being. Being with Clytie, Miss Ella and Nellie seemed to put Emily into a better frame of mind. She was much more talkative and slept in Nellie's spare bedroom with Hurley her cat, while Clytie slept with her mother and Miss Ella.

"You alright Miss Emily?" Nellie asked.

"It hurts so much Miss Nellie."

"Where is it hurting?" Nellie asked.

"It's Papa. I miss him so much."

"I miss him too," said Nellie as the words blurted out of her mouth, but it was too late.

"You knew Papa?" she asked.

"Yes, I used to work in the kitchen at Bottomsley."

"Why did you leave?"

"It is a long story Miss Emily."

"Tell me Miss Nellie."

"Well I lost my baby and it was real hard for me to work with Miss Sarah because she just had a baby and it would remind me of my own poor baby. So I left and came to live up here."

"Was I that baby Miss Nellie?"

"Yes Miss Emily. That baby was you."

"So you've known me for a long time Miss Nellie."

"Yes child, I know you from the first minute you were born. I even help to hold you and to feed you."

"I didn't know that Miss Nellie. Papa never told me, neither did Mama."

"It was not so important Miss Emily. We are friends now. That's what is important and I am really glad that we are friends."

"Me too Miss Nellie."

"So what are you going to do now? Are you going back to school and later run the plantation?"

"That's Mama's decision. It is now hers."

"Why do you say it is hers?"

"Because normally Miss Nellie, when the husband dies, everything goes to the wife."

"And what about the children?" asked Nellie

"If you mean me, I'm much too young to take over the running of any kind of business."

Nellie was becoming confused and was extremely afraid that her daughter might lose her inheritance. JB had told her everything he owned would be passed down to Emily, but it seemed as if her daughter knew nothing about it.

"Miss Emily, I don't mean to meddle in your business, but they ain't read the will yet?"

"Not as far as I know Miss Nellie or perhaps Mama just hasn't said anything."

Fear gripped Nellie's heart and she sat with Emily until she fell asleep. Then like a bolt of lightning, she dashed over to see Clytie.

"Something happen to Miss Emily?" asked a panic stricken Clytie.

"No, she alright. I have to ask you something Clytie."

"What Nellie?"

"When JB take Emily from me, he make me sign a piece of paper and I think it still somewhere inside the house."

"Calm yourself Nellie. It isn't anywhere in the house."

"How you know that Clytie?"

"I burn it."

"But how Clytie?"

Clytie told her the story of the safe and the document, at which point Nellie sat down and started to cry. Someone else was crying too. She did not see Emily enter the room with Hurley in her arms.

"Why are you crying Miss Nellie?" she asked.

"Miss Emily, I thought you was sleeping," said Clytie.

"I was dreaming about Papa. He said I should go and talk to Miss Nellie, but I couldn't find you."

Nellie held the child in her arms and they both cried as Nellie rocked her back and forth. Then she lifted her and Clytie accompanied them back to the house, where Nellie lay beside Emily until she was sound asleep.

"They ain't read the will yet Clytie?"

"Not as far I know," she replied.

"Why you asking?"

"Because Emily think the plantation belong to Miss Sarah."

"Who it belong to then?" asked Clytie.

"It belong to Emily. Sarah is only the caretaker until Emily turn twenty one."

"Well that is sure going to turn Thomas Hurley hair grey, because he think that it all belong to Miss Sarah."

"Well he going to be in for a big surprise."

"What you think JB want you to tell Emily?"

"I don't understand what you mean Clytie."

"Just a few minutes ago," said Clytie. "Emily say she had a dream and her father say she should go and talk to you."

"She say that Clytie?"

"You didn't hear that?"

"No. Not a word."

"I forget to tell you that he was in the house one night last week," said Clytie.

"You mean he was in the plantation house?"

"That was the same night when I went to look for that piece of paper. I went into the bedroom and I hear footsteps coming in my direction. I was so frighten Nellie, I didn't know what to do, so I keep real quiet and then he turn around and went out again. Then poor Miss Emily start to cry because she too hear her father's footsteps. I think he was making sure that I was getting rid of that piece of paper."

"So he looking after Emily even though he is gone."

"It sure look so Nels."

"But he never come to visit me Clytie. I have never had a dream about him, nothing at all. I longing for JB to come and visit me Clytie."

* * *

# 34

Her father's death seemed to strengthen and make her an even more independent young woman, in spite of bouts of sadness and loneliness, but she clung to the hope that one day she would reach adulthood, and be away from the clutches of her mother and her soon to be step-father. He had proposed marriage to the widow and she had accepted.

One day John Bottomsley's solicitor finally called his wife to his office. It was now time to let her know how the property would be dispersed. Thomas Hurley insisted upon attending, but since he was not a family member, the solicitor denied his presence there. The widow was dressed in mourning attire, black from head to foot although she had accepted another man's marriage proposal. Emily walked nervously behind her mother, not because she thought there was nothing left for her but because she would hear her Papa's words spoken through another. Grandpa Bottomsley, realising how nervous she was, held her hand firmly and continued to do so even after they were seated in the regal mahogany chambers with all its legal books sitting from one end of the room to the other.

Mr. Yates, John Bottomsley's solicitor greeted them as they took their places. He was not one for beating around the bush and started to recite John Bottomsley's Papa's will verbatim. Sarah sat silently as the words were read. Her daughter was the sole inheritor of Bottomsley plantation but could only take ownership when she reached the age of twenty one. The widow would administrate the running of it until her daughter was ready to take over. Sarah was not at all pleased, but Grandpa Bottomsley was delighted. He squeezed his granddaughter's hand even tighter and smiled when she was told she was sole executor of her father's will. Of course Sarah could still live in the house and continue her charmed life but she was also to keep John Bottomsley's parents in the lifestyle to which they had grown accustomed.

Needless to say, the cavalier Mr. Hurley was not amused when he was told the news. He and Sarah sat in silence consuming drink after drink and wondering what their next move should be.

"I am a penniless woman," she said to her intended.

"Don't be so dramatic Sarah. Of course you're not penniless. The plantation is still yours until Emily turns twenty one. Have you thought about my proposal?"

"If you'll still have a penniless widow," she replied.

"You know I will, but I was speaking about sending Emily off to boarding school."

"I did find a couple schools but haven't made a decision yet."

"Why are you waiting?"

"Because my dear Thomas, I haven't told her yet that we intend abandoning her."

"But you are not doing that. You want her to grow up to be a respectable young woman."

"I'll tell her soon."

* * *

"Are you Nellie Peterkin?" asked the man as he entered the shop.

"Yes," she answered.

"My name is Gus Ridley."

Nellie waited for him to continue, but he didn't.

"What can I do for you Mr. Ridley?"

Miss Una sitting at the cashier's cage heard the name and listened more intently. She knew his face was familiar and now she knew exactly who he was, but what did he want with Nellie?

"I take it you don't know me," he said smiling with her.

"Should I know you Mr....Sir?" she said since she had forgotten his name.

"I knew your mother Hilda Peterkin."

She had no idea what he wanted or why he was referring to her mother.

"Nellie," said Miss Una. "Come here."

"Just a minute Miss Una," she said.

"You did know my mother?" she asked him.

"Very well," he answered.

"Nellie excuse yourself, and come here for a moment."

"Yes Miss Una. What is it?" she asked feeling a little irritated.

"That man is your father."

"What? You sure about that Miss Una?"

"As sure as there is a God, he is Gus Ridley," the old woman replied.

"How you know my mother so good?" asked Nellie staring at him.

"Well enough to have a daughter with her," he replied with a smile.

"You trying to tell me that you is my father?"

"I am Nellie."

"And what you want from me after all these years?"

"I wanted to meet you and to see if you looked anything like your mother," he replied.

"And now that you see me. I look like her?"

"Exactly like her Nellie. Exactly like her except your skin is lighter."

"To tell you the truth, I didn't have much to do with that," she replied.

He laughed uneasily and stared at her.

"But tell me Gus, why you really looking for me after all these years and how you find me?"

"Like I said, I wanted to see if you looked liked your mother and John Bottomsley told me about you. God rest his soul," he said making a sign of the cross.

"What John Bottomsley tell you about me?"

"You know I used to be the overseer at The Henley Place. Well John and I became pretty good friends and even though I retired a while ago, he was looking for someone to replace that Hurley fellow. Seems Hurley had an eye on his wife. It never materialised because the poor man died before he had a chance to do it. I don't mind because I really didn't have the strength for it. As a matter of fact, I was just going to do it to help him out."

"But you still ain't say what he tell you about me."

"He was a good friend of mine Nellie. Friends talk about things."

"What things?" she asked again.

"Everything."

"So what you want? You trying to get money from me?"

"Not at all! Well perhaps you can help me. Things haven't been going well for me since I left the job."

"So that is why JB was offering you a job running the plantation?"

"Well you could say that."

"Well Mr. Gus or whatever your name is. When my poor mother was hungry, we couldn't find you. You was hiding when I had to go to work in the Bottomsley kitchen when I was only eleven, and now you coming to ask for help. I helping two old people already. You don't remember Miss Una? What about Miss Ella? These two women help my mother when she had no where to turn."

"Amen," shouted Miss Una from behind the cashier's cage.

"So Mr. Gus, do whatever you want. I don't have a father, never had one. I ain't a young woman no more and I don't have a thing to hide," she said, in case his intention was to blackmail her.

"You misunderstand me Nellie. I'm not looking for help."

Nellie knew she was gambling, but she had to take a chance. Somehow she knew JB had never disclosed anything about their child. He was much too clever a man.

That evening the telephone rang in her house and Nellie jumped up to answer it.

"Nels? It is me Clytie. I got some good news. Miss Sarah isn't home so I taking a chance to call you. The plantation belong to Miss Emily."

"They read the will?"

"Yes and Miss Emily and only Miss Emily own Bottomsley."

"Praise the Lord!" she exclaimed.

"There is more news Nels."

"It look like if Miss Sarah planning to send Miss Emily overseas."

"Where she sending her?"

"Somewhere to study some more," said Clytie. "I think they say England."

"Who is they Clytie?"

"Miss Sarah and the Hurley fellow," she replied. "And by the way, they getting married next week. No big thing. Just a few friends!"

"He ain't even move in yet and he making decisions concerning Emily?"

"But he was making decisions ever since Nels."

"And how Emily taking the news?"

"I don't think she know yet Nels. I think Miss Sarah frighten to tell her anything."

"I lost Emily father and now I am going to lose Emily too?"

"Only until she is twenty one, and then they don't have nothing more to say."

"But she still going to be so far away."

"She still here Nels and she can be real stubborn."

"What do they call children around Emily age?"

"What you mean Nellie?"

"When they can't make decisions for themselves?"

"You mean under age."

"That isn't the word but you know what I mean. She got to do what Miss Sarah say."

"We got to wait and see Nellie."

"Clytie, my father come by to see me this morning."

"Your what?" asked a shocked Clytie.

"My father."

"What he want Nels?"

"I not so sure but I know he isn't coming back."

Little did Nellie know that her last words to Clytie in that telephone conversation would come to pass. Two weeks after Gus Ridley's visit, he passed away. Although she had known him only for two weeks, she felt a bit of sadness for the poor man. She wondered about the cause of death. She hoped he hadn't died of hunger but she knew no one on the rock ever died of starvation. There was always someone willing and ready to share whatever there was to eat. Perhaps he knew he was going to die and that was the reason for paying her that visit. Was it a dying man's way of trying to make things right? She was sorry she had treated him the way she did, for after all he was her father and seemed to have had a good relationship with JB.

"You think I should go to the funeral Miss Ella?"

"I don't know Nellie. You got to do what you think is right."

"After all he was my father."

"Like I say Nellie, you got to do what you got to do."

In comparison to JB's funeral, this one was rather small. Nellie could identify many of the faces standing over the casket. In all there were no more than fifteen persons in attendance. What kind of a man was this who had only such a small gathering at his last farewell? Did he have children? Where was his wife?

"As a man liveth, so shall he die," was Miss Una's only explanation why Gus Ridley's farewell was not well attended.

"But it still sad to see him go like that Miss Una."

"Well he had a wife when me and Hilda was working at that first plantation where he was."

"He didn't have no children?"

"Not that I can remember. Could be he had some later but I don't remember any."

"Well he gone home to heaven."

"He isn't in heaven Nellie. That man gone straight to fight Lucifer to take over hell."

"We should not talk bad things about the departed."

"That is true Nellie."

***

# 35

"Grandma," wailed Emily. "They're trying to get rid of me."

"Emily, stop crying and tell me what's going on."

"They want to send me away Grandma."

"Emily, your Grandpa and I are coming over right away."

"Miss Emily, don't cry like that," said Clytie. "Your Grandma is coming over and she is going to fix everything."

"Nobody can help me Clytie. They want to take my inheritance away from me."

Although they were both in their sixties, the Bottomsleys sprang up the steps like two young people. Millie Bottomsley rang the door bell and never let it go until Clytie opened the door.

"Where is she Clytie?" asked Millie.

"In the kitchen with Ursy," replied Clytie.

"Emily?" her grandmother called out.

She ran into her grandmother's arms, her face redder than a beet and still wailing.

"Where is Sarah?" asked John Bottomsley.

Clytie did not answer but pointed in the direction of the front porch where he trotted off and an argument ensued.

"Sarah, how dare you send my granddaughter out of the island? If my son were alive, you'd never dream of doing it."

"Like your wife always said John, she needs to grow up among her peers and become a lady. That's exactly what I'm doing."

"Didn't you think you could've consulted us since we too have something to say regarding her upbringing?"

"You weren't listening," she said. "Your wife always thought it was a good idea."

"Sometimes I have this feeling that you are not Emily's mother. How could you treat her this way just after her father's death?"

"I won't have you talking to my wife this way," said Thomas Hurley who had been silent throughout the conversation.

"Well! Well! If it's not the free-loader," he said to him.

"If you weren't such an old man, I would thrash you," said Thomas.

"I'm not too old to take you on my boy. Here you are standing on my granddaughter's property and threatening to thrash me. Why don't you get a place of your own and take her with you?"

Sarah Bottomsley broke down and started to cry, thus softening the old man's heart.

"I think you ought to leave," said Thomas Hurley.

"If anyone's leaving, it will be you. Sarah I didn't come here to hurt you. I'm just so worried about my granddaughter. Why don't you sit down with her and discuss things. She's only a child and a child with a broken heart. She needs you now more than ever Sarah. Be a mother to her. Don't allow her to turn to Clytie each time she needs someone to talk to."

"I didn't mean to forsake her Father Bottomsley. I too am suffering from John's death. Maybe you're right. I have probably left her alone too much and never noticed how much she needed me."

"I'm glad we understand each other Sarah. But tell her you are not trying to get rid of her. Tell her you love her and what you are doing is just to give her a foundation for the future, and to make her a lady fit to run Bottomsley."

Emily and her grandmother stood in the doorway and heard the interaction between John Bottomsley and Sarah. He persuaded Sarah to go immediately to her daughter and talk to her, but when she saw the state her daughter was in, she held out her arms and Emily ran into them.

"I'm so sorry Emily. So sorry," she said hugging her.

"Will you still send me away Mama?"

"We will talk about it together when you are feeling better."

"Mama may I spend the night with Grandma and Grandpa?"

"Of course you may darling," said her mother as she walked with her daughter to her bedroom.

"This is your doing Thomas Hurley," said John Bottomsley. "Sarah would never have tried to push her child out of her life if you hadn't put the idea into her head."

"You may think what you like. If you hadn't spoilt her, she would be a better child."

"Young man, don't forget you are speaking about my granddaughter, and Hurley, if you intend to live here with Sarah, you'd better stay out of my granddaughter's affairs."

Thomas Hurley got up, walked to his car, got in and drove out into the night, returning only after Emily and her grandparents had left. It seemed as though he had been drinking.

"Clytie," he shouted.

"She has gone home already Thomas," said his wife.

"And who will serve my dinner?" he asked, his words slurring.

"It is ten thirty and you know Clytie goes home at seven."

"It is unbelievable how you run this house," he said looking at his wife. "There is absolutely no discipline in here. The servants do whatever they want; your child does whatever she wants and you, you sit idly by and allow all this to happen. You need a housekeeper and one who knows what's she's about."

"There has never been a housekeeper here Thomas and I don't need one. I ran this house alone for many years and will continue to do so."

"Then you need better help. You must get rid of Clytie and Ursy."

"Never Thomas!" she replied. "Clytie has been with me for many, many years. I trust her and I know she'll never let me down."

Thomas did not hear the last thing his wife said for he had fallen asleep in John Bottomsley's plantation chair. He seemed to be taking over everything which belonged to John and was rather cocky and indifferent about it all. Morning came and he was still fully clothed and asleep in the chair.

Clytie opened the kitchen door, but quickly closed it when she saw his outstretched body in the chair.

"Things like they not so good with the newly married couple," she said to Ursy.

"Why do you say so?" asked Ursy.

"Peep in there and you will see why."

Ursy looked in and heard the snoring coming from the plantation chair.

"I'm sure it got something to do with Miss Emily," said Clytie.

"He put that notion in Miss Sarah's head to send Emily away."

"I don't understand that at all. Miss Emily ain't depending on him for nothing. Emily father left her good. She don't want nothing from nobody."

"He can't get his fingers on Emily's money and he must be upset, so to punish that lovely child, he is trying to put distance between her and Miss Sarah. The master must be rolling over in his grave."

"They say money is the root of all evil, and it sure look like it," Clytie replied.

"He isn't anything like Mr. Bottomsley. He had his funny ways but he was a good man. God rest his soul."

"I got to phone Nellie. She don't know what happening to Emily. Ursy look out and tell me when he is coming."

"You better hurry. He is still snoring," she replied.

"All I can say is that I real glad that Miss Emily got grandparents that love her."

"Amen to that Clytie. She really doesn't deserve what is happening to her. I really don't want her to suffer anymore."

The old black telephone was extremely heavy, but she managed to slide it through the kitchen door and dialled Nellie's number.

"Nels, I phoning to see how things are up there."

"Everything is alright. I just getting ready to go to the shop."

"Ma ain't opening the shop today?"

"Yes, but Miss Ella didn't feel too good, so I going to open it myself this morning. Where is Emily?"

"The grandparents take her home with them last night because there was too much commotion around here. It was better for the child."

Clytie related the last evening's happenings to Nellie who was listening intently, when suddenly they both heard a click on the line.

"I got to go. I will talk to you again," she said and put the receiver down. "I think somebody was listening to me Ursy. I thought you did keeping a eye out for me. He still sleeping?"

Thomas Hurley was nowhere to be seen and Clytie was now concerned that he might have been listening and secondly, she hadn't asked permission to use the telephone. She hurried to make the breakfast while Ursy set the table. Thomas Hurley came out and sat down hardly acknowledging her presence.

"Morning Mr. Hurley," said Ursy.

He did not reply, but started to drink his tea.

"Send Clytie in to see me," he commanded.

"He wants to see you Clytie," Ursy said.

She went in and stood at the bottom of the table.

"Morning sir, you want to see me?"

He ignored her and kept on eating. She stood there like an inanimate object while he ate and she shook in her boots. She despised the gold digger who had taken John Bottomsley's place.

"As long as I am here in this house, things will change," he told her. "You are never to touch the telephone without permission and if I hear you've been discussing the affairs of this household, you will be fired immediately."

"What you talking about sir?" she asked trying to play the innocent part.

'Don't make it worse by denying it. Just remember what I've said or you will have to go. Now get out of my sight."

Clytie opened the kitchen door and almost knocked Ursy over. She was listening at the keyhole and didn't realise the conversation was over.

"Don't bother about him Clytie. If he let you go, I will be going too. I never once heard Master Bottomsley talk to nobody like that. He thinks that this plantation belongs to him."

"Ursy, he can't frighten me. I know how to deal with him. After today, he got to be careful with me. He can say whatever he want, but he will pay the price."

"What you planning to do Clytie?"

"Keep your ears to the ground and your mouth shut," she said sounding very much like her predecessor Miss Ella. "I can only say he is a lucky man because of Emily."

"You are making me real nervous Clytie."

"Don't be nervous. He is going to get only what he deserve."

* * *

# 36

Things went from bad to worse. Thomas Hurley treated the plantation workers as if they were his property. He insisted on firing one quarter of them and then expected the others to carry the full workload. From sunup to sundown, they toiled like slaves in the sugar cane fields; then were too tired to cook and eat their evening meals or even sit around in front of their huts like they normally did. He raised the rent on the little hot huts they lived in and stationed a watchman in the orchard close to the huts. Under John Bottomsley, they could consume as much as they wanted, provided the family in the great house, received the best of the harvest. Now they were expected to purchase even the little plums, although the fruit sat rotting on the trees. The children would still take the opportunity to throw stones in the trees and then gather up the fruit, but he threatened to expel the parents from the land if they did not take control of their children. Then to add insult to injury, he closed the school putting the teacher, Clytie's son Jonas out of work. Many of them now could not afford to send their children to school, because they couldn't afford the fees at the new schools which had opened up. He then tried to encourage the workers to take their children to the fields with them, but they refused. They wanted better lives for their offspring and working in the fields certainly didn't fit that bill.

"Master Bottomsley never counted anything that came in here," Ursy complained. "Now he is asking about what happen to the mangoes and what happen to this and to that. He should be ashamed that he is so stingy.

"Although I like the master parents now, I didn't like them at the beginning. They used to behave the same way Thomas Hurley behaving."

"They didn't come from anywhere, so they have to behave like if they better than we."

Ursy pulled the air in between her teeth, something which she did when she was annoyed and it penetrated throughout the house.

"Tschuuuuuuups!"

"You make me laugh when you do that Ursy. I wish I could do that as good as you."

"I learn that from the old cook where I used to work after I left school. Whenever anything went wrong, she used to let out this long chewps and we used to keep out of the way. If you didn't, the Cou Cou stick would be flying past your head."

"What happen to her?" asked Clytie.

Ursy pointed down and her laughter rang out like that of a frightened hen.

"I don't understand Ursy."

"She is down there with the devil. She was a wicked old woman."

A door slammed and Clytie looked out hoping it was Emily back with her grandparents. Instead it was the Lord of the manor rushing up the steps as fast as he could. A minute later, he was running back down with a shotgun and Sarah Bottomsley-Hurley in hot pursuit.

"What's going on?" she asked as he slammed the car door leaving her standing in the dust the car had created.

She stood there for a moment as if lost and then hurried up the stairs and made a phone call.

"I think something is wrong Father Bottomsley. Thomas just came home and took the shotgun with him."

"Where did he go Sarah?"

"I suspect out to the fields. He has been having a hard time with the workers recently and I'm afraid he's going to do something terrible."

"Alright Sarah, I'll see what I can do. In the meantime we'll keep Emily here until we find out what's going on."

John Bottomsley arrived at the sugar cane fields where there seemed to be a standoff. Thomas Hurley stood poised with his weapon and the workers with their hoes and cutlasses.

"What's going on here?" the old man asked.

"Nothing that I can't handle," he replied.

"Looks to me like you're outnumbered," said the old man.

"The first one to make a move in my direction will get a bullet right between the eyes," he threatened.

"That won't be necessary. What is going on?"

Thomas Hurley did not answer, but concentrated on the weapon he had cocked in their direction. Soon other plantation owners, along with their weapons were coming to his assistance. Fear was in the eyes of the workers and they were happy to see John Bottomsley on the scene. At least he seemed to be on their side.

"What seems to be the problem Thomas?" one of them asked.

"I seem to have a mutiny here on my hands," he replied.

"One wrong move and we'll shoot the pack of good for nothings," said one of his friends.

"There won't be any shooting around here," said the elder Bottomsley. "My son ran this plantation for over twenty years and it has never come to this. Thomas I demand to know what the problem is."

One of the workers whom John Bottomsley had schooled answered the old man.

"It is like this sir, since the master pass on, nothing ain't the same around here. We getting less money and we got to pay for everything; the school for the children shut down, and now we can't leave de fields to pee.

"What do you mean you can't leave the fields to pee?"

"If we go, he say don't come back, so we decide that we going to stop working and he say he will shoot us."

"I know I speak on behalf of my dead son. Go back to your homes and take your guns with you," he said to Thomas' friends. "Thomas and I will handle this."

It took a bit of coaxing, but the old man managed to bring order out of the chaos and ended an impending war which had been looming on the horizon."

"I know we don't see eye to eye Thomas, but for goodness sake, you can't treat them like that. They are human beings and won't tolerate things which their grandparents tolerated.

"It's his fault," he shouted at the worker Stanley Alleyne.

"Let's not start throwing blame around Thomas. Let's see if we can get them back to work."

"If he didn't go against my wishes and allow them to leave the field during their work time, this would never have happened."

"You can't stop a man from going to pee Thomas. Slavery is no more. You have to understand that."

"I need a new overseer. I can't work with him anymore. And if you insist, I will leave this plantation in their hands."

'Let's not be hasty Thomas. You need a job. You can't live without a job and Bottomsley plantation cannot thrive without these people. That's where your wife's bread and butter comes from, and the money to keep us in the lifestyles we all have."

The two men walked off together, leaving the workers to ponder their fate They hoped the elder Bottomsley could at least talk some sense into the hot-headed Thomas Hurley.

And the bush drums travelled all the way north because Nellie made a call to Clytie, who was afraid to pick up the telephone. Only after it rang unceasingly, did she take it. Nellie had heard the news and wanted to know if there really was a shooting at Bottomsley. Clytie knew nothing, but promised she would get back to her when she had a bit of news. She knew Thomas Hurley had come home and picked up a shotgun, and Miss Sarah had called upon her father in law for assistance. That was all she knew.

* * *

# 37

Although the fuse had been dislodged from the ticking time bomb, there was still tension in the air, because the workers had lost their benefits and there was less money for them to try to support their families. It was also not easy for Thomas Hurley, for since he had lit the fuse, it kept on smouldering although there was never an explosion. There was tension between him and his new bride which caused him to drink and to stay out late. Sarah Bottomsley was making an effort to get closer to her daughter, although she had convinced her that going away to study was the best thing for her. Emily seemed to understand and believed it would be a positive thing for her in the long run. Her departure would be hard on everyone especially Nellie, Miss Ella, Grandma Bottomsley and all the people who loved her. Clytie made sure she was leaving with a suitcase packed with clothing which was crisp and clean.

It would've been unheard of, if she left without saying goodbye to her friends living in St. Lucy. So along with Clytie, she visited them all to bid them farewell.

"You too young to be going off by yourself," said Nellie.

"I'm going to a boarding school. Most of the children there will be around my age and I will make new friends," she said.

"Miss Emily, you ain't going to see me when you come back," said Miss Ella.

"Where are you going?" she asked.

"To meet my Lord," she said.

"Don't talk like that Miss Ella. Of course I'll see you again. I'll write to you and Miss Nellie can read it for you."

"That is nice that you would remember an old woman."

"You're not an old woman. You're my friend."

As if it understood Emily was leaving for a long time, Hurley hid under the table and his meowing resembled that of a very sad child. She lifted the animal and held it close to her bosom.

"Miss Nellie, please take good care of Hurley," she said. "I will miss him very much."

As the evening sun sank in the west, Emily and Clytie started the journey back to Bottomsley. She sat behind Clarence the driver and waved until she was out of sight. Nellie's tears flowed like rain. Her daughter was leaving for a distant land where it was sometimes so cold that they had to light fires inside the house to keep themselves warm. Miss Ella dabbed her eyes with a handkerchief while Miss Una tried to comfort her.

"I don't have nothing left," said Nellie. "JB left me now Emily gone too."

"She going to come back one day," said Miss Una. "Everything in life does happen for a good reason."

"The reason is that man Thomas Hurley," Nellie replied. "If he didn't want Emily money, she would be here with us now."

"He is going to get what he deserve," said Miss Ella. "He sure will."

"I know how Nellie feel. When my one sister went off with that family to Carlina up there in Amurca, I didn't know what to do. She did all the family I had, and since that day I never hear one word from Ida. I ain't know if she living or dead."

"I just don't understand why she wouldn't send a letter to you Una."

"Don't forget that we all in the same boat. Ida didn't know how to read or write."

"But she could find somebody who could write two lines to you. It is real hard when you don't know if the only people that you could call family still on God earth."

"Ella there ain't a thing I can do but leave it in God hand. If I am to see Ida again, God will send my sister back to me."

Nellie was tired and worn out from crying, so she went to bed earlier than usual. She was actually feeling rather depressed. The lamp on her bedside table was burning low and the shade which read 'Home sweet home,' was covered with soot. She had forgotten to clean it earlier, but it would have to wait until the following morning. She closed her eyes and her thoughts started to wander when she thought she heard something moving in the drawing room.

"Come Hurley," she called out, as the cat sprang onto the bed with its shoulders raised in the air.

Her heart started to pound. Was there someone in the house? She quietly opened the bedroom door and peeped out into the darkness where she saw a shadow move across the window.

"What you want?" she asked.

There was no answer, but the sweet aroma of pipe tobacco lingered in the air; the kind of pipe tobacco JB had always smoked.

"JB? Is that you?" she asked, her knees trembling.

There was no answer. Just that sweet smell was now penetrating her senses and kept wafting past her nose. She returned to her bed, put out the light and continued to inhale the sweet fragrance. That was the first time since he had left her that he had returned to visit. He too was probably grieving for his daughter who would be leaving the rock for unknown parts, leaving the only place she had known all her life. Nellie kept inhaling deeply but after a couple minutes, the smell went away.

"I know he did not forget me. I know it," she said hugging her pillow and going off to sleep.

The following morning, she couldn't wait to tell the news to Miss Ella and Miss Una. They too were convinced that John Bottomsley had finally come back to visit Nellie and equally convinced it was because his heart was breaking over his daughter.

"You think the ship carry Emily away yet?" Miss Ella asked.

"She is not going by ship Miss Ella. They fly now and it don't take as long as it used to. It only take a whole day now."

"I would be frightened to go up in one o' those things," said Miss Una. "Tell me something, how the driver know to find the way to the other side?"

"I don't know," replied Nellie, "but they know how to do it and I hope they do it right today and take Emily where she going."

In spite of her selfish ways, Sarah Bottomsley's heart seemed to be breaking. In a couple hours, her only child would be leaving her to go to England. She knew it would hurt, but never realised there would be so much suffering.

"John must be very angry with me," she said to his father who along with his wife was accompanying them to the airbase.

"Pull yourself together Sarah," said John Bottomsley. "Don't let the child see you in this state. It would bother her tremendously."

"You're right Father Bottomsley. I don't want her to see me crying. Do you know where she is?"

"She went to the kitchen to say goodbye to Clytie, so Millie went to get her."

The scene in the kitchen was no better than that in the drawing room. Clytie cried and cried and that threw Emily into hysterics.

"Don't forget me Miss Emily," said Clytie through sobs. "Come back home real soon. Look after yourself and learn good."

"I will. I will Clytie. You must write to me too."

"Come Emily. It's time to go," said her grandmother.

Later that evening, the atmosphere in the house was similar to that following John

Bottomsley's burial. The family sat around and no one spoke, and Thomas Hurley as usual made himself scarce especially since John and Millie Bottomsley were there. He had no desire to be anywhere around them and neither did they want to be in the same room with him. Clytie as usual served them tea and biscuits and they sat quietly listening to the BBC as if they thought it would bring them closer to Emily.

* * *

Emily had never seen so many white faces before, and fear gripped her little heart. She now understood the hopelessness of some of the characters in the books her mother had forced her to read. She felt like Jane Eyre. She felt like David Copperfield and like many of the orphans in the Dickens' novels. She had never seen her grandparents and had no idea what they looked like. She looked from face to face as loneliness and fear crept through her tiny body. How she longed for Clytie's gentle voice and loving smile.

"Emily Bottomsley?" asked the wrinkled, gentle old woman.

"Yes, I'm Emily Bottomsley."

"I'm your grandmother."

She bent and kissed her and Emily noticed that she bore absolutely no resemblance to her mother. Her fear departed because they were there to take her to a nice warm place and to look after her. She didn't have to spend the night like so many of the orphans she had read about

"Put your coat on dear," said her grandmother.

"But the sun is shining Grandma," said Emily.

The old woman smiled down at her.

"In spite of the sun, you will need your coat Emily."

"Papa said when he lived here he hardly ever saw the sun. "That's true. But now and again, we do get a bit of sunshine."

"Where is Grandpa?"

"He's waiting outside in the car."

They slowly made their way through the sea of faces, with the old lady pushing her valise on a cart. Everyone around them spoke just like her mother did. Sometimes it was difficult to understand what they were saying although they were speaking English. They stepped out into the British air and she gasped. It was deathly cold. Her little body trembled and her teeth chattered.

"This is your Grandpa," said her grandmother Louise Bonnett. "Hurry up and get into the car. You're not used to this kind of weather and must find it very cold."

The old man seemed just as kind as the old woman but he was dressed a little too formal for the occasion, in his long black coat, a felt hat and a pair of gloves. He was not as wrinkled as the old woman, but his skin seemed weather beaten. So these were the people who never wanted to set foot on the rock where she grew up and who considered such places not fit for human habitation. The old man kissed her, opened the car door and she climbed in.

"How was the trip?" he asked.

"Much too long Grandpa," she replied

"How is your Mama?"

"Mama is fine but was sad yesterday when I left."

"I remember when Sarah left us. I felt exactly the same way," her grandmother said. "Sometimes I still feel sad about it."

Emily looked out at tall buildings, some of them with smoke rising from chimneys. The streets were full of cars and big buses. It was all new to her. She wanted to consume everything with her eyes because she was going to describe it all to Clytie when she wrote to her. She chatted along the way until fatigue gave way to sleep.

A good night's sleep was all she needed but she awoke feeling rather homesick. There was no sunshine and everything seemed dreary, dark and cold in spite of the fact her grandfather had lit the fire to warm the room. She sat in the chair closest to the fire and watched as the flames danced over the firewood. She found out her school was about one hundred and fifty miles away, but she would be spending the weekends with her grandparents.

"Tomorrow we will take you into London. I'm sure your mother has told you lots about London."

"A bit Grandpa,"she said. "Mama told me about places like Trafalgar Square and Buckingham Palace.

"I'm sure you would like to see them before you go off to school. You know Emily, you look so much like John Bottomsley. Turn your head and let me see. Not a shred of evidence that you are Sarah's child," he said with a smile. "But you speak like her and remind me so much of my daughter when she was your age."

"Grandpa," she said, "why did you and grandma never visit us?"

"We would've loved to have seen you child, but we were not up to those long voyages, which meant spending six weeks or more on the high seas. Besides your Grandma cannot stand the heat. However that didn't change our love for you and our daughter. How is Sarah really?"

"Mama is fine, but sometimes I think she misses Papa."

"But she is married to Thomas Hurley now, isn't she?

"Do you know him Grandpa?"

"Not very well my child. I saw him twice when Sarah was here the last time and that was about fourteen years ago."

"He's not like Papa."

"Of course he isn't. No one can ever take the place of a father and don't you forget it."

"Look what I've found for you," said her grandmother as she entered the room with her hands full of clothing. "All these were Sarah's when she was about your age."

She couldn't believe her grandmother had held onto her mother's clothing for such a long time, and Sarah Bottomsley was perhaps the same size because the clothes fit her daughter perfectly.

* * *

# 38

Life was returning to normal in the Great House although Emily's absence seemed to affect everyone. Sarah's life was returning to normal and she had left the house to have her beauty treatment while her husband was away looking after the plantation. Ginger Hurley had shown up late the previous evening and had spent the night with her brother and his wife. With her employers away, it was only natural for Clytie to pick up the telephone when it rang.

"Morning Nels," she said. "You sleep good last night?"

Ginger Hurley was about to ask Clytie to hang up since she had already picked up the phone in the hallway between the drawing room and the bedrooms, but decided against it when she heard Clytie conversing with the caller. It was good to know what was going on, so she listened in on the conversation.

"Not a wink Clytie," Nellie replied. "All I could think about was that poor little girl all alone in some far away country."

"She alright Nels. Miss Sarah mother and father looking after Emily."

"I glad to hear that Clytie, but the strangest thing happen last night. JB visit me for the first time since he pass away."

"What you telling me Nels? Master Bottomsley was there in the house visiting you?"

"Yes. I know he was there because I smell the strong sweet smell of that tobacco he used to smoke."

"That must be real frightening Nels."

"At first I was frighten, but after I realise it was JB, I know he wouldn't do nothing to hurt me."

The conversation was confusing to Ginger. Nellie spoke as if she and John Bottomsley were good friends or more than just friends.

"So what else happen?"

"He frighten poor Hurley, but I just lay there in my bed and inhale that sweet smelling tobacco until he left.

"You think he upset because his daughter is now in that cold England?"

Ginger Hurley was now convinced that John Bottomsley and Nellie had had some sort of an affair. But why were they so concerned about Emily? She waited until Clytie put the telephone down before she placed the receiver on the hook. Her brain started to race at top speed. She was going to find out what it was all about, but she first had to talk to her brother. She also wanted to talk to Clytie to see what she could find out. She opened the kitchen door and looked in.

"Good morning Clytie," she said in a very friendly way.

Clytie's knees almost buckled beneath her. She had no idea Ginger Hurley was in the house. She wondered how much she had heard, if she had indeed heard anything. Ginger was much too friendly. She probably hadn't heard anything.

"I didn't know you was here," she said. "You want some breakfast?"

"That would be nice. I would like two scrambled eggs with toast and jam, and a nice hot pot of tea."

"Yes ma'am," Clytie replied.

"By the way, I heard the telephone ring. Who was it?"

"It was for me."

"I see," she replied. "I thought you weren't allowed to have personal telephone calls Clytie."

"Sometimes Miss Sarah let me take calls, especially since my mother live up in St. Lucy."

"She lives with the maid Nellie, doesn't she?"

"Nellie is not a maid no more. She is looking after my mother."

"Nellie must have done well for herself to be looking after your mother and Ella."

"She doing alright. She got a good heart."

"What does she do if she is no longer working as a maid?"

Clytie felt proud of Nellie's achievements and her pride did not allow her to keep her mouth closed. She had forgotten Miss Ella's warnings. Keep your ears open and your mouth closed.

"Miss Nellie got a big shop up north and she and my mother working in it."

"Sometime when I'm in the neighbourhood, I should stop by and say hello.

Clytie suddenly realised she had spoken too much because Nellie never did like her nor her brother. And as if she wanted to warn Clytie, her last statement made her stomach churn.

"And by the way Clytie, I don't know if you've heard anything about it, but I will be moving into Bottomsley in another couple of weeks."

It was difficult enough having her brother around, but now they would have to contend with his conniving sister. Things would never be the same, especially without Emily being there. While Clytie put her scrambled eggs in front of her, she landed one parting blow.

"Do you believe in ghosts Clytie?"

"I don't know Miss. I hear people talking about them, but I never see any."

"I'm sure Mr. Bottomsley was here last night."

"Why you say that?"

"Last night I was reading before I went to sleep, when suddenly the smell of his pipe tobacco floated through the room.

"You sleep in Miss Emily room?"

"I did."

"Maybe he was looking for Miss Emily. He frighten you Miss Ginger?"

"No! I have heard of things like that, but never really experienced any of it. Well that explains it. He was probably looking for Emily."

"Is that all Miss?" Clytie asked eager to get away from Ginger Hurley.

"Brother Dearest," said Ginger. "I have some news that will make your hair stand on end."

"What is it? I know you're dying to tell me."

"How much is it worth to you?" she asked.

"Does it have anything to do with me?"

"Not directly."

"Well then, I don't really care."

"You'll be sorry."

"Come on then, tell me," he coaxed.

"Not before you tell me what it is worth to you."

"I've allowed you to move in here with Sarah and me."

"You'll have to raise the stakes Brother."

"Alright, what would you like?"

"A little house somewhere on the east coast, where I can see and smell the beautiful ocean," she replied.

"Are you out of your mind?"

"Let's forget about it then," she said.

"I'll see what I can do," he replied eager to hear the news his sister was holding so close to her heart.

"A gentleman's word?" she asked.

He nodded.

"You won't believe what I heard this morning. Nellie the maid had an on-going affair with John Bottomsley."

"You're out of your mind. Where did you hear that?"

"A telephone conversation between Nellie and Clytie," she replied.

"I told her she was not supposed to use the telephone."

"Your wife allows her to use it to telephone her mother who lives with Nellie."

"I'm going out there and send her packing right now," he shouted.

"Don't be so hasty Thomas. If you kill the goose that lays the golden eggs, there won't be any more omelettes; besides Sarah gave her permission."

"I guess you're right. What else did you find out?"

"Nellie no longer works as a maid. She owns some big store somewhere in St. Lucy."

"I wonder if it's that 'Nellie's Bar and Grocery' on the way to the Henleys?"

"Maybe! We should find out about that as soon as possible."

"What makes you think she and Bottomsley were having an affair?"

"She referred to him as her JB?"

"JB?" asked her brother with a questioning look.

"John Bottomsley's initials," he said tapping his fingers on the table.

"Do you think he gave her the shop?"

"I don't know, but we should also find out about that."

"If it had been still in his name when they read the will, his daughter would also have inherited it."

"And speaking of his daughter, there is also something quite mysterious about that relationship, but where do we start our treasure hunt?"

* * *

# 39

It was no big surprise to anyone when Stanley Alleyne the overseer was dismissed. His crime was that he had taken sides with the workers and had not supported Thomas Hurley in his efforts to control the lives of the people who worked for him. Having such a position was unheard of for a black man and this was blamed on John Bottomsley, although it was his plantation and he had the right to hire whomever he pleased. His dismissal led to another confrontation because the workers refused to enter the fields, leaving crops to rot on the ground. Food prices were also now reaching heights that the workers could not afford and some of them made the decision to return to work. This pleased Thomas Hurley greatly because he knew he could now pit them one against the other, which he succeeded in doing.

Life became very hard for those who decided against working for him and no one else would hire them, because they were deemed trouble makers. They could not get anything on credit from Mr Polgreen since they had no means of repaying him, and to add insult to injury, Thomas Hurley decided those who could no longer pay the rent for the huts at Bottomsley would be evicted.

Stanley Alleyne decided he had to take matters into his hands to help himself and his friends who were hungry and penniless. He decided to hold a meeting and invite the workers from the surrounding plantations to tell them how to protect themselves against the likes of Thomas Hurley. He had no idea what he would do, but he had to do something before they were all forced to endure the conditions of the times of slavery. Unfortunately there was no unity among them. Almost all of them decided that it was every man for himself. No amount of persuasion could convince them there was strength in unity. It failed miserably and so their rough and unfair treatment continued, although no one thought it could get any worse than it already was. Stanley Alleyne decided he wouldn't give up so easily. He planned another meeting but those who were still employed did not want to take the chance of being ostracised, so they suffered quietly through their humiliating working conditions. The ex-overseer now had no choice but to look after his own skin and so he packed his bags and joined the police force. At least he would have a better idea of peoples' rights and his family wouldn't die of hunger.

While Thomas Hurley penalised the workers, his sister was making plans for Nellie Peterkin's life. She drove up north to see where Nellie lived and was truly surprised at how far Nellie had come. Her shop was twice the size of Polgreen's and in addition, she had a very lovely home. Parking in an advantageous position, she waited to see if Nellie would appear. She did not have to wait too long, because Nellie left the shop and went to her home. Then on the pretence of purchasing something, she entered the shop and ordered a cold drink. This she drank from the bottle while standing at the counter. Miss Una didn't recognise her.

"How much do I owe you?" she asked.

"Seven cents," said the elderly woman, charging her two cents above the normal price.

"Is this your shop?" she asked Miss Una.

"This shop belong to Nellie. It say that on the name outside."

"It's a nice shop but where is Nellie?" she asked.

"Do you know Nellie?"

"Could be. I knew someone called Nellie. Perhaps it's the same person."

"I don't know," said Miss Una growing a little suspicious since no white people ever entered the shop. They always sent their servants when they wanted to buy anything.

"Thanks," Ginger said and left.

Miss Una watched as she jumped into the car and drove off. She was sure nothing good would come out of the visit, but then she was suspicious by nature.

***

"I saw Nellie today," Ginger said to her brother.

"Did you go up to St. Lucy?"

"Better than that," she replied. "I even went into the shop."

"Didn't she see you?"

"I waited until she left and then I decided to look around. There was an old woman there who served me."

"It must've been Ella."

"It wasn't Ella. I know Ella. It could've been Clytie's mother."

"So what happened?"

"I asked the whereabouts of Nellie, but she suddenly didn't want to talk anymore."

"You should be careful Ginger."

"I've got a plan that will work. We must find out what is going on."

She told her brother what she had decided to do and he was totally in agreement. Whatever it was they both had planned seemed to be quite hilarious, since they both laughed hysterically.

Ginger seemed to be taking over the running of the household and Sarah Bottomsley-Hurley was being left out of the decision-making.

"I feel real sorry for Miss Sarah," said Clytie. "She is not the nicest person but she ain't the worst either. That Ginger really taking advantage of Miss Sarah weakness."

"Don't feel sorry for Sarah. If she is foolish enough to let them do it, it isn't nobody fault but her own."

"Don't be so hard Ursy. The husband gone, her daughter gone and she ain't got a soul left."

"She's got that Hurley man. I am sure he is only here to see what he can get."

"He know he can't get nothing. He know that everything belong to Miss Emily."

"I don't trust that man as far as I can throw him. Look at all the trouble he cause around here. A lot of my friends are gone because he throw them off Bottomsley. And Bottomsley don't even belong to that idiot. I will be glad when Miss Emily come back and get him out of here."

"You got a real long wait Ursy. She is not coming back until she turn twenty one, and she is only fourteen now."

"Only the good Lord knows if there will be anything left by that time."

"We can only pray Ursy. That is all we can do."

"There is more we can do Clytie. You know it and I know it, and we waste too much time already."

"I was thinking about it Ursy, but I am a Christian and don't like to meddle in those things."

"The good Lord understands and knows we have to look out for one another and he will forgive you and me."

The tinkling of a bell broke their intense conversation. It was Ginger Hurley asking to have tea brought in for the family. She sat across from her brother and his wife, all the time taking the leading role of the mistress of the manor. Ursy noticed that while the brother and sister chatted, Sarah sat listlessly, hardly concentrating on what they were talking about.

"Don't you agree Sarah?" her husband asked.

"Sorry I wasn't listening," she replied.

Ursy was beginning to worry. In spite of the harsh way she sometimes spoke about her employer, she really felt sorry for her. She was never a bad woman, only self-centred and uncaring, but now she sat alone while the two carried on their conversation oblivious to her presence.

* * *

# 40

A letter arrived in the mail for Nellie and there was great excitement because she thought it was from Emily. She was so filled with anxiety that her hands trembled as she tried to open it. Miss Una hovered over her as she too was eager to know how the child was settling in. It was now six weeks since she had left and they hadn't heard anything from her, except the occasional tidbit Clytie would pass on.

"What it say?" asked Miss Una.

Nellie read in silence and disappointment showed on her face.

"Something happen to Miss Emily?" she asked impatiently.

"It isn't from Emily. It come from some solicitors named Bantree and Bertrand."

"What they want Nellie?"

"I don't know Miss Una. They want me to come down to their office Friday morning."

"You think it got something to do with JB?"

"I don't think so. Everything belonging to JB settle and it all belong to Emily."

"Well you better go and see what is."

"I don't know Bridgetown too good so I better ask Nora to go with me."

"Yes, you should not go down there by all by yourself. I hear down there worse than a two cent whorehouse," said Miss Una.

"It worried Nellie all day. She read the letter over and over again, scrutinising every word as if it would help her to find out what it was all about. She called Clytie to see if she could shed some light on the mysterious letter, but she was as much in the dark as Nellie was.

"You didn't hear Miss Sarah say nothing?" Nellie asked.

"Miss Sarah don't say too much these days."

"What you mean?"

"Child, Ginger Hurley move in and she running the house now. I can't even get a biscuit to go with my tea. She count everything and ask a lot of questions when we take anything."

"Lord havis mercy. They running a real tight ship down there. I remember when me and Miss Ella could take whatever we want so long as they were finish."

"Not now soul. Whatever left over, got to get warm up for the next day. Girl it isn't easy anymore."

"So why Miss Sarah don't say something?"

"She must be frightened for the two of them."

"Why?" asked Nellie.

"I don't know, but she ain't opening her mouth. If it keep on like this, Ursy and me planning to fix the two of them."

"What you planning to do Clytie?"

"It is for we to know and for them to find out."

"I can't believe my ears. You should not get mixed up in that foolishness Clytie."

"Anything I can do to help Miss Sarah, I going to do."

"Be careful Clytie."

"It is them who got to be careful."

"When I find out what this letter is about, I will let you know Clytie."

Nellie and her sister Nora arrived at the solicitor's office. She had put herself together very well. No longer did she wear the white head tie or the long dress covered by an apron; she now dressed more fashionably. Today she wore a beret cocked over her right eye, the way a French person would wear it and a stylish dress which reached halfway down her legs. Her court shoes and stockings were also fashionable, but she sported just a tad too much makeup, which minutely detracted from the stylish woman who stood in front of the office waiting for someone to open the door. Nora was not as nicely dressed, but courage replaced style.

"Yes?" asked a brown-skinned woman rudely.

"Morning," said Nellie, "Mr. Bertrand expecting me. I have an appointment with him this morning."

"For what?" asked the woman, her demeanour no better than before.

Nellie looked into her purse, pulled out the letter and handed it to the woman, who read it and disappeared without saying a word. Nora was becoming agitated and threatened to tell her off, but Nellie was afraid they would be thrown out of the office before she had a chance to find out what the letter was all about. Shortly after the woman disappeared, a man opened the door and greeted them. He was as good looking as he was polite. Tall, but not overly so! He had a medium build, olive complexion and beautiful black hair, which was brushed away from his face towards the back of his head. Nellie was trying to guess his age because a little white showed around his temples. He had a strong nose and large brown eyes. She was still thinking about his age when he stretched his hand out to Nora. His shirt sleeves were turned halfway up his arms and she couldn't help noticing how hairy his arms were.

"Good morning. I'm Francois Bertrand," he said with a strange accent. "Which one of you is Miss Peterkin?"

"I am Nellie Peterkin and this is my sister Nora Peterkin."

He stared at them both as if he didn't believe her. They didn't look like sisters; so vastly different were their appearances. One was as black as night, the other almost as white as he was.

Nellie could not take her eyes off him for he was indeed such a handsome specimen.

"Please have a seat," he said. "I'll be with you in just a moment."

"He real good-looking Nora."

"I ain't blind Nellie but you don't have to let him know that you notice. Anyway you can't take good-looking to the shop Nellie."

"That is a new one Nora. I never even hear Miss Ella with that one."

"It mean that good looks just ain't everything."

"Mr. Bertrand is ready to see you," said the impertinent woman to Nellie.

"Come on Nellie," said her sister.

"Not you," said the woman to Nora.

"Who is going to stop me? I want to know why you all want to see my sister."

The woman could only step to the side as Nora flew past her like a gust of wind. She followed them, along with the lingering smell of Nellie's Khus Khus perfume, straight into the solicitor's office. She hoped Mr. Bertrand would see it her way and confine Nora to the waiting room.

"I told her she could not come in," the woman said.

"It's alright. Miss Peterkin can stay," he said looking to Nellie for confirmation.

"He smiled at them as he studied the stack of papers that lay in front of him. The brown skinned woman sat across from them with a pencil and note pad and waited.

"Miss Peterkin, I'm sure you're wondering why I asked you to come here today."

"Yes sir. I was wondering what you want from me."

"Were you acquainted with a man named Gus Ridley?" he asked.

"I see him only once sir, but I really didn't know him."

"Do you know he was related to you Miss Peterkin?"

"I understand so, but I don't really know."

Nellie began to tremble. What if Gus Ridley had died leaving lots of debt and as the only living relative, she had to pay for everything he had incurred.

"What Gus Ridley got to do with Nellie?" asked Nora. "Nellie isn't paying for nothing for him. He never give my sister nothing so don't think that Nellie is going to pay for nothing."

The unfriendly woman seemed to be taking down word for word everything the solicitor and the women said.

"She got to sit in here with Nellie and me?" asked Nora.

"Yes, I need my secretary here Miss Peterkin."

Mr. Bertrand never seemed to lose control. He kept on being polite in spite of Nora's outbursts, although the same could not be said for his secretary.

"It's not at all like that Miss Peterkin," he continued. "Mr. Ridley had no other relatives, but he had some money in the bank and a rather handsome house way up north, close to where you are living."

"Why are you telling me that sir?" Nellie asked.

"You have inherited everything Gus Ridley owned."

"You sure about that sir?" a stunned Nellie asked.

"Nellie don't want nothing from him. Nellie work hard and got everything she want."

"That is not your decision," said the secretary.

"Miss Peterkin, I will read Mr. Ridley's Will to you and you can decide what you want to do with the property."

In addition to what she owned, Nellie had now come into a small fortune. Still sitting in her father's bank account was thirty thousand dollars and an empty house about three miles away from where she lived, just waiting to be claimed.

"This is all so sudden," she said. "You have to give me time to think about this."

"That's not a problem Miss Peterkin. Do you have a telephone?"

She gave the number to him and they parted company.

"I can't believe this Nora. After all that man do to me, he turn around and left everything to me."

"Everybody got a conscience Nellie. His kill him when he see that you make something of yourself."

"I still don't believe it Nora."

* * *

# 41

"All I can say is that he had a conscience," said Miss Ella after hearing about Nellie's good fortune. "He take your mother and treat her very bad. Although he like her pretty skin, she still wasn't good enough for him to .......

She was rudely interrupted by Nora.

"All due respect Miss Ella, but all you ever talk about is pretty skin. When you ain't singing about a Brown girl in the ring, it is either, Brown skin gal stay home and mind baby or that stupid song, Sees my little brown gal."

Everyone watched and listened as Nora continued to as berate the old woman.

"If my sister didn't bring you out of Bottomsley kitchen, you would still be scrubbing Sarah pots. What your pretty skin do for you?"

Before anyone else had a chance to say anything, Miss Una stopped Nora in her tracks.

"What ever happen to respect Nora? Why you treating Ella so?" she asked.

"Because she think I ain't nobody. Just like that brown skin woman in the solicitor office. She was trying to treat me the same way."

"What brown skin woman?" Miss Una asked.

"The secretary," said Nellie. "She didn't want Nora to come into the office."

"That is what I keep saying," said Miss Ella. "We all got our place in this life."

"What is yours?" asked a very upset Nora.

"Ella, don't throw more gasoline in the fire. You see how bad Nora feel. Leave her alone."

"Thanks Miss Una. I think I should go home now, before I say something that would not be too nice."

It was obvious that being put down for so many years was beginning to take its toll on Nora. No sooner was she out the door, than Miss Una turned on her dear friend Miss Ella.

"Ella, it is time you stop talking all this foolishness about pretty skin and trying to put down Nora. I didn't want to disrespect you in front of her, but she was right. We were friends for many years and I look just like Nora. Why you don't tell me all those funny things?"

"Because you know where you belong. You don't try to push your head where your body can't go."

Seeing where the conversation was headed, Nellie intervened.

"What you think I should do with that house Miss Una?"

"Take it child. Tell yourself it is payment for your mother suffering."

During the conversation between the two women, Miss Ella said nothing. She was still brooding over the tongue lashing she had received from Nora and Miss Una. Recently she had not been feeling her chipper self, and Nellie was spending the evenings with them and going home only when it was time for bed. She would always be welcomed by Hurley who would spring from his favourite chair by the window and wrap himself around her legs as if to welcome her home. The animal would then follow her around and purr until she picked him up. After he was fed, he would once again take his place on the chair and wait until she went to her bedroom and then he would follow. He slept at the foot of her bed neatly rolled up in a ball, moving only when Nellie's legs moved.

Tonight her head was filled with lots of different thoughts. Miss Ella, the woman who had helped to mould her didn't seem to be doing very well. What would she do with her father's inheritance? What had happened to Emily? She had heard nothing from her since her departure although she had promised she would write. Suddenly the sweet smell of pipe tobacco came floating into the room.

"Hurley," she whispered. "JB come to visit again."

The cat did not move even though Nellie shifted her body around to face the bedroom door. Tonight the tobacco smell was stronger than usual.

"JB, I'm glad you come to visit again. I have a lot to tell you."

"Nellie," whispered a voice.

She was startled to hear a reply and started to tremble, but she wasn't about to let the opportunity slip by.

"JB, let me see you," she said.

"You can't see me Nellie," whispered the voice again.

"Why not JB?"

"Because I've passed on," he replied.

"But can we talk just like we used to?"

There was no answer and no matter how she tried to coax him, it seemed as if he had returned from whence he came. The next morning she related the story to Miss Ella and Miss Una, but they didn't believe it had happened.

"Nellie, I see my mother a few times after she left me, but she never open her mouth to say one word to me," Miss Ella said.

"Ella is right Nellie. I never hear anything about the dead talking. When I was small, there was a man that say the duppy talk to him and even slap him in his face, but we know it wasn't true," Miss Una said.

"So you trying to tell me that JB didn't talk to me?"

"That was a dream," Miss Ella replied.

"And where was Hurley when this was going on?" asked Miss Una.

"Sleeping at the bottom of the bed by my feet," she replied.

"So you mean that when JB was talking, Hurley was still sleeping?"

"Hurley didn't move."

"Well they say that a cat can see and feel ghosts and if Hurley didn't move, that mean you had to be dreaming Nellie."

"I know what I know and I know that JB and I was talking with one another last night."

"What he tell you Nellie?" asked Miss Ella.

"Not much. First, he call my name. Then when I say I want to see him, he say that I could not see him because he had pass on. Then when I ask him if we could talk some more, he went away."

"That is real strange Nellie. I never hear nothing like that since I was on this earth."

"Believe me, I was not sleeping and I know he was talking to me, so there. How you feeling today Miss Ella?" she asked.

"So-so Nellie. I won't say I am the best, but I am alright. I have this longing for some Cou Cou. I can't remember the last time I taste a little bit of that good food."

Miss Una and Nellie looked at each other, because on the previous weekend, Miss Ella had requested the same meal which they had prepared for her.

"I will cook some for you today, but I got to look to see if I got any okras."

"Bring over everything and I will get it ready for you."

"Alright Miss Ella, give me a minute while I run to get the corn meal."

"Wait Nellie, you decide yet what you going to do with the things your father left to you?"

"I didn't have time to think about it Miss Una, but I think I will keep it. After all he put us through, I think I deserve it."

"You talking like a sensible woman," said Miss Una. "He left it for you, so you keep it and tell yourself that it is for all the years he forget you and your mother. Go and get the okras because I am longing to put my lips on that Cou Cou."

The women discussed what they would eat with the meal and Miss Ella set about with the preparation. She sliced the okras thinly and then started to make the salt fish sauce which she was craving. The pungent odour of the salted cod which was boiling on the stove, permeated throughout the house. She poured the salted water from the fish, added more water and set it to boil again. She then sliced onions, thyme and tomatoes, shredded the boiled fish and thus began the accompanying sauce for the Cou Cou. When Miss Una and Nellie arrived, the fragile old lady was standing over the stove cooking her favourite dish.

"What you doing Ella?" asked Miss Una.

"What it look like to you? I am stirring Cou Cou."

"You ain't able Miss Ella. Let me do it," Nellie said trying to take the Cou Cou stick from her hand.

"I am old but I'm not dead yet Nellie."

"Leave her alone Nellie. She is stubborn," said Miss Una. "Besides Ella can turn a wicked Cou Cou."

After a hearty meal, the three women sat on the porch. Nellie sat at their feet while they sat in their rocking chairs and watched the setting of the evening sun. Miss Ella was unusually quiet, but so was everyone else because the heaviness of their meal seemed to put them into a lethargic state. Miss Una was the only one who spoke and she related a dream she had the night before. She had been gathering flowers from garden beds with beautiful black earth piled high between the flowers. Each time she picked a flower, she had the hard task of putting the rich, black earth back in its place.

"What you do with the flowers?" asked Nellie.

"I don't remember," she said after a moment's thought.

"That ain't a good dream," said Miss Ella.

"I know that Ella," she replied.

At eight o'clock, Nellie decided to go home, because Hurley had to be fed. The old ladies kept rocking, but still not saying too much. Suddenly Miss Ella started to cough uncontrollaby and her head slumped to one side.

"Ella," said her friend. "Let me get you some water."

When she returned, Miss Ella was quite still. That evening, just where the sky met the sea, Miss Ella suddenly went on a long journey. At first Miss Una thought she was just resting but then she realised her best friend for so many years, had taken her last breath.

Does one lose one's fear of death with age? Did Ella know she was about to leave the earth? She had asked for her favourite meal and after eating, was rather quiet, because she had been recalling the days of her youth. Una probably also knew for she too was totally in control. There were no hysterical outbursts or loud wailing as was usually the case when someone died suddenly. She calmly walked over to Nellie's to impart the bad news. Nellie ran bare-footed to the house, while Miss Una followed at a quick pace, and just as they reached the front steps, a car which had been parked a few yards away suddenly drove off, but they paid little attention, and kept their focus on the matter at hand. Together they lay Miss Ella on her bed, her body still warm to the touch while Nellie set out to call the doctor, who said he couldn't be there until the following morning.

"I have to wash Ella body," said Miss Una.

She sang a hymn as she wiped Miss Ella's body clean and then together, they dressed her in a clean white night gown and covered her body.

"Just like that," said Nellie sadly. "Just like that!"

"When he call, we can't say no Nellie. We just have to answer the call."

"I know," said Nellie bursting into tears.

The Matriarch had left a great void in the hearts and minds of those who knew her. Una had lost a friend, a friend she had known almost all her life, but she did not cry. Did she cry in the sanctuary of her room? Or was the grief too much for her to bear? She never showed it. Clytie arrived to comfort her grieving mother, leaving Ursy to bear the brunt of Hurley's cruelty.

"Heavenly father, we commit to thee the body of thy daughter Ella Louise Burnett. Dust to dust. Ashes to ashes," said the priest.

"I can't believe Miss Ella left us," said Clytie. "Ma you think she run into the Master yet?"

"Who knows Clytie? Could be, but I hope she won't have to cook for him where ever it is they happen to be."

"Don't let Nellie hear you talking like that."

"I just making a little fun child. I just trying to lighten the atmosphere."

"Anything interesting going on over at Bottomsley Clytie?"

"Ma, it ain't what it used to be. They measure every grain o' rice. They give me three tiny chicken legs to cook, so that means there isn't anything left for Ursy or me. I tell you Ma, they change Bottomsley forever."

"And what Miss Sarah got to say?"

"I tell you already Ma that Miss Sarah don't have nothing more to say. Miss Ginger running the household and Ma, I think Hurley does beat Miss Sarah."

"You see that Clytie?"

"No, but she always in her room and she always crying."

"She must be lonely, and that is why she cry a lot."

"Ma, last week one side of Miss Sarah face was almost as black as yours."

"You sure she didn't tumble down?"

"If she did tumble down, she would ask me for help. Not only that, he was hollering and then he left the house real quick. It is then that I could hear Miss Sarah crying."

"That don't sound too good Clytie."

"I got to ask you for a favour Ma."

She explained what she wanted and her mother promised to assist her, in spite of the fact that her daughter was a novice in what she was getting into.

"Don't worry Ma. Ursy going to help me."

"You just be careful. When are you playing with fire, you have to know how to put it out, in case it get out of hand. And another thing Clytie, you don't want no witnesses to these things. What you have to do, do it by yourself, but be careful."

"I will be careful Ma," she said as she pushed her hands into the pockets of her dress.

She pulled an envelope out and looked at it.

"I forget to give this to Nellie. It is a letter from Miss Emily."

"Why she didn't send it to Nellie address?"

"I don't know, but I get it from the postman since last week."

"Hurry and get Nellie. She was worrying a lot about not hearing nothing from Miss Emily."

"I got a letter too,"said Clytie, "and she say she write to Nellie before but never get no answer."

"Nellie never get no letter. Hurry, I want to hear what Miss Emily got to say."

* * *

# 42

"Emily say this is the second letter she is sending to me. That is very funny. I never get the first one."

"You must find out where she send it because all of your letters come here to the shop and I pass them on to you."

"She must be sending them to Bottomsley," said Clytie. "If I don't get to the postman first, Miss Ginger get the letters and then she give them out."

"You think she keeping my letters?"

"I am sure Emily is putting your name on them, just like she put it on this one," said Clytie."

"Well I will write to Emily tonight and tell her to send all my letters here to the shop."

"But what she had to say Nellie?" asked Miss Una.

"She say she settling in good in the school. The other children are very nice, but she still miss everybody especially Clytie, Miss Ella and Miss Sarah."

"Lord I have to give her the bad news about Miss Ella. I wish I didn't have to say nothing, but she isn't a little girl no more. She would understand, especially since she went through it with her father. She's going to be fifteen in a few weeks. She is almost a woman now."

Tears ran down Clytie's face as Nellie continued reading the letter. Emily wanted to know about Hurley and also asked if Nellie knew anything about her Mama. Could it be Sarah Bottomsley told her child of her unhappiness? Clytie was no longer her jovial self. She too seemed to be suffering under the strain and pressure the Hurleys had inflicted upon the household.

"I was thinking Ma that since you now by yourself, I could leave the job at Bottomsley and come to live with you."

"What about Jonas? You can't leave him down there by himself."

"Jonas ain't a child no more Miss Una. Tell your daughter yes. Tell her that she can come," said Nellie.

"You know it would do my heart good to have you close by Clytie. With Ella gone, it would be good company for me especially at night."

"That is a yes Ma?"

"Yes child. Come and keep your old mother company."

"I got an idea Clytie."

"What is it Nels?"

"That house that my ....Gus Ridley left me, we could turn into a school."

"What house?" asked Clytie.

"Girl I forget to tell you. That man that say he was my father left me a house up the road."

"What you telling me Nels?"

"You could have knock me over with a feather Clytie. I get a letter from the solicitor as I tell you and when I went down there to see him, he tell me that I inherit some money and a house."

"Girl, you ain't only born good looking, you born lucky too."

"Don't fret Clytie, one day good things will happen to you too, but you can't leave Bottomsley before you finish that job you start."

"What job is that?" asked Nellie.

"As Miss Ella used to say, keep yer mouth shut and your ears open," replied Clytie.

"That mean you ain't going to tell me?"

"You will hear about it Nels. I don't want to spoil it by talking about it."

"What is going on at Bottomsley?" Nellie asked as her curiosity peaked.

"Well it look like Thomas Hurley is having some kind o' affair."

"Why you say that Clytie?" asked Nellie.

"Because about two times a week, around half past six in the evening, he drive away and come back around eleven. I think she must be married."

"Why you think so?" asked her mother.

"He don't sleep out and when he come back he and Miss Ginger always whispering. Either that or he up to no good."

"I wonder where he going," asked Nellie. "He must be looking for another widow to latch on to, because he can't get at the Bottomsley money."

"All this foolish talk about those white people," said Miss Una. "You was talking about how you want to turn the house into a school Nellie."

"Yes, as I was saying, if I do that, then Jonas could come up and open the school there, so that the children don't have to walk so far."

"That is a good idea Nels. I will tell him as soon as I get back and hear what he got to say."

"Not so fast Clytie. I have to talk to Mr. Bertrand first."

"Who?" asked Clytie furrowing her brow."

"He is Gus Ridley solicitor."

Nellie sat on her bed and by lamplight, she started the letter which she promised she would write that night. After many greetings which she deemed inappropriate, she finally started the letter.

My dear Miss Emily,

I was wondering if you forget poor old Nellie...

Suddenly she heard her name.

"Nellie," a voice came from outside the bedroom.

She knew who it was. Without a doubt JB was visiting her again, for the smell of his tobacco filled the air.

"JB? You're here again? I'm glad to hear you."

"I'm sorry I had to leave so quickly the other night," he whispered.

"I hope you don't have to leave so soon tonight JB."

"You said you had lots to tell me," he whispered again.

"Yes JB. First I want to tell you that I get a letter from Emily today. She send it to Bottomsley and Clytie bring it over for me. It look as if she is happy so you don't have to worry about her. Then that Gus Ridley pass away and left me a house and thirty thousand dollars. Imagine that JB? He didn't care nothing about me when I was a little girl and now he left me everything. I am sure you know all about this, but I will mention it anyway. You see Miss Ella yet? She left us and gone to meet her Lord."

There was absolute silence and Nellie called out to him.

"JB, you still there?" she asked.

"Yes Nellie. I'm still listening to you."

"So what you got to say about Gus Ridley?"

"About whom Nellie?" the voice asked.

"You know Gus, my father."

"Oh Gus. All I can say is that it was a good thing which he did. Anyway Nellie, I will be back to see you again. Take care of yourself," came the hoarse whisper.

"You too JB," she replied.

Nellie looked at Hurley who in spite of the ongoing conversation did not even open his eyes. He was still rolled up in a ball and breathing heavily. Nellie felt happy to hear from JB again, but she felt drained after the visit and decided she would finish writing the letter the following evening.

"I am telling you Miss Una, I talk with him again last night."

"I still say that I never hear anything like that," said Clytie. "I know they come back to visit, but I never hear that they talk too."

"What you need is a witness to all this Nellie. Why you don't ask Nora to come by and sleep a couple nights with you?"

"I going to do that so I can show all of you doubting Thomases that he really does talk to me

Later that day there was a phone call from Francois Bertrand the solicitor. He wanted to know if Nellie had made a decision regarding her father's estate and since he was going to be in the neighbourhood he said he would stop by. He was just as handsome as the first time she had seen him and his manners were just as impeccable.

"Would you like me to represent you Miss Peterkin?"

"You think I need that?"

"I think it would be wise to have a solicitor Miss Peterkin. There should be someone who can represent you and advise you in your financial matters. You have a handsome sum of money sitting in the bank and a home that has been left to you. Do you own this home too?"

"Yes this belong to me. I own that hotel you see when you turn the corner, but seeing the tourists don't come this far, I had to shut it down. I had another shop my sister Nora was running, but there was no need for two shops, so I had to sell that. You remember my sister Nora?"

"Yes I remember her," he said with a smile.

"She help me now in the shop next door."

"Do you mean the shop with the adjoining house?"

"That belong to me sir."

"You do need someone to look after your interests Miss Peterkin."

"Do you want to do that sir?"

"Mr. Bertrand," he said correcting her. "And yes I will be willing to represent you. Do you have papers for all these properties?"

"Yes."

"Do you mind if I have a look at them?" he asked.

It was a very hot day and the lemonade she had made to offer him, sat untouched on the tray with the two glasses. She returned with the case JB had given to her and started to look through the several compartments.

"May I have a drink?" he asked.

"Sorry sir. I forget my manners."

She poured him a glass of cool lemonade and set it down on the table next to him. He thanked her and drank it down all at once. She watched as he slowly emptied the glass. He was really thirsty.

"I want to ask you something Mr. Bertrand."

"Of course Miss Peterkin, feel free to ask me anything."

"How much it going to cost for you to rep....

"To represent you?" he asked.

"It all depends," he answered.

"On what sir?" she asked.

"On how much work I have to do for you, but have no fear Miss Peterkin, my fees are very reasonable."

Nellie was not a fool and she knew she shouldn't trust anyone, but there was something about Mr. Bertrand she liked. He treated her like a lady and he just had that gentlemanlike quality she admired.

"One more thing Mr. Bertrand, there is something about confident....

"You mean the confidentiality clause Miss Peterkin. Of course, anything that transpires between us would not be repeated to anyone. I could be brought before the court if I told anyone anything about your business."

"Good and what about that secretary?"

"She must also abide by that law."

"Alright then Mr. Bertrand, I giving you my life here in these papers."

The solicitor took out the papers and read them one by one. The expression on his face never changed as he read.

"What is this property you own on the island of St. Lucia?"

"That is my little vacation house that I get about three years ago."

He stared at her and then smiled.

"Something wrong Mr. Bertrand?"

"I am amazed Miss Peterkin. You are an amazing woman."

"What you mean sir?"

"Mr Bertrand," he said again smiling. "It means you are a very strong, smart woman. I am really surprised at what you have accumulated in such a short length of time. I see you are only forty two years old."

"I work hard Mr. Bertrand, and I also had a bit of help along the way."

"So many people get a helping hand and it doesn't seem to make any difference. I truly admire you Miss Peterkin. I have one question though. Where is your daughter Emily right now?"

"She is at school in England."

"I see," he said. "Why did you send her there instead of to France?"

"She can't speak French Mr. Bertrand."

"France would've been so much better. It must be difficult for someone with her complexion to be living in England."

"But I thought everybody over there was white."

"Are you trying to tell me she doesn't look like you?" he asked.

"Emily whiter than you Mr. Bertrand," she said laughing.

"Now I'm totally confused Miss Peterkin."

"It is a really long story and one day I might tell you, but you have to remember that confidential thing."

"Not a problem Miss Peterkin, but then I assume her father is a plantation owner?"

"Yes he was a plantation owner."

"I'm sorry."

"What you sorry for?" she asked

"To hear that her father passed away."

"How you know her father is dead?"

"Because you said he *was* a plantation owner, which led me to believe he had passed away."

"You're right. He left Emily and me."

She stared at him for a moment and tears welled up in her eyes.

"I know it must be difficult Miss Peterkin to be alone at such a young age."

"You don't understand Mr. Bertrand. You just don't understand."

"What don't I understand Miss Peterkin?"

"Emily, my daughter, she don't know that I am her mother."

"That must be very difficult for you."

"When we go through my papers, I will have to explain it to you."

* * *

## 43

Along with their melodious singing, the Casuarinas were constantly whispering secrets to each other as they swayed in the breeze. Clytie stopped and looked at the dried needles which lay scattered underneath their beautiful canopies and she gathered a few of the seeds which in time would spring to life, bringing a new generation of whisperers who would be there to welcome her grand children and great grand children.

It was a pleasant day, full of sunshine and she could hear the sound of the waves in the distance as they lashed against the rocks. There were hardly any beautiful beaches on that side of the island; everywhere one looked there were only cliffs and caves, where the mighty ocean would send the water crashing into every hollow. She remembered when she was younger and they would all have a day off together. Miss Ella, Nora, Nellie and her mother would walk to the beach very early in the morning and would wade in the cool waters and even catch some the sea urchins which would be floating around at that early hour. After a couple hours of splashing around and having a good time, the rising sun would find them walking back to their huts where Miss Ella and Miss Una would make fried bakes and salt fish and good rich coffee to wash it all down. In spite of all this beauty, she was afraid; afraid of what she was now embarking upon.

As if she had forgotten something, she quickened her pace and tightened the grip on parcel she held under her arm. When she arrived at her destination, there was no one in sight so she hurried to a chattel house which was built next to a big mango tree, which hung heavily with green mangoes. She knocked and called out to the owner who pushed the door open without showing his or her face. She timidly stepped into the darkened room, where one candle gently flickered.

"You bring all the things I ask you to bring girl?" a gruff voice asked.

"I got it all," she replied. "It here in this package."

He took the package from her and opened it. Wrapped in a small piece of paper there were bits of blonde hair; in another something which resembled a man's dirty under shirt, a pair of socks and a small bottle containing a clear liquid.

"This is the simmy-dimmy water?" he growled at her. "And did you bring the coppers?"

"Yes sir," she said with great respect as fear gripped her heart. "I have the coppers here in this kerchief."

The man didn't talk too much. He spread the items onto the table in front of him and started mixing and pouring and his incantations scared her out of her wits. She remembered her mother's words about starting a fire she didn't know how to extinguish.

"Help me Lord," she whispered under her breath. "Forgive me for what doing, but you know I just trying to help Miss Sarah."

After about thirty minutes, he dismissed Clytie telling her it wouldn't be long before the powers start to work for her. She handed him the kerchief with an unknown sum of money and started on her trek back to her mother's house and later that day, back to Bottomsley. The next morning, she made breakfast for the Bottomsley clan and found herself trembling when Thomas Hurley sat down to breakfast. She felt sorry for what she had done, but his arrogant and impolite manner soon made her forget any regrets she might have had.

She kept staring at him out of the corner of her eye. What was she looking for? She had no idea what to expect. Would his teeth fall out? Would his eyes bulge out of his head? So far he still looked like Thomas Hurley; tall and good looking, but sadly a man with no conscience. Sarah sat in front of him, her eyes fastened on the poached egg on her plate. She didn't eat. Sarah Bottomsley-Hurley would normally still be in bed at that hour, but he insisted they sit together at the breakfast table each morning, like a normal married couple.

*"It isn't going to be too much longer Miss Sarah before you get some peace," Clytie thought.*

"Did you hear me?" he shouted. "I want another cup of coffee."

"Yes sir. I hear you," she said with contempt.

* * *

"Sarah, look at the condition you're in," said Millie Bottomsley.

"My God Sarah, you are so thin. Aren't you eating properly?" asked John Bottomsley.

"I'm alright," she replied.

"I'm so glad Emily isn't here to see you looking like this."

"I haven't been feeling well recently Mother Bottomsley."

"Why didn't you call us? We still think of you as a daughter in law."

"I was thinking of coming by to visit you sometime, but I wasn't up to it."

"Sarah," said John Bottomsley softly. "We've come to discuss a very delicate matter with you."

"What is it?" she asked.

"You know my son used to look after Millie and me, and in his will he said that should continue until the day we both die."

"I know that. What seems to be the problem Father Bottomsley?"

"You know how expensive it is here. Why did you cut our money in half Sarah? We have been good to you."

"I'm sorry Father Bottomsley. I was not aware that had happened. I'll speak to Thomas tonight when he comes in."

"I should've known it was that no-good bastard. This is my son's money he left for us. He knows nothing about the hard work and long hours my son invested on this property."

"I'm sorry Father Bottomsley and you too Millie. I will see to it that you receive every penny that was taken from you."

"Sarah I would like to talk to him myself," said John Bottomsley. "You know I'm not afraid of him. He is a spiteful man who would stop at nothing to ruin what my son worked so hard for."

After chatting a little longer, the couple reluctantly left Sarah, mystified and alone. Instead of continuing on their way home, Millie Bottomsley found herself at the back entrance to the house.

"Good day Miss Bottomsley," Clytie greeted her

"Shhhhh!" she said putting her finger to her lips.

"Something wrong Miss Bottomsley?" she whispered.

"Clytie, please tell me what is going on with Sarah."

"I don't know ma'am."

"Clytie, I know you know things are not what they used to be. Is Sarah afraid of that Hurley man?"

"I don't know, but I think so."

"Does he beat her Clytie?"

"I never see anything, but I feel he beat Miss Sarah sometimes."

"I knew it. I knew it," she said.

"Ma'am, please don't tell them I say so."

"No Clytie. They will never know I heard that from you. By the way, are you alone now in the kitchen?"

"No Ursy is still here with me, but I don't think Mr. Hurley like her too much. She tell him what she think and he always telling her that she not only black, but she real rude. That don't bother Ursy at all. Anyway if she want to keep the job here in the kitchen, she got to work every Thursday out in the cane fields weeding out the grass."

"My son must be rolling over in his grave," Millie Bottomsley said as she hurried out to join her husband waiting in the car.

* * *

# 44

Clytie and Ursy pressed their ears to the kitchen door because there seemed to be a full fledged war going on inside the living room. Thomas Hurley's voice was loud against the whimper of Miss Sarah's.

"You have no right to decrease their money," she said.

"You seem to think we are running a poor house here. If I don't make some cuts, this damn plantation would never make a profit."

"It always did before Thomas. Anyway you should have consulted me before you interfered with their money. John left it in the will that his parents should always be looked after and you seem hell bent in driving them into poverty."

It had been a while since Ursy and Clytie had heard Sarah Bottomsley stand up to her husband and it seemed she was not about to let him get away with his schemes to gyp her ex in laws out of their monthly allowance.

"Why don't you run the plantation yourself?" he asked.

"You do a great job Thomas, but I can't allow you to send John's parents into the poor house."

"What do they do to deserve that money anyway?"

"It doesn't matter Thomas. It was in the will. Please abide by the terms that were set down for those two elderly people."

"Sarah, I have heard enough of your diatribe. I need some fresh air. I'm getting out of here and don't expect me back before tomorrow."

"Where on earth are you going at this ungodly hour?" she asked.

There was no answer. He just slammed the door and the sound of the motor told them he could be on his way to drink himself into oblivion. After such a confrontation, Sarah Bottomsley usually retired to her room to cry herself to sleep.

* * *

"Sea eggs! Come and get your sea eggs," cried out the hawker with the heavy basket on her head.

Nellie rushed out to purchase as many as she could, so she could share them with Nora and Miss Una.

"How much they cost?" she asked the woman.

"Twenty five cents for one," replied the portly woman.

"That too expensive," replied Nellie.

"Miss you want me to give them away? Look! See how I full them up? They can't hold one scrap more. One of my sea eggs would feed a whole family."

"I still say they are real expensive, but I will still take eight."

"Eight?" asked the woman her frown turning to a smile. "God bless you. One more stop and I can go back home."

Nellie took the prickly delicacies and went back to her home. She knew what she would have for dinner the next day. White rice with sea eggs garnished with some cucumber and avocado pear. Just thinking about it made her mouth start to water.

"Nellie," her sister called out.

"I'm out here in the kitchen."

"Sea eggs?" shouted Nora with glee as she noticed the shells on the counter.

"I have some for you too."

"I would like to eat some right now," said Nora. "I'm going to have a whole one for myself and tomorrow I will still share what is left between Percy and the children."

Nellie brought out a bottle of pepper sauce and some biscuits and the two women ate to their heart's content. It was getting late and time for bed, so they cleaned up the kitchen while talking and laughing.

"I going to walk through the back with you Nora."

"You forget you asked me to sleep here tonight?"

"It is the sea egg Nora. They make me forget everything."

The two sisters burst into laughter and decided they should go to bed. After all Nora was there to witness the presence of the talking ghost.

"What is that?" Nellie shouted looking at the thick piece of wood positioned on the inside of the bedroom door.

"I have to defend myself against the talking ghosts that run around here at night."

They started to laugh again and settled down in Nellie's bedroom for the night, with Hurley curled up in his usual position at the bottom of the bed. Shortly after they put the light out the rich smell of tobacco started to penetrate the bedroom walls.

"Nora," whispered Nellie. "JB out there!"

"Keep quiet," Nora said as she felt Hurley jump from the bed and start a strange purring.

"Call his name," said Nora.

"JB, you come back to visit?" she asked.

There was no reply, just the aroma from his tobacco swirled through the air, and after a couple of minutes, it was gone.

"I tell you he always come to visit me, didn't I Nora?"

"But he didn't say nothing this time Nellie."

"I don't understand it. When I talk he always answer."

"I think he frighten poor Hurley."

"Hurley don't behave like that when JB come to visit."

"Anyway, we should try to sleep. The thought of that sea egg waiting for me is like finding gold."

The two women were just on the verge of falling asleep when the pungent aroma of tobacco once again floated through the air.

"JB come back Nora. He come back again."

"Shhh," said Nora.

"This is the first time he come by twice in the same night," Nellie whispered.

"Shhh," said Nora again. "Somebody walking around out there," she whispered. "It must be Hurley."

"No Hurley lying down on my feet."

"Call out his name Nellie."

Strangely enough, Nellie was now afraid, but she plucked up the courage to call out to him.

"JB, is that you?"

"Nellie, are you waiting for me?" the hoarse whisper came.

"Yes JB. You alright?"

"I'm happy Nellie but you said you had a lot to tell me the last time I was here, but I had to go."

"I understand JB."

"Did you want to tell me something about Emily?" he asked.

"All I want to say is that she write me a letter and also that I take on Mr. Bertrand to do all the legal work for me."

"What legal things?" asked the voice as it were just outside her bedroom door.

"Don't say nothing else Nellie," said her sister.

"Nellie," said the voice again. "Tell me about the legal things."

Nora slipped out of bed, grabbed her piece of wood and with Nellie behind her, she opened the bedroom door and came face to face with someone. Nora struck out with her weapon and the intruder fluttered like a dying turkey to the floor.

"Bring the lamp Nellie," Nora said to her sister who was too afraid to move. "Bring the lamp!" she said in a loud whisper.

The intruder lay motionless on the floor. Nora brought the lamp close to his face and there lay Thomas Hurley lifeless on Nellie's floor.

"Lord havis mercy," said Nellie. "Thomas Hurley? I think we killed him."

"What he doing in here?" asked Nora.

"I don't know, but he was doing this to me all this time," said a trembling Nellie.

"He isn't breathing Nellie. I think I hit him too hard."

"What we going to do now Nora?"

"Get a sheet Nellie. We got to get him out of here."

Together they wrapped him in a sheet, and dragged his lifeless body out the back door and through the mango grove, where JB used to park his car.

"He is real heavy Nellie."

"That is what they call dead weight Nora. I can't believe we get ourselves in this predicament. Where we taking him?"

"The only place is down to the cliff and then we can throw him over into the sea."

"I can't do that Nora. Suppose he is still living?"

"We have to do it Nellie. You don't want the police to find out we had something to do with him."

"I was never so frightened Nora. JB where are you when I need you?" asked Nellie, the tears running down her face.

Luckily it was late and everyone was in bed as the two women reached the cliff. They rolled the lifeless body out of the sheet and with all their strength, pushed it into the turbulent shark infested waters below.

"My God Nellie, somebody just see us."

"Who?"

"In that car that park over yonder," said Nora.

"That look like Hurley car," said Nellie.

They crept up to the vehicle and realised it was indeed Thomas Hurley's car which he had parked out of sight.

"Hurry Nellie, we have to get home to see if he left any blood on the wall."

They scrubbed and they cleaned until everything sparkled, but then Nora realised that her weapon of death was still lying on the floor next to the spot where Thomas Hurley's body had fallen.

"What we going to do with this?" Nora asked.

"We should throw it in the sea."

"I ain't going back out there. I can't believe this happen Nellie."

"Nora we can't tell nobody about this. Not even Miss Una. The two of us will have to keep this secret until the day we leave this earth."

"I can't tell nobody Nellie. Don't forget I hit him with that piece o' wood."

"What we going to do now?"

"Nothing Nellie, there isn't a thing we can do now, but behave like nothing ain't happen."

Nothing was thought of Thomas Hurley's absence from the breakfast table. He had pronounced he wouldn't be back until the following day, but when he didn't show up for dinner the following evening, his wife and sister became suspicious. He had no change of clothing with him and if he didn't want to call Sarah, he would've gotten in touch with his sister.

After not showing up again the following day, the police were called in and they questioned the family. Of course there had been a row at home, but it was nothing new for him to stay out for one night. Two nights had passed and no one had heard anything from him and worst of all, they found out he hadn't shown up for work. They now suspected foul play and decided to look for his car. No matter how long and hard they looked, nothing could be found.

The morning newspaper carried the news of the missing plantation overseer, his description and that of his car. Anyone seeing the car or the person in question should contact the nearest police station. Sarah roamed around the house all day in her morning robe, while Ginger Hurley spent much time on the phone trying to find her brother. She had no idea what could've happened to him. When he became angry with Sarah, he usually spent the night binging, but this time it was different. He would never miss work, nor would he go so long without contacting anyone. The next best thing for her to do was to drive around and try to find his car. She eventually found her way driving past Nellie's shop and thought she should go in and see what she could find out. Nellie saw her and quickly went into the back room leaving Miss Una to serve her.

"What can I do for you?" asked Miss Una.

"I would like a cold red Ju-c."

"Ain't you the young woman who been here a couple weeks ago asking about Nellie?"

"Yes," answered Ginger.

"You live around here?" asked the old woman.

"No, but I'm driving around looking for someone."

"I see," Miss Una said. "If you still looking for Nellie, she isn't here today neither."

"No, I'm looking for my brother."

Nellie thought Ginger could hear her heart beating from outside at the counter. So afraid was she that she took a seat and started to fan herself with a piece of cardboard. The young woman drank her Ju-c and left the shop.

"You can come out now," said Miss Una.

Nellie watched as the car drove away with Ginger Hurley at the controls, and while she watched the car drive away, Miss Una's eyes were focussed on her.

"Something wrong with you Nellie?" the old woman asked.

"No Miss Una. Why you think something wrong?"

"You hiding from that Ginger girl?"

"No Miss Una. It is just that I don't trust her at all. I think she spying on me."

"I wonder why she would do a thing like that?"

"I don't know, so it is much better if I stay out of the way when she come around."

"It is a strange thing that they can't find hair or hide of her brother Thomas."

"He must be somewhere blind drunk."

"Nobody stay drunk so long, and from what I understand, he was not the type to miss work. So they say."

"Don't worry about that devil. He is going to show up sometime."

* * *

# 45

It was a restless night for Clytie. Her imagination was getting the better of her. She wanted something to hinder Thomas Hurley, but nothing as severe as what had happened. He was missing for five days and had had no contact with his family. She never thought of obeah as being so powerful a force, that it could make someone disappear without a trace. She could hardly look Ginger Hurley or Miss Sarah in the eye. She blamed herself for the misfortune which had befallen him, but could not share her misdeeds with anyone. Although she had originally asked for Ursy's assistance, she had turned to her mother instead because she knew her secret was safe with Miss Una.

"Ma, I real worried," she said in a telephone call.

"You should keep your mouth shut Clytie."

"Alright Ma."

"When you come up next time, we can talk."

"Alright Ma."

Around five o'clock that evening, five days after Thomas Hurley was reported missing his car was spotted on a cliff in the parish of St. Lucy. The door was unlocked and a half bottle of rum lay on the front seat, but there was no sign of him.

The police investigation began. Had he been drinking and accidentally fallen over the cliff or had he intentionally jumped over and taken his own life? Why would he have chosen such a remote area so far away from home?

Everyone suspected of a possible murder had an alibi which had checked out, so it was decided that under the circumstances,

Thomas Hurley had taken his own life, although there was no body to confirm the suspicions. Ginger Hurley knew her brother had had no plans to terrorise Nellie that evening, and had only left home because of the quarrel with his wife. But why did he choose that part of the island to drown his sorrows?

Although she was deeply distraught, Sarah had to find someone reliable to take over the running of the plantation, so she requested the help of the elder John Bottomsley to find a replacement for her missing husband.

"I didn't care for him very much Sarah, but I certainly didn't wish him any harm."

"I know Father Bottomsley. I just wish I hadn't quarrelled with him that evening."

"There are quarrels in every marriage Sarah. You don't think that Millie and I have a perfect marriage? Sometimes I want to throw her out of the house, but common sense usually prevails and I put distance between us."

"The thing is not knowing if he is alive or dead Father Bottomsley."

"I know. It's always the unknown. At least when you see the casket going into the earth, you know where he is, but only God knows that right now."

Sarah broke down and had to be helped to her bedroom, and Clytie could not help but cry along with her, such was the heavy load on her conscience.

"It is so sad to see her Millie," said John Bottomsley to his wife. "That poor child is nothing but skin and bone."

"She has lost two husbands in such a very short space of time. It seems as if she's doomed to be the eternal widow, but I must say he brought many things upon himself."

"Millie, I was thinking," said her husband.

"What are you thinking John?"

"What if he is not dead at all? What if he decided to park that car on the cliff so everyone would think he took his own life?"

"He was an unscrupulous fellow, but I don't think he would go so far as to feign his own death. What did he have to gain by doing that?"

"I wouldn't put it past him Millie."

"So what you're telling me is that you expect to see him appear again one day?"

"Yes I do."

"I don't think so John."

"Maybe Sarah should take a trip back to England. She needs to get away from all this for a little while. That way she can see Emily again."

"Why don't you suggest it to her then?"

"I think I'll do just that Millie."

"You should do it soon before she has a nervous breakdown."

***

"Why ain't you coming to work Nora?" asked Nellie.

"I so frightened that I can't think straight."

"If you don't come, I'm going to have to deal with Miss Una all by myself and you know how suspicious she can be. She know you sleep by me the night Hurley vanish and she can put two and two together, especially since they find the car so close to where we live."

"You ask yourself why he was doing that to you?"

"I think he was suspicious about Emily and me but he was not sure. That is why he was asking me all those questions."

"You think he wanted to take the plantation from Emily?"

"I don't know Nora. All I know right now is that we two will be in a lot of trouble if anybody find out that we know what happen to him. We shouldn't even talk about it, because we don't want nobody to overhear this conversation."

Nora decided her sister was right, so she went to the shop to work with Miss Una. Clytie was also there and didn't seem to be herself. As a matter of fact, it looked as if she had been crying.

"What's wrong Clytie?" asked Nellie.

"It is Thomas Hurley."

"But you say you didn't like him."

"That is true. I didn't like him at all, but still I didn't expect that."

"What it is you didn't expect?" asked Nellie.

"Keep yer mouth shut girl," said Miss Una.

"I can't keep it no more Ma. I have to tell Nellie."

"What you want to tell me?" Nellie asked.

"I went to the obeah man for Thomas Hurley and now he dead. I did expect his teeth to fall out, or his hair, but I think the potion Dootie put on him was too strong and now he dead," Clytie wailed.

In spite of her fear, Nora turned her head and a.smile worked its way across her lips; so did Nellie! Poor Clytie was blaming herself for Thomas Hurley's demise when she was not at all guilty of anything.

"You just don't know when to keep your mouth shut," her mother chastised her, while giving the two sisters a suspicious glance.

"You should go and lay down Clytie," Nellie suggested. "You don't look good at all."

And so at lunchtime, they all went to Una's house to have lunch.

"You feeling better Nora?" the old woman asked.

"Yes Miss Una."

"You in the family way?" she asked.

"I am through with that," Nora replied. "God give me two children and they are more than enough."

"With everything that was going on, I forget to ask you what happen the other night when you sleep at Nellie? JB come by?"

Nora felt every orifice in her body tingle. She had tried to forget that night completely and here was Miss Una bringing it all back to the forefront of her mind.

"Nellie didn't tell you he come by? We smell the sweet smell o' that tobacco he used to smoke."

"He didn't talk to Nellie?"

"No Miss Una. He was real quiet. It look like all he want to do was smoke. He even frighten poor Hurley."

"Hurley?" asked Miss Una.

"You forget Emily cat Hurley? He fly off the bed and start one strange set of meowing."

Just as the words left her mouth, Nora realised that when Thomas Hurley was in the house, Hurley had slept through the whole episode; something he hadn't done earlier that evening when there was the strong smell of tobacco in the house. Perhaps John Bottomsley did visit Nellie occasionally, but how had Thomas Hurley found out about it? Nellie had always said she knew when JB was visiting because of that smell and it did seem as if Thomas Hurley had found out about it and intended to blackmail Nellie. .

* * *

# 46

Nellie raced up the steps to answer the telephone which had been ringing off the hook. She was totally out of breath when she finally reached it.

"Miss Peterkin?"

"Yes?"

"This is Francois Bertrand."

"Yes Mr. Bertrand, what can I do for you?"

"I was wondering if I could come by to see you sometime this week."

"Is something wrong sir?"

"No Miss Peterkin, I just have a few questions in regards to your father's estate."

"What is wrong with it?"

"Nothing, but may I come by tomorrow afternoon around two?"

"Two o'clock would be just right."

"I'll see you then."

She wondered what could be so pressing regarding her father's house, but that was not the number one priority at the moment. She kept her ears open for any bit of news concerning Thomas Hurley.

On her way back to the shop, her mind kept turning to Miss Una. She was not an uneducated woman but what she lacked in education, she made up for with common sense. Did she suspect something regarding Hurley's disappearance? Nellie was sure she knew that someone was trying to terrorise her because she had advised her to allow her sister to sleep with her as a witness to this strange phenomenon of a talking ghost. Since that night, there was no mention of JB conversing with her.

Miss Una's eyes followed her everywhere she went. Was Thomas Hurley the culprit who had pretended to be JB? Was he killed accidentally? No mention was made of a talking ghost since his disappearance. She felt sure that the two women knew something about the missing man, especially since his car was found so close to where they lived. Miss Una felt that if he had been trying to ruin Nellie's life, he really deserved what he got.

"Something wrong Miss Una? You keep looking at me in a funny way."

"I ain't looking at you Nellie. Must be your mind playing tricks just like those talking ghosts," she said with a chuckle.

Nellie did not answer, but kept on behaving as though she was extremely busy.

"You been talking to JB recently Nellie?"

"For some strange reason Miss Una, he just stopped talking."

"But he does still come around?"

"He was there last night, but never said a word."

"I find that most strange, but thank the Lord he stop that talking, because I was getting real worried about you Nellie."

"But why Miss Una?" she asked.

"Because I really thought you was going off in the head. I thought you was losing your mental faculties, and would end up in Jinkins."

"I am as sane as you are Miss Una. I know what I hear."

"Well if he isn't talking no more. So be it."

*"She ain't believe a word I say," thought Nellie.*

"Miss Una the solicitor coming by today. He want to talk to me about Gus Ridley house."

"Maybe he want to talk about the school."

"You could be right Miss Una. I was wondering what he want to talk to me about. He coming around two tomorrow so I got to get those papers that I stash away."

"You like him Nellie?"

"Yes, he is a real nice fellow. He ain't like those high and mighty people who think we ain't nothing."

"That isn't what I mean Nellie. You always get real dress up when he coming around."

"You talking foolishness Miss Una. The only man for me was JB and he gone; but you expect me to wear my shop clothes in front of the gentleman?"

"You still young Nellie and you is a beautiful woman. Don't sell yourself short."

"I ain't interested Miss Una," she said. "I got love for only one man."

"He can't do a thing for you down in that grave Nellie. Life does go on. When I dead and gone and Clytie find herself a nice husband, you going to be here all by yourself."

"Miss Una, he don't have any interest in me. He coming by to talk about business."

"Don't forget that Jonas will be running the school, just in case he want to bring somebody else."

"It is none of his business who I choose to run the school. I know Jonas didn't go to any high school, but everybody know he is a good teacher."

"Well we shouldn't start jumping to no conclsions. Wait until he come by and see what he want."

* * *

Sarah Bottomsley and her ex father in law put their heads together and came up with a new overseer for the plantation. He had worked on two other plantations before and was trying to decide if he should go back to England, when they made him a very attractive offer. Sarah Bottomsley couldn't have been happier because she was desperate to get away from the island for a vacation. She had not seen Emily in three years and would be there for her entry into another school, where she would take her higher level exams and after that, it would be on to Law School. She was proud of her daughter. It was one of the few sensible suggestions Thomas Hurley had made, not because he had loved Emily but just wanted her out of the way. She also promised Clytie she could visit her mother, but should at least visit Bottomsley once per week to make sure everything was in order even though Ursy would be there. It seemed as if a load had been lifted off her shoulders. She would once again go for her beauty treatments and read on the porch just like she used to. Clytie made sure everything she needed for the trip was packed in her two cases along with some Barbadian specialities; six brown sugar cakes, six comforts, six nutties, two glassies and two sugar apples in a parcel with Emily Bottomsley's name written on it. Gone were the days of the steamer trunk and the long six week ocean voyage. She would be flying on an airplane for the first time and was very nervous. Her daughter had completed the trip a few years before and she was sure her journey would be just as uneventful. She would stay with her parents which would give her the chance to see her daughter every weekend.

What would she do with Ginger Hurley? Staying in the big plantation house meant the use of water, electricity and food, and since she had learnt to be frugal from Ginger and her brother, it would be wasteful having her stay in such a big house especially since she never contributed one penny to the household finances. Therefore Ginger had to go. She was not happy about it, but there was nothing she could do. With the disappearance of her brother, it meant the power she once wielded was a thing of the past.

Two weeks after sending Ginger on her way, Sarah Bottomsley boarded a flight for London for a two month stay, leaving Clytie and Ursy to take care of the house during her long absence. They covered the furniture with white sheets and made sure every window was tightly closed to keep those ghastly insects out and to prevent them for destroying the furniture and drapes. Ursy would come by now and then to make sure everything was in order and Clytie would come to Bottomsley once per week to see that Ursy was doing what she was supposed to be doing.

One day when Clytie least expected it, Ursy reminded her of a long made promise.

"Miss Nellie promised me that I could come to visit. Now that Sarah isn't here, I think this is a good time to ask her."

"I don't know Ursy. You will have to ask Nellie yourself."

"After making the call, she came back to say that Nellie was busy and couldn't talk to her.

* * *

# 47

It was a very warm day, much warmer than usual, but Nellie kept her lookout on the porch for the arrival of her solicitor Francois Bertrand. She was curious to know what was so important regarding her inheritance.

"It was two fifteen when she saw his car driving up the street and she waited to greet him.

"Good afternoon Miss Peterkin," he said his lips barely touching hand. "I'm sorry to be late but I was detained by another client."

"Never mind Mr. Bertrand. You only a couple minutes late. Would you like a glass of cool lemonade?"

"That would be nice," he said wiping the perspiration from his forehead with a handkerchief.

"It real hot today, ain't it" she asked.

"It's only hot like this when there is really bad weather in the area. You haven't heard anything, have you?"

"I didn't listen to the radio all day, but Miss Una is always listening, and when she hear something she always tell me."

He drank his glass of lemonade and Nellie refilled it as he took some documents from his case.

"Miss Peterkin, I told you that your father had left you his home and a sum of money in the bank."

"I know," she said. "It was a big mistake."

"No Miss Peterkin. I would like to take you down to the house to look around."

"Why Mr. Bertrand? Something wrong?"

"Nothing's wrong. I want to show you around the home. Do you have time today?"

"We can go now if you want."

Nellie went to inform Miss Una where she was going while Mr. Bertrand waited for her at the opened front door of his car. She had always sat in the back when she was being driven around by Sarah Bottomsley, so it came as a great shock to her to be sitting up front next to him. They drove along partly in silence until they arrived at Gus Ridley's home.

"I don't think this big enough for a school house," she said looking at the structure.

"That's not the main house you can see from here. That used to be a stable. The main house is behind those trees."

"Those horses had a good life," she said trying to make him laugh.

"They certainly did," he replied. "Now you can get a good view of the house."

She put her hands over her eyes to keep the sun out, and what she saw made her gasp. It was by no means as big or as grand as Bottomsley, but it was quite a beautiful home."

"He used to live here all by himself?" she asked.

"I can't be sure," replied Mr. Bertrand. "It's quite big isn't it?"

"I don't think I would want to turn this into school house," she said staring at it.

"Let's go inside, you will get a better idea what you would like to do once you've seen the inside."

He opened the door and Nellie followed closely on his heels. The inside was even more of a pleasant surprise. Gus Ridley had collected the most precious mahogany antiques and paintings. There was even a plantation chair which reminded her of JB's chair at Bottomsley plantation. Nellie couldn't believe her eyes as she looked at all the luxurious things in the home. The china cabinets were filled with crystal wine glasses and beautiful porcelain, like those she had seen at the expensive stores in the city.

"Are you sure he left all this for me Mr. Bertrand?"

"I read the will to you Miss Peterkin. It's all yours. You've got to make a decision what you're going to do with it. You certainly can't leave it here like this to fall apart."

"This is just too much for me to digest all at once. I know you say he left this house for me, but all of this?" she asked stretching out her arms and spinning around. "I can't make this decision all by myself."

"Would you like my help?" he asked.

"That would be very nice sir."

"Why don't you move into this house, sell or rent the house you're living in along with the shop and adjoining house?"

"What about Miss Una? Where she would live? And what about the school?" she asked.

"I've thought of everything Miss Peterkin. There haven't been any horses in the stable for a very long time. You could fix that up for the old lady and instead of leaving the hotel closed, you can turn that into the school."

"When I sell my shop Mr. Bertrand, what I going to do?"

"You have always told me how hard you've worked all your life. Now is the time to start enjoying some of it."

"You mean I should just stop working?"

"It really wouldn't be necessary. You've got enough money to last you two lifetimes."

"I have that much Mr. Bertrand?"

"If you want me to show you everything, I can list it all for you and let you know exactly how much you're worth."

"That wouldn't be a bad idea. I need to see it on paper."

"That won't be a problem. I'll see to it that you have the figures by next week."

They were so busy looking around the house they didn't notice that it wasn't the setting sun which had brought the darkness on, but the storm that was brewing outside. Reality did set in when a clap of thunder seemed to land on the roof of the house and a bolt of lightning sizzled to the ground striking a tree and causing a big branch to fall off.

"I know this was going to happen. It was just too hot today," she said.

"We'll have to wait it out Miss Peterkin. It is much too dangerous to go out there now."

"Especially with all that lightning," added Nellie.

"Let's look around to see if there are any lanterns or lamps we can use. It's really getting dark now and I know there is no electricity."

"You mean to say he used to live in such a big house and he didn't have no electricity?"

"Since he passed away, there was no need to keep it connected and paying bills for something which was not being used."

"I see," she said as another clap of thunder made her jump.

"We'd better hurry and find that lamp before it gets any darker."

Looking around, they found a pair of lanterns and a box of matches on a shelf in the kitchen and they lit them both and carried them into the drawing room. By this time the rain was coming down in torrents and it was difficult to see anything outside.

"You like the rain Mr. Bertrand?" she asked.

"Only when I'm at home and in bed," he replied.

"When I was a little girl, I used to be frightened for thunder and lightning, but it don't bother me no more. I used to like it when the sun was shining and the rain was falling. As children we used to say that the devil and his wife were fighting with the Cou Ccou stick."

He started to laugh.

"Why a Cou Cou stick?" he asked.

"I don't know, come to think of it. Ever since I was little, everybody used to say that."

"What about your sister?" he asked. "Her name is---?"

"Nora good. She is a very good sister. Not everybody is lucky to have a good sister like Nora."

"I take it she is only your half sister."

"If you mean that we don't have the same father, no we don't. Nora father was like my own father. He looked after me just like if I was his daughter. Things were hard Mr. Bertrand. Real hard! My mother went every morning to weed the hedgerows after Nora father pass away. Then when I was eleven, I had to help my family so I went to work in the kitchen at Bottomsley. I was real young with no education at all."

"And how did you learn to read and write?"

"Mr. Bottomsley open a school for the children at the plantation and Clytie son Jonas show me how to read and write and then Mr….."

"You were saying Miss Peterkin?"

"Never mind," she said as she almost spilled the beans.

Francois Bertrand went to the window and looked out. It was no longer just bad weather, but a full fledged storm.

"I take it Mr. Bottomsley was a good man," he said turning around and looking at her.

"Yes he was a very good man."

"Did you like him?"

"Why you asking me all these questions?"

"You are a very intriguing woman and I'm just trying to understand you better."

"What about you sir, you are not from The Rock?"

"I have been here for many years but I wasn't born here."

"I know that."

"How did you know that?"

"You talk different. You have a soft sweet voice."

"Thank you. My mother came from one of the French islands and my father from France and they sent me to England to study."

"And they still living on that French island?" she asked.

"No they passed away some time ago. They both died in an accident while I was in England."

"That is very sad. I always wonder about my daughter. What if something happen to her mother, what would she do then? She isn't twenty one yet."

"She will be looked after. You've got enough money to see that she finishes school. What is she studying?"

"She is going to be a solicitor just like you."

"Do you have any contact with her Miss Peterkin?"

"Know what? Call me Nellie. We waiting here for the storm to stop and talking like old friends."

"Alright Nellie, and you may call me Francois."

"Fran who?" she asked.

"Francois."

"Alright Francois," she said. "Emily write to me about once every three months but just like friends."

"When do you intend to tell her you are her mother?"

"I don't know. She got a mother already."

"But that's not her mother."

"It is the only mother she know Mr. Bertra……Francois."

"Since we are sitting here and talking like friends Nellie, may I ask you something personal?"

"It all depend how personal it is," she said as another clap of thunder interrupted their conversation.

"Very personal," he replied. "Was John Bottomsley Emily's father?"

"Why do you think that?" she asked.

"Who else could it be? You are a very beautiful woman and having worked in the Bottomsley household, he was the only European man with whom you had any contact."

"You don't know that," she said not looking at him.

"But my guess is correct, isn't it?"

"You are right Francois," she said looking away.

"But how did he get Emily away from you?"

"It was like this," she began, and so she told Francois Bertrand the story of how Emily was taken away from her and her relationship with John Bottomsley.

"In spite of what he had done, it seemed as if you still loved him."

"I did love him Francois. I did and I think I still love him although he is long gone."

"That's a very sad story Nellie. Truly sad!"

They sat in silence after she opened her heart to him. Neither one seemed to know what else to say, so they sat quietly and waited for the storm to blow over.

"You have children Francois?"

"No Nellie. I have never been married and neither do I have any children."

"But you don't have to be married to have children."

"That's true Nellie, but having children is a great responsibility and I think every child needs a mother and a father."

"So since we are asking personal questions, I want to know why you never get married. A handsome man like you," she said.

"Thank you Nellie. I spent all my time trying to build up a law practice and really never had time for a social nor family life."

"What about Mr. Bantree? He got a wife and children?"

"Yes he does."

"Forgive my asking Francois, but how old are you?"

"I don't mind telling you Nellie. I am forty seven."

"You just a little bit older than me," she said.

"Now it's my turn to ask you a question."

"What sir?"

"Why are you asking me so many personal questions?"

"Because just like you Francois, I want to find out more about the person who is going to be looking after my money."

Francois Bertrand could not help but laugh. Here was a woman, not very educated but extremely sharp. She was a kind woman, a woman with substance. He liked her, and although she was what people would say, not in his league, he knew that with a little guidance, she could be a force to be reckoned with.

"Did you know Thomas Hurley, the man who disappeared about a month ago?"

She was surprised by his question but kept her wits about her.

"Not really but I see him one or two twice around the place and Clytie tell me he was Miss Sarah new husband."

"What do you think happened to him?"

"I really don't know. All I know is that they find his car over by the cliff where we used go to watch the sharks."

"Do you go to watch sharks Nellie?"

"Not as much as I used to. We take the insides of chickens and ducks and throw them in the water just to see them swimming around."

"You must show it to me sometime."

"You really want to see something like that?"

"Of course," he replied. "I have never seen a shark."

"Alright, I will carry you over there one day I will show it to you."

The bad weather lifted and they were able to run to the car through the drizzling rain.

"Let me know your decision Nellie," he said as they reached her home.

"I will think about it and let you know. Francois, I am making something to eat. Are you a little hungry? I know I am."

"Are you inviting me to stay for dinner Nellie?"

"Seeing there ain't a Miss Bertrand to cook nothing for you, it wouldn't be good manners to send you home with an empty stomach."

He accepted the invitation and together they entered the house and he sat down.

"You like sea eggs Francois?"

"It's one of my favourite meals and I love the way they prepare them here."

"Make yourself comfortable. I have to run next door for a minute. I have to check on Miss Una."

After a five minute absence, she returned with the news that Miss Una was fine and her daughter was spending the night with her.

"I have some good Bottomsley rum in the kitchen. You like a drink?"

"Wouldn't mind if I do," he said. "It would certainly warm me up a bit."

"You drink it straight like----? How you like it?"

"On the rocks with a piece of lime," he said.

"On the rocks? What is that?" she asked with a quizzical expression.

"With some ice," he said laughing.

"I see. All those English people used to put a shot in a glass and drink it just like that."

"I prefer to have a little ice with it. It makes it smoother for me."

"While you enjoying that drink, you can turn on the radio," she said. The BBC news will be starting soon."

Dinner was prepared and they sat together at the table and ate.

"It's very tasty Nellie. I love it the way you prepared it; with lots of lime."

"My mother always used to serve it with cucumber and pear."

"They go very well together. Very, very good, the taste is so similar to something I used to eat when I was a child. Has anyone ever told you, you look like a Creole woman from the French Islands?"

"You really think I like one of those French ladies?"

"You certainly do Nellie."

* * *

# 48

"Be careful Nellie," said Miss Una. "You got a lot of money. You got to be careful who you let in your life."

"I don't have anybody in my life Miss Una. All I say was that Francois and me had supper together last night."

"See what I mean? Just yesterday he was Mr. Bertrum."

"Bertrand," said Nellie correcting her.

"Bertrand, Bertrum. As I was saying, just a couple days back, it was Mr. Bertrand. Now it is Francis."

"Ma, leave Nellie alone. Let Nellie enjoy her life."

"Thanks Clytie. I don't know why your mother making such a fuss. We are only friends."

"Ignore Ma," Clytie whispered under her breath.

"What you say Clytie?" her mother asked. "I old but I ain't deaf."

Clytie and Nellie had a chuckle about it and then Clytie became quite serious.

"You like the solicitor Nellie?"

"He real nice. He different from JB, but he talk real gentle and he don't behave like these idiots from the plantations."

"You got to be careful with those married men," Clytie continued.

"He ain't married."

"What?" asked a rather surprised Clytie. "Such a good-looking man with all that learning and he don't have no wife?"

"He say he spend all his time trying to get his business going."

"He don't have no girl friend neither?"

"Not that I know."

"Find out if he got a brother Nellie. Lord you is one of the luckiest women on this earth."

"Clytie, I didn't say that something going on between Francois and me."

"If you ain't interested Nellie, you can invite him over so I can meet him?"

"I did not say that if I had a chance I won't take it. I like Francois, but I don't think he even think of me that way; not only that, it won't make JB too happy."

"Wake up Nellie. JB long dead and gone. And I know he wouldn't want to stand in the way o' your happiness."

"You right Clytie," she said thinking out loud. "You right."

"I almost forget to tell you that you get a letter from Emily today."

"Give it to me," she said running towards Miss Una. "Where is Emily letter?"

Miss Una took it from the cash cage and handed it to her. She sat down and looked at the writing on the front and ran her fingers over it. Miss Una was beginning to run out of patience because she too looked forward to Emily's letters although they were meant for Nellie.

"Open it Nels," said Clytie. "Open it."

Dear Miss Nellie,

I can hardly find the time to do much writing anymore since I've got so much studying to do. Next week I will be taking my final exams and then it will be time for me to start Law School. I am so looking forward to coming back to that precious little rock than I can hardly stand it. Of course it won't be the same without Miss Ella. I can hardly believe she is no longer with us. Mama said Clytie would be spending lots of time with you since she

is here. It was so good to see Mama and all the nice things she brought from Clytie. I especially loved those brown sugar cakes. I could almost smell the molasses floating through the air, just like it used to at Bottomsley. It is possible Mama may stay a little longer since Grandpa is not at all well. They say he's going senile. I guess that means he is slowly losing his mind. You would love him. He is a very kind and gentle man. How is Hurley? Does he miss me? I hope he will be there when I return. Does he still steal the flying fish when you leave the kitchen? I must go now. Mama is waiting for me to go into London and I am hurrying to post this letter when I'm there. Please tell Clytie I will write to her soon and give my fondest greetings to Miss Una.
Warmest wishes,
Emily Bottomsley

Nellie read the letter over and over and cried each time she read the words on the page.

"Just yesterday she was a little child and now she is a woman and talking about becoming a solicitor. If only her father was still on this earth, he would be a happy man," Miss Una said.

"You right Ma. It would make him real happy."

"Nobody ain't hear nothing else about that demon that disappear?" Miss Una asked changing the subject.

"Ma, you know how I feel about that. Don't even talk about Thomas Hurley. I get the nerves whenever I think about what I do to him."

"You ain't do nothing child. And even if you do something to that demon, he deserve it," Miss Una said hoping her words would lighten Nellie's load.

"I don't know Ma. Nobody ain't say a word more about him and it is more than three months now."

"I never trust that man. Suppose he ain't dead."

"Why you say that Miss Una?" asked Nellie.

"Suppose he park that car out by the cliff and then walk away, so we would believe he jump over?"

"He was bad Ma, but I don't think he had enough gumption to do something like that."

"Miss Una, you could be right," said Nellie. "That didn't even cross my mind."

The old woman was now totally confused because of Nellie's reply. If Nellie and her sister had accidentally killed Thomas Hurley, Nellie would never have agreed with her or was Nellie trying to trick her?

"I think the sharks eat him ever since," said Clytie. "That potion Dootie the obeah man put on him was just too strong."

"Clytie, you talking foolishness," her mother said. "You think that if obeah could kill, we would suffer so much hardship in this life?"

"But I thought you believe in obeah Ma?"

"I didn't say that I don't believe, but girl there is something much stronger than obeah and it is he," she said pointing to the sky. "If you believe something will hurt you, you bet it will hurt you."

"But Hurley didn't know I went to the obeah man for him."

"He didn't know, but he was no good, and they say that if a man live by the sword, he will certainly die by the sword."

"What sword Ma?"

"Sometimes I worry about you Clytie. What I mean is that as a man live, so shall he die, and he was a right bastard. He only get what he deserve."

Nellie no longer took part in the conversation, because she was busy re-reading Emily's letter while the mother and daughter conversed about Thomas Hurley and his untimely demise.

* * *

"I have drawn up all the papers for you Miss Peterkin. I wanted to know if I could stop by this afternoon or would you rather I sent them to you?"

"You can stop by Mr. Bertrand. I am not busy this afternoon. What time do you think you will come by?"

"Around four thirty if that's alright with you."

"That is alright."

She was suddenly as nervous as a cockroach in a hen house. She could only remember having such feelings when JB was going to visit her. She wondered why she seemed to be losing control. She was sure Francois Bertrand was not interested in her as a partner, but only as a friend or advisor. She was getting herself head over heels in something which she thought would amount to nothing.

"Nice to see you again Miss Peterkin," he said making the motion of kissing her hand.

"Thank you sir."

"Have you got one of your nice glasses of lemonade for me?" he asked with a smile.

"No I didn't make any today. Would you prefer something like coconut water instead?"

"That's refreshing too. I would love some."

"Would you like a tip of gin in it?"

"No thank you. Just the coconut water would be fine."

He seemed so different from the last time they were together. He was much more formal and businesslike. She did not trust herself to say anything for fear of saying the wrong thing. After a moment of organising his papers, he gave Nellie a summary of all her assets.

"How much is this?" she asked staring at all the zeros.

"Your worth is about three hundred and fifty thousand Miss Peterkin.

"That is a lot of money."

"It certainly is. I want to ask you about the property you own in St. Lucia."

"What do you want to know?"

"I know it says on the plan it is about twenty eight hundred square feet. Is it in good condition Miss Peterkin?"

"Mr. Bertrand you was calling me Nellie the other night. Why you suddenly calling me Miss Peterkin again?"

"There is no reason to worry. When I'm on business, I try to address my clients in a businesslike manner. If it makes you happy, I'll address you as Nellie."

"I don't want to mess up nothing, so you should go on calling me Miss Peterkin, and I will say Mr. Bertrand."

"You don't have to do that Nellie. You can continue to call me Francois."

"I think that is a good idea. For business we will say Miss Peterkin and Mr. Bertrand."

"As you wish Miss Peterkin," he said with a smile.

"What you want to know about the vacation house?"

"I was just wondering if it was in good condition and what happens to it when you aren't there?"

"Well I don't get down there too often, so it remain empty."

"I have a suggestion. Why don't you rent it out to clients who want to get away for a weekend or for long vacations?"

"And what would happen when I want to go and spend some time over there?"

"You can set aside the time you want to spend in it and then it wouldn't be available for rent for that period of time."

"Like if I want to go for Christmas, I wouldn't rent it out then?"

"That's right. If you want to go from let's say the fifteenth of December right through until the new year you'll set that time aside for yourself."

"How much would I get for rent?" she asked.

"I don't know. I have never seen it and I don't know what condition it is in."

"It is in good condition."

"I do believe you Miss Peterkin, but you must think of the clients who may want to rent it. It must be in tip top condition. Perhaps there all well-to-do people who might want to get away for a weekend and want to have a nice place to stay."

"If you don't believe me, you can go and see for yourself."

"That wouldn't be a bad idea, but I can't go away until next weekend."

"That is alright with me."

"I expect you'll be going with me Miss Peterkin?"

"That isn't a problem. Miss Una daughter Clytie is spending a couple weeks up here and Nora don't live too far away, so the business is not going to suffer."

"Alright Miss Peterkin, I'll get the tickets for the boat and we'll have a look at the house next week."

As she walked him to the porch, she realised what she had done. She was going away with him for the weekend. On business of course!

The whole week was spent packing and unpacking her little valise. She was not sure what she should carry because she wanted to look her best. She was extremely nervous and Miss Una's comments didn't help.

"I know you will like him Miss Una. I will bring him into the shop and let you meet him."

"I was wondering when we would get a chance to see him. You sure you ain't hiding him from me and Clytie?"

"Ma why you don't leave Nellie in peace?" asked Clytie.

"Thanks Clytie."

"When he coming back Nellie?"

"I don't know if he coming back before we go on the trip."

"It don't matter, as long as I get to see his face," the old woman said. "Don't talk," she said putting her finger to her lips. "Listen," she continued. "You hear that dove? He is saying that God is calling home somebody."

"But doves coo all the time Ma."

"But listen to the way it is cooing. Hoo! Hoo! Hoo hoo hoo!"

"They coo like that all the time."

"No Clytie, not like that. That is the Lord calling home one of his children," she said, as Clytie and Nellie just looked at each other.

"You two don't believe me. Just wait and see."

* * *

# 49

The new overseer at Bottomsley turned out to be better at handling the workers than Thomas Hurley. He was by no means a pushover, but he was fair. Nicholas Bellamy had spent many years on the island and knew the mentality of all the people; the workers and their employers. He did not have to worry about Sarah Bottomsley because she had given him full rein of the plantation. He had been highly recommended as someone who got the job done by fair means and also known for increasing production as well as profits.

Now and again John Bottomsley would stop by to see how things were progressing and he was usually quite pleased. Then he would pass on his observations by letter to Sarah Bottomsley. The shop where the workers bought their groceries was now much bigger and more produce from the plantation could be purchased at a cheaper price for the families who toiled in the fields. Mr. Polgreen who was now much too frail to carry on the business was replaced by one of the workers with the ability to read and write. He did not go without a fight, but Nicholas Bellamy saw to it, that he was well looked after, even though he swore and shouted each time his pay packet was delivered.

Ursy kept everyone up north up to date with the happenings at Bottomsley. She was calling that day to tell them that Mr. Fitz had passed away.

"He was carrying one of the little boys with him every time he went out to pick bush. I think he had a feeling there was not too much time left. Just in time he passed down everything he had in his head about bush and bush teas to that boy."

"That is too sad," said Nellie.

"Miss Sarah isn't here, but Mr. Bellamy helping with the funeral because Mr. Fitz was still working in the garden although he was old and bent over."

"Something happen to Mr. Fitz?" asked Miss Una.

"He is up there," answered Nellie pointing to the sky.

"He is there with Ella and the angels. Have mercy on his soul Father," she said making a sign of the cross. "He was sick long?"

"Ursy say his condition get worse last week and they rush him to the hospital. He was on life water for two days before the Lord call him home."

Nellie continued her telephone conversation with Ursy who informed her that she would like to visit Miss Una and Clytie.

"You can come next week Ursy, but I ain't going to be here, but you can talk to Clytie because she know when I am coming back."

* * *

Nellie stood by the docks waiting for Francois Bertrand to arrive. She was receiving all kinds of stares for she was beautifully dressed and did indeed look like a Creole from one of the French islands. Some of the men would smile at her while the women went by as if she were invisible. She was feeling more and more self conscious and was relieved when Francois arrived. He picked up her valise and the two started walking in the direction of the lighter boats, which would in turn take them out to the larger boat.

"You don't have to carry my valise," she said. "It ain't heavy. I can carry it myself."

"What kind of gentleman would I be if I allowed a lady to carry her own case?"

"Thank you. What I calling you today? Mr.Bertrand or Francois?" she whispered.

"Whatever you like Nellie," he replied. "But I would prefer Francois."

She remembered when she went away with JB and they couldn't sit together. They couldn't even speak to each other.

*"What would it be like this time?" she wondered.*

The boat ran into bad weather and it rocked from side to side. Nellie was afraid, so afraid that she was turning all the colours of the rainbow. Francois stayed beside her and comforted her. They were indeed glad when the voyage was over and they set their feet again on firm land. They hailed a taxi to take them to their destination.

"It isn't as pretty as The Rock," she said to him.

"Nothing is as pretty as The Rock," was his reply.

"This is it. This is it," she said as the taxi driver almost drove past the house.

Together they climbed the steps while Francois kept looking around at the property. It was just as Nellie had left it the last time, except that the housekeeper wasn't there. She knocked and since there was no reply, she opened her purse to get her key, but had forgotten it at home.

"I forget to bring the key," she said feeling like a fool. "I am sorry Francois."

She really wanted to impress him, but now she was afraid he would think she was not as smart as she pretended to be.

"Isn't there anyone else here who can let us in?"

"Stop, Stop!" she shouted to the taxi driver who was about to drive away.

"What are you going to do?" he asked.

"I think I know where I can get a key."

They climbed back into the taxi leaving their cases on the porch while Nellie tried to explain to the driver where Mr. Applewhite the former owner lived. They drove through narrow streets where Casuarina and Flamboyant trees lined the roadways, but she had to admit she had forgotten where he lived. Nothing seemed familiar to her. However after making a couple more wrong turns, they finally found Mr. Applewhite's home. He was very happy to see Nellie again and promised he would come by the following day to say hello and to meet her companion who was still standing beside the taxi. Mr. Applewhite's children were nowhere in sight and Nellie felt it a little forward to inquire about them especially since she had never met the mother.

"The housekeeper coming around tomorrow?" she asked him.

"I don't know Miss Nellie. Since I sell the house, I haven't seen a lot of Meta."

"I am just asking because I don't know if the house is in order and I may want her to fix up a bit."

"No problem Miss Nellie. Before I come by tomorrow, I will stop by to see if I can find her."

"Thank you Mr. Applewhite."

"Call me Teddy Miss Nellie. After all, those days gone when we had to be so formal."

"Thanks Teddy."

Key in hand, they climbed the steps to the house again and after a couple tries, Francois was able to open the door.

"So what do you think?" she asked as he surveyed the living room.

"It has possibilities. It is charming with a beautiful view."

"What you think we should do?"

"We'll have to get a carpenter and mason around to tell us what needs to be done."

"It look alright to me," said Nellie also looking around.

"If this house is repaired properly, you can command a good rental income."

"Well, you always give me good advice, so I will let you handle it."

"That's the sensible thing to do."

There was not a scrap of food in the house. Nellie had not written to say she would be arriving, so the housekeeper had not done anything for her arrival. The kitchen door creaked as Francois pushed it open could see through the window panes that most of the fruit trees were hanging heavily with fruit. A lot of it had already been destroyed perhaps by monkeys who were still sitting high in the trees and calling out to each other.

"At least we won't starve before tomorrow," he said.

She grabbed a basket from the counter just in time to see a cockroach scamper into the sink and down the empty drain.

"There ain't nothing here for it to eat," she said as it made its exit.

"We should also get the pest control to rid the house of any pests. In the meantime, it can go on enjoying its life here without interruption."

Mangoes, paw paws, sugar apples and also a couple coconuts found beneath the trees would serve as dinner.

"We definitely won't starve," he said with a smile.

She prepared the fruit and they sat on the porch and looked out onto the beautiful

Caribbean sea. It was still except for the occasional wave which made its way to the shore and trickled out again. There was no one in sight. It was rather peaceful.

"This is what visitors would enjoy," he said still gazing out at the water.

"You don't find it too quiet?" she asked.

"This is just perfect Nellie. After working around people all day, this is what I would love to come home to."

She did not reply. Out of the corner of her eye, she stole a glance at him. He did look rested and well tanned and as she had noticed from the first time she had seen him, he was a very handsome man.

"Do you know Mr. Applewhite well?"

"Not really. We buy the house from him. He is a nice man. That is all I know about him. Why are you asking?"

"I thought his face looked familiar, that's all."

"You can ask him tomorrow when he come by."

"I was just curious. I don't think I should be so forward Nellie."

"You can ask him. He is a real nice fellow."

"I'll think about it."

"Whatever you say," she replied.

Nellie was beginning to feel rather nervous. It was getting dark and she had no idea what to expect from Francois. Suppose he wanted her to sleep in the same bed with him? What would she do? He was handsome enough but she felt she still had an obligation to JB. She wouldn't want him to think she had forsaken him for another man. He helped with the drying of the dishes while Nellie washed in silence.

"Do you have a radio here Nellie?"

"Just a little one in the first bedroom upstairs," she replied.

He disappeared and she could hear the static emanating from the radio as he tried to find a station. She climbed the stairs and saw him sitting on the floor, still fiddling with the knob and trying to get some kind of reception.

"I just can't find anything," he said to her.

"Let me try," she said brushing against his arm as she tried moving the antenna back and forth as JB had done. Suddenly in the place of static, there was quiet music. She had found the BBC. After the music, the announcer brought the news in that familiar voice which comes only from the BBC.

*"This is the British Broadcasting Corporation. Here is the news read by Tom Smith."*

Everyone listened to the BBC to find out what was happening in the world. There was news about Africa and the other British colonies and Nellie listened intently, as she sat on the floor close to Francois' feet.

"You used to live in England?" she asked.

"Yes, but I spent a lot of time in France too. You would love it in France."

"But everything is so far away. When I think of Emily out in that cold country, I could really sit down and cry."

"It's not that bad. There are nice hot summers too."

"Really? I thought it was always cold."

"Maybe one day you should travel and see a bit of Europe."

"I don't know. If Emily don't come back, then I will have to go and see where she is living."

"I'm sure she will return," he replied.

"I am going to bed," she said. "That trip on the boat made me real tired."

"I am a little tired also," he said getting up from the floor.

She pointed him in the direction of one bedroom and she went to the other.

"Goodnight Nellie. Sleep well," he said to her.

"You sleep well too," she said repeating what he had said.

They both lay in their beds wide awake, just listening to the waves come in and go out. The fresh smell of the ocean permeated the rooms and thoughts of JB came flowing back into her mind. Not only did she smell the ocean breeze, but also the sweet smell of tobacco intermingling with it. She was petrified. The last time she had smelled tobacco that strong, was the same night Thomas Hurley met his untimely death. The smell kept getting stronger and the stronger it got, the more her heart raced.

Usually after five minutes, the smell went away but tonight it just lingered. She got out of bed and looked out the window. There was no one there. She looked down the stairs and on to the landing. No one, but the aroma was quite intense.

"Francois," she whispered.

"Yes Nellie. Is something wrong?" he asked appearing at the bedroom door.

"I think somebody is in the house."

"Did you hear or see anything?"

"No, but whoever it is, is smoking a pipe."

He started to laugh and returned to the bedroom and came back with a pipe stuck between his teeth.

"You smoke?" she asked.

"Not too often," he replied.

"I feel so much better. I was very frightened."

"Are you alright now?" he asked.

"Yes, goodnight Francois," she replied.

* * *

## 50

A new day found Nellie and Francois in St. Lucia with nothing to eat for breakfast. She was still lying in bed and wondering where they could find something when someone started hammering on the door. It was still rather quiet because Francois was still asleep, so she got out of bed and went to the door. It was Meta, the unfriendly housekeeper.

"Morning," she said with not a hint cheerfulness in her voice. "Mr. Applewhite say you want to see me."

"I want to know where I could find some food and some oil for the stove.

"Mr. Applewhite could tell you where to get those things."

"Isn't that what I pay you for?"

"If you had let me know you that you was coming, everything would be in order, but you didn't say nothing," said the surly woman.

"Howdy," another voice called from outside.

It was none other than Mr. Applewhite. This time he had his two children in tow; both still dirty and unkempt.

"Top o' the morning to yer," he said.

"Good morning Mr. Applewhite," Nellie said.

"Don't forget. Teddy."

"Good morning Teddy."

"Where is the mister?" he asked looking around.

"Still sleeping," said Nellie as Francois came down the stairs.

"Top o' the morning to yer sir," he continued in his jovial voice.

Francois introduced himself and he introduced his two children, while the housekeeper looked on in amazement. Nellie knew what she was thinking.

*"She is wondering where I find this good looking fellow."*

Nellie excused herself and reappeared a few minutes later fully dressed. She told the housekeeper what she wanted and she set off to purchase the necessary breakfast items.

"Don't yer offer a fellow a grog?" Mr. Applewhite asked.

"I would love to," said Francois, "but I don't think there's any in the house."

"It's a poor house when a man can't have a drink," he said laughing.

Nellie brought out a bottle and a glass and set it down in front of him. He filled the glass and threw it back in one gulp. Francois couldn't take his eyes off him. At such an early hour, the man consumed enough alcohol for three men.

"Which one are you?" Nellie asked one of the girls.

"Jenny and my sister is Rose."

"You want some mangoes?" she asked.

"Yes thanks," said the one who said her name was Jenny.

"School's out?" asked Francois.

"I teach the girls myself. They don't go to school."

"Don't they want to mix with their friends?" he asked.

"Now and again some friends come out to visit, but as you can see, we live far out."

Francois noticed the girls didn't say too much unless they were directly addressed, and they seemed to fidget quite a lot with their hands.

"Do you like to read?" Francois asked the older one.

"Not really," she said. "I like to play outside."

The housekeeper returned with the groceries and Mr. Applewhite and his daughters set out for home.

"There is something strange about that man," said Francois. "Fancy him keeping the children at home and not allowing them to mix with other children.

"He drinks too much. That's all I can say," replied Nellie.

"He does live with them," said the housekeeper suddenly.

Nellie's face turned bright red and she turned to look at the woman.

"What you say?" she asked.

"I say he does live with them," she replied.

"Where else should he live?" asked Francois.

"You don't understand," Nellie said to him. "He sleeps with those two little girls."

"Are you trying to tell me that he actually goes to bed with his two daughters?"

"Everybody on the island know that sir," said the housekeeper.

"Did you know that Nellie?"

"I didn't know a thing," she replied.

"Aren't they going to do anything about it?"

"What can they do? He is rich and he know everybody on this island. When he drink too much, it is hell to pay especially for those two children," said Meta.

"Where is the mother," Francois asked.

"We don't know. He showed up here about ten years ago with those two children. The little one was just a baby then."

With only one day to do all the things which had to be done, Francois and Nellie set out for the solicitor's office. They would still need his services, but Francois was now handling all of Nellie's affairs and they needed to inform him. Mr. Taylor was quite an affable man who moved rather slowly and regretted the loss of the bulk of his client's business. Although he wanted to tread carefully, Francois decided to ask about Mr. Applewhite and the two girls who never crossed a school door.

"I'll give you a piece of good advice," he told Francois. "Since you are just passing through and know very little about this island and the things that go on here, see nothing, hear nothing and most of all, say nothing."

He didn't understand the man's attitude, but he decided to take his advice. Nellie too was afraid and told him he should take Mr. Taylor's advice.

"It just bothers me that he can get away with doing such an awful thing," he said to her on the way home.

"He is just plain nasty."

"I wish there was something I could do," he said.

Later that evening Mr. Applewhite dropped in again for his uninvited visit.

"Where are your daughters?" Francois asked.

"Doing their homework," he answered looking around.

"I thought they didn't go to school."

"Because they don't go school means there is no homework. I make them study every evening. What does a man have to do to get a drink around here?"

Nellie placed the bottle and glass in front of him and he swallowed one drink after the other, while Francois carefully studied him.

"Got a plantation too Mr. Francois?" he asked.

"No I don't."

"And what does a handsome fellow like you do to keep himself busy and I don't mean with pretty Miss Nellie."

"Please show respect to Miss Peterkin," Francois told him in no uncertain terms.

"No disrespect meant my good man, but Miss Nellie sure is a pretty woman."

"I am Miss Peterkin's solicitor as well as her friend."

"I see. I see," he said now carefully studying Francois. "Got any children?" he asked.

"No," answered Francois. "Why do you ask?"

"Just trying to understand yer," he replied.

"And you Teddy, how long were you on the island?"

"Ten long years," he said as he threw back another grog.

"Where did you come from?"

"I can tell you are a solicitor by profession my good man. You certainly ask a lot of questions," he said as he picked up his hat and headed out the door bowing to Nellie as he left.

"He left in a real hurry, didn't he? He hiding something. You notice he never say where he come from," said Nellie.

After an evening meal of roasted fish, plantain and rice, they packed their bags for the early boat ride back to The Rock. It was a short but sweet visit.

* * *

That evening Ursy telephoned to say that Sarah Bottomsley was back and had given her letters for Nellie and Clytie. Miss Una was a little sad because it meant that Clytie must now return to Bottomsley to resume her duties.

"I didn't even get a chance to ask how things went with the solicitor," said Clytie.

"Everything went alright, but girl you remember that man named Mr. Applewhite?"

"Yes."

"You wouldn't believe what that nasty man is doing with those two girls he got."

"What he doing Nels?"

"He sleeping with them."

"What you mean, he sleeping with them?"

"I always have to spell out everything for you Clytie. He doing to those children what JB and me used to do."

"You mean he fooping those little girls?"

"What kind of language is that?" asked Miss Una. "That is not a respectful word. It was better when they used to talk about carnal knowledge, but nowadays everybody talking about fooping. No respect," said the old woman gruffly.

"Beg your pardon Ma. I forget that you sitting down over there."

"Anyway, that isn't nothing new. A lot of that does go on not only with those people, but some of our people do that too."

"I never hear nothing like that Miss Una," said Nellie.

"It real hush-hush, but does happen. Nobody don't talk too much about it. You remember Mamie Watkins from down in the village? You remember how Mr. Watkins used to beat Mamie? It was all because of that."

"But that was his wife Miss Una."

"But they had a daughter and when he was interfering with the daughter and Mamie say anything, it was licks galore."

"Do you mean Cora, the girl that was so foolishy- foolishy?"

"Yes, and they say that the first child she had was her father child."

"What a thing!" said Clytie shaking her head in disbelief and disgust.

"Let us talk about something else. That make me want to vomit," Nellie said. "I am thinking of moving from this house."

"Where you going?" asked Miss Una with big eyes.

"I moving into the house that Gus Ridley left me."

"Why so sudden Nellie?" asked the old woman.

"I was thinking about it and then after I went with Francois to look around, I decide I would like to move in. It is a real pretty house Miss Una. It got electricity, a lot of pictures on the walls like at Bottomsley, and a lot of china in the china cabinet. There is even a big chandelier like that one Miss Sarah got in the dining room. I will carry you all to see it."

"And what going to happen to the shop and my little house?" asked Miss Una.

"Don't worry Miss Una. I was thinking that if Clytie want to, she could come up here and work with you and Nora in the shop. That way everybody will have a chance to get some free time. Anyhow it is time you left Bottomsley kitchen Clytie."

"What about Miss Sarah?"

"She can look after herself."

"You tell Nora yet?" asked the old woman.

"Not yet, but she know I was thinking about it."

"Don't worry Ma. Nellie never let you down."

"I just don't want to sit around like an old shoe."

"Miss Una and Nora could carry on with the shop and if you decide to come back, that would be even better."

"When all this going to happen Nellie?"

"I ain't sure yet."

What used to be an area with three houses had now turned into a full fledged village. More and more people were leaving the plantation tenements with their families and settling in villages. There was now a shoemaker, who scoured the countryside for old car tyres which he made into shoes and sold to the families; the barber who sat under a mango tree with his stool, razor, calabash and bucket of water to attend to his clients; the hawker, fat and round sat with wide open legs in front of her tray filled with sugar cakes, nutties, comforts and packages of nuts waiting for eager buyers to taste her wares; there was also the maubywoman with a can full of that bitter-sweet drink, which she dispensed from a spigot at the front of the container.

These families all collected their water from the standpipe, and at night they burned their smut lamps in the street. They never seemed to use them anymore in their homes, since they were all using oil burning glass lamps with chimneys that read, Home Sweet Home.

On one visit to her home, Nellie asked Francois about making life better for the villagers who spent their money in her grocery store. She asked him about electricity and running water to ease their burdens. He promised he would look into it and after six months of struggles, anxiety and telephone calls, the underground pipes were laid and posts and overhead electric wires were installed.

The only thing left to do was to start the school for the village children. The village carpenter was now a well off man since he was called upon to furnish the school rooms with benches and tables. They were not the most comfortable looking pieces of furniture, but education was the thing which counted. Francois set out to inquire which text books the other schools were using and along with Nellie's financing, he and Clytie's son purchased the books and the school was ready to be opened when the new term began.

Nellie was very proud of her achievements and rightly so. It was named Miss Peterkin's Private school, but there was a hullabaloo coming from the colonial school board whether the teachers were qualified enough to teach. Again Francois came to the rescue helping her to find two qualified teachers. This did not bother the children one bit because they were free to play instead of sitting in a stuffy classroom. Two weeks behind schedule, the school was finally opened much to the annoyance of the school board.

She found herself depending more and more on Francois and he on her for different reasons. One could say their relationship was a little more than a friendly one, but still there was no intimacy between them.

* * *

# 51

She had made the move and was now living in the house which Gus Ridley had left her. Nellie was a contented and happy woman, although she still didn't know what to make of the relationship with Francois. Although happy, she still needed companionship which he sometimes provided.

"Peterkin," she said picking up the phone one day.

"I'm coming out to see you later," Francois said.

She didn't know what to make of the call, because he seemed quite serious. She waited patiently for him to arrive after he had closed his office for the day.

"Is something wrong?" she asked.

"I wish I didn't have to tell you this Nellie," he began.

"Then tell me what it is. If you getting married, I can handle it."

"It's nothing like that. I was contacted today by another solicitor who informed me that a client of his intends to contest Gus Ridley's will."

"What that mean?"

"It means that they will fight you for this house and the money."

"But Gus Ridley left it to me."

"Don't worry too much Nellie. I will fight for you."

"What can I do?"

"Nothing at the moment," he said. "Oh yes, there is something. Is there anyone who knew your mother and knew of her relationship with Gus Ridley?"

"Just Miss Ella and she is gone."

"What about Miss Una? Doesn't she know anything?"

"I think so but how can that help?"

"We need proof that he really was your father. Can I speak to Miss Una later?"

"If you want, we can go there now."

"I am extremely hungry," he said. "After I got the letter today, I began to do some research it, and forgot all about lunch."

"I'll fix a little something for you and then we can talk to Miss Una."

* * *

"I was not there when it happen, but I know for sure that Gus was Nellie father."

"How can you be so sure?" Francois asked.

"That man used to spend more time with Hilda than with his own wife. He used to sleep in Hilda little hut. That was something we didn't understand. He had a beautiful home somewhere else but prefer to sleep with Hilda in the tenement."

"If he was there so often, then why didn't he look after her and her daughter?"

"Francis, listen to what I have to say. Men are men, all due respect. When it sweet, they stick around, but when the water get too hot, they run. After Hilda was in the family way, he stop coming around so often, and when Nellie was born, he stop coming altogether."

"Are you saying that after Nellie was born, Hilda never saw him again?"

"Yes, that is what I saying. The only time she see him was when he pass by in his car and she was working in the fields. That was when she would see him."

"So he never supported Nellie at all?"

"Francis, if Miss Ella was not around, Hilda and Nellie wouldn't have nothing to eat. Ella used to bring whatever they had in the big house to feed them. After Nellie was a couple months old, Hilda went back to weeding the hedgerows, so they wouldn't starve. But why you asking me all these questions?"

"Someone is trying to take the house away from Nellie."

"That house belongs to Nellie. She deserve it after that no good man didn't raise a finger to help her when she was growing up."

"Would you be willing to go to court to testify on Nellie's behalf?"

"I would do anything for Nellie. She is one o' God angels. Francis, I don't know if you know this, but Nellie bring me up here so I wouldn't have to work in the sun at my age, so there ain't a thing I wouldn't do for that child."

"I will talk to you before we go to the court. Thanks Miss Una."

"Alright Francis, I waiting here for you."

Nellie knew it was too good to be true. A couple of weeks before he died, Gus turned up on her doorstep and then left her everything he owned. Now someone was going to take it all away from her.

One day she was out looking for Hurley when a car stopped outside the gate, then the driver reversed to get a better view of the house. Inside the car, sat a man and a woman.

"Nice house!" said the man.

"Thanks," she replied.

"Who owns it?" he asked.

"I do."

"I could give you a handsome price for it," he said.

"It ain't for sale."

"Come, come. What is a woman like you going to do with a house like this?"

"The same thing you would do if I sell it to you. Live in it."

She had never before seen the couple before and had no idea who they were. If they had wanted to buy the house after Gus had died, why did they wait for such a long time?

She related the story to Francois and he also could not understand why they had chosen that particular time to show interest in the home.

"I have to prepare Miss Una for the court case," he said. "It's in a week from today."

"What she got to say?"

"The same things she told me."

Miss Una was dressed in her Sunday best and sat with Nora behind Nellie in the court house. Looking around, Nellie saw that the same couple who wanted to buy her home was also sitting across from her, and she passed the information on to Francois, who turned to look at them. He also did not know them. He had done his homework and since no one had made any claims on Gus Ridley's property, naturally it was all Nellie's. He had been Gus' solicitor for about six years and was in possession of the copy of his will.

The court was in session and Miss Una was called upon to testify.

"Take your time and don't be afraid," Francois whispered to her.

"I ain't frightened Francis. Don't worry about me.

"State your name please," the opposing solicitor said.

"Una Prescott."

"And do you know why you are here?" he asked.

"Yes I do," she said emphatically.

"Do you know the defendant?"

"The who?" asked Miss Una.

"Do you know this woman?" he asked pointing at Nellie.

"Of course I know Nellie. I know Nellie since the day she born."

"Just answer yes or no Miss Prescott."

"You ask me if I know Nellie and I am telling you I know her since day one."

Francois did not intervene. She was handling herself well.

"Did you know a man called Gus Ridley?" he asked.

"Yes."

"And how did you come to know Mr. Ridley?"

"That man more or less used to live in the tenement where I used to live at the Fielding plantation."

"What do you mean more or less?"

"Well he had a girlfriend over there and he used to spend more time there than with his wife."

The onlookers in the court broke into sniggers. The old lady was giving them more entertainment than they had had in a long time.

"Did you know the girl friend?"

"Yes, I know the girlfriend."

"And?"

"And what? You ask me if I know the girlfriend and I say yes, I used to know her."

Roars of laughter now came from the back of the courtroom, prompting the judge to threaten to clear the court if there was such another outburst.

"I want to know if you knew her name."

"Yes."

"Will you tell the court what her name was?"

"Hilda."

"Did she have a last name?"

"Yes."

Again there was laughter. Even the judge too was smiling.

"What was it Miss Prescott?"

"Peterkin."

"Was she related to the def.... this woman sitting here?"

"Yes."

There was muted laughter from the onlookers.

"Please tell the court the relationship between the woman sitting here and Hilda Peterkin."

"They didn't have no relationship. They did family. Nellie was Hilda daughter and Hilda was Nellie mother."

Una Prescott had brought the court to its knees. The judge banged his gavel and ordered a recess.

"I doing alright Francis?"

"You couldn't be better," he replied.

Nellie was anxious but she knew Miss Una was doing her best to help her.

"All rise," said the court clerk, and Miss Una once again took the witness stand.

"State your name," said the opposing attorney.

"You sure you know what you doing?" she asked. "I tell you about half hour ago my name is Una Prescott."

There was more laughter from the crowd and gavel pounding by the judge.

"Miss Prescott," said the judge. "Just answer the questions."

"Yes sir."

"And now that we have established that you are Una Prescott, I want to ask you something. Was Gus Ridley Nellie Peterkin's father?"

"I wasn't in there with the two o' them, but I know he was Nellie father."

"How can you be so sure Miss Prescott?"

"My name is Una. That would do. As I was saying, I was not there when it happen, but Hilda wasn't sleeping with nobody except Gus. Look at Nellie. Who else you think could be her father?"

"Well was he a good father?"

"You should never speak bad about the dead, but he was a good for nothing brute who left Hilda and that poor child to suffer. Not even a grain of salt he offer that child you see sitting there, but Nellie got a good heart and the Lord does smile down on her every day."

The onlookers were now quiet as Miss Una poured her heart out.

"My good friend Ella," she said making a sign of the cross, "save Nellie and Hilda from destitution and starvation. When Nellie wasn't but eleven years old, she had to go to work to help the family and end up in Bottomsley kitchen cleaning and cooking. She was only a young girl, but today she make something of herself. Now that man Gus Ridley walk into Nellie shop a couple days before he pass way. He did want to see what Nellie look like. He say to Nellie that day that he was her father. I hear that with these two ears. I'm a little blind, but the ears still working real good. Nellie deserve that house. After all the struggles she and Hilda went through, I say shame on whoever want to teef (steal) that house from Nellie."

"Now sir," she said turning to the judge. "I can't read or write, but I got a good memory and I know that that man who walk into the shop was the same man who used to sleep with Hilda. We used to call him Gussy. He used to drive all the way from the St. Lucy plantation just to be with Hilda. Now tell me, she ain't deserve that house?"

There was silence in the court and the solicitor said he had no more questions and neither did Francois; but Francois addressed the court and showed as evidence the documents which he had received from Gus Ridley which made his daughter Nellie Peterkin his sole heir.

It was now a matter of waiting for the judge's decision.

* * *

# 52

It was October second and Nellie's fiftieth birthday but she was in no mood for celebrating. She decided to spend the day quietly doing things around the house. There was no news from the judge and she was also disappointed since she hadn't heard anything from Francois and she really believed he would have remembered her birthday.

"Remember what Ella used to say," said Miss Una. "Don't hang your hat too high, you will only get disappointed."

There was too much going on in her life and she wanted to lash out at Miss Una, but she kept her cool out of respect for the older woman. She knew Miss Una was probably right and perhaps Francois had no such feelings for her. After all, he was an accomplished solicitor, and she an uneducated black kitchen hand who in spite of her accomplishments, was still a black woman.

She got into the four poster mahogany bed and thought of the times when she wished she could have had such a life. Here she was living that life and still not happy.

*"If only JB was still alive," she thought. "He would never forget my birthday."*

She remembered the difficult times she had had; of the long days spent in the Bottomsley kitchen doing chores; of her dark steamy hut and then there was her daughter Emily. This brought her to tears. She had everything in the world that she needed but she could not claim her daughter as her own. She wondered if she should answer the telephone. She was wrapped up pretty cosily in her bed, because it was cool on the rock at that time of the year. She picked up the heavy black receiver and Francois' voice caused her heartbeat to quicken. He was coming over to see her and would be there within an hour. She must look pretty. After all it was her birthday and Francois might be coming with a gift. She fussed and primped, looking in the mirror at each turn. Finally she liked what she saw.

*"Nellie Peterkin, tonight is your night," she thought.*

Francois Bertrand did arrive within the hour, but was empty-handed.

"Is that a new dress Nellie? It looks lovely on you."

Thanks," she replied trying not to show her disappointment. "I buy it for my birthday."

"Is today your birthday?" he asked pretending he was surprised.

*"How could he forget?" she thought.*

"I'll be back in a minute," he said going out the door.

He returned with an envelope which he handed to her.

"Open it Nellie."

She did as he instructed and looked at the contents.

"I don't understand," she said.

"You said one day you would like to travel and so I decided we should go together."

"Where we going?" she asked.

"To France. I told you lots about France. Those are our airline tickets. See here where it says Paris?"

"We are going to Paris? You mean where they drink a lot of wine and only talk about love?"

"That's the same Paris Nellie. So are you going with me?"

"I'm so surprised that I don't know what to say."

"All you've got to say is yes."

"Yes. You think I will like it in France?"

"Of course you will. You will like them and they will love you."

"You think so?" she asked with doubt etched across her brow.

"Not only do I think so, but I also know so. I have another surprise for you Nellie, so close your eyes."

She closed her eyes.

"Open your eyes now."

She opened them but there was nothing.

"I don't understand," she said. "I don't see nothing."

"What about this beautiful house? The judge has awarded the house to you."

She couldn't contain her happiness and rushed over to him, threw her arms around his neck and hugged him.

"You do so much for me," she said.

"Don't forget how much Miss Una also did," he said smiling. "Nellie Peterkin, I knew you were special from the first day I met you in my office. You are a very strong-willed woman and a woman I admire greatly."

"Do you mean all those things you are saying?"

"Of course I do."

"But I don't have any nice clothes for Paris. I will have to get Harriett to make some for me."

"You don't need any more clothes," he said.

"Why not?" she asked.

"Because Paris is the city of fashion and you can buy some new clothes when we're there. You can even have your hair cut in the latest style."

"Francois, you trying to tell me that in that beautiful city, they got people who know what to with my hair?"

"You're in for the surprise of your life Nellie."

"I have to start getting ready. When we leaving?"

"In a month or so," he replied. "Do you have a passport?"

"No, I don't have no passport."

"You must have a birth certificate. Look for it and we are going to have some photos taken."

"I know where my birth certificate is, but why do you want photos?"

"In order to get the passport, you will need a couple photos. There will be a photo of you in the front of the passport. On Monday morning we'll go the Passport office together."

No sooner had Francois left, than Nellie started looking through her wardrobe. She examined her shoes and decided some of them needed fixing. So bright and early on Saturday morning, she decided to walk the three miles from her house down to the village where she once lived. Halfway there she saw a black car and its driver surrounded by many of the villagers. She had no idea what was going on, but as she got closer, she saw that the car was filled with bolts of cloth and the driver, once he had measured the cloth, wrote the information in a book. She noticed that he did this every time he cut a length of cloth for each villager. The material was very pretty and she thought she could put her sewing skills back to work, especially since she thought she needed some more dresses to take to Paris. Not only did she want buy a couple lengths for herself, but also for Nora, Clytie and Miss Una. When she looked into her purse, there wasn't enough money there.

"You don't have to pay me now," said the man. "I will come by every Saturday morning and you can pay me some of the money if you have it."

He then wrote her name in the book and the amount of money which she owed him. She liked the idea of the man selling his cloth from the car, because that would save her and the poor villagers a trip to Bridgetown.

"I never see you about here before," she said to the man.

"I'm from Trinidad, although I'm really a Syrian."

"A what?" asked Nellie.

"Syrian! All my relatives come from Syria. That is in the Middle East."

"Well, I don't know what you talking about, but I like the cloth. If you can't find me, go to the shop down the road and Miss Una will pay you. You say you coming by every Saturday morning?"

"Yes."

"Stop by the shop with my name on it. Nellie's Bar and Grocery."

"So you are Nellie. I'm Mr. Patel."

Nellie bade the man goodbye and continued on her way. She finally reached the shoemaker's shop with all of her parcels under both arms.

"What you so busy doing?" she asked the little boy in front of the shoemaker's shop.

"I am putting wheels on my scooter Miss Nellie," he said carrying on with what he was doing.

"Where your father?" she asked.

"Inside the shop," was his reply.

"You studying good at school?" she asked him as she headed for the open door.

"Yes Miss Nellie."

"Morning Miss Nellie," said the shoemaker jumping up to greet her. "What bring you here so early this Saturday morning?"

"I got some shoes that need fixing."

"Sit down Miss Nellie," he said dusting off a bench which read, Product of Halifax, Nova Scotia.

The resourcefulness of the villagers was amazing. His bench was made from the wooden crates in which salted cod was transported to the island. He examined each shoe and explained to her what he would do. She was dying to let it out. She was going to Paris and she knew he would be fascinated, since he could not even afford a trip to the downtown area, furthermore to Paris.

"Fix them properly. I taking them to Paris with me."

"You going to Paris Miss Nellie?"

"Yes. I going on a little vacation."

"That ain't no little vacation Miss Nellie. That place is overseas and far away. You think you going to like it there?"

"I know I will like it. When I come back, I will tell you everything about it."

In no time word had spread throughout the village that Miss Nellie was going to Paris on vacation.

"Morning Miss Una," she said to the old lady.

"Morning Nellie," she answered in a gruff manner.

"You don't feel well this morning Miss Una?"

"We alright," said Nora. "It is just that we always the last to hear anything."

"What you talking about girl?" asked her sister.

"A little birdie just tell us that you going to Paris and we don't know a thing about it."

"I only mention it to Blackie the shoemaker because I take some shoes for him to repair."

"You know how they are around here. You say something and by the time you turn your back, the whole village know. News don't lack a carrier. Anyhow I got some bad news Nellie."

"What happen now?" she asked expecting the worst.

"That son of mine tell me he want to go away."

"What do you mean, go away? Where he going?"

"Some white man was in the village yesterday and he say he looking for young people to work in England."

To Nellie, the word England was not one she liked. When she thought of it, it was usually with a shivering cold thought. She pictured dark days, cold days and most of all the country which took Emily so far away from her.

"What he going to do once he get there?"

"They looking for people to work on the buses and some kind o' trains."

"When he leaving?"

"I don't know. He tell me the man say he is going to send him a letter."

"I am going to ask Francois what that is about. He used to live in England."

"So you going to Paris with him?" asked Miss Una.

"He invite me to go. It was a present for my birthday."

"I hope you coming back before Christmas Nellie."

"We only going for a month. Francois got his office to run. But back to the man who sending these people to England. Who else going?"

"Girl if you did here to see how they line up to see him, you would think he was giving away money. So many o' the young people turn up at the school to hear what he was going to say that they did not have room left inside. He didn't take everybody because some o' them didn't pass the test."

"They had to take a test too?" asked Nellie. "And what about the women? He carrying them too?"

"Yes. He say they want nurses, but Harriett say isn't going nowhere. She say that England too cold."

"She right," said Miss Una. "Those places too far. She can't go away and leave Nora all by herself."

"What you talking about Miss Una? She still got Percy there. Don't you Nora?"

"Yes, but it really isn't the same. She is the only child that I am going to have here."

"Toby got to make a life for himself Nora. What he going to do around here? Work on the plantations like all the rest until he old and grey?"

"I know it better for him, but I am going to miss my boy."

"You just have to think about all those pounds he is going to send home to help you."

"Pounds o' what?" asked Miss Una.

"That is the money they use in England Miss Una. We have dollars and they got pounds. I think it must be ten dollars to a pound."

"You making sport Nels? One pound is ten dollars?" asked Nora.

"That is what Francois tell me."

"Let him go Nora," said Miss Una laughing. "Think about all that money he will send home to you. We used to have pounds and shillings here at one time, didn't we?" asked Miss Una.

"But now we have our own money," said Nellie.

"Listen everybody! I forget to tell you that Francois say I win the case and the house is mine."

"Amen," shouted Miss Una.

Nellie hugged the old woman.

"Tell me something Nellie. Who is these people who come to teef your birthright?"

"Francois say they is really Gus family, but they didn't have no contact with him since he did living here on the Rock. It seem as if Gus wife pass way many years ago and when they find out she was gone and then he was gone too, they thought they should get Gus property."

"These people really got gumption," said Miss Una. "Them didn't know if he was eating or starving, but as soon as they find out he had something, they come to collect. And that man who did asking me all those question, and pushing out his long neck like this," said Miss Una imitation the actions the opposing solictor had made. "I would swear somebody did give him a dose of Kruschan salts."

"What is Kruschan salts?" asked Nora.

"We both born on this Rock and if you never hear about Kruschan salts, then I ain't got no explaining to do."

"Thanks Miss Una. You really help me to get what was really mine."

"That was something though. He did trying to trip up a poor old woman. My grandmother always used to say, you should never show your hand. He look at me an old woman and think he could mess me up. I was on this earth too long to have these people making a laughing stock of me. I was too much for him, wasn't I Nellie?"

"I don't think they had a good laugh since then. Anybody hear anything from Clytie? She real scarce these days."

Miss Una and Nora started to laugh.

"Why everybody laughing?" asked Nellie.

"You don't know yet?" asked Miss Una smiling. "Clytie find herself a young man. She courting, if you please."

"Who she courting or who courting her?" asked Nellie putting the receiver back in its place.

"There got a new postman who taking the letters to the plantation and he take a liking to Clytie."

"And why I am the last to know?" asked Nellie.

"Same reason she don't know you going to Paris," said Miss Una.

"That was what I want to tell her today."

"Well you better call quick before she leave Bottomsley for the evening."

The voice on the other end was that of Sarah Bottomsley. Nellie identified herself and asked if it were possible to speak to Clytie. Sarah Bottomsley was happy to hear Nellie's voice and chatted with her like an old friend. She seemed to be very well-informed, because she knew that Nellie had inherited Gus Ridley's estate and had moved into his home. When Nellie asked about Emily, she said that her daughter was on the verge of getting married and would be returning home to The Rock just in time for Christmas. Nellie couldn't contain her excitement and told Sarah Bottomsley she hoped she would have a chance to see her when she came home for her vacation.

"It won't be a vacation Nellie. My daughter and her husband are coming home to stay."

"That is real good news Miss Sarah. That is good news."

"That's how I feel about it Nellie. You have been gone for such a long time and I still miss you."

"I miss you too Miss Sarah," she replied.

"You know that anytime you want to come back to Bottomsley, there is a place here for you. But I know you will never return Nellie because your life is just as good or better than mine."

"Thank you for understanding Miss Sarah."

"You know what I miss most, especially with Christmas coming Nellie? Those wonderful Christmas cakes you and Ella used to bake. Clytie's are not as good. Do you think you can come by and make some for me for Christmas?"

"Sorry Miss Sarah, but I just don't have the time. I am going to Paris and I ain't coming back until just before the Christmas season start."

"You're going to Paris Nellie? What, what for?" she stammered.

"It is a birthday present Miss Sarah."

"You must introduce me to him Nellie. You are a lucky woman."

Nellie didn't give Sarah Bottomsley an answer and never did get the chance to speak to Clytie.

"What she had to say when you tell her you are going to Paris?" Nora asked.

"She say she want to meet him."

"She know who you are going with?"

"I don't think so."

"She must be real jealous," said Nora.

"Ella," said Miss Una looking up to heaven. "You see our little Nellie. She going to Paris. The Lord really does look after the children and the unlucky ones."

* * *

## 53

Nellie returned from the city where she had met Francois and where she had applied for her passport. The clerk had told Francois she would receive her passport within two weeks. She pretended Nellie wasn't there and communicated only with Francois, but Nellie was beyond caring. She needed that passport in order to go to Paris, so absolutely nothing was going to dampen her enthusiasm.

As she opened the garden gate a car with a couple stopped in front of the driveway. The couple did not greet her. They just stared at the house.

"Is the Mistress or Master in?" the woman asked.

"I am the Mistress," she said.

The two grumbled something to each other and then drove away. They had broken her trend of thought because in her head, she was already in Paris.

Her wardrobe lay scattered all over the bed, and she was trying to make a decision when the phone started to ring.

"Just when I trying to concentrate," she muttered.

"Nels," said Clytie. "I hear you going off to Paris."

"And I hear you courting strong," she replied.

"My mother and your sister talk too much."

"Why you didn't tell me? Is he a good man Clytie?"

"I don't want nothing more to do with him Nels. He expect me to leave Bottomsley plantation after working the whole day and then go to the house to cook for him. You ever hear such a thing Nellie?"

"But we used to do that all the time Clytie."

"It isn't the same now Nels. Times changing Nels. I want somebody to carry me to Paris too. I don't want nobody who expect me to stand up over a wood fire when I get home from working so hard."

"That is true Clytie, but I don't think we men see it that way."

"Well I will be Clytie the old maid until I die because I don't intend working like a slave no more, especially for a good for nothing man."

"That mean you done with him Clytie?"

"To tell you the truth Nellie, it ain't only that. All he want from me is to jump in the bed and I too old for that. He seem to think that we on the Garrison Savannah and he is a jockey. All night long that old brute does confuse me. And he getting vex and want to hit me if I don't want to give him a little piece. A little bit now and again is alright, but he think that all I good for is cooking and jumping in the bed. You and Francois do anything yet?"

"I don't like talking about my bedroom business, but I could tell you Clytie. We ain't do nothing yet."

"See what I mean Nels? He treating you with respect. You can think of one of we men who would take you to Paris without wanting something for it?"

"You can't compare them Clytie."

"Why not Nels? A man is a man."

"Well I can't blame you Clytie. Leave him where he is. No man ain't got no right to lay his hands on a woman. Take your time. Somebody else will come along."

"I want somebody to respect me and show me love. Just like you and Francois. That man always behaving like a stray dog in heat."

"You right Clytie. Like I just say, take your time. Something good will happen to you."

"That is what Ma always saying, but not a thing ain't happening. Whenever I find somebody, he looking for a slave. Anyway Nels, I was calling to tell you that Emily going to Africa on her honeymoon."

"I don't understand why she want to go to Africa. People go to Paris for their honeymoon. I wish she would go to Paris. Clytie, think how good it would be if we meet up on the street in Paris."

"I hear Africa is real pretty Nels."

"Where you hear that? I don't believe a word."

"Wait until Miss Emily come home and then she can tell all of us what it really like in Africa."

***

The valise was packed and placed at the door for Francois' arrival. The flight was leaving at eleven and seven o' clock found her pacing back and forth.

"How I look?" she asked Nora for the umpteenth time.

"How many times you going to ask me that? I tell you already that you look like a Frenchwoman."

"Don't make fun of me Nora. You sure I look good enough to go to Paris?"

"You got those papers?" Nora asked.

"Yes I have them here in my bag with my powder."

"How much money you carrying with you?" asked Nora.

"I don't know. Francois say he would get it for me and I give him five hundred dollars."

"That is a lot o' money, but you have to pay to sleep somewhere and don't forget you have to bring some of that sweet smelling perfume for me."

Francois finally arrived and complimented her on her attire. He too looked extremely dashing with the grey around his temples and his well-tanned skin. He wore a light grey suit and carried a coat over his arm.

"Take good care of my home," Nellie said to her sister. "We will see you when we get back."

"Goodbye Nora," said Francois. "I'll take good care of your sister," he told her as he noticed her tears.

They climbed into the car and Clarence sped off to take them to the airbase for their flight to Paris with a stop in London. Francois handed her a coat which he said she would need once she was there.

"You mean it going to be so cold?" she asked.

"It will be cold, but not too bad at this time of the year."

"It don't matter. If it is everything you say it is, I will not let a little cold spoil my vacation."

"That's the right attitude Nellie. At last you will be able to say you know what winter is like."

"After lunch, Nellie who was tired from waking up so early fell asleep somewhere over the Atlantic ocean. She wanted to be awake for the complete journey, but her body was not co-operating. Soon Francois was also asleep and snoring lightly. The air hostess in her tight skirt and stiletto heels patrolled the cabin regularly and each time she addressed Nellie as Madame, she became extremely excited.

"Everyone says Madame in Paris," Francois said.

"Then I will really like it there."

She rested her head on her pillow and was once again fast asleep.

The trip to Paris was a turning point in Nellie's life. She learnt what grace and gentility meant. After being a second class citizen and being treated like a child for so many years, she now realised what it meant to be equal. She loved being called Madame and she loved the way Francois behaved when they were together. When she went shopping, he would sit and wait until she came from the fitting room and give his oui or non, depending on how he felt about her choice. The store clerks would open the doors for them and say their 'Au Voir', which Nellie learnt to say as her confidence grew along with her self esteem.

He introduced her to wine drinking. She thought she would love red wine since she was used to the sweet cheap port wine they would drink on the Rock at Christmastime, but she was disappointed. She found it much too sour, so she drank white instead and pretended to like it, just to please him.

In Paris there were many women who looked like her and were all on the arms of Frenchmen. There were also Black people whom Francois referred to as Artists who had left America because of persecution and settled there. It was a city of glamour. The women were dressed in beautiful hats, gloves and long coats to ward off the cold. Some of them wore berets and they spoke as if they were afraid to open their mouths too wide. She watched as Francois conversed with them, and it seemed as if he too suddenly became afraid to open his mouth too widely. It was a mind blowing experience for her.

"I think that hairstyle would really suit you," he said as he noticed the woman seated at the next table.

"I am not so sure about that."

"I think it would make you even more beautiful," he said. "Let's find out where she had it done."

Nellie was much too shy so he approached the woman who spoke French, but also perfect English. She invited Nellie over to her table and the three had a wonderful time together especially since she kept referring to Nellie as Francois' wife.

Two days later, a stunning Nellie Peterkin walked out of the beauty salon. Even Francois couldn't get over the change in her appearance.

He wanted to make a special evening in remembrance of her long gone birthday and decided to take her to a show and then dinner.

"Is it too cold for you?" he asked as they walked along the Champs D'Elysee.

"You know something Francois? I could really live here. The people so nice and I don't have to worry if anybody staring at me because I am with you."

"I guess you had to see it for yourself to believe it," he replied. "The show starts at seven, so we should be ready to go by six fifteen and watch out for that hair."

She smiled at him as he opened his door and entered the adjoining room. Heading for the window, she looked out onto the main street and gazed at the well-lit, famous tower which they had climbed only the day before.

"JB, Nellie here in Paris. Can you believe it?"

This was the first time since she was there that she had thought of John Bottomsley. However, there was no time to waste because she had only thirty minutes before Francois would come knocking on her door.

* * *

## 54

Arm in arm, they climbed the steps to the theatre and walked into the foyer which was filled with patrons waiting in the queue to enter while others were milling around enjoying glasses of champagne. Feeling a little self-conscious, Nellie started to fidget, and Francois realising this held her arm even tighter. Men were openly smiling with her and the women were acknowledging her presence.

"No need to worry," he whispered. "They all think you are someone famous," he said reassuring her.

"There ain't any famous people who look like me."

"Then let's pretend there are, because they are all staring at you."

The lights were dimmed and the show began. She felt as though she was in some kind of a dream. Never in her wildest dreams did she think that one day Nellie Peterkin would be sitting beside a handsome man enjoying a show in the city of lights and love. The sparkle and the glitter made her feel dizzy. She couldn't understand how the showgirls did everything in unison without making mistakes. She pictured herself sprawled across the stage and embarrassed because she had made a mistake and messed up the production. A few minutes later she was applauding and shouting when the other patrons showed their pleasure. Francois looked at her out the corner of his eye. So engrossed was she in the show that she never noticed how much he was admiring her.

"Did you really enjoy it?" he asked over the dinner.

"I never see anything like that before. Only when there was a play in the church for Christmas, but it wasn't anything like that."

"You seem to feel so much better about yourself now that you're here," he said.

"I feel good, real good. You wouldn't understand. All my life I dream about being somebody and you make me feel real special. You make me feel important. The problem is that when people keep putting you down for so long, you don't have no self worth. I remember when I used to tell Miss Ella that I want a better life, she used to say I was foolish. She didn't mean anything by it because that was all she was accustomed to. She thought we were good only for cooking and scrubbing and washing pots and running behind Miss Sarah."

He did not interrupt her. He allowed her to free her soul of the heavy baggage she had been carrying for such a long time.

"I remember when I ask if Nora could work in the kitchen but she couldn't do it because she was too black to serve Miss Sarah."

"Nellie, will you marry me?" he asked.

"What you just say?"

"I asked if you would marry me."

"You only had one glass of wine. You know what you saying?"

"Wine never affects my thinking Nellie. Will you consider marrying me?" he asked again.

"I feel real confuse," she said.

"Alright, if you won't marry me, then I'll ask the young lady sitting at the next table."

"You laughing at me. If you mean it, I would like to marry you."

"Does that mean yes Nellie?"

"What will I tell Nora and Miss Una?"

"Tell them I asked you to marry me and you accepted."

He reached across the table and kissed her on the cheek just as the waiter brought them a bottle of Champagne."

"How he know we want Champagne?"

"We are in the city of love. They know when the time is right to bring Champagne."

"You laughing at me again," she said reaching out to touch him.

"When we leave Paris, we will be leaving as husband and wife Nellie."

"I can't believe this is happening to me. Me Nellie Peterkin!" she said as tears streamed down her face.

He wiped them away with his thumb and forefinger.

"In Paris, a lady is expected to smile when a gentleman asks her to marry him."

"These are tears of joy Francois! Tears of joy because I real happy."

She didn't know if she needed them, but she had brought every single personal document with her. She could produce her birth certificate, baptismal, passport and even the copy of the liquor licence she kept for the shop. Francois could only smile. She had had a difficult life and it was his goal to make her happy and keep it that way because he knew her trials might not be quite over. He had fallen in love with the ex-kitchen maid Nellie Peterkin.

Back in the hotel, he was opening his room door when she stopped him.

"You just ask me to marry you and you going to leave me alone with all these thoughts running around in my head?"

"Are you inviting me to your room Nellie?" he asked.

"Come in and we can talk again like that that night when we were in Gus Ridley house in that horrible storm."

"What should we talk about?"

"Things like where we are going to live, what my new name will be and when we will come to Paris again."

"You make me laugh Nellie. Just like my mother did."

"Your mother used to make you laugh a lot?"

"She was funny Nellie. Just like you."

How she longed to be touched by him. She remembered how she felt when JB would hold her and make love to her after she had left Bottomsley. Then he had become gentle and caring and she knew that Francois would be just the same.

"You want to spend the night here?"

"Maybe it's not such a good idea," he said.

"You mean we should only stay together after we are married?"

"Don't you find that a good idea?"

"We are not children Francois, but it is up to you."

"If you would like me to stay, then I'll stay."

She was elated, but didn't dare show it. She had known him for more than eight years and yet they had not consummated their relationship. She was afraid that he might find her too cheap if she gave into him too easily.

They talked and talked and then both lay across her bed. He hugged her and kissed her. He was taking his time and she loved it. She loved the way he touched her, the way he whispered in her ear and most of all, his gentleness. It seemed like an eternity since they had started making love to each other, and now their bodies united with both passion and fervour. It had been such a long time since she had been with a man that she was afraid. What could she expect from Francois? Every touch brought her dream of being with him closer to reality. She knew he cared about her.

What she had experienced with JB could not be compared with the wholesome feeling she was now experiencing. There was no hurrying nor was there any roughness. She knew what it felt liked to be loved and to have someone make love to her.

Heartbeats quickened, pulses raced and breathing grew louder and shallower. Then like an exploding volcano, there was eruption after eruption until they both were completely exhausted. Neither one spoke. Nothing seemed to matter anymore. They just lay in each other's arms and snuggled until they both fell asleep.

Nellie opened her eyes and saw Francois beside her. She was on the verge of panic when she remembered what had happened the night before. He had asked her to marry him. It was definitely not a dream. She was in Paris in a hotel room with Francois Bertrand beside her and he had indeed asked her to marry him.

The sunlight was streaming through the sheer curtains as they had failed to darken the room the night before. She was naked. Last night was one thing, but today this was reality and she must cover herself before he awoke. Moving his hand from her shoulder caused him to stir. She waited and slowly began to slip away from the bed when his hand quickly tightened around her arm.

"Where do you think you're going?" he asked.

"I coming back," she said.

"Are you trying to get away from me?"

"How could I do that after you ask me to marry you?"

"Don't stay away too long. I'll miss you."

Nellie stared at the half-naked woman in the mirror. She reached up to touch her hair which was no longer nicely coiffed but a mess. She had no idea what to do with it since she had always worn corn rows or a beret. That was the answer. She would wear a beret until she could return to the beauty shop. Lots of people in Paris wore them and looked quite fashionable in them. Turning on the water, she stepped into the shower to wash away the sweat from the previous night, when Francois stepped in with her. He held her and closed his eyes allowing the water to beat down on them. Then they slowly washed each other and not wanting to miss a moment in the city of love, got dressed and were on the way with every document Nellie had brought along with her.

A quick continental breakfast followed and they entered an official looking building where Francois spoke to the clerk in French. As Francois passed the documents to him, the clerk looked over at Nellie and smiled. Congratulations and an approval on their impending marriage.

There was one week left of the holiday. She was sad because it had flown by too quickly, but she was now Mrs. Bertrand. What would they all say when she returned as his wife. She knew her friends would be happy for her, but she would no longer be in Paris, but on The Rock where she was considered nobody. Would the marriage raise her status in the eyes of those who despised her? She was not considered as an equal among the whites and among her own who had achieved something, she was still the kitchen hand who would never be good enough.

Francois no longer occupied his room. He wanted to be close to Nellie and she to him, so together they packed their valises because early the next morning, they would be boarding a plane for London. There they would spend one night there before returning home the following day.

"Francois," she suddenly said.

"Yes Nellie," he said as he was about to close his valise.

"Stop for just a minute," she said.

"This sounds serious."

"Yes, it serious," she said. "I want you to help me to speak better and to write better. I didn't go to school and I don't want you to be ashamed of me. So I want you to show me how to do it better, so I can be proud and make you a proud husband."

"I could never be ashamed of you Nellie. I would be more than happy to help you improve your English. I'm so very proud of you Nellie. You've made this decision all alone without my trying to influence you."

"So when we going to start?" she asked looking up at him.

"As soon as you think you are ready."

"Can I learn French too? I like these French people. They make me feel good about myself."

"Didn't I tell you they would love you Nellie? And they did, so let's go to sleep. We must be up bright and early tomorrow morning."

This was truly the turning point in Nellie Peterkin's life. She had no desire to return to The Rock but knew she had to be realistic. She would have no trouble living in Paris because Francois was a French citizen, but there was that life she left behind and must return to. She wondered about Emily. Suppose they ran into each other in London? That was not at all possible since they were staying close to the airport and a trip into the city would just be too exhausting as a sixteen hour flight lay ahead of them the following day.

* * *

Emily's thoughts turned to her father, John Bottomsley. She was now twenty five years old and had just married Alastair Chambers, a fellow solicitor. After a brief ceremony, they flew to Southwest Africa, where they would spend their honeymoon. It was not Alastair's first choice of a honeymoon location, but he gave into his wife and settled for a cultural experience. Emily had studied African Literature before she had decided to enter into law. Now she yearned to see parts of Africa before her return to the Rock. No one understood why Africa was so entrenched in her being and neither did she. She concluded that it was because she had read so much about it and was intrigued by everything she had read.

"So much of this country reminds me of my home, that little paradise in the Caribbean," she said to her husband. "I see Clytie, Miss Ella and Miss Una and so many of the faces that worked on Bottomsley plantation."

There were indeed many Clyties in their long white dresses with their aprons and head ties. The same postures, the same beautiful faces and their lot seemed no different from that of the people who attended the whims of her mother and endured the hostilities of her stepfather. So far apart and their lives were so intricately intertwined. Those women who loved and her and had treated her as their own, could have been from that part of the world. She also found out that their staple food was very similar to that which Clytie had forced her to eat so many years ago. They called it Mealy Pap.

She would sometimes stop and stare and wonder if some of the people could be Clytie's long lost relatives. Her husband Alastair Chambers found it difficult to understand why she found the people so fascinating, but one must understand that he had for the first time in his life encountered people of African descent.

She wanted to see the different tribes she had read about; the Herero, the Nama and the Himba. They tickled her thoughts and she was not at all disappointed when she finally met them face to face. Amazingly so did Alastair. She thought so often of her father and wondered if he would have enjoyed the journey as much as she did. Perhaps he would have. In her childhood dreams, she had seen her father escorting her down the aisle, but it was not to be. Instead she and Alastair settled for a civil ceremony with her grandma and grandpa in attendance.

In three months she and her husband will travel to the Rock to see what has happened to Bottomsley plantation.

*Mama is not at all happy with me since I married Alastair before she had a chance to meet him, and I'm afraid she may not like him. He is so much like Papa.*

* * *

# 55

Sarah Bottomsley grew more and excited as she read her daughter's letter. She was coming home in just under six weeks and was expecting a baby. She needed something to hold onto. Something to make life worth living and this was more than she had expected. She called John and Millie Bottomsley to give them the good news.

"Can you believe it? I'm going to be a grandmother."

Ursy pressed her ear to the kitchen door and she too was excited, but unfortunately couldn't let on that she had overheard the conversation. Things had improved between her and Sarah Bottomsley. Clytie was spending the time in the north with her mother while Nellie was on her trip to Paris.

"You seem real happy Miss Bottomsley," Ursy said to her.

"That's because my daughter is finally coming home and I'll soon be a grandmother. I'm so happy Ursy. If only John were alive to see our daughter," she said with resignation.

"That is real good news Miss Bottomsley. You want me to start preparing anything? Like getting the room ready or buying Miss Emily favourite food?"

"No Ursy. Clytie will be back soon and you can do it together. Clytie knows more about these things than I do. What would I do without her?"

"But Miss Bottomsley, Clytie's mother is getting old and she is hoping she could go and live with her."

"Did she say that to you?"

"No, but I think that Miss Una eyesight is getting real bad and she might need Cytie with her."

"I hope not. I know Emily is so looking forward to be back here and to have Clytie with us."

Ursy realised Sarah Bottomsley would never change. She was number one and it didn't matter at what cost. The first opportunity she got, Ursy called Clytie with the news.

"You mean my Emily is going to be a mother?" she asked.

"That is what Miss Bottomsley say. She is coming home in about six weeks and she is in the family way."

Clytie did not notice her mother sigh and make the sign of the cross. She listened carefully to the conversation and did not interfere.

"Ma, Emily going to have a baby," she said.

"Well she is married and when they get married, soon after that, they are in the family way."

"Wait until we tell Nellie about this," she continued.

"Ain't Nellie coming back today?" Miss Una asked.

"I think so, but I don't know the time," said Clytie. "Anyway, Clarence is going to the airbase to pick them up."

"I hope she had a real good time," said Miss Una as if something unforeseen would be awaiting her at home.

"Why you talking so strange Ma?" she asked.

"I am not talking strange. All I say is that I hope she had a real good time wherever she went."

"Paris Ma, Paris."

Clarence sped past the shop with the newly-weds in the car. Normally Nellie would have gone straight to see Miss Una, Clytie and Nora, but she was extremely tired. She had been used to long working days and knew what it was to be tired, but this was really different. She could hardly keep her eyes open and her body felt like it was not her own. She could hardly wait to tell her friends and family the good news, but it would have to wait.

"I feel real funny," she said to her husband.

"You're suffering from jetlag," he replied.

"You feel the same way?" she asked.

"Probably worse," he replied. "Let's get a shower and go to bed."

"But it is only half past six," she replied.

"It doesn't matter. I can't keep my eyes open. I need to sleep for a week," he said.

Francois and Nellie Bertrand settled into bed for their first night at home as man and wife. Before they could fall asleep, Hurley jumped onto the bed and purred his little heart out.

"You miss me Hurley?" she asked as Francois' breathing grew shallower. "You got a new Daddy," she said to the cat.

"Hurley?" called someone from outside. "Come Hurley."

It was Nora. She had brought some foodstuff for Nellie since there was none in the house. She was suddenly quiet perhaps because she had seen the valises at the door.

"Nellie?" she whispered. "You home?"

Her sister got out of bed and went to greet her.

"Why you didn't phone to say that you come back? When you get home Nellie? Look at your hair Nellie. You look so good."

"Shhhhh," said Nellie putting her finger to her lips. "We just get home."

"Who is we?" Nora asked.

"I got some good news to tell you Nora. Francois and me get married in Paris."

"You and Francois married?" a shocked Nora asked. "How that happen?"

"He ask me and I say yes. Pinch me Nora. I can't believe it myself. You ain't happy for me?"

"You know I real happy for you, but that come as a real big surprise."

"I was surprised too."

"You happy Nellie?" her sister asked. "Happy like when you and JB did together?"

"Happier than that Nora. I real happy," she said showing her sister the ring on her left finger. "In Paris, they wear the rings on the right hand, but I didn't want nobody here to think we wasn't really married."

"Did you tell Clytie?"

"We didn't have a chance to tell nobody because we was real tired. Francois say that is normal. He call it jetlag."

"I am going home and let you sleep then," said Nora.

"I think I get a second wind. Don't go yet. Tell me what was happening around here."

"Where is Francois?"

"As soon as his head hit the pillow, he was gone. He is real tired too. How is Miss Una?"

"She is still there. Can't see a thing but pretending she could see everything. Oh Lord Nellie, I forget to tell you. Emily coming home in about six weeks and she in the family way."

"My daughter going to have a baby?"

"Yes Nellie. You going to be a grandmother."

"How you find out?"

"Ursy overhear Miss Sarah telling somebody and she call to tell Clytie."

Tears of joy flowed down Nellie's cheeks.

"When we was in London, I look everywhere to see if I see Emily but that place is so big, that even if she was there, I would not see her."

"So tell me about Paris. It really pretty like everybody say?"

"Prettier Nora. And if you see the people who look just like you and me, it would do your heart good."

"You mean they got black people like me and you living in Paris Nellie?"

"A lot o' them and they look good. They wear real nice clothes and a lot o' them married to Frenchmen."

"What you telling me Nellie?"

"That is the truth as my name is Mrs. Bertrand."

The two sisters became just a little bit noisy causing Francois to stir. He reached out but Nellie wasn't there. Then he heard voices and knew it was Nora, so he turned over and went back to sleep.

"Anything else happen? What about Toby? He hear anything yet?"

"I feel so sad Nellie. Toby taking off for England before Christmas. I was hoping he would spend the holidays here but he didn't want to miss out because the man say he didn't know when he would come back to pick more young men. Anyway he is going off at the end o' this month."

"That isn't so good, but he got to spread his wings and fly Nora. He is a man and he got to be independent. We girls different, we stay at home forever. You will miss Toby but it is all for the best."

"I can't take this talk about Toby going away. We could talk about something else? So Francois is going to live here with you?"

"Yes, we talk about it and thought this would be the best place. We are far out in the country and he will have a long drive to town, but he don't mind at all. How Percy?"

"Child, Percy open a carpenter shop in the back of the house. He see how much people moving about here and he and decide he could make some quick money."

"That is real good Nora. It don't sound like if you too happy."

"I happy about it, but he keep forgetting he is a old fowl cock."

"How old Percy is now?"

"He going to be fifty five on his next birthday."

"So you think I ain't no spring chicken either?"

"I don't mean it so Nellie. You do those things when you young, not when you getting old like Percy."

"Leave him alone. As long as he happy, that is the important thing."

"You didn't forget my French perfume?" asked Nora.

"Girl when you go in those perfume stores, it smell like heaven and you have a real hard time making up your mind, but I got something real nice. Francois help me to pick out one for you. You should hear how he speak French with them. I learn to say 'Au voir' and that make him real happy."

"What that mean?"

"It mean goodbye and you should see how those French people make their mouths real small to talk. Even Francois do it. Girl they not like these redlegs we got around here. Everybody say 'bonjour'. That mean good morning. It don't matter if you black or if you blue."

"That sound like a real nice place Nellie."

"It nice, but I have to tell you more about it another time because I going back in my bed. I don't want my husband to miss me," she said as they both started to cackle like two laying hens.

"I still like your hair Nellie. It look real good. It make you look like one o' those rich Amercuns."

* * *

# 56

Nora did not go straight to her home. The news was good and she needed to share it with Clytie and Miss Una.

"What you telling me Nora? Nellie is married to Francois?"

"Yes, now she is Mrs. Bertrand if you please."

"That is the best news I hear in a long time. How she look?"

"She look like a rich Amercun. She got a new hairdo. I didn't see anything else because they was tired."

"It ain't like Nellie to go straight home and not stop by to see if we living or dead," said Miss Una.

"Miss Una, it was a real long trip and the two of them real tired."

"But she could phone to say she get back," the old woman complained. "I hope she ain't going to forget we now that she married to Francis."

"Francois Ma. And Nellie would never do that."

"You tell Nellie that Emily in the family way?"

"Yes, and she was real happy."

"Hmm!" grunted Miss Una.

"Nellie say she coming by first thing tomorrow morning. She buy something for everybody. I can't wait to smell that nice French perfume that Francois pick out for me."

"Why she didn't give it to you when you was over there?"

"She ain't unpack the valises yet Miss Una. They was still by the front door."

"Nellie still on her honeymoon. Leave her. I am so glad that I am going down on my knees and pray for a good man to come along," said Clytie.

"What happen to that postman? You mean he gone already Clytie?" asked her mother.

"Yes Ma. He gone already," she said without further explanation. "I want somebody just like Francois."

"Cat luck ain't dog luck Clytie. You have to hold on to what you can get. You ain't as young as you used to be."

"Ma Nellie is older than me."

"I tell you cat luck ain't dog luck. Nellie ain't only pretty. She real lucky."

"It wasn't always so Miss Una," said Nora. "Me and Nellie and my mother had a real hard life. It is only right that we find some kind o' happiness. So don't keep putting down Clytie. She work hard and deserve something good. Anyhow I have to go home. I tell Percy that I was only going for half hour and it is nearly two hours now. I coming back early tomorrow morning to open the shop."

"Alright Nora."

* * *

"Francois, your breakfast ready and the newspaper here too," shouted Nellie.

"What's good for breakfast?" he asked embracing his wife.

"Eggs like those we had in Paris and croissants."

"You made poached eggs? Where did you get the croissants?"

"I make them myself," she said proudly. "Read the paper while I get the tea," she said thinking of what the plantation owners would have done.

He sat down and picked up the paper. On the front page was an article which he started to read to Nellie as she poured the tea into his teacup.

"It says here that the case of the missing Thomas Hurley has finally been closed. They have decided that he committed suicide and since there was no evidence to prove otherwise, they are closing the case."

Nellie sat down but was still gripping the handle of the teapot.

"Is that all I'm getting Nellie?" he asked.

"What?" she asked.

"Is that all I'm getting?" he asked as he saw the two drops of tea she had poured into his cup.

"Sorry," she said as she continued to fill it.

"What's wrong Nellie?" he asked.

"Nothing," she replied.

"You're suddenly behaving quite strangely. Tell me what's wrong. You know you can tell me anything. Remember I'm your husband Nellie."

"Nothing is wrong," she replied. "Nothing at all!"

"We have a lot of paper work to do today. The bills have piled up and we have to make some decisions regarding us."

"What you mean?" she asked.

"I have a housekeeper who will be out of work, and you need someone to help you around this big house. Do you mind if I bring Otty to work here? She's honest and hardworking."

"But I don't need a housemaid Francois. I know how to clean this house."

"Come over here Nellie," he said pulling her onto his lap. "This is quite a big house and when we have guests, we will need someone to help us. We need help with the cooking, the washing, the cleaning and the ironing. Besides that, Otty needs the money. She is alone and has no family."

"Well since you put it that way," she said trying to get a glimpse of the article about Thomas Hurley. "She must be just like Miss Una and I don't want nobody to suffer."

"So can I tell her she has a new job?"

"Yes. When you going to start to help me with my English?"

"That's another reason why you will need help around here. You won't have time for all these household chores."

"So when we starting?" she asked eagerly.

"As soon as I can speak to Jonas."

"What Jonas got to do with it?"

"He's a teacher Nellie. I want him to come here two or three times a week to teach you English grammar. When I come home in the evening, we can discuss certain topics and I will teach you good pronunciation and correct any mistakes you are still making. How does that sound Nellie"

"And what about the French?" she asked.

"Paris has really made a great impact on you Nellie, but we've still got to take it one step at a time. When I think you're ready, I'll start teaching you a bit."

Francois had given her reason to feel alive and she had completely forgotten the Thomas Hurley incident. She cleared the table and he deposited a stack of unopened letters where his breakfast plate was. One month of unopened bills and letters were opened one by one.

The vacation house in St. Lucia was proving to be profitable and the grocery store was still proving to be a lucrative business. Francois' worries were the school and the two houses beside the grocery store. Nellie had been paying the teachers at the school and she also had the added expense of the property taxes.

He persuaded his wife to charge a nominal fee for each school child and move Miss Una into the home which she had vacated. Jonas was now living with his grandmother and Clytie was leaving Bottomsley to look after Miss Una. There would be enough room in Nellie's old home for the three of them. That meant another bit of income from them and also from Miss Una's house which they would put up for rent.

Nellie did not want an added burden on the poor parents of the children, but she understood that she couldn't carry the burden forever, and a nominal fee was just enough, as Francois had put it, to make their parents realise that they had a responsibility towards their children. He also explained that both Clytie and Jonas earned a salary and it was only fair that they paid towards the upkeep of her home.

"You couldn't go on like that forever Nels," he explained. "What about your will? Your daughter is expecting a child, your grandchild!"

"You will tell me what to do?" she asked.

"What do you want to do?" he asked her. "The decision has to be yours."

"But I want you to advise me. I don't know what to do."

"Is Bottomsley plantation profitable?" he asked.

"I don't know."

"If you can find out, then I can give you my opinion."

The telephone rang and interrupted their conversation.

"Yes I coming, but Francois is helping me with all the papers and my bills."

"You better Hurry Nels because Ma is real upset."

"What is she upset about?"

"She say you didn't even pass by to see if she was living or dead."

"Tell Miss Una I coming down there soon, and when I show her what I bring her from Paris, she ain't going to be upset no more."

"Hurry Nels. It feels like I ain't see you for years."

"Clytie, I have to ask you something. You know how Bottomsley doing?"

"I don't understand what you mean?"

"Is it making money? I know they still making rum and sugar. I just want to know how Emily stand with money."

"From what I hear, I think they doing real good. Nicolas Bellamy was only supposed to be there for a couple years, but he running it so good that Miss Sarah beg him to stay on. He ain't a thing like Thomas Hurley."

"What about Thomas Hurley?" asked Nora who was attending to a customer.

"We only saying that the Bellamy fellow ain't anything like that thief Thomas Hurley. By the way Nels, in this morning paper, the say they going to close the case because they think he kill himself."

"I hear that too. I am real glad he ain't going to be there when Emily come home. At least she is going to have a bit o' money to be able to eat."

"That is true Nels. If he was still at Bottomsley, Emily wouldn't have a penny."

"God works in mysterious ways," said Miss Una. "What you say to that Nora?"

"You right Miss Una. Although I ain't no Christian I got to agree with you."

Francois was on his way to home to collect his clothing and whatever personal items he needed; and also to give his housemaid the news while Nellie went to visit her friends and relatives. They were all there to see what Paris had done to their Nellie. Even Percy who never showed his face anywhere had put in an appearance. They were all pleasantly surprised by Nellie's new look. They touched her hair which was now straight and styled around her shoulders with a fringe at the front. She gave

Nora a bottle of perfume and a heavy iron comb with a wooden handle and another contraption which Nora had never seen.

"What is this?" she asked her sister.

"That is to make your hair straight and this one is to put curls in it."

"I never see anything like this," Nora said.

"This is what they use in Paris. The lady in the beauty shop wash my hair. Then she put this one on something to make it hot and then she pulled it through my hair, a little bit at a time and that is what make my hair straight. Then she heat up this one and roll the hair around it. She call this one a curler."

"Why you make it straight and then want to curl it up?" asked Clytie.

"We ain't got straight hair Clytie, so we have to straighten it out first to make it look nice."

Everyone was pleased with the gifts Nellie gave them, but what intrigued them most was the hot comb and the curling iron and Nellie's marriage. Miss Una held her stockings and her blouse up close because her sight was now really bad.

"You like them Miss Una?" asked Nellie.

"Yes, they real pretty, but I need to talk to you about this getting married."

"What you want to know?" Nellie asked.

"You happy Nellie?"

"I real happy Miss Una."

"Francis treating you good?" asked the old woman, as she emptied a bag of rice onto the table and all the women sat down and started to pick the bad grains out of it.

"Yes."

"And you sure he got his own money and ain't after yours?"

"Yes Miss Una."

"Then everything in order. I just want to know that you are happy."

"I was never so happy Miss Una. Francois is a good man."

"Amen," whispered Clytie to Nellie. "That was bothering Ma. She keep on saying that she didn't want nobody to steal nothing from you."

"He look after me real good Miss Una, so don't worry. He even going to give me English lessons so that I can talk good."

"Whatever make you happy child, make me happy. You can't find a good man for my daughter?"

"Ma?" shouted Clytie. "Stop trying to marry me off."

"Look how happy Nellie is. You don't want to be happy too?"

"Nothing don't happen before the time Ma."

"I don't understand those people from Demerara. We used to get good rice before and now look at the amount of bad grains and shells we pick out of this little bag. They should be shame to do that to poor people."

"It was always so Ma. I think that you don't see so good. Some o' those grains you pick out is good rice."

"I ain't so blind that I don't know bad rice from good rice."

"Alright Ma," said Clytie winking at Nellie.

"Miss Una, I think it is time for you to get some glasses. They will help you to see better."

"I can see alright Nellie. Don't listen to my daughter."

"Look Miss Una. How these look on me?" asked Nellie pulling a pair of spectacles out of her purse and putting them on.

"I didn't know you had trouble seeing," said the old woman.

"I can see far off, but when I have to read something, I can't see a thing on the paper, so Francois say that I should get glasses for reading, so I get these in Paris."

"Let me try them," said Miss Una as she sported Nellie's glasses. "Girl you look real rich and important, and your hair look real good too."

"Now you know what I was saying is true. She can't see anything Nellie,"said Clytie.

"Miss Una, I taking you to the glasses place to get some glasses. See how good you can see with my glasses?"

Nellie returned home to find that Francois had already returned and had brought his house helper Otty, who was already setting herself up in the refurbished stables. Francois' clothes were already neatly hanging in the closet and everything else that he brought was neatly packed away. Otty seemed to be a good housekeeper.

"She'll be here in a few minutes," he said to Nellie.

"She clean up the house so you could rent it out?"

"It's all done Nellie."

"What you have in those two big boxes?" she asked.

"It's a surprise."

"For me?"

Francois opened the box and carefully lifted a big black contraption from it. He had brought his gramophone along with the heavy vinyl records which were in the second box. They all featured a dog in the centre howling into a loudspeaker. Nellie was elated.

"Miss Sarah had one like this but she hardly ever play it."

"But we are going to play this one," he said as he placed one on the records onto the gramophone and then lifted the heavy head with the needle onto it. "This is my favourite song," he said.

"I know that song," she said. "I like it. It is Tennessee Waltz."

"May I have this dance Madame?" he asked.

"You making it sound as if we still in Paris," she said smiling and walking into his arms.

"You're a beautiful dancer Mrs. Bertrand. Where did you learn to dance like this?"

"My mother was a real good dancer and we used to dance around in front of the hut. All the people in the village like to dance when we hear good music."

Before they could continue their conversation, someone knocked on the kitchen door and Francois quickly removed the needle from the record and they sat down..

"Come in Otty," he said.

A buxom black woman entered and stood in front them.

"This is my wife Mrs Bertrand," Francois said to the woman who seemed for some reason to be totally surprised. "Is something wrong?"

"No sir," she replied hardly looking at Nellie.

"Since I no longer have to worry about looking after a home, my wife will instruct you in whatever needs to be done."

"Yes sir," she answered.

"I know you will look after my wife and me just as you have looked after me for such a long time. She knows you've been with me for several years and allowed me to bring you here at my request."

"Thank you sir," she replied.

Francois went to his office for a few hours leaving Nellie with the woman who never ventured from the kitchen. She was sitting at the kitchen table when Nellie opened the door and she jumped up and pretended to be looking through the pantry.

"You looking for something Otty?" she asked.

"Just trying to see where everything is," she replied.

"You going to like it here," said Nellie feeling a little uncomfortable.

"Yes please," replied the woman. "Tell me what you want me to do."

"Whatever you used to do at Mr. Bertrand, you can do here. Back then it was only Mr. Bertrand, but now it is the two of us and there might be a little bit more to do, but not a lot."

"Yes please," she replied again. "What you want me to cook for Mr. Bertrand? He like chicken and fish."

Nellie thought of Sarah Bottomsley and the way she had behaved towards her. She didn't want anyone to be treated the way she had been treated and so she began to treat the woman like a friend and not a paid helper. She tried to converse about Francois and where the woman had come from, but she received only one word answers and finally gave up.

"I don't think she like me," she said to Francois.

"Otty? She's only shy since she doesn't know you very well."

"I don't know."

"Has she been rude to you?"

"No, but she doesn't want to talk to me."

"If she is ever rude to you Nellie, then she must go. I did not bring her here to disrespect you and if she ever does, then she must go. Maybe I should have a little talk with her."

"Don't be so quick to judge her Francois. You say she need the money and that she don't have any family. I could carry her to the shop to meet Miss Una in case she get lonely."

"Nellie, she is much younger than Miss Una."

"Then Clytie and Nora?"

"I don't know Nellie. Let's wait to see how it works out."

Nora turned the key in the door and entered Nellie's kitchen. The door to the backyard was ajar and she looked out and saw a woman standing over a galvanized wash tub and a jucking board. Francois' white shirts had already been laid out in the sun to whiten and she was carefully hanging more of his clothing on the line to dry. She picked up a couple of Nellie's dresses and flung them to the side. Nellie had said that Francois would be bringing his helper to work for them and she thought this must be the woman. She looked around her as if she was missing something and not finding it, made her way to the kitchen door. Nora quickly sat down to remove her shoes when Otty entered the kitchen.

"Morning," said Nora. "I didn't know Nellie had somebody working here."

"Nellie?" asked Otty with scorn. "I here to work for Mr. Bertrand. You work here too?"

"No, but I come to do Nellie hair."

"She got a hairdresser too?" asked the woman. "I used to work with Mr. Bertrand for a lot o' years and he ask me to come and work for him and his wife. He just get married you know. I come here expecting a English lady and he show me this woman and say that it is his wife. I was never so disappointed in all my life."

"Why you so disappointed?" asked Nora pumping the woman for information.

"I really don't want to work for no black people. As I was saying, I was expecting a white lady. He could do a whole lot better than what he got."

"Why you take the job if you don't like his wife?" asked Nora.

"Because it hard to find a good job," she replied. "I like Mr. Bertrand. He is like a son to me."

"If he is like your son, then you should like his wife. He make that decision."

"I thought I hear your voice," said Nellie opening the kitchen door. "Otty, I see you already meet my sister Nora."

"Yes please," she said, realising she had made a big mistake.

Nora stared at her as she and Nellie left the kitchen together.

"What you think about Otty Nora?"

"Not much," answered Nora.

"You ain't even giving her a chance. You don't know her."

"And I don't want to know her neither."

"What is wrong with you this morning Nora?"

"She don't like you Nellie."

"Why you say that?"

"Because she tell me so. She thought I was the hairdresser and she open her mouth wide and tell me what she think about you."

"I didn't do nothing to the woman."

"You is a black woman Nellie. She thought she was coming to work for a white English woman."

"She didn't say that," said Nellie feeling let down by her own.

"You have to tell Francois. You should kick her backside out. This is your house."

"I feel sorry for Otty. She don't have no family and she is real poor. I know about being poor Nora."

"Don't make that your business Nellie. You better be careful she don't put one o' those castor oil seeds in your food. Get rid o' her. Don't worry about that woman. You just call me if she give you any trouble."

"With all that talk, I didn't even notice your hair," said Nellie. "It looks real good."

"I tell Harriet what you say, and she fix it. It really look good Nellie?"

"It look like if somebody in Paris fix it."

"Everybody who see it, want to have the same hairdo. I come to ask you if Harriet can rent Miss Una house. She want to turn it in to a little hairdresser shop. The only problem is that she only got one o' those hot combs and the other thing."

"Well I got a comb and a curler that I can lend Harriet to make a start, but she got to ask Francois how she could get some from Paris."

"Why we don't go over there and pick them up Nellie?"

The two women laughed loudly at Nora's remark.

"So that mean Harriet can rent the shop?" asked Nora.

"I don't see no problem, but let me talk to Francois and hear what he got to say."

Her sister was a little disappointed in her final remark but realised she was no longer a single woman and must perhaps share decision- making with her husband.

"I am real thirsty," said Nora. "She don't bring in tea nor nothing so?"

"When I ask," said Nellie.

"Well your sister thirsty, so tell that woman to come in and serve something to drink. If you don't want to ask, I will have to ask."

Nellie reluctantly got up and asked her to serve some beverages.

"You have to get a little bell Nellie. You don't want to get up every time you want something. Just ring that bell and make her come in here."

"I can't do that Nora."

"She want to work for white people Nellie and that is what they do," said Nora laughing out loudly.

* * *

# 57

The corn-row and corkscrew hair-styles had now been replaced by the hot comb and the curling iron. The women were all trying to imitate Nellie's hair-style and Harriet was spending long hours in the beauty shop and earning a good income. She also had made a little invention. She collected old newspapers, and cut and rolled pieces into long strips for her clients to purchase. They could roll their hair at night, so that they would have curls the following day. Each night, almost every man in the village slept beside a woman whose hair was neatly wrapped in Harriet's improvised hair rollers. Even Nellie took her niece's advice and was able to style her own hair as time went by. Francois teased her about it, but she reminded him it was better to look pretty beside him during the day, since no one saw her when she slept at night.

The re-education of Nellie Bertrand began with a whimper but soon broke into a hefty storm. As promised, Clytie's son tutored her twice per week and Francois helped her and corrected any mistakes she made during their discussions. He was proud of her and she became more confident as time went by.

The so-called upper class could not understand why Francois had married her. A charming lawyer and an ex-kitchen hand? That was the question on all their lips. He's just interested in the house left to her by Gus Ridley they said, but Francois did not allow their pettiness to get in the way of his happiness. Secretly, the white men were jealous of him while the white women ignored Nellie; the educated brown-skinned ones envied her and the black ones like Otty despised her. Her refuge was her husband and very close friends.

Nora's son Toby departed for England to work on the buses leaving his mother somewhat depressed. It was a difficult time with Christmas approaching because the family had always spent the time together. Luckily she had the loving shoulders of her sister and daughter who reminded her of the British pounds that would soon be rolling in.

She was not the only mother saddened by a son's departure. The London transport had taken away many sons from the village. Their consolation was that their sons would at least have companionship as they knew each other and could possibly live together.

All was not lost. A vibrant colony of entrepreneurs had sprung up. Starting with Nellie's Bar and Grocery, there was now the hairdresser's shop run by Harriet, Nora's daughter; there was the snowball man with his collection of bottles of food dyes and his ice and ice shaver, the ice cream man, the shoe-repairman, hawkers with their legs sprawled open behind their trays of toffees, nuts, mints, comforts and sugar cakes, the carpenters, fishermen, and those who continued to work on the plantations as cane cutters. Many of them, although they had no interest in living in the countryside, had fled Bottomsley when Thomas Hurley had made life unbearable for them. At least they could eat when there was no money because Nellie allowed them to take their purchases on credit and pay at the end of every week.

The Bottomsley great house was a flurry of activity. A pregnant Emily Chambers was returning home after many years in England. It was the fifteenth of December and Sarah Bottomsley was excited at the thought of seeing her daughter again and the expectation of her grandchild made it even more exhilarating.

She summoned Clytie back to Bottomsley to help with the preparations. There were Christmas cakes to be baked, chickens and ducks to be slaughtered, the house was to be decorated and the baby's room to be sparkling and free of mosquitoes. In addition there would a party just before Christmas for the homecoming and also to celebrate the festive season.

The plantation hands were also getting into the spirit of things. They were cutting the casuarinas or mile tree branches as they were better known, to be used as Christmas trees which they then decorated with cotton batten to resemble snow and their home-made decorations were proudly hung with care. They had already bought their hams and had them soaking to remove some of the saltiness. The currants, prunes, raisins and other dried fruit were ground and soaked in the cheap red port wine just waiting to be made into Christmas cakes. Sometimes there would be nothing left when it came time for baking, because the children would climb to where their parents hid this tasty treat and consume most if it. Of course this brought them a lashing they would not soon forget.

The smell of fresh varnish lingered in the air as each one tried to make everything sparkle for the holiday season. New net curtains hung at the windows and gently flew in and out with the breeze.

Nellie turned over in her bed and called out to Hurley, but he was not there. He had been running in and out between her legs as she was preparing Francois' breakfast, and waiting for his to be served to him. After Francois left for the office, Nellie usually returned to bed and slept a while longer. She was learning to enjoy the prosperity in her life. It was time to get up, get showered and dressed. Otty came in to find out what she had to do that day and then returned to the kitchen.

The Christmas season was on her mind. She and Francois had not yet discussed any plans, so she decided to wait before she made any. Her mind was also on her daughter and her impending arrival and the delivery of her baby.

"Please," said Otty. "There is a white gentleman looking around outside."

Nellie looked out and saw the old man who had parked his car on the street, inspecting the house from outside the gate. He looked up at the canopy of Flamboyant trees with their red flowers which had formed an archway over the gate. He ran his hand along the mahogany tree which was slightly to the right of the gate and then he opened it and slowly put the latch back in its place. He then made his way towards the house and seemed to be admiring everything as he approached the entrance.

"My God," Nellie said under her breath. "It's John Bottomsley. What does he want?"

She stepped outside and greeted him.

"Nellie, I haven't seen you since my son passed away."

"How are you sir?" she asked him.

"For an old man, not too bad," he replied.

"How is your wife?" she asked.

"Millie's not too good. The doctor thinks she's got St. Vitus dance. It's really hard for her to control her limbs, but just like me, for an old woman, she is still alive."

"I'm sorry to hear that sir."

"You haven't done badly for yourself Nellie. I heard you had inherited Gus Ridley's house, but I wasn't sure if it was true."

"As you can see sir, it is true."

"I didn't know Gus was your father."

"Neither did I," she replied.

"I also heard you got married to a solicitor," he said looking past her and trying to get a glimpse into the living room.

"If you're looking for him, he's not here right now. He went to his office."

"Nellie my girl, you've done well for yourself."

"Thank you sir."

"You know that Emily is coming back next week, don't you?"

"Yes Clytie told me. Would you like a cup of tea or something cool?" she asked.

"Got anything stronger?" he asked with a wink.

"I've got some rum. Would you like that?"

"Yes and straight up."

She poured him a double. He threw his head back and he swallowed it in one gulp. Nellie fixed him another and then sat down to hear what had brought him to her home.

"I know you're wondering why I'm here," he said.

"Yes."

"Nellie, I know you and my son had something going on. I could see it whenever he looked at you, but there is one thing I'm not sure of."

"What is that?" she asked.

"I want you to tell me the truth. Are you Emily's mother?"

"You know Miss Sarah is her mother," she replied. "Why would you ask me such a question?"

"I asked my son the same thing just before he passed away and he was behaving just the way you're behaving now; beating around and around the bush and never giving me a straight answer."

"Even if I was Emily's mother, what good would it do now to bring it into the open?"

"I don't intend to bring it into the open. I just want to know if she is your child. You know Sarah never brought a living child into this world and you had a child almost the same time she had hers; then you disappeared."

"I left because my child died."

"Nellie I know that you are Emily's mother. I don't have the proof, but I know you and my son had a child together."

She did not reply.

"I knew it Nellie. Your secret is safe with me," he said standing up and going out the door. "But Nellie, I'm proud of you. You've done well for yourself. By the way, you know Emily's expecting a child?"

"I also heard that sir."

He paused for a while as if he wanted to say something, but changed his mind and started down the path. She was happy to see him go because his visit had turned her into a basket of nerves. The engine roared, he waved and then drove away. He was a shadow of what he used to be. A smile crossed her lips as she remembered the hambone incident with Miss Ella. Those were days long gone. However, she needed to talk to someone and that someone was Clytie. She telephoned Bottomsley and Sarah answered. Nellie greeted her and then asked if she could speak to Clytie.

"Nellie, did you hear that Emily's coming home?" Sarah asked.

"Yes I heard."

"I'm going to throw a party for her and her husband."

"I'm sure she would like that," replied Nellie.

"Is that really you Nellie?" she asked unaccustomed to Nellie's perfect grammar.

"Yes Miss Sarah," she replied.

"Nellie would you be interested in coming over to help with the party?" she asked.

"I don't think so Miss Sarah. I now have a husband to look after."

"Clytie never told me you got married."

"We got married in Paris Miss Sarah."

"I hope I get to meet him one day. What is his name?"

"Francois Bertrand."

"Is that the same Francois Bertrand the solicitor?"

"Yes Miss Sarah."

"Alright Nellie, I'll get Clytie for you."

Nellie could hear the disappointment and contempt in her voice. She had not congratulated her. It seems as if her success had annoyed her former mistress who believed they could never be on the same level socially. She knew Sarah Bottomsley and she knew her way of thinking.

She thought better of discussing John Bottomsley's visit with Clytie at that time. With Sarah Bottomsley in the house, it would be foolish to discuss such a personal matter which could affect the lives of so many.

Unable to find Hurley, Nellie opted to stay at home and search for him. Otty hadn't seen the cat when she came in and now they both searched and searched, but it was all in vain. Hurley, like his namesake, had simply vanished.

"What you looking for?" asked Nora as she saw her sister looking up into the mahogany tree.

"I can't find Hurley," she said.

"If you got a minute, I have to tell you something."

"What?" asked Nellie with fear written all over her face.

It was one of those days when everything just seemed to be going against her.

"Don't get so worried," she said. "Nothing bad ain't happen."

"Then why you left Miss Una alone in the shop?"

"Harriet is there waiting until I get back."

"What happen?" she asked forgetting all about grammar.

"Percy and me do it this morning."

"Do what?" asked Nellie.

"We get married this morning."

"After all these years and two children?" her sister asked. "Nora, I am very happy to hear that. Why did you decide to do it now?"

"We did together real long Nellie. We went through thick and thin together. We see how happy you is and Percy thought it was a good idea."

"But why you didn't tell me Nora? I'm your only living relative."

"We just want to do it real quiet. We didn't want no fuss nor nothing."

"Well Mrs Trotman, how does it feel?"

"To tell the truth Nellie, nothing ain't feel no different. Maybe if I went to Paris to do it, it would feel different."

"We will celebrate for Christmas, but I will have to talk to Francois first."

"That will have to wait. Percy and me going on a little trip."

"Where?" asked Nellie.

"We hoping we could stay at the holiday house in St. Lucia."

"I will still have to ask Francois, because I'm not sure if anyone has rented it yet."

"Talk to him and let me know."

"John Bottomsley was here this morning."

"You ain't see him for a long time. He ain't know you happy? I thought he did staying away from you especially now you married to Francois."

"I am talking about JB's father."

"What did he want?"

"To tell me he knows that I am Emily's mother."

"How he find that out?"

"He isn't sure. He's only guessing. He said he knew there was something going on between his son and me, and that Sarah Bottomsley had never brought a living child into the world."

"What you tell him?"

"I didn't say yes or no, so he wished me well and left. I tried calling Clytie to tell her and got Miss Sarah on the telephone. She asked me to come and help out at the big Christmas party she's giving for Emily."

"I hope you tell that woman that your kitchen days done."

"I told her I now a husband to look after, and that we got married in Paris. When I said I had married a solicitor, she asked me for his name. You won't believe how upset she got and didn't say another word to me."

"She is upset because you got as much as she got and you ain't going back in Bottomsley kitchen."

"But what am I going to do when Emily comes back?"

"You wait for her to come and visit you. Don't go down to that plantation. You got to hold your head high and get respect. As Francois wife, you can't be running down to Bottomsley plantation no more."

"What would I do without you and Clytie?"

"So tell me what happen to Hurley."

"He was in the kitchen this morning, and then he suddenly disappeared."

"He is going to come back when he get hungry. He must be out there running around behind the sparrows and blackbirds. Is that Otty behaving herself?"

"Since she realised it was a big mistake she made by talking to you, she's trying to be really nice."

"She ain't foolish. But don't trust that woman and don't sleep when she is in the house; and if you have to sleep, keep one eye open."

"Nora you aren't going to change at all. But I love you because you are my only sister."

"Alright Nellie. Don't forget to talk to Francois about the holiday house."

* * *

# 58

Emily and Alastair Chambers arrived on the island one week before Christmas. It had been eleven years since she had last set foot on The Rock, so there was much jubilation at Bottomsley. The plantation workers lined the pathway to the house, although many of them didn't know her. When she stepped out of the car, it was obvious to everyone she was in the family way. Clytie stared out the kitchen window at the beautiful young woman who slowly climbed the steps while looking around her. Sarah Bottomsley could not contain her happiness. She fussed over her daughter and her husband as if they were two little children.

"He is real tall," said Ursy.

"You right. He is even taller than Master Bottomsley and he was a real tall man," Clytie replied.

"Miss Bottomsley is real happy," said Clytie. "I ain't see her this happy for a long time."

The two kitchen helpers cracked open the kitchen door and peeped in. Emily was down on her knees in front of Millie Bottomsley who had arrived for the momentous occasion. Unableto control her movements, Millie Bottomsley cried like a baby while her granddaughter hugged her.

"Grandma this is Alastair my husband," she said.

He took her hand and spoke to her while the once feisty Millie Bottomsley could only smile at him. John Bottomsley hugged and kissed his granddaughter while Sarah looked on smiling like a Cheshire cat.

"I really missed all of you," she said.

"Let's get you undressed and comfortable," said her mother.

"I've made up your father's room for both of you. Your old room is much too small. By the time you've washed up, Clytie will have dinner on the table."

"Oh I've got to see Clytie," she said heading for the kitchen, giving the two servants just enough time to dash back to their duties.

"Clytie," she said softly.

Clytie looked around and pretended to be surprised.

"Miss Emily, oh Miss Emily, I miss you so much," she said running to her and hugging her.

"I missed you too Clytie. I have so much to tell you. How is Miss Una?"

"She is still there. She can't see too good, but Nellie got her some glasses and now she can see better. She is real, real proud Miss Emily."

"Good day Miss Emily," said Ursy feeling a little neglected.

"I don't remember you," said Emily.

"I take Miss Ella place. I am Ursy."

"That's right. How could I forget? How is Miss Nellie Clytie?"

"She get married Miss Emily. She went to Paris and get married," Clytie replied.

"We really have a lot of talking to do Clytie, but first I must rest a bit. That was the longest journey I have ever experienced."

"Come on Emily," said her mother opening the kitchen door.

"She is still sweet," said Ursy as Clytie wiped the tears away with her apron.

"I know that child from the first day she was born, and now she is having a child of her own. I hope he is a good husband."

"Emily isn't foolish like her mother," said Ursy. "You remember how she used to hide under the table here and nobody could find her?"

"If that Thomas Hurley did never come into this house, she would never have gone to no England."

"She back now so we should be happy," Ursy said.

"I have to call Nellie and tell her the news."

"Just be careful Clytie. They are waiting on us to put dinner on the table."

"It ain't going to take too long. I just want Nellie to know Emily get here safe."

Of course there more tears shed over the telephone. Nellie wanted to know if Emily had asked about her and when told she had, a fountain had opened up and water flowed. Realising the stress his wife was under, Francois took the telephone away from her and spoke to Clytie, who was a little worried she had over stepped her boundary.

"Come come, Nellie," he whispered in her ear. "It isn't that bad. You will soon see her and I will be here with you when that happens."

"Will you?" she asked through a tear-stained face.

"Of course I will be here with you."

"I must tell you something Francois. John Bottomsley came here two days ago and I think he knows I'm Emily's mother."

"How did he find that out?"

"He's not sure but he said Sarah Bottomsley never brought a living child into the world and he finds it strange that I disappeared just after my child was born."

"Was he nice about it or did he threaten you?"

"He was nice. I gave him a drink of rum and he told me he was happy that I had made something out of my life."

"Do you think he will tell anyone?"

"I don't think so. He said my secret was safe with him."

"Don't worry Nels. If anything happens, I will handle it."

"I am the luckiest woman in the world. What did I do to deserve you Francois?"

"What did I do to deserve you? I do it all because I love you Nellie and I don't want anything to make you unhappy."

"I love you too Francois and I will try my best to make you really happy."

The two of them sat on the couch with eyes closed, hugging each other tightly.

"Have you made any plans for Christmas Nellie?"

"Nothing yet. I was waiting to see if you wanted to do anything special, like going to Paris," she said with a giggle.

"But it hasn't been that long since we were there."

"I was just making fun Francois. What do you want to do?"

"I thought we could spend the time with your sister and her family and Clytie and Miss Una."

"I forgot something Francois. Nora and Percy asked if they could go to the holiday house for a honeymoon."

"Over the Christmas holidays?" he asked. "Did they get married?" he asked.

"Yes, they did it yesterday morning."

"I don't think it's rented, but I can check and let you know."

"If it isn't rented Francois, could we all go to St. Lucia for Christmas?"

"That's a good idea, but we have only two bedrooms."

"We could rent the house next door from Mr. Applewhite for Clytie and Miss Una and Harriet could stay there too."

"Not a bad idea. That means we will all have a chance to spend Christmas together."

"What about the shop?" she asked.

"You will close at midday on Christmas eve, won't you? Then we can leave on Friday night, spend Saturday, Sunday and come back on Monday evening."

"That's a long time to keep the shop closed."

"Monday is a bank holiday Nellie."

"That's true, so I should hurry. I have to package out what I'm going to give to the customers."

"What are you giving to them?"

"I ordered ten salty hams. Those are for the big families. Then I thought I could give each customer a little parcel with a pint of rice, a pound of flour and a pound of sugar. What do you think?"

"Don't you think you are giving away too much?"

"Without these people my business would be dead, so I don't mind giving back a little."

"You're such a wonderful woman," he said kissing her on the forehead. "I will never try to tell you what you should do unless I see you headed for disaster."

"Do you think I'm heading for disaster?" she asked raising her head to look him in the face.

"Not at all, I just want you to be careful with your money."

"I'll be careful.

"Do you think Clytie will get the time off to go to St. Lucia?"

"Knowing Sarah Bottomsley, I'm not too sure. You think I should phone her to find out?"

"You should. She has to know ahead of time."

Nellie called and this time it was Emily on the telephone.

"Miss Emily?" she asked in a really soft voice.

"Yes, this is Emily."

"It's Miss Nellie," she whispered.

They spoke for about a minute and then she spoke to Clytie who promised to ask Sarah Bottomsley for the time off.

"No way!" Sarah Bottomsley shouted. "What will I do if you take off leaving me here in the lurch?"

"Ma is getting old Miss Sarah and it would be good to spend this Christmas with her."

"I understand all that Clytie, but what would I do without you?"

"Ursy know what to do and she could find somebody else to help."

"I don't want strangers sniffing around my dinner table especially at Christmas."

Emily could hear her mother's raised voice and came to investigate.

"But Mother, I don't see why you won't allow Clytie to go with her mother."

"Who's going to look after us?" Sarah Bottomsley screamed.

"We can look after ourselves. Ursy is still there and she seems quite capable."

"Well Clytie, all I can say is that if you decide to abandon us at Christmas, you're never to set foot on Bottomsley again."

"Mama!" shouted Emily. "You can't do that to Clytie."

"Yes I can," she replied. "What will Alastair think? That we can't afford help over the Christmas season?"

"Don't worry about him. I will explain it to him," she said as her mother disappeared behind the bedroom door.

"She didn't mean that Clytie. Go ahead and enjoy yourself."

"I'm only here Miss Emily because I know you were coming back, but Ma is old now and she need me. I can't let Ma spend Christmas by herself again."

"I will talk to Mama."

"Miss Emily, when I leave here, I ain't coming back."

"I'm sorry Clytie, but I understand. After the holidays are over, I'll come up to see Miss Una and Miss Nellie. But you'll be staying for the party?"

"Yes Miss Emily."

"I have something for you that I picked up in Africa, but I've still got a little unpacking to do."

"Thank you Miss Emily. I want to hear about Africa. I could help you to unpack and you can tell me everything then. It would be just like old times."

"You will enjoy the stories I have to tell you, but I will do it tomorrow when I feel a bit more rested."

* * *

Nellie's customers were all lined up at the shop door since word had gone out that all those who had patronised her business, would receive a little parcel for Christmas. The bush drums had spread very far and wide, because some of the people who turned up, she had never ever seen. However the parcels were only for the long standing customers. Nellie and Nora had to keep their eyes peeled because Miss Una knew voices but she couldn't recognise faces anymore. The village people showered praise upon Nellie for her kindness and all she had done for the villagers, like providing them with a school for their children and having trust in them when they could not afford to pay for their goods until the end of the week. Some of them even brought their children in to recite poems to thank Miss Nellie for her kindness, although some of the same parents had been upset with her when she announced they were to pay a nominal fee for their children's lunches.

It had all been forgotten and Nellie felt good. Although not a church-goer, she knew there would be a place for her somewhere, when she left the earth.

* * *

# 59

Sarah Bottomsley stopped at nothing to make the party one the invited guests would never forget. Clytie and Ursy could only stare out the kitchen window at them as they arrived in their finery for the celebration. There were faces Clytie had not seen for many years because Sarah did not socialise too much anymore due to Thomas Hurley's disappearance. Gossip had it he had deserted her and this was much too painful for her to endure. Now she had a reason to celebrate and could once again show her face in public. Perhaps they too now thought he had really committed suicide since some of those who had turned their backs on her were now among the invited guests.

"People is people," said Clytie. "Don't matter the colour of their skin. Some of these people didn't want nothing to do with Miss Sarah after that Hurley man disappear, but now they back because Miss Emily come home with she English husband."

"Those people are real strange. You should know that by now Clytie."

"I don't understand why Miss Sarah didn't invite Nellie and her husband. They are rich people too."

"You have to understand that Miss Bottomsley don't think that she and Nellie on the same level. Don't forget Nellie used to work here just like the two o' we," said Ursy.

"You think Nellie would come if Miss Sarah had send a invitation?"

"I don't think so Clytie."

Clytie was glad it had only been a cocktail party and not a sit-down dinner. They were both extremely tired by the end of the evening, but it had been a great success. She remembered that after a party like that one, John Bottomsley would give them a couple extra shillings, but she really didn't expect it from Sarah Bottomsley.

"Thank the Lord this is my last party here at Bottomsley."

"I just don't understand how you could pack up and leave me here alone Clytie. I don't like Miss Bottomsley, but her daughter is a real lady. However I am packing my things and moving out of here too."

"You can't do that Ursy. Miss Emily is going to need you."

"What will she need me for?"

"Now that she is in the family way, she is going to need a lot o' help."

"Look how many o' we used to be in the family way, but still had to work like mules."

"It is different with Miss Emily. We got to look out for that girl. I thought you like Miss Emily."

"I like Miss Emily, but I got to think about myself."

"Just promise me you going to wait till Miss Emily got the baby."

"Then I am going to move to St. Lucy with my family."

"Just wait until the time come Ursy."

They didn't know what to make of Alastair Chambers. He seemed pretty quiet and spent lots of time on the telephone. Sometimes he and Emily would meet with Nicholas Bellamy and they would spend hours looking over papers spread across the table. Still Sarah Bottomsley showed no interest in what they were doing. Emily was now over twenty one and it seemed as if she and her husband were getting ready to take over the running of the plantation. Rumours spread among the plantation workers that Emily Chambers had no interest in the plantation and was going to sell it. What interest would two solicitors have in sugar cane production? However selling Bottomsley was the last thing Emily intended doing. She had seen her father work long hours just to leave her this legacy and she would never consider selling it.

The plantation was more profitable than she had expected. Nicholas Bellamy was an honest man who had put his energy into keeping it running and out of the hands of the creditors. He was now ready to let it all go and return to England; something which he wanted to do for a while. Did that mean a new overseer or would Alastair Chambers be taking over the running of Bottomsley for his wife? He knew nothing about sugar cane nor the running of a plantation, but Nicholas Bellamy could teach him all he knew in the little time he had left on the island. With Christmas so close at hand, they decided to wait until the holidays were over before they tackled such an important decision.

Sarah's mood was not a very good one. Clytie had packed her things and left Bottomsley; never to return.

"It's your fault," she said to her daughter. "These people must be treated like children. You must think for them, make decisions for them and tell them when to come and when to go."

"Mama, I can't believe you still think that way. Clytie has been faithful to you all these years and the least you could have done was given the fours days off to spend with her aging mother."

"You have been away from the island for much too long. You have forgotten how things work here. Clytie was happy working here with me. You have brought your new ideas and put them into her head."

"Mama, you know Clytie is not a stupid woman. She can read and write and think for herself. She was very good to me when I was growing up. Sometimes she put everything aside just to be with me and that I will never forget."

"My child, she was paid for it. She didn't do it out of the goodness of her heart."

Alastair Chambers listened to the mother and daughter and did not intervene. His mother in law didn't seem to be a very giving or caring person, but he was new on the scene and held his opinion to himself. His wife on the other hand, was a lovely and big-hearted-person. She always gave and gave and he knew there was a special place in her heart for Clytie, the woman she said had cared more about her than her mother when she was growing up. If Emily loved her, so did he.

Emily related to him about the years when her mother spent most of her time socialising, much too busy to think of a child, and Clytie along with Miss Ella would sit with her in the kitchen, or even take her to their little huts especially when she felt lonely. Clytie was definitely not paid for that. She had done it because she loved Emily. Not only because she happened to be her best friend Nellie's daughter, but because she was a lovely little girl.

"After Father's death, Clytie was the only friend and consolation I had Mama. I would never, ever forget how much she helped me to get over my loss."

"She forgot her place Emily."

"What do you mean Mama?"

"She forgot she was only a servant here in this house."

"Because she asked for a couple days to go away with Miss Una?"

"I can see nothing has changed in our relationship. You are still as stubborn as before."

"Let's change the subject ladies since you both seem to be getting nowhere. And Emily, you shouldn't get yourself into such a state."

"You tell her Alastair," said Sarah Bottomsley.

"Why don't we go for a drive Emily? I haven't had any time to see much of the island."

She agreed and they both set out in her mother's car to do a little exploring. Alastair was fascinated by the fields and fields of sugar cane. He found it hard to believe this was where the sugar came from for his cup of tea. The chattel houses with their little gardens intrigued him. He had had quite a different picture in his mind's eye about the island. Some of those who had moved away from the plantations and had learnt carpentry skills had emulated the styles of the colonial homes, but on a much smaller scale. He saw the children playing in the street, and stopping to wave to them whenever the car passed by. Most colourful was the horse and cart and its driver. The bent over figure of the driver with his whip and the clop-clop of the horse's hooves on the hot tar made him feel sorry for the duo. What was so colourful about the whole thing? As soon as the horse dropped its load of dung onto the street, children would run out with their pans and scrapers to fetch it for their gardens.

"It makes the roses beautiful," said Emily.

He could now understand his wife's passion for the island where she was born and also for its people.

"It's so beautiful," he said as they drove through the lonely country roads.

"I think we are quite close to where Clytie lives," said Emily. "Let's stop and say hello to her."

"But she's not expecting us," said her husband.

"That's not necessary," she replied. "An invitation is hardly ever needed. We can drop by to say hello."

"I know you would love to see Clytie," he said.

When they reached the house, Alastair got out, climbed the steps to the entrance and knocked. Clytie came quickly to the door but did not recognise him, but after seeing Sarah's car, realised it was her son in law.

"Afternoon Mr. Alastair," she said wiping her hands on her apron.

"Good afternoon Clytie. We were in the area and my wife wanted to see how you were."

She saw Emily stepping out of the car and rushed past Alastair to help her.

"Miss Emily," she said as she hugged her. "It so nice of you to come by. Ma keep asking when she is going to see you. She is going to be real happy."

"I hope you don't mind us dropping by. We were driving through the country and when I realised we were so close to your home, we just had to stop in."

"Don't worry about it Miss Emily. We happy to see you anytime you feel like stopping by. You and the baby alright?" she asked.

"We're both fine. Where is Miss Una?" she asked stopping on the last step to catch her breath.

"Come in Mr. Alastair," said Clytie still hanging on to his wife.

He could see how much the woman really loved and admired Emily, and he knew there was nothing Sarah Bottomsley could do, to put a wedge between this friendship.

"Ma, Miss Emily come to see you," she said as Emily sat down.

The old lady came slowly in the living room. They could all tell that her sight was extremely poor.

"Miss Emily?" she said headed in the direction of Alastair.

Her daughter guided her towards Emily who hugged and kissed the old woman.

"I hear you in the family way Miss Emily. I remember when you was a little thing. Only a few days old! You did look just like Master Bottomsley. Your little nose could pick a chigger. I can't see too good no more Miss Emily. You still look like your father?"

"I think so Miss Una. Let me introduce you to my husband Alastair."

"You is a real tall one," she said holding on to his arm and looking up at him. "Be a good husband to our Emily."

"I intend to do that," he said to her.

"You like it here on this little Rock?"

"Very much," he said. "Some things remind me a lot of England."

"Why you think they call it Little England?" asked the old woman. "There are more British people here than in England. Did you hear about the joke that during the last war, the people here was telling England, 'go forth, we are behind you.' We was a real laughing stock. This little David telling Goliath he could count on we for support."

Alastair laughed uneasily as Emily explained the story to him.

"Yes, yes. We couldn't stop laughing," continued the old woman.

Clytie came in carrying a tray with lemonade and biscuits and they talked for a little while. Clytie then reminded Emily that they were leaving the following day for St. Lucia.

"You should stop by and see Nellie. She would be real happy. She only live five minutes from here and Mr. Alastair you could talk to Francois, Nellie husband. He is a solicitor too. Lord it would do Nellie heart good to see you."

"If Emily's not too tired, I wouldn't mind stopping by to meet them."

"I would love to see Miss Nellie and Hurley."

"I got some bad news for you Miss Emily. Since two weeks now, Nellie can't find Hurley. He just disappear. But you know this is not the same Hurley as when you left. He was old and Nellie got another one just in case you come back."

"Who is Hurley?" asked Alastair.

"That was Miss Emily cat. He was real old and half blind, and then one day he just wasn't there no more."

"He do what we all have to do one day," said Miss Una. "He is up in cat heaven."

No sooner had the couple left, than Clytie telephoned her friend.

"I am just calling to let you know that Miss Emily on the way to see you."

"Francois," Nellie shouted. "Emily and her husband are coming to see us. How do I look?" she asked.

"As beautiful as you always look."

She ran to the kitchen calling out to Otty as she ran.

"Make some fresh lemonade Otty. Make a pot of tea and get out some fresh biscuits. We are having visitors in a couple of minutes."

She ran between the verandah and the mirror, while Francois did all he could to calm her frayed nerves.

"They're here," he said as she stood in front of the mirror for the last time.

She peeped out from behind Francois.

"He's extremely tall," she said. "Just a little taller than you.are."

"Miss Emily," called out Nellie going down the pathway to greet them.

"Hello Miss Nellie. This is my husband Alastair."

"Hello Alastair," she said shaking his hand. "And this is my husband Francois."

"Pleased to meet you Francois," said Alastair.

Alastair was amazed at Nellie's home and so was Emily. He looked around at all the beautiful things and commented to Francois on some of them. Then the two men sat together and chatted while Nellie showed Emily around her home.

"This is a beautiful home Miss Nellie."

"Thanks Miss Emily. My father left it for me."

"You are a lucky woman. This is indeed beautiful; even more beautiful than Bottomsley."

"Bottomsley is just as beautiful Miss Emily."

"Miss Nellie, there is something different about you. You speak so well now and tell me where did you find that handsome Francois?"

"He used to be my solicitor Miss Emily."

"Oh Miss Nellie," she said hugging her. "I'm so happy for you. You did so much for Miss Ella and Miss Una, I just knew something good was going to happen for you."

"He is such a good man Miss Emily and he makes me very happy."

"I know he and Alastair will get along well together."

The two men were indeed getting along fabulously. They had something in common. They had both studied law in England and Francois could advise him on the way things were done on the island. Emily couldn't get over the change in Nellie. Her hair was beautifully styled and she raved about her trip to Paris and how Francois had asked her to marry him in the city of love; she also explained about the house and Gus Ridley. Nellie felt as if she were talking to her daughter in a good mother-daughter relationship and that her daughter had been gone for a while and was being brought up-to-date with everything that had gone on in her life during her daughter's absence. Nellie was very proud of her daughter but unfortunately was unable to tell her anything regarding their relationship. They spoke about Sarah Bottomsley and the way she treated Clytie and finally they spoke of Hurley the cat and Hurley the cad.

"He was responsible for Mama shipping me off to England," she said. "But Miss Nellie, it did me a lot of good getting off the Rock for a while. I see things differently and would never have met Alastair if I hadn't left here, but it is so good to be back in the sunshine and warm weather."

"I can understand Miss Emily. As much as I loved Paris I don't think I could live in that cold weather."

"I didn't fully understand the British way of life. It was all just too different."

"I understand what you mean Miss Emily."

Not seeing them return after half an hour, Francois excused himself and called out to his wife.

"We'll be there in a minute," she called back. "I'm just bringing Miss Emily up-to-date on everything that's been happening."

He breathed a sigh of relief. Things seemed to be going well. Soon they returned to the living room where Otty had already placed the lemonade and glasses on a side table and had returned to the kitchen to get the tea. Francois had already introduced the favourite libation of the island people to Alastair. Rum! At first he found it a little too strong but as they continued to converse, it just seemed to slide down his throat.

"Nellie tells me you're also a solicitor," said Emily.

"Three solicitors all under one roof," said Nellie nervously.

"I was telling Francois you've both got a beautiful home," said Alastair looking around.

"You'll have to come over to Bottomsley one evening for dinner," said Emily. "I would love us all to be good friends."

"Thank you," said Francois quickly glancing at his wife who was playing with her hands as she usually did when she was nervous. "We are going away for a few days and will be in touch when we return."

"Does that mean you'll be spending Christmas away from here?" asked Alastair.

"Yes, Nellie has a little vacation house in St. Lucia and about six of us will be spending Christmas there."

"Sometimes it's good to just get away without relatives and enjoy the holiday season away from home."

"Yes. Nellie works very hard and so do I. I leave home at seven in the morning and return at seven at night. Nellie also spends long days in the grocery store and I just don't want her making a big fuss for Christmas."

"I wish Mama would think like that," said Emily. "I'm not used to all this fuss anymore. We have spent quiet Christmases together, haven't we Alastair?"

"Yes but we must understand your mother. You've been gone for a while and she thinks that what she's doing is making you happy."

"You're right. I'm just too critical of Mama."

"Someday you'll invite us to go along with you to St. Lucia I hope," said Alastair.

"Just say the word my friend," said Francois.

* * *

## 60

Needless to say Sarah Bottomsley's mood had deteriorated by the time the couple reached home.

"I was so worried about you," she shouted.

"There was nothing to worry about Mama. We were visiting Clytie and Miss Nellie. You should visit Nellie sometime. She has done quite well for herself. Her home is beautiful and she is married to a solicitor."

"One of the reasons you were sent off to England was to mix with people of your own standing. You have returned home but you have learnt nothing. I cannot send you away again but please do not embarrass me by fraternising with the servants."

"Mama!" she shouted and turned on her heels, leaving Alastair standing with her mother.

"You've upset her Mrs. Bottomsley," he said.

"Please call me Sarah," she said sweetening her tone. "You must talk to her. She cannot be seen with any and everyone. She is Emily Bottomsley. Servants are here to work and provide for us. Not to be socialising with."

"Do you know how much your daughter loves Clytie?" he asked.

"I am aware of how much she cares for Clytie, but that doesn't change anything. Both of those women were servants here in this house. How could she expect to sit down at the same table with them?"

"You know Sarah, Emily tried to explain this to me and I thought I had understood it, but this goes beyond understanding."

"What do you mean?" she asked as she tinkled a little bell which brought Ursy running into the room.

"Yes Miss Bottomsley?"

"Bring me a couple phensic and a glass of water. I have a terrible headache."

"Maybe we can continue this later," he said to her.

"I'm fine," she said. "See that Ursy? She has been in this house for many years, but has never called me ma'am like the others. She is proud. She always calls me Miss Bottomsley."

Ursy returned and handed her the two pills on a little tray and a glass of water. She hardly looked at her but took the pills and the water. As Ursy turned to leave, she called out to her.

"Tell me Ursy, why is it that you call me Miss Bottomsley?"

"Because it is your name," said the woman as she disappeared behind the kitchen door.

He had fight to hold the laughter back and at the same time he realised how vindictive Sarah could be.

"If I may continue Sarah, I want you to know that my wife is not the same little girl who left this island all those years ago. She is now an adult with a mind of her own and you cannot tell her who her friends should be. If she chooses to have Clytie as a friend, it should be none of your concern. And as for Nellie, when was the last time you saw her?"

"I don't remember, but I can see my daughter has also poisoned your mind against me."

"Emily hasn't poisoned my mind against anyone. It is not in her nature to be like that. The Emily I married is a kind, loving and gentle person."

"I can see that I'm once again the rogue here."

"All I'm asking is that you leave her alone to do what she wants to do and to live her life the way she sees fit."

"This is going to be one wonderful Christmas," said Sarah Bottomsley. "Goodnight Alastair."

"Goodnight Sarah," he said shrugging his shoulders.

The kitchen door squeaked gently and long. He knew that Ursy had been listening to their conversation.

***

It was the twenty fourth of December and Nellie and her friends and family had just landed on the island of St. Lucia. It was dark and almost midnight when they finally found two taxis to take them to their destination. With the exception of Nellie and Francois, none of the others had ever left the Rock, and were excited to be on another island.

"Can't see too much," said Miss Una.

"Tomorrow morning we will see a lot more," said her daughter.

"I wish Ella was here to make this trip too," the old lady said.

"I am sure she is somewhere around here looking down," said Clytie.

"I hope so," replied Miss Una. "And Ella, if you can hear me, I want you to know that I will soon be joining you."

"What foolishness you talking Ma?"

"We ain't here on this earth forever Clytie. One day I got go whether you like it or not."

"I know that Ma, but you don't always have to keep talking about it."

The four days were gone before they could bat an eyelash and it was time to go home. Christmas was over and they all had enjoyed themselves to the fullest. Miss Una went as faras to tell Francois that she hadn't trusted him when he first married Nellie.

"I thought you was after Nellie money," she said to him.

"Ma," shouted Clytie. "You can't talk to Francois like that."

"And what do you think now Miss Una?" he asked.

"You is a decent fellow. Nellie is lucky to have a husband like you."

"Thank you Miss Una," he said kissing her on the cheek.

"Don't kiss me too much," said the old woman. "I might just take you away from Nellie."

"We'd better hurry," he said after they had all had a laugh. "The boat leaves in two hours."

* * *

Nellie and Francois returned home to find the kitchen brimming with all kinds of foodstuff.

"Where did this come from?" she asked examining some of the items.

"We'll find out tomorrow when Otty comes in. Let's go to bed."

Otty had forgotten who had brought what, and not only had they brought foodstuff, but they were chickens, rabbits and even a little piglet tied up in the backyard.

"What am I going to do with all this?" she asked.

"The pig must go," said Francois. "You can give away most of it and send the rest to the church to be distributed among the villagers."

"There is something else," said Otty. "I have to go home to get it."

She returned with a little kitten which was about three weeks old.

"This one I'm keeping," she said to Francois. "And I'll call it Hurley. The next time Emily comes, she can see we have another little kitten just like Hurley."

Francois could only shake his head. Nellie's mind was always on her daughter and hardly anyone else. He drove off for the office and dropped Nellie off at the store. The others were already there. Miss Una was in usual spot behind the cash cage and although she wore very thick glasses, she constantly squinted in order to see. Clytie and Nora were busy packaging a pound of this and a pint of that.

"How everybody this morning," Nellie called out forgetting everything about speaking the Queen's English.

"We here abiding in the name of the Lord," answered Miss Una. "How is my Francis?"

"He is fine," she answered. "He gone off to the office."

Nora and Clytie nudged each other. Miss Una had not even asked Nellie how she was. Her sole interest was Francois.

"What are you two smiling about?" asked Nellie.

"You can't come between Ma and her Francis. The two o' them like two peas in a pod."

"I nearly died when she told him she thought he was only after my money."

"What is wrong with that?" asked Miss Una. "It is good to get things off your chest sometimes and let people know we ain't fools."

"Ma there is nobody in this world that would think you are a fool. Your mouth frighten me sometimes."

"Miss Una, I thought I was happy when I was with JB, but now I know what it is like to have somebody who cares about you. I thought JB loved me, but I know that Francois loves me. He shows me that in every little thing he does."

"You is a lucky girl. You remember I tell you one time that a bright light is going to shine down on you, and you didn't believe me. Now you know it is true."

"I was so unhappy back then Miss Una, that nothing anyone said would have made a bit of difference."

"Men is real strange creatures," continued the old woman. "I had one a long time ago, and after him I didn't want to see another one."

"You talking about my father Ma?"

"Yes Clytie. I am talking about that no-good brute. Don't even call him your father. Had not for Ella, we would drink water and eat dry bread many a day. Ella was a true friend. She was more than a friend to me."

Nora stopped her work and listened to Miss Una. Staring at Nellie, she raised her eyebrows and waited for Miss Una to continue. Curiosity was getting the better of them. Gossip had it that Una and Ella had been lovers, but no one knew for sure, and today the old woman seemed to be purging her soul of everything.

"Things wasn't so bad Ma," said Clytie.

"What you know? You was just a little child when he spend every single cent on rum. He didn't want nobody to know he was my child father although he wasn't that much better off than we. All he had was his red skin. When there wasn't a cent left to buy food, and I quarrel, he would drop a lash in me, but I learn to get tough and I promise to give him some arsenic if he ever try it again; and Ella would bring down the hambone from Bottomsley kitchen so I could make some soup to feed you."

Nellie burst out laughing when Miss Una mentioned the hambone. Tears ran down her cheeks as she remembered the episode of John Bottomsley Senior, Miss Ella and the hambone. As soon as she stopped laughing, she told the three women the story and soon they too were all laughing hysterically

"That was my friend Ella," said Miss Una. "But back to what I was saying, I could only say that the men today seem better. Look at Percy. He make a honest woman out of Nora. A little bit late but he is still making the rest o' the village show respect to Nora."

"What is wrong with you today Ma? You talking non stop. Your mouth keep running and running."

"Times really changing. Look at Nellie and Clytie. Once upon a time, you had to look like them to work in the kitchen. They didn't want nobody who look like me nor Nora near the back door, but they had better change their ways. I remember when they used to say, if you white, you alright; if you brown, you could stick around; but if you black, you had to stand back. Yes they were hard times for my people; real hard times."

Nellie cringed as Miss Una continued to tell her tales of woe. They were all beginning to feel just a little uncomfortable, because they too could recall some of the stories she was telling and it was nothing but the truth.

"Anyway I know that most women want a man to make them feel like they is somebody, but Clytie as long as you happy and you got something to eat, you should not fret yourself."

"I ain't fretting Ma."

"Anybody hear anything from Miss Emily?" she suddenly asked changing the subject.

"You know that Ursy call yesterday Ma and Miss Emily alright."

"That poor child!" she said and was then quiet.

"Why did you say she is a poor child Miss Una?" asked Nellie.

"Nellie girl, you will have to be strong; for yourself and for Miss Emily."

"What do you mean by that Miss Una?"

"Just prepare yourself Nellie. Just prepare yourself well."

* * *

# 61

That evening Francois told Nellie he had had a call from Alastair Chambers. He was taking over control of Bottomsley and needed his assistance. Against Sarah Bottomsley's wishes, he was taking his business from the antiquated law firm which had handled it for years and was passing it over to Francois. Nellie was pleased but knew it would make the distance even wider between herself and Sarah Bottomsley. The two men had become quite friendly which was a great thrill for Nellie, because it it meant she would be seeing Emily more often. She would have the chance to foster a better relationship between her and her daughter and grandchild. Francois went on to say he would be accompanying Alastair on business sometime during the following week. It would only be for three days, but Nellie had not slept alone since she and Francois had gotten married and she would miss him; but it was all in her daughter's best interest.

"He asked me if Emily could stay with you while he was gone because Sarah Bottomsley makes it very stressful for her."

"And what did you say?" she asked bubbling with excitement.

"I said Emily should talk to you, but he called back later and said Emily preferred to remain at home, since she did not want to antagonize her mother nor hurt her feelings."

Disappointment was written all over Nellie's face.

"Come on Nellie. Perhaps it is for the best. Look at how close we have all become. When the baby is born, I'm sure she'll be spending more and more time with us."

"I hope so Francois, I really hope so."

"Try to see the bright side," he replied.

On Friday evening, after calling Nellie, Alastair, Francois and Nicholas Bellamy headed for the airport to take a late flight to St. Lucia. Alastair was meeting another plantation owner on Nicholas Bellamy's advice. Up-to-date methods were being tried which would increase sugar cane production and Alastair was eager to keep Bottomsley a success. If time permitted, Francois was eager to show him the vacation house which he and Nellie owned, but for the time being they would all stay in a hotel in the city, in close proximity to the plantation where they would see the new experiments.

They were happy Nicholas Bellamy had accompanied them, because they both found it rather time-consuming and for lack of another word, boring, but Alastair decided it was in his best interest to learn as much as he could, boring or not.

After dinner Alastair invited the three men for a drink in the hotel bar, but Nicholas Bellamy declined the invitation and went to his room. The two men sat and talked until around midnight and then went to bed. The following day brought more instructions on cane production and since both men weren't as enthused as Nicholas Bellamy, they still needed to show some interest in sugar cane cultivation.

"Do you know the man sitting alone at the bar?" asked Alastair.

"It was none other than Teddy Applewhite who had drunk a bit more than he could handle, if that was at all possible.

"Nellie bought the vacation house here on the island from him."

"What is his name?" Alastair asked.

"Ted Applewhite. He's not the sort you would want to mix with. Why do you ask? Do you know him?"

"No I don't, but his face seems rather familiar."

Francois related the story about the man and his two unfortunate daughters whom he sexually abused. It was more shocking to Alastair to find out that no one was interested or too afraid to do anything about it.

"Those girls should have been taken away from him long ago," he said.

"I wanted to do something about it, but was told by a solicitor that it was better if I minded my business. I would have taken the matter further, but Nellie was afraid and begged me to stay out of it. It still bothers me that this man can get away with such abuse and everyone turns a blind eye."

"What about the mother of the children?"

"No one has ever seen her. It is a big mystery."

"I know I have seen that face somewhere before. I will ask Emily. Perhaps she may remember something."

It was six thirty in the evening and Clytie was preparing dinner for her family, when the telephone rang. It was Ursy on the other end and she was panic-stricken.

"Slow down Ursy and tell me what happen."

"Miss Emily is going to have the baby and she is asking for you."

"What you mean she asking for me?" asked Clytie.

"She keeps saying she wish you was here."

"I'm coming," said Clytie without another thought to dinner.

When she was ready to go, she realised she had no way to get to Bottomsley and Clarence was called upon to take her there. She paced back and forth and ran down the steps as soon as she saw the car approaching. On the way, she remembered she hadn't called Nellie to tell her the news. She wasn't sure if Sarah Bottomsley would allow her onto the premises, but she was willing to take the chance. Had Alastair been called, she wondered. When they reached the plantation, without a second thought, she jumped from the car and made her way towards the kitchen where she was met by Ursy.

"I'm so glad you come," she said. "They can't find Mr. Alastair but the doctor is in there with her."

"Miss Sarah is there too?"

"She in the drawing room."

"She know that I'm coming?" asked Clytie.

"I don't know, but she know that Miss Emily was asking for you."

"Evening Miss Sarah," said Clytie as she opened the kitchen door.

"Good evening Clytie," she answered nervously. "Emily has been asking for you."

"You think I could see her?" she asked.

"I would have to ask Dr. Sims," she said as she got up and gently knocked on the bedroom door.

The doctor went to the verandah and lit a cigarette while Clytie went in to see Emily.

"Miss Emily?" she said as she held her hand.

Emily opened her eyes and smiled.

"How you feeling?" Clytie asked.

"I never knew there would be so much pain," she said. "My baby's feeling too comfortable and doesn't want to come out."

"It does take time Miss Emily," she said as Emily screamed bringing her mother and the doctor to the door.

"You'll have to leave now," said the doctor as he started to examine her.

"This is it Mrs Chambers. I think the baby is now ready," he said with a smile. "You've got to help me now."

Twenty minutes later, Emily Chambers gave birth to a healthy baby boy. She could see the look on the doctor's face as her child entered the world.

"You seem worried Dr. Sims," she said raising her head to see what was wrong.

"I think I'll get your mother," he said without replying.

Sarah entered the room and the moment she saw the baby, shock registered across her face.

"What's wrong with my baby?" asked Emily.

The doctor took the little child and put in on the mother's stomach. Emily took one look at the baby and shock also registered across her tired face.

"The baby's healthy," said the doctor. "Now I'll be on my way."

"How did this happen?" asked Sarah Bottomsley afraid to touch the child.

"I have no idea Mama."

"The child is black Emily. How could this have happened?"

Without waiting for an answer, Sarah Bottomsley wrapped the child in a blanket and left the room, leaving her daughter in hysterics. Clytie was on her way to see Emily and ran into Sarah Bottomsley. She pushed the blanket into her hands and told her to take the child away from the plantation.

"What you mean Miss Sarah?"

"Don't ask any questions. Just take it away from here. And Clytie, if anyone asks about Emily's baby, please say it died."

"Yes Miss Sarah," said Clytie as she pulled the blanket away from the child's face and was totally in shock by what she saw.

She jumped into Clarence's car and they headed to the north.

"Go directly to Miss Nellie," she said to the driver.

The child started to squirm and cry. He was obviously hungry and had not had a chance to suckle. He was tossed from the arms of his mother into the unknown.

"Don't worry little fellow," said Clytie. "You soon will get something to eat."

Nellie was surprised to see Clytie at that hour of the night and wondered what was in the parcel she carried so gently in her arms.

"Nels we got trouble; this is Emily baby."

Nellie was confused but quickly took the blanket and its contents away from Clytie.

"Why are you bringing Emily's baby up here at this time of the night?" she asked.

No answer was needed because Nellie had lifted the blanket and saw the child who was obviously very hungry. She stuck her finger in the child's mouth and it sucked and sucked.

"Clytie, get Clarence to take you back to the shop and bring two baby bottles and some baby milk"

Nellie held the child in her arms and swayed from side to side to console the hungry infant. She was happy when she saw the headlights of the car and knew Clytie had returned. They mixed a bottle of milk and fed the naked hungry child who then slept peacefully in Nellie's arms.

"What we going to do Nels?"

"This is Emily's son and I'm keeping him."

"I don't understand how Miss Sarah could do that to an innocent child. I wonder how Miss Emily doing?"

"Lord have mercy. My poor child! I know exactly what she is going through," Nellie said as she cried and stared at the baby. "I wish Francois was at home."

"I have to call Ma and I tell her I am staying here tonight."

"Just a minute; let me think," said Nellie through her tears.

"I will phone Otty tomorrow morning, but I think I should spend the night by you."

"I don't understand Nels."

"I still don't trust Otty and since nobody knows where you took the child, I have to think before she sees it."

The sleeping child was gathered up and they headed for Clytie's home, where Miss Una waited anxiously to see him.

"I know something like this was going to happen," she said as she gently pulled the blanket away from the sleeping bundle.

"Why didn't you warn me about this Miss Una?" Nellie asked.

"I try to warn you a couple days ago but you didn't listen."

"What are we going to do Miss Una?"

"First we have to get the child some sort of clothes. He can't lie down in just this blanket."

"Then we have to do something bright and early tomorrow," said Clytie. "Why you don't call Nora? Harriet make clothes when she has the time. I am sure she got something that would fit this poor child."

"Don't keep calling him a poor child. He will never be poor as long as I got anything to say about it," protested Nellie.

"You understand what I mean Nels. I know he ain't poor. It is just the way that Sarah Bottomsley kick him off the plantation."

"Lord how I wish Francois was here," Nellie said.

"Well he ain't here Nellie, so we got to think about the next step. When Francis coming home?"

"Tomorrow evening."

Nora quickly arrived with two little outfits that would fit the baby and of course was curious to know where they got the child.

"That woman should be ashamed of herself," she said staring at the copper-skinned sleeping infant. "I never see a child with that colour hair and that colour skin," she said.

"How Miss Emily could do that?" asked Clytie.

"How she could do what?" asked Miss Una. "Sometimes you could be real foolish. You ain't see what happening here?"

"What do you mean Miss Una?" asked Nellie.

"I thought you understand what I was saying Nellie? Who is Emily mother?" asked the old woman.

"Lord have mercy!" said Clytie.

"I just don't understand the young people. You always have to spell out everything for them," the old woman muttered.

Everyone took a seat as they were all shocked by Miss Una's explanation.

"That didn't even cross my mind Miss Una," said Nellie.

"So that means you all think that lovely girl was running around behind her husband back?"

"Miss Una, I didn't have time to think about nothing so," said Nellie again forgetting about the Queen's English. "Don't open your mouths about this to nobody. I want to wait until Francois comes home before I do anything."

* * *

# 62

Francois and Alastair decided to forget about the drunken Teddy Applewhite and settle in for the night. As Alastair flipped his light switch, he noticed there was a sheet of paper which had been pushed under his door. He picked it up and read it.

*This is of the utmost importance. Please call your home. There has been an emergency.*

He called the operator who tried to connect him to his home on the Rock but was unsuccessful. He then asked to be connected to Francois' room and related the contents of the message he had received. Francois then decided to call Nellie since he was sure his wife would know what it was all about, but there was no answer at his home. They both decided they should return to the Rock leaving Nicholas Bellamy behind to finish the project. They also had no success in reaching the airline at that late hour, but decided to pack their bags and head for the airport early the next morning.

There was only one available seat and Alastair was on board vleaving Francois behind, with no hope of returning home before his scheduled flight departure. The little propeller plane seemed to make a stop on every little dirt patch, which made Alastair more and more frantic.

He rushed directly to a telephone at the airport to call his wife, but instead got Sarah Bottomsley on the phone.

"Emily has miscarried," she said through tears. "It was a little boy."

"Where is she now? How is she taking it?" he asked.

"My daughter is tired and as expected is still sleeping."

"I'll be home within half an hour," he said.

"Are you on the island?" she asked, her lips trembling.

"Tell Emily I'll be there soon."

Ursy was on the telephone with Clytie and she was totally distressed.

"So Miss Emily lost the baby," she said to Clytie.

"I know Ursy. How she is this morning?"

"I haven't seen her yet, but it must be real hard for her."

"Who is it?" asked Nellie.

"It is only Ursy."

"What does she want?" asked Nellie holding the baby in her arms.

"She is only asking me about Miss Emily and the baby she lost."

Nellie stared at Clytie as if daring her to say a word, and breathed a sigh of relief when the conversation came to an end. Before she could say anything the telephone rang again and it was the operator looking for Nellie Bertrand.

"I slept here last night," she said to him.

She listened for a while and then she replied.

"Hurry home Francois. I have trouble. Emily's baby is here with us."

He seemed to be asking lots of questions until the baby started to cry.

"I am going home when Otty leaves," she said. "I'll see you later this evening."

"Bring him here," said Miss Una. "I want to wash him. He is crying bcause he is feeling hot and miserable. What you going to call him Nellie?"

"That is a good question."

"Well while I bathe him, you better think about a name and Clytie, get the milk ready before he cry down the house."

"I always liked the name Douglas. Francois' father was Douglas too. That name makes him sound important."

Miss Una cleaned the child and talked to him as she took care with his navel. She wiped under his neck and under his little arms while he protested. Then she dressed him in one of Harriet's little creations and he settled down to a bottle in Nellie's lap.

* * *

"I'm so glad you're home Alastair," said Sarah Bottomsley running to meet him at the door.

"Is Emily still in her room?"

"Yes," she said running after him.

"I want to be alone with my wife for a few minutes Sarah."

"Of course," she said. "Please forgive me."

Emily opened her eyes and started to cry when she saw her husband. He took her in his arms and tried to console her.

"We'll have other children," he said kissing her on the head.

That tatement seemed to throw her into hysterics and she wept and wept. Alastair climbed into bed next to her and held her until she fell asleep.

"Did the doctor give her anything to calm her nerves?" he asked her mother.

"No he didn't."

"Then I think I should get her something."

"I'll do that," said Sarah. "You stay here with her in case she wakes up."

"Please hurry Sarah."

* * *

Dr. Sims came out and called Sarah Bottomsley into his office. She sat uneasily in the chair and stared at him.

"I came to get something to calm my daughter's nerves," she said.

"How is Mrs Chambers?" he asked.

"As to be expected," she answered.

"It is none of my business Mrs Bottomsley…..

"And I hope it remains that way," she said looking him directly in the eye. "I've sent the child away and told everyone that it had died."

The doctor leaned back in his chair and looked at her.

"She must take one of of these pills every four hours. If there is any problem, you can call me."

Sarah Bottomsley got up and walked to the door. She then turned and gave the dfoctor a cold stare.

"Thank you," she said.

"Mrs Bottomsley," he replied.

Francois walked to the pay telephone after he left the customs area. He wanted to speak to Alastair but thought it better if he spoke to his wife first. Clytie and Nora were also at the house when he arrived. Nellie jumped up and clung to her husband while he stared at the little bundle lying on Clytie's lap.

"What on earth is going on," he asked.

"Look at the baby," Nellie said to him.

As he lifted the bundle from Clytie's lap, all eyes were focussed on him.

"Emily wasn't running around behind her husband's back," said Nellie trying to protect her daughter.

"Iknow," he answered as he stared at the child. "Don't you see he's got your nose Nellie?"

She gazed at the sleeping child.

"Is that my nose?" she asked putting her hand to her face and feeling her nose.

"I'll take you both home," he said to Clytie and Nora. "You are both probably very tired from all this."

Nellie could only stare at her husband as he walked to the parked car to take the two ladies to their homes.

* * *

"I will not give him away," said Nellie.

"Who said we should give him away?"

"You mean it is alright to keep him?"

"I wouldn't have expected you to give him away Nellie."

"I love you so much," she said clinging to him.

"He is your grandchild. He is a part of you and he is also a part of me."

"Oh thank you Francois," she said breaking into tears.

"Alright Nellie; there is no time for tears. We have to think about what we will tell Otty and most of all, what we will tell Alastair and Emily."

"I never thought that something like this would happen again. I thought everything would be alright, but it is a real mess."

"When anyone sees us with the child, they will probably think we are the grandparents."

"I want to call him Douglas."

"Why Douglas?" he asked.

"You said it was your father's name."

"That's why I love you Nellie Bertrand. You always think of others before you think of yourself. I really appreciate the thought, but there will be lots of questions, but you owe no one an explanation except the two people concerned and I will talk to them."

"Thank you Lord," said Nellie looking upward.

And so Douglas slept in the bed alongside his newly acquired parents until they could furnish a room for him. Their story was ready for anyone who asked about the child, but the truth had to be told to the child's parents. They were not stupid people and Francois was sure they would put two and two together. However Nellie was very grateful to have her husband by her side for he gave her the confidence and security she needed in this tenuous situation.

"Nellie I will tell you a story one day," he said.

"Why don't you tell me now?" she asked.

"Because the time is not right," he replied.

* * *

# 63

Although his wife was still in a depressed state, Alastair's hands were still full with the imminent takeover of the plantation. He had to meet with Nicholas Bellamy that morning because of very pressing matters.

Sarah Bottomsley knocked on her daughter's door and gently opened it. Emily was lying with her face to the window and staring glassy-eyed at the sky.

"How are you this morning?" her mother asked as she sat on the edge of her daughter's bed.

Emily did not reply, nor did she look in her mother's direction.

"I know you're not happy with me or my decision, but something had to be done Emily. How could you have done such a thing? How could you have done that to Alastair and to me? We would have been the laughing stock of this island."

"How dare you Sarah Bottomsley? How dare you accuse me of such an indiscretion? Do you think think I was having affairs behind Alastair's back like you did with Papa? Tell me Mother. Do you think that's what I did?"

Sarah Bottomsley was in shock. She felt that at any moment her daughter would jump out of bed and strike her.

"I'm sorry Emily. I just don't understand it. How could such a thing have happened?"

"You tell me mother. What have you hidden from me all these years? Are you really my mother?"

"How could you say that to me Emily?"

"You never really cared anything about me. Clytie was the only one I could go to when I needed help. You were too caught up in your own world to care anything about me."

"That's not true Emily. I really loved you then and I love you still."

"You loved me so much that you allowed Thomas Hurley to throw me out of your life; to abandon me. Are you really my mother or is Clytie my mother?"

"Now you're talking absolute nonsense Emily. How on earth could Clytie be your mother?"

"Mother, something isn't right here. I know I haven't been unfaithful to my husband, so how could this have happened to me?"

"I don't know Emily. I just don't know."

"Could you call Clytie? I would like to see her."

"Why do you want to see Clytie?"

"It's none of your business Mother."

"Alright then; I'll get Ursy to call her on the phone."

"I asked you Mother. Is she so socially beneath you that you cannot make a call to her?"

"Don't worry Emily. I'll do it. I'll do it."

Sarah was on the receiving end of her daughter's bitterness and it was hard for her to accept. In the long run, it was better if she did make the call to Clytie. She had no idea what the woman had done with the baby and she knew her daughter would probably want to know, and so did she.

Alastair Chambers found it difficult to see his beloved Emily in such a depressed state and decided to visit Francois that evening to ask his advice.

"We're just having dinner," said Nellie. "I'll set a place for you."

"Thank you Nellie," he said, "as long as it's not too much trouble."

"Will it be the usual?"Francois asked him.

"Yes, the usual," he replied.

"How is Emily?"

"She's not doing very well. She is absolutely depressed."

Nellie got up from the dinner table and quietly entered the bedroom and closed the door. Douglas was still fast asleep. He had had his bottle about half an hour earlier and was contented as could be. His friend and companion Hurley also slept peacefully in his favourite place at the foot of the bed. The two men were deep in conversation when she returned.

"I really don't know what to do," he said.

"Maybe you should take her away for a couple of days. A change of scenery would do her good."

"Are you talking about Emily?"

"Yes Nellie. She's very depressed.

"Why don't you take her to St. Lucia. The house is empty until March," Francois said.

"I've got so much to do. Nicholas Bellamy is anxious to leave and is trying to teach me all he knows before he departs."

"Sweeten the pot for him Alastair," said Francois.

"Do you mean I should bribe him to stay?"

"That word is never used in our profession," said Francois in a teasing manner.

"Maybe he would stay if I paid him well for another month.

"You can only try my friend," said Francois.

"Excuse me for a moment," she said getting up to answer the telephone.

"Nels," said Clytie. "I am real worried."

"About what?" she asked.

"Sarah Bottomsley just call and say Emily want me to come by."

"Yes," said Nellie.

"What you think is going to happen Nels?"

"I am not sure," she replied.

"She probably want to know what happen to her baby."

"I think so too. When are you going there?" asked Nellie.

"Nels, you sound real funny. You can't talk?"

"No I can't right now. I'll call you later."

"Don't forget Nels."

They hadn't noticed how quiet Nellie had become and that her face had taken on a very worried look and since Alastair was anxious to get home to his wife, he thanked his friends and set off for Bottomsley.

"I have to phone Clytie. We have trouble Francois."

"What kind of trouble?"

"Sarah phoned Clytie and told her Emily wants to see her."

"Don't panic at everything Nellie. She is depressed and needs to see a kind face."

"I hope that is all."

Nellie tried to convince Clytie there was nothing to worry about, but Clytie was not easily convinced.

"What if she ask me about the baby? What am I supposed to say?"

"That is a hard one Clytie. Let me talk to Francois and call you back."

"She must tell Emily the truth. She must tell her where the baby is."

His wife seemed shocked by his answer.

"Are you sure you want her to know that?"

"We promised the only people who would be told the truth are the child's parents."

"Francois, you know I always look to you for advice, but do you think this is the right thing to do?"

"We can't hide it for too much longer Nels. She will sooner or later find the truth out."

"What if she hates me then? I wouldn't be able to bear it if she stopped speaking to me."

"Let them take a little vacation first and then we'll tell them."

"Lord knows I'm not looking forward to this," Nellie said.

"Listen Nellie, tell Clytie not to visit her right now. She must find an excuse not to go. Then Emily and Alastair will be out of the island and that will give us a chance to get our thoughts together."

"That is a good idea."

Needless to say, Clytie was relieved to know she wouldn't have to face Emily just yet, for it was a moment she had really dreaded.

Alastair convinced his wife that a change of scenery would be good for her and Francois' advice on handling Nicholas Bellamy did work out well. Alastair believed with or wthout the extra money, Nicholas would have stayed. He was a man with strong moral fibre and would never have left his employer stranded.

Word had spread that Emily had lost the baby and the rumour mills had started to spin. She was compared to her mother who had had great difficulty in presenting a child to John Bottomsley. She knew she had to get away from the wagging tongues of the rumour mongers on the island. So it was not long before she and Alastair were sitting on the front porch of Nellie's vacation home in St. Lucia. They sat quietly listening to the silence when a car drove by and the driver reversed and stepped out.

"Morning to yer," he said lifting his hat. "I thought it was Miss Nellie."

"Good morning," said Alastair. "I'm Alastair Chambers and this is my wife Emily."

"Morning ma'am," he said again lifting his hat. "Teddy's the name. Anyone ever told you look just like Miss Nellie?"

"No, you're the first," said Emily with little enthusiasm. "Do you know Nellie well?"

"Of course I do. She and her husband, God rest his soul, bought this house from me about twelve years ago."

"But Nellie wasn't married," said Emily. "She married Mr. Bertrand only a short while ago."

"I know I sold this house to Miss Nellie and her husband John."

"It doesn't matter. It probably happened after I left for England. But why didn't she tell me?" she asked aloud.

"Don't know ma'am. You would have to take that up with Miss Nellie."

Alastair, who had been pretty quiet up to this point, spoke to him.

"Your face seems so familiar. Why do I think I've seen you somewhere before."

"I've got one o' those faces. Everybody thinks they've seen me before. Probably got a twin brother and don't know it," he said with a grin. "Anyway I must run. I have a lot of business to do today. Say hello to Miss Nellie and that new husband of hers."

Like a flash of lightning, Teddy Applewhite had disappeared.

"Don't you think he left in an awful hurry?" Alastair asked. "And doesn't his face seem very familiar?"

"He is Thomas Appleby?" said Emily without batting an eyelash.

"And who is Thomas Appleby?"

"He murdered his wife and then disappeared with the two children."

"You're right Emily. I thought his face looked so familiar. We should inform the authorities," he said.

"Don't you think we've got enough of our own problems?"

"Do you mean we should let him get away with it?"

"Alastair, I just can't cope with anything else. I just want to sit here and watch the ocean."

"Sorry Emily. I didn't mean to place added any burden on you."

"Thank you for understanding Alastair," she said reaching out and holding his hand. "I never knew Nellie had been married before," she continued her mind miles away.

"Ask her when we return. I'm sure they will invite us over."

"Yes," she said closing her eyes and leaning her head on his shoulder.

Sometimes a little rest and relaxation is all one needs and it certainly seemed to have taken Emily's mind off her troubles. Together they strolled along the beach hand in hand, picking up shells or just sat watching the setting sun. Meta the housekeeper had their meals on the table punctually and catered to their every wish.

They did see Teddy Applewhite or Thomas Appleby drive by on three other occasions, but he never stopped nor did he even wave to them.

"I wonder what happened to his children," Alastair said as he sat enjoying his dinner.

"They were two girls, weren't they?"

"Yes, they must be about sixteen and eleven."

"Thank you Meta," said Alastair. "That was a delicious meal."

"Thank you sir," she replied. "I am glad you like it."

"Tell me something Meta. Do you know a man called Thomas Appleby?"

"No, can't say I do," she replied.

"He lives somewhere around here and he has two daughters."

"You mean Teddy Applewhite. Yes, he lives about ten minutes from here with his two children."

"Are they two girls?"

"Yes, I don't mean to be forward sir, but why you asking me all these questions about him?"

"He dropped in here two days ago and I just wondered if you knew him."

"Stay way from him. He isn't a decent man sir. He sleeps with his two daughters."

Emily raised her head and looked at Meta as if she hadn't clearly understood what she had said.

"Did you say he sleeps with his daughters?" she asked.

"That is what I say ma'am. He don't send them to school and he really like his grog. He didn't ask you for a drink?"

Alastair did recall that he had left in a dreadful hurry and perhaps didn't have the chance to ask. They didn't discuss the subject anymore in Meta's presence, because they didn't know her and didn't know if they could trust her.

"Is everything alright?" asked Francois as Alastair picked up the telephone.

"We were already in bed," said Alastair. "It's beautiful here and Emily seems to be coming around."

"I'm glad to hear that. We were a bit concerned about you."

"Another two days and we'll be home again. I hope Emily can spend some time with Nellie. She needs good friends right now."

"Don't worry. Nellie would be more than happy to have her come around."

"Francois, do you remember the drunken man we saw sitting in the bar about a week ago and I said his face looked familiar?"

"You're speaking about Teddy Applewhite?"

"His name isn't Teddy Applewhite. It's Thomas Appleby and he's wanted for murder on the continent."

"What? I knew he was a strange character. But murder?"

"This happened over thirteen years ago, and as you know he also has an incestuous relationship with his two daughters."

"Please be careful Alastair. You can do something about it when you're back here, but don't get involved in anything there. It seems as if he's got everyone in his pockets."

"Thanks I'll be careful."

"Say hello to Emily from Nellie and from me."

"By the way Francois, was Nellie married before?"

"No, this is her first marriage. Why do you ask?"

"Thomas Appleby dropped by and during the conversation he told Emily that Nellie had been married before to someone named John."

"He's mistaken. I'm the first man to whom Nellie said, I do," he answered with a chuckle.

Francois knew what it was all about and decided not to tell Nellie because it would only bring her more unwanted worry.

* * *

# 64

"What you doing here Miss Sarah?" asked Clytie.

"I'm using this opportunity now that my daughter is out of the island to get some information."

"What kind of information you want?"

"What did you do with the child Clytie."

"I can't say Miss Sarah. You tell me to get rid of it and I carry it somewhere safe."

"Don't be silly Clytie. Just tell me what you did with Emily's baby."

"You didn't think about that before you abandon that innocent child," shouted Miss Una from behind the cashier's cage.

"You stay out of this. I'm speaking to Clytie."

"I ain't staying out of nothing. You throw that child out without even a diaper. What you want now? Stop confusing my daughter."

"How dare you speak to me like that?"

"I can say whatever I want. I ain't on Bottomsley property, but you on private property."

"It is alright Ma," said Clytie.

"It ain't alright. She showing up here and giving orders? You don't work in Bottomsley kitchen no more. You don't know how long I wait to tell you that. You is a selfish woman. You only think about yourself and nobody else. You better change your ways or you ain't going to have no daughter."

"What do you know about my daughter?"

"Alright Ma, Miss Sarah going to leave now."

"Are you throwing me out before telling me what you did with my grandson?"

Miss Una cackled like a setting hen when Sarah Bottomsley referred to the child as her grandson.

"You is grandmother in name only. What you know about being a grandmother?"

"I will find out," threatened Sarah Bottomsley. "And when I do, God help you two."

"You ain't going to do a thing," said Miss Una. "You mean to tell me that you will tell the people on this Rock that that little boy is your grandson? You wouldn't find that a little too shameful to call him a part o' your family?"

Without another word, Sarah Bottomsley got into her car and drove off.

"You didn't have to be so hard Ma."

"It is time somebody put that old harlot in her place," said Miss Una. "She is used to everybody jumping when she say jump, but I ain't jumping. The old bones ain't going to let me jump even if I want to. You don't think you should tell Nellie in case she find herself at Nellie house?"

* * *

"How was your holiday darling?" asked Sarah Bottomsley trying to be friendly.

"Good thank you," said Emily brushing her mother aside.

"I should visit St. Lucia sometime. I've been here in the Caribbean for such a long time and have never visited another island."

"I'm not surprised Mother," she said.

"I thought you would've come back in a different frame of mind, but you seem as bitter as the day you left."

"Where is my child mother? What have you done with him?"

"Forget about him Emily. You and Alastair will have more children."

Anger and hatred seemed to consume Emily. The very sight of her mother seemed to enrage her and without another word, she grabbed a hat, jumped into the car and drove off. She drove and drove until she found herself in front of Clytie's door.

"Good morning Miss Una," she said looking inside.

"I know the voice. Is that my little Emily?" she asked.

"Yes Miss Una. I thought I'd come by for a visit. Where is Clytie?"

"Come in child and sit next to an old woman. Clytie is in the shop."

Emily did as she was told.

"How you feeling child?" Miss Una asked.

"Not very well Miss Una."

"I help to bring you into this world. Tell me what bothering you child."

"Were you present at my birth Miss Una?"

"I was present at the birth of every child on Bottomsley plantation."

"But I thought Dr. Sims had brought me into the world."

"I used to help out with everybody. Not only the plantation workers. Tell me what on your mind child"

"Is Sarah really my mother?"

"Why you asking a question like that?"

"You know the story about my baby?"

"Yes Miss Emily. I know that story only too good."

"Then would you please explain to me what it is all about, because I'm very, very confused."

"The person who is responsible for this mess long left this earth."

"Who are you talking about Miss Una?"

"Your father! John Bottomsley. He was a good man, but he sure left a mess behind him. Oh what a tangled web we weave, when we first set out to deceive."

"Please explain what my father had to do with this Miss Una."

"You ever hear about something name 'Striking Back' Miss Emily?"

"I think so."

"And you know what it mean?"

"I think I do Miss Una. What are you trying to tell me?"

"You think you having a hard time Miss Emily? I can think about another young girl who was about the same age as you and who went through the same hell."

"Who was that Miss Una?"

"I will get to that in a minute. When you ain't born with a gold spoon in your mouth, your life can be as hard as hell. I hope that now you come back to this rock, you will remain as sweet as you always was. Life can be rough when you come from the other side, if you understand what I mean. You belong to the plantation and we was just the workers trying to make ends meet."

The old woman took Emily's hand in her wrinkled black hand; a hand wrinkled from years and years of toil in the sugar canefields.

"You believe in angels Miss Emily?"

"I think I do."

"I do, not only in heaven. We got angels down here on this earth. Nellie Peterkin is a angel. She see the good in a stray dog. You know she take me in when I had nowhere else to go; now that I am old and wrinkled. As I was telling you Miss Emily, your father left a real mess behind. You come to ask me who your mother is. That mean you got doubts."

"I just want to know how Alastair and I could have a child who is blacker than he is white."

"We was talking about 'Striking Back.' Remember what I am going to tell you, only three other people know. That girl I was telling you about was Nellie. She used to work in the kitchen at Bottomsley. She was a pretty little girl and Master Bottomsley always had an eye for pretty women. So he had his eye on Nellie. She was only about fourteen at the time, but it didn't matter to Master Bottomsley. That was the way things was back then. She was the Keep Miss. That mean that she had to be there whenever he want her. Well next thing you know Nellie was in the family way and so was Sarah. Nellie never ever did want to give away her baby, but he make a agreement with Nellie that if Sarah child should be born dead, he and Sarah would raise Nellie child as their own. He promise Nellie her child would inherit the plantation. When I think back on those times, and poor Nellie, I get cold bumps all over my skin. It was a real hard time for that child. Everybody hear that Nellie baby only live for ten days. On top o' that, Sarah Bottomsley did want Nellie to look after the baby even though she hear that Nellie baby did pass away a couple o' days earlier. But what I neglect to tell you is that Sarah didn't know that all this was going on. After your father carry out Sarah dead baby, she did real tired and went to sleep. When she wake up, you was in the bed next to her."

Tears flowed down Emily's face. For so many years she thought Sarah was her mother, only to find out the woman she had referred to as Miss Nellie was really her biological mother.

"And what happened to Miss Nellie?"

"I think John Bottomsley did really love Nellie. In time, you would own the plantation if Nellie would give you up and in turn, he would move her far from Bottomsley into she own house."

"Did he do that?"

"Yes he live up to his word. Nora and Nellie move up here and we been up here ever since. Nellie work real hard and she look out for John Bottomsley and care for him when he was so sick."

"So when Papa died, it must have been very hard for her."

"Words can't tell you how much Nellie suffer. She couldn't eat and she couldn't sleep. Then when they send you off to England, it was a terrible blow. She lost the man she did love and then that Thomas Hurley send you away out of Nellie life, but Nellie used to say how John Bottomsley used to visit her at night. She say he always used to smoke his pipe."

"That is true Miss Una. I remember Papa visiting us one night. I was really frightened, but Clytie also knew he was there and came to my room to make sure I was alright. Miss Una, I thought it was Clytie who was my mother and not Miss Nellie. I knew that Clytie loved me and cared for me, but never in my wildest dreams would I have thought of Miss Nellie."

"Nellie is happy now. God send Francis for Nellie. A proper gentleman. They all want to know why Francis married Nellie. It ain't that Nellie ain't pretty, she just like my Clytie. But Nellie got a heart of gold and Francis likes that. I wasn't very happy about that marriage. I thought he married Nellie to get her money, so I had to ask him."

"You didn't Miss Una."

"Oh yes. I ask him if it was Nellie money he was after, but I find out he had his own money."

"I've never met anyone who was as straight forward as you Miss Una."

"Nellie wasn't going to ask him, so I had to. I really didn't want nobody to unfair Nellie after all those hard knocks she had already."

"So tell me Miss Una. Do you know where my son is?"

"I do Miss Emily. He is with his grandmother. I give you a whole lot o' information Miss Emily. Not it is up to you to use it accordingly. Just remember that Nellie is a good person and she couldn't help the situation she find herself in."

"That means that I am also black Miss Una."

"That don't mean nothing child. You got a gold heart and nobody looking at your skin can say that you black, but you have to be honest and tell your husband. I know he is going to understand. I can feel it right here," she said pounding at her heart.

"Thank you Miss Una. It will be difficult but I must be honest and tell him. What if he doesn't understand Miss Una?"

"Then he ain't worth it. Love is love, don't care what colour it is."

"One more question Miss Una, was Miss Nellie married before she met Francois?"

"Nellie married? Never! She did love your father, but he had a wife. Sarah Bottomsley. She would never marry nobody else. You planning to go up by Nellie when you leave here?"

"No Miss Una. I'm going home. I know my child is in safe hands, but I must talk to Alastair at once."

"You was always a sweet child and you is a nice woman. Don't ever change Miss Emily. I know I don't have too long before I get up there with my friend Miss Ella. She listening to this conversation right now and she know I am right about everything I am telling you."

"I'll come and see you again Miss Una. Tell Clytie I'll come back to see her. By the way Miss Una, do you think I look like Miss Nellie?"

"Child, you is the spitting image of your father."

Emily looked at the old woman and smiled. She had remembered Thomas Appleby's words.

*Anyone ever tell you you look just like Miss Nellie?*

It seemed as if Thomas Appleby was the only one who had noticed the resemblance.

* * *

# 65

It was her intention to head straight for home to speak with Alastair, but on the way fear took a strangle-hold on her and she decided to go to the little beach bar where her father had always taken her when there was something important to be discussed. She ordered a glass of lemonade and watched the waves as they broke on the shore, bringing with them all kinds of twigs and branches from the ocean floor. As if in a daze, tears streamed down her face and she wiped them away with her hands. Her thoughts were totally concentrated on the man she had loved more than any other, her father John Bottomsley. It seemed as if his good intentions had just about ruined her life. He too had loved her more than he loved himself and she knew he had done it all with her best interest at heart. But how could someone steal another's child? She was sitting there for more than an hour when she realised all eyes had been focussed upon her. Her drink lay before her still untouched. It was time to go. Her mind was in a fog and she headed for the next person she knew she could trust. Grandpa Bottomsley.

The old man was very happy to see her, but looking at her face he knew something was really wrong.

"Come in," he whispered, putting his finger to his lips. "Your grandmother is asleep. She hasn't been feeling very well. What's wrong?"

"May I look in on Grandma?" she asked.

"Yes, but you've got to be very quiet."

She looked at the old woman lying on the bed. The no-nonsense Millie Bottomsley was now a shadow of her former self. Even in her sleep, she no longer looked alive. This brought more tears to her granddaughter's eyes.

"She looks so helpless Grandpa."

"I know," he answered. "Tell me what your problem is Emily."

"Grandpa, do you know everything about me?"

"That's a silly question Emily. Of course I know everything about you. You are my only grandchild whom I love more than anything else."

"Then why didn't you tell me that Mama isn't really my mother?"

The old man's legs almost gave way as he struggled to sit in the nearest chair.

"Where did you hear such a stupid thing?"

"It is true, isn't it Grandpa?"

"Come and sit next to me child. I don't really know the truth Emily, but I suspected something wasn't right when my son was dying."

"So who do you think my mother is?"

Again the old man paused and wondered if he should tell all that he knew.

"You've been through so much with the loss of your baby and all that. Why don't we speak about it at another time?"

"I want to speak about it now. How could Papa do such a thing? How could he steal someone else's baby?"

"I'm sure he thought he was doing the right thing child. He knew you would be well looked after."

"So who really is mmy mother Grandpa?"

"I suspect it is Nellie," he said breathing a sigh of relief.

"You suspected it all this time?"

"I'm sorry to say I did, but what was I to do Emily?"

"Tell me the truth."

"How did you find out?"

"Miss Una told me."

"And now that you know, what are you going to do?"

"I don't know Grandpa. I must tell Alastair."

"No need to tell him child. What good would it do if you told him that Nellie is your mother?"

"You don't understand Grandpa. My son did not die. Mother was ashamed of him and got rid of him before Alastair could see him. Then she said that he had died."

"Are you saying my great grandchild is alive? Where is he?"

"Why do you think Mama got rid of him?" she asked.

"I don't know Emily."

"He doesn't look like a child with two white parents."

"Do you mean he looks black?"

"What do you think Grandpa? He is such a beautiful baby."

"My Lord!" said John Bottomsley. "This is a real predicament. I have to think. What are we going to do?"

"I will tell Alastair and then I'm going to get my baby."

"Where is the baby right now Emily?"

"With Miss Nellie and her husband Francois."

"The child is in good hands Emily. Why don't you leave him there for a while until things sort themselves out?"

"I have to think of my husband and my mother. She is ashamed of him and hates him. He is only a little innocent child."

"So why did Sarah conspire with John and do it in the first place?" he asked.

"Mama knows nothing about it."

"Do you mean Sarah thinks you are really her child?"

"As strange as it sounds Grandpa, it is really true."

"Did Una tell you all this?"

"She was there at my birth and at the birth of Mama's child which died. She has no reason to lie to me Grandpa."

"I don't know what to say," replied the old man. "This is one of the strangest things I've ever heard."

"I must be going Grandpa," she said. "Give Grandma a kiss for me when she wakes up."

The tough old man seemed on the verge of tears. His granddaughter was in a predicament and he had no idea how he could help her. She kissed him goodbye and started on her way home, her body and mind still gripped with fear.

"Papa," she shouted. "Why did you do this to me? Why Papa? Why?"

She drove and drove until she arrived at the casuarina-lined driveway of the parish church. Climbing from the car, she made her way through the cemetery to her father's tombstone. She read the words that were written there and then sat down and spoke to him as if he could hear her.

"I need your help Papa. I don't know what to do. I need you now more than ever," she said as the tears sprung like a river which had overflowed its banks.

She didn't know how long she had been there, but it was now getting dark when she made her way back to the car.

"I was so worried about you," said Alastair. "Where were you? Your grandfather called to say that your grandmother passed away in her sleep."

"But I just saw Grandma," she said as the dams burst open again and the water came gushing out again.

"Were you over there?" he asked.

"I left a little while ago," she said as she went to her bedroom, with Alastair on her heels.

"Shhhh," he said trying to console her.

"Why does life have to be so difficult?" she asked.

"She wasn't very well for a long time Emily. You know that."

"But I didn't expect her to die."

"She is no longer suffering Emily. She has gone to join your father and her son."

"That's true," she answered as if that statement brought her some relief.

"I'm glad you understand," he said hugging her closely.

"There is something I must discuss with you," she said.

"This sounds serious. What is it?"

"I don't know where to begin," she said looking into his face as he tried to wipe away the tears.

"Does it have anything to do with your mother?"

"It concerns us all," she said as she looked away.

"Tell me what it is. There is nothing we cannot handle together."

"Where is Mother?" she asked.

"She went over to your Grandfather. I wanted to go but couldn't because I had no idea where you were. Tell me what's troubling you."

"Maybe I should wait until after Grandma Bottomsley's funeral."

"Emily," he said taking her face into his hands, "if it is something which concerns our lives, I want you to tell me now. We will face it together."

"You will hate me Alastair. When I tell you, you will hate me. You won't have anything more to do with me. I am not who you think I am."

"What are you trying to say?"

"I found out today that Mama is really not my mother."

Alastair could hardly believe his ears and pushed her to tell her story.

"If Sarah is not your mother, then who is?"

"Nellie is my mother."

"You mean Nellie, Francois' wife?"

"Yes," she said staring at him to see his reaction.

"I don't understand. How did this happen?"

She related the unbelievable story to him as he stared at her. She had no idea what he was going to do and she was totally consumed with fear and started to tremble. There were no more tears. She had none left.

"It doesn't matter Emily. Nellie is a good woman. Have you spoken to her about it?"

"No, I found out today and I've spoken only to Grandpa."

"Did he know?"

"He said he had suspected something all along, but was not really sure."

He walked to the open window and looked out.

"How could Sarah have done such a thing?"

"She knows nothing about it. Papa was trying to help her out of her depression."

"But she should never have taken someone else's child."

"She knew nothing about it. She was asleep and when she awoke, I was lying beside her and she thought I was the baby she had given birth to."

"Unbelievable!" he said strolling back and forth.

"There is something else Alastair. Our baby is alive."

"What do you mean?"

Again Emily had to tell her husband the gory details of their child's disappearance. This time Alastair was not as forgiving.

"How could you allow Sarah to do such a thing to my child? How could you keep it a secret from me Emily? Where is my son?" he shouted.

"At Nellie's," she answered as he was halfway through the door.

She ran after him, but he jumped into the car and sped off. She was left alone with her troubles and no one to console her.

* * *

# 66

"I don't believe you Ma," said Clytie. "How you could do that to Nellie and to Emily?"

"I ain't do nothing wrong. That poor child was suffering and nobody had the heart to tell her the truth. If I didn't open my mouth, she would be in the mad house by now. I know exactly what she was going through. I see the same thing happen to Nellie."

"But Ma you had a right to tell Nellie and Francois what you was going to do."

"Child, it happen real sudden and I just couldn't see that child suffer no more."

Nellie ain't going to be too happy, and I ain't know what Francois is going to do. After all Nellie do for you Ma, you had a right to say something before you do it."

"Child whatever a man do in the dark, always come out in the light. You don't think she would find out? It was better to find out from somebody who was there when it happen and who could explain it and explain it real good. She ain't going to have any problem with Nellie nor Francois."

"I have to tell Nellie and you can start explaining what you did."

"Give me the telephone. I ain't frighten. I can stand behind whatever I do."

The telephone was ringing as Alastair Chambers walked up to the entrance. He called Francois onto the porch while Nellie spoke with the caller and then suddenly sat down, her hands trembling. The two men continued talking and Francois knew that the cat was finally out of the bag. Poor Nellie was beside herself with fear and did not trust herself to stand up again.

"Come in and sit down Alastair," Francois said.

He poured a measure of rum into two glasses, one of which he handed to Alastair.

"Can I have one too?" his wife asked.

Her husband poured her a small drink and the three of them sat in silence for a while.

"That was Miss Una on the telephone, wasn't it?" asked Francois.

"Yes," replied Nellie.

"Alastair knows the whole story Nellie, and I am glad this is finally out in the open. It is so difficult when a man has to lie to his best friend and a mother to her daughter."

"I didn't know what to do," said Nellie with tears streaming from her face. "I would never have given up Emily, but I wanted her to have a better future. Better than the one I had. I didn't want my daughter to go through the same hell I went through. I wanted her to go to school and have a good education. I didn't want her scrubbing pots in a kitchen and having to sleep with the Master of the house to make ends meet. I am so sorry Alastair. It wasn't Emily's fault. She didn't know anything about it. She's not to blame. You can put all the blame on me, but please don't hurt my child. I love her."

"Nellie," said Alastair calmly, "that you are Emily's mother makes no difference to me. What bothers me is how she allowed Sarah to get rid of my child without my having a say in it."

"Speaking of your child," said Francois as Douglas awoke and started to cry.

Nellie wanted to get him, but Francois was faster and brought the little bundle of joy out and put him in his arms.

"This is your son," he said to Alastair, who took the baby and gazed down into its face.

"He's a beautiful child," he said as he tenderly looked down at Douglas.

"I'll get his bottle and you can feed him," Nellie said.

"I'm glad Clytie brought him here. What would've happened if he had just disappeared? I would never have forgiven Sarah Bottomsley."

"Do you forgive Emily?" asked Francois.

"Of course I have forgiven her. I am just angry that she allowed her mother to manipulate her and then never said a word to me about it."

"Sarah Bottomsley seems like a very scheming person, but I think I can understand Emily's shock also when she realised that your child and her child was anything but white. She was probably afraid of what you might think. I think that's why she turned to Miss Una. She too needed answers, so don't be too hard on her."

"There is so much intrigue on this little island that I cannot stand it. Sometimes I really regret that Emily and I came here."

"You will learn that to live here, you must do what you want and not what other people expect or want you to do."

Nellie brought the bottle in and the hungry child drank while still in his father's arms.

"What are your plans now Alastair?" Nellie asked. "I hope you won't take Douglas away tonight."

"There is just so much going on. I forgot to mention that Emily's grandmother passed away this evening, so it won't be a good idea to take him away now."

"Millie Bottomsley passed away?" asked a shocked Nellie.

"She died in her sleep."

"Poor Emily! Everything is happening to my poor daughter all at once. Do you think I should call her Alastair?"

"She wasn't in a good frame of mind when I left."

"I'll call her," said Francois. "I'm sure she needs some comforting words at this time."

Emily was still alone and Francois' voice and his words helped to ease the pain she felt. He told her that her husband was there and had seen the child.

"What did he say?" she asked.

"It makes no difference to him. He loves his child."

If words could cure all ills, those words from Francois certainly dismissed Emily's fears and eased her troubled mind.

"I know I have no right to ask,"said Nellie, "but must you take Douglas away from us?"

"Who is Douglas?" he asked.

"My grandson," she said, her eyes looking bigger than usual.

"He is my son Nellie. I want him with us," he said as he looked at the sleeping child.

"And what about Miss Sarah?" she asked.

"I don't know what we'll do about her. There is so much on Emily's mind right now that I just don't want to ask her about her ---- Sarah."

"When is the funeral for her grandmother?" asked Francois.

"I think Sarah has gone over to talk to her husband tonight. I should be on my way home. I have been rather harsh with Emily and she needs me right now."

"Thanks so much for understanding," said Nellie.

"I will always care for Emily. She is not to be held responsible. So much in her life has changed and only a strong person could endure the things she has gone through and still be sane."

He kissed the sleeping child on its forehead and then handed it to Nellie who disappeared into the bedroom. The two men stood up and looked at each other.

"Thank you Francois. You have been a good friend. Without you, my son would probably be in the arms of a stranger. Thank you my friend."

"Thank you for not being hard on Nellie. I know she has suffered for a very long time and as you can see, she loves Emily more than she loves herself."

"I just cannot understand how he got away with it and I find it very difficult to believe Sarah knew nothing about it."

"Perhaps she did know, but closed her mind to the fact. Now after so many years, she actually believes Emily is really her child."

"I just don't know what to do about Sarah, because I will definitely take my son home with me soon. She has to accept the fact that he will live there with us."

"And if she doesn't accept him?"

"I'm sorry to say, but she will have to find some other means of accommodation or we will."

"I hope it won't come to that," replied Francois.

"Let's wait and see. Goodnight Francois. Say goodbye to Nellie. I'm sure Emily will want to come by soon to see Douglas."

"Does that mean you will keep the name Douglas?"

"I will and I'm sure Emily will too."

"Nellie will be happy to hear that. She chose the name."

"And one more thing Francois, I was in touch with the CID and they will look into the Thomas Appleby matter."

"What does that mean?"

"It means that they now know where he is. With all the confusion, I had forgotten to tell you."

"Let's hope he doesn't get a chance to escape before they reach him."

"Has Alastair left already? It wasn't as bad as I had expected," she said hanging onto her husband's arm.

"Sometimes it is better to tell the truth. The only one I feel sorry for right now is Sarah Bottomsley. How on earth is she going to explain all this?"

"Knowing Miss Sarah, she will be alright."

"Nellie please do something for me."

"What?" she asked.

"Please stop calling her Miss Sarah. She is either Sarah or Mrs Bottomsley."

"You're right as usual. Douglas is fast asleep. Let's sit and talk a little longer."

"I think you've got something on your mind Nellie."

"I was wondering what we would do without Douglas."

"You must get used to the fact that Emily is soon coming to get her son."

"It will be so different around here. Even Otty will miss him."

"I'll tell you what we'll do. We'll go to St. Lucia for a couple weeks or we can go back to Paris."

"I don't want to go so far right now. What if Sarah decides she doesn't want Douglas in the house?"

"It is no longer her house and Alastair wants our grandson home with him."

"That makes me feel good when you call him *our* grandson Francois."

"Unless you would rather not have me as his Grandpa," Francois teased her.

"You know I love it."

"Let's go to bed. He will wake up screaming any minute."

* * *

Millie Bottomsley was laid to rest next to her son. Francois went to the funeral to pay his respects leaving Nellie at home with Douglas. He couldn't help noticing how drawn and pale

Emily was. With Alastair on one side and Grandpa Bottomsley on the other, they made their way to the graveside. Sarah Bottomsley sat in the car and watched from a distance. As usual, it was too much for her and she needed to sit. Emily smiled when she saw Francois. He nodded to her and continued to sing along with all the friends and the workers who had also come to pay their respects. John Bottomsley was frail, but brave. He watched as his wife's casket was slowly lowered into the earth. Only then and for just a moment did he seem to grow weak, but his granddaughter held onto him. Millie Bottomsley had been a force to be reckoned with. She was never afraid to speak her mind. Sometimes she made her husband's life a living hell, but he would certainly miss her. She had always said she wanted to go back to England someday, but she never did and here she was buried on a tropical island beside her son.

Emily reached out and wiped a bit of earth from the inscription on her father's grave and was about to sit when Alastair tightened his grip on her arm. Still Sarah Bottomsley watched from afar. Emily, her grandfather and Alastair Chambers were the last to leave the graveside and make their way slowly back to the waiting car, where Sarah Bottomsley sat.

"I'm taking you home with us Grandpa. I won't allow you to sleep alone tonight."

"You are your father's child; always thinking about someone else. I'm happy you're my granddaughter," he said still holding onto her arm. "Alastair you've got a good wife. Take care of her. Millie and I had our differences, but I wouldn't have traded her for anything."

"Yes sir, I know Emily is a treasure," he said looking at his wife.

Francois was still waiting by his car when the family drove past. Alastair stopped and spoke to him.

"Thank you for coming," said Emily as she jumped out and hugged him. "Grandpa, this is Francois Bertrand, Miss Nellie's husband."

"Glad to meet you," he said.

She also tried to introduce her mother to him, but she kept looking straight ahead, but glanced at him through the corner of her eye. He was more handsome than she had expected.

*Nellie Peterkin was indeed a lucky woman.*

He offered his condolences and then spoke quietly with Alastair.

"We'll come to see you on the weekend," he said to Francois.

"I'll tell Nellie."

* * *

# 67

The moment had arrived when Alastair decided it was time to confront his mother in law. He chose a late evening when the servants had all gone to their homes. Emily sat beside him, her palms sweaty from fear, while Sarah sat in her late husband's plantation chair.

"I know you must be wondering why I have called this family meeting."

"I did wonder," she said as she sipped a glass of sherry.

"I want to talk to you about my son. The child you forced my wife to give up, when she was in a very vulnerable state."

Sarah Bottomsley opened her mouth to speak, but Alastair raised his hand to silence her and he continued.

"You had no right to make such a decision without first consulting me. I am Emily's husband and the father of that child. You abandoned a helpless child, and chased it out into the dark of night. My child Sarah! My child!"

"I thought …..

"What did you think?" he asked interrupting her. "That my wife was unfaithful to me? You really don't know Emily, do you? I trust her and I know she would never do anything to undermine our relationship."

"Then why was the child…….

"So dark Sarah?" he asked. "You answer that. You owe your daughter an explanation."

"I don't understand what you want me to tell her."

"Tell her the truth. Tell her you are not her mother."

"You are totally mad. What do you mean I am not her mother?"

"Sarah, think back carefully to the night your child was born. Was there anyone else on the plantation that was also in the family way or had had a newborn baby?"

"What has that got to do with anything?"

"Think back Sarah. Was there anyone?"

"Yes there was Nellie my maid."

"Isn't Nellie Emily's mother?"

"No she isn't. I'm Emily's mother," she said breaking into tears.

"Mama, you had two miscarriages before I was born, didn't you? And did the doctor not say you shouldn't ever try to have anymore children?"

"Yes but you were really healthy. You didn't die like the others."

"Sarah, why did Nellie leave the plantation?"

"Because her baby died."

"Or is it because your husband stole her baby and gave it to you?"

Sarah was now reduced to a trembling, tearful woman, who tried reaching out to her daughter.

"Tell me the truth Mama. I know the truth. Someone who was present told me the story."

"Was it Clytie?"

"No Mama, it was Clytie's mother Miss Una. She used to help the women on the plantation to deliver their babies. Don't you remember any of this Mama?"

"After so many years, I just can't remember," she said sobbing loudly.

"I know where my son is Mama and I'm bringing him back here with me."

"What will people say?"

"I don't care what people will say Mama. We do not intend to tell this story to any of the gossipmongers on this island. Life will go on as it did before, but you must stop your manipulating ways. Mama I love Miss Nellie and have from the first time I met her. She will always be Miss Nellie to me, and you will always be my Mama."

"Thank you Emily. Thank you. I don't deserve it."

"I have also been thinking of bringing Grandpa here with us. He is alone and needs company. I want to tell you that Nellie and Francois will also be our house guests and I want you to treat them with respect. It doesn't matter where Nellie started, but where she has ended. She has done a lot with her life and is well-respected by the community."

"I will do whatever you say my child."

"Mama, I want you do it because it is the right thing to do, not because I say so."

Alastair could see his wife's strength and allowed the two women to converse without interference.

"I'll say goodnight now Emily. This has been a rather hard evening for me."

"Goodnight Sarah," said Alastair.

"Will you be alright Mama?"

"I'll be alright. You go to bed. It was a hard day for you too."

Sarah closed her bedroom door and sighed as she threw her body against it.

"Next thing, Clytie and her mother will also be guests at my dinner table," she said with scorn.

"Do you think she will agree with what you said?" Alastair asked.

"I don't know, but I hope so. I would hate to have her leave."

"Do you mean you will ask her to leave?"

"It will hurt, but if I have to, I'll find her a comfortable home away from here. I cannot allow her to destroy my life and our relationship."

"Did she really think I was unfaithful to you?"

"She certainly did."

Nellie and Emily were seeing each other for the first time since the truth was known. Nellie as usual, was very nervous. Each time she heard a car go by, she rushed onto the verandah to see if they had arrived. When the moment came, she hung onto Francois' hand like a frightened child.

"Hello Miss Nellie," she said.

"Hello Emily. How are you?"

"I am very well, thank you," she said with a broad smile.

They were both very nervous and could not seem to get past their words of greeting.

"Have a seat," said Francois. "What will it be Alastair? The usual?"

"Yes and a sherry for my wife."

"And for you Nellie?"

"I'll have a sherry too," she answered with a nervous giggle.

"Miss Nellie, may I see Douglas?"

"Yes," she replied springing from her chair. "He is trying to stand up in his crib and I think he has one little tooth."

"Really? I can't believe it."

Douglas' big black pram stood proudly in the corner of the verandah with the hood pushed all the way down. Emily got up and looked inside. There was a rattle and a little sock which no doubt was her child's. She picked it up and put it to her nose and inhaled. She thought she could smell the soul of her child through the piece of clothing.

"Someone's here to see you Douglas," said Nellie as she returned with the child who had since grown somewhat.

"He is so big," said Emily.

"Do you want to hold him?" asked Nellie, trying to wipe away the dribble which was now oozing from the corner of the child's mouth.

"Oh yes Miss Nellie. I have to get used to holding him."

The child wriggled and reached for Nellie as Emily did her best to comfort him.

"Don't dribble on Emily's dress," said Nellie. "Since he got that tooth, his mouth is always wet."

"It doesn't matter Miss Nellie," said Emily trying to hold on to him as he struggled to get away from her.

"If you give him his bottle, he might calm down," said Francois.

As soon as she heard the child's cries, Otty was there with a bottle which Emily took and fed him. He looked up at her and his little fingers played with hers. The tears ran down Nellie's face. She was already losing Douglas.

"He won't be far away Nellie," said her husband trying to console her.

"Yes Nellie. You are welcome at Bottomsley anytime you choose. Of course you may bring your husband with you."

There was a bit of nervous laughter from the two women, but the men laughed heartily.

"When can I take him home Miss Nellie?"

"You can call me Nellie and whenever you choose, but you can leave him here as long as you like."

"I would like to Nellie, but then he will never get to know Alastair nor me."

"I understand."

"We will take him home next Sunday. That's the same day Grandpa will be moving in. May I bring him to see where you live Nellie?"

"He has been here already."

"Was Grandpa really here Nellie?"

"Yes."

"What did he want?"

"He said he heard I had inherited this house and wanted to see for himself."

"Oh well, you don't mind if he comes along, do you?"

"He's welcome to come along anytime," Francois replied. "And Nellie, Grandpa knows the whole story."

* * *

## 68

There was a new addition to the Bottomsley household. Emily brought her grandfather into the home since he would be well-looked after there. She couldn't bear the thought of him spending his time alone. At Bottomsley, he would have companionship. Sarah was not very happy about it, but there was nothing she could do. Although they were a little nervous, they had to be bring little Douglas home; the sooner the better.

Grandpa Bottomsley was dressed and waiting since he was accompanying them to bring the child home. Sarah sat alone on the verandah, deep in thought. She was paler than normal and when John Bottomsley spoke to her, she never replied. She hadn't heard him. He sat on the rattan chair across from her and spoke to her again.

"What did you say?" she asked.

"Grandpa," shouted Emily. "We are ready to go."

"I'mon the verandah," he replied. "I'll stay with you if you want," he said turning to Sarah.

"Thank you," she whispered.

"I'll tell Emily," he said as he left her and entered the drawing room.

"Thank you," she said again.

"Emily, I decided I'd stay with Sarah. She is a little under the weather."

"What's the matter with her?" asked Alastair.

"I guess too many changes all at oncetoo," whispered the old man.

"Don't worry. She'll get used to them," said Emily as she walked onto the verandah to speak with her mother.

"Don't take too long," said Alastair. "Our son is waiting."

"What's wrong mother?" she asked.

"Just feeling a little tired today," she replied. "It must be this dreadful heat."

"We'll be on our way to pick up our son. I hope you can at least try be a grandmother to him."

Emily did not wait for an answer, and no sooner than they were out the door, Sarah Bottomsley broke down and wept.

"Come, come Sarah. It's not so bad. You'll get used to having the little one around. Would you like Ursy to bring you a cup of tea?"

She shook her head and continued to wail; something which she had never done before.

"No one wants or cares about me Father Bottomsley."

"Of course they do Sarah. They are just a little disappointed and I'm sure in time they will forget. I'm going to get myself a drink. Would you like just a little one?"

"No."

"A little one will make you feel better."

"Just a little one," she replied.

For a little while, the two sat in silence, until Sarah began to speak.

"You know my husband worked hard to make this plantation a success. He had hoped that one day his offspring would inherit it and continue to make it work."

"I know that Sarah."

"He would be so disappointed to see the way things have turned out."

"What do you mean? The plantation is still a success; more so than before."

"He didn't think that a bunch of Negroes would be taking it over."

"Sarah Bottomsley. Are you referring to Emily?"

"Not so much Emily, but the people she has chosen to call her friends; people who have absolutely no social standing."

"I am disappointed Sarah. If Emily hears you speaking that way, you would be out on the street."

"She would never do that to me."

"Don't forget you've already annoyed them Sarah. You don't want to do anything stupid."

"Could I have another one?" she asked holding up her glass.

He returned with two drinks and sat down.

"You know John, I could fight her for the plantation."

"You don't want to do that. What would people say when you tell them your husband slept with the servant and they produced a child?" he said hoping to bring her to her senses.

"Yes, you're right. I couldn't do that. I would be a laughing stock. Nellie and my husband together? I just can't picture it."

"Are you trying to tell me you didn't know John was having an affair?"

"I knew he was having affairs, but I thought it might have been some plantation owner's daughter, but never with a servant. How could he have belittled me so?"

"These things happen Sarah and don't forget Nellie was quite an attractive girl."

"But she was a servant John."

"My son obviously didn't see it that way."

"Did you know he was seeing her?"

"You mean Nellie?"

"Isn't that who we are speaking about?"

"I didn't but just before he died, I found out."

"Did you know that Emily wasn't my child?"

"I didn't Sarah, I really didn't. Didn't you know?"

"If I had known, I guess I pushed it out of mind."

Come Sarah, you couldn't forget something that important."

She started to weep again.

"I knew Emily wasn't my child, but as time went by, I thought everything was alright. I didn't know she was Nellie's daughter."

"Whose daughter did you think she was?"

"Someone from another plantation," she replied. "She's just as white as I am John."

"That's what Mother Nature does Sarah. These things happen. Now look at Emily's son; a child from two white-skinned people. Before they return Sarah, I want to tell yo something."

"What?" she asked.

"It doesn't matter what the child looks like, it's Emily's son and my great grandson and I'm looking forward to spending my last years playing with him. I would advise you to do the same."

"But he isn't my grandson."

"He is your husband's grandson and you are still living here as Emily's mother."

"That means nothing to me."

"For your own good, you must change your way of thinking Sarah. My granddaughter will never put up with anyone not treating her child well. And Sarah, he is just an innocent little one. You can't hold him responsible for anything."

"Doesn't it bother you that you may have to sit down to dinner with Nellie and the rest of them?"

"To be honest with you Sarah, it will not bother me in the least bit. Have you seen Nellie since she left Bottomsley?"

"Yes, a couple of times."

"Nellie is no longer the Nellie of long ago. She is a respected member of her community and she has a husband who loves her; a solicitor at that Sarah!"

"She used to be my servant and I just don't want to sit down with them."

"And what will you do when they are invited?"

"I'll just stay in my room."

"You're making it harder on yourself Sarah. Lighten up and enjoy being around your family."

"They are not my family John. Do you hear me? They are not my family."

"If you are so adamant, maybe you should consider finding a home of your own."

"This is my home and I will not leave it."

"Remember everything here belongs to Emily. Do not put her in the position of asking you to leave Sarah."

"Would she throw her own mother on to the street?"

"You're being irrational Sarah. First you say she's not your family, then you say you are her mother. Take my advice and try to get along with them."

"Do you really think she would put me on the street John?"

"I don't know Sarah, but if I were you, I wouldn't put it to the test."

* * *

Nellie paced back and forth and kept looking into the street because Alastair and Emily had not yet arrived. They were late and the evening sun was beginning to set. She went back to the bedroom where Douglas and Hurley were trying to communicate with each other. Those two were really going to miss each other.

"Sit down Nels," said Clytie. "You are making me real nervous."

"Why you don't bring out Douglas so we can play with him for the last time?" asked Miss Una.

"He and Hurley are trying to talk to each other," Nellie replied.

"As long as they are only talking," replied the old woman. "I never did like that name. It reminds me of that beast that used to run Bottomsley. He and the devil must be fighting to see who is in charge."

"How you know he ain't gone to heaven Ma?"

"People like that only got one way to go, and that is down."

Normally Nellie would have reacted to the name Hurley, but her mind was so preoccupied that she didn't hear the conversation between the two women.

Alastair and Emily arrived in the village to find crowds of people blocking the way.

"What's going on?" he asked.

"I don't know, but it doesn't seem to be anything serious."

As they got closer, they realised the whole village had come out to see a film on the mobile cinema. It was not due to start for another couple hours, but they all wanted to be up front and close to the screen, because they thought they would be able to see better. Slowly the group made way for the car to pass, each one of them peering in and waving as they drove by. It was now too late to visit Miss Una, so they continued directly to Nellie's home.

"What took you so long?" asked Nellie as Francois came through the door. "I thought Emily would take Douglas before you got back."

"The villagers are getting ready for the show."

"What show?" she asked.

"The show you begged them to put on because six of your students have won scholarships to enter high school."

"I just have too much on my mind. I really did not remember."

"I understand," he said hugging and squeezing her.

"But what has that got to do with your being late?" she asked.

"I couldn't get through the village."

"My Francis?" said Miss Una. "Come here and let an old woman touch your flesh. I ain't see you for a real long time."

He greeted Clytie and then hugged the half-blind lady.

"We losing little Douglas, but a child belong with the mother. I know it is going to be hard, but Emily is a good girl and you going to see that child more often than you think."

"I hope so Miss Una," he replied.

"They're here," said Nellie running in and heading straight for the bedroom. She returned with Douglas who had already been dressed for the journey. "You want to hold him one more time Miss Una?"

"Let me feel his flesh for the last time," she said as she suddenly called out to Nellie.

"You need to clean him Nellie. Lord his pants full of doo doo."

"Let me help," said Emily as she and Alastair came in the door.

"Yes, it would be a good experience for you. You going to have a lot of that to do."

Alastair greeted them, and went over to Miss Una. He had grown rather fond of the straight-forward old lady. He took her hand.

"You must be the tall one; Emily husband. I can't see so good so you have to excuse me."

"That's alright. I hope you come down to visit. We don't want you to forget Douglas."

"If it is alright with you, I would like to see him again before I leave this earth."

"I hope that's a promise."

Nellie and Emily appeared once again with Emily carrying the child who was struggling to get out of her arms and into Nellie's.

"We should be going soon," said Alastair. "It's dark and we want to get him home to bed."

There was a knock on the kitchen door and Otty came in. She was crying and this threw everyone else into hysterics.

"When I going to see Douglas again?" she asked. "I would help to look after him. Miss Bertrand say she is too old. She isn't too old and I don't mind running behind him. Now he is going and I ain't going to see him again."

"You will see him," said Emily. "I promise I will bring him by at least once a week."

"Sorry but we've got to go," said Alastair.

Everyone stood on the verandah while Douglas' things were packed into the car. Emily held him in her arms but he cried and stretched out his little arms to Nellie, who could no longer watch as the family climbed into the car and slowly drove away.

"This is a real sad day," said Clytie. "I can't believe the little one is gone for good."

"Don't worry about that child. We know he in good hands," said Miss Una. "That Alastair is a good man."

Nellie buried her face in Francois' chest. She felt as if her heart would break. It reminded her of the day when JB had taken Emily away from her and handed her to Sarah Bottomsley. She looked at the empty pram which still stood in the corner of the verandah and knew she would no longer be pushing Douglas around it.

"I have three weeks holiday," he whispered to her. "I'll take you back to Paris."

"I don't want to go to Paris right now," she said sadly. "Suppose something happens to Douglas when we are so far away."

"Nothing will happen. Besides he is with his parents."

"What if Sarah does something bad to him?"

"Nellie, the woman is selfish, but she isn't wicked. Besides she doesn't want to be on Emily's bad side."

"Alright, we can go away, but only as far as St. Lucia."

"It would be good for you to get away from here for a while. So when should we go?"

"Next week?"

* * *

## 69

Under his mother's watchful eye and John Bottomsley's doting, Douglas was quickly settling down. He was the apple of Ursy's eye, but Emily wanted to have a part in her child's upbringing. She recalled how her mother had left her with Clytie and Miss Ella, and she would not allow the same thing to happen to her son. It wasn't that she didn't care for the two women who showered her with love, but she had so yearned for her mother's affection. Sarah Bottomsley smiled with him, but never did take him into her arms to feed him or to comfort him. She seemed afraid. The more he grew, the more he resembled his departed grandfather.

There was a question on the lips of the island's people.

*"Where did the child come from?"*

The parents offered no explanations, except he was their child. Many considered him to be adopted, but The Chambers thought it none of their business.

Nellie had grown used to the child's absence, but Hurley didn't. He sat on the bed and stared into the empty crib in the corner of the room. Then he would purr like a crying child.

The Bertrands took off on their vacation to St. Lucia, a much needed diversion from the sadness of losing the child. Meta was there to cater to them and she had bought everything she thought they would like. She now respected Nellie, but it was difficult to say if she really liked her. There was no question when it came to Francois. She not only respected, but adored him.

"He's gone Mr. Francois," she said.

"Who's gone?" he asked Nellie who just raised her shoulders. "Who's gone Meta?"

"Mr.Applewhite. He just disappear."

"Why do you say disappear?" he asked.

"Because some white men come by looking for him, but a couple days before that, he left the island. I hear they were policemen from overseas. I did always think there was something strange about Mr. Applewhite, and his real name wasn't even Applewhite."

"What about his home? Did he sell it?"

"I hear that when they went there, there was a pot o' food still on the stove. He didn't have time to sell anything."

"Are you trying to say they didn't find him?"

"When they went there, he was gone. They think somebody tell him and he just disappear."

"What about his daughters?"

"It look as if they left with him carrying along the baby too."

"What baby?" asked Nellie.

"The first daughter was in the family way and had a baby about two months before they disappear."

"I don't believe it," said Nellie. "He is really a nasty man. He should be in jail."

"Well he ain't in jail and nobody ain't know where he is."

"Too bad!" said Francois, "and Alastair did all that work for nothing."

"What you say Mr. Francois?"

"Nothing, I was just thinking out loud."

Nellie and Francois sat on the verandah discussing what they had heard earlier regarding Ted Applewhite.

"I wish they hadn't changed his name," she said.

"His real name is Appleby, not Applewhite," said Francois. "He changed it himself to avoid the authorities."

"Not him," she said. "I'm talking about Douglas."

"I think they did the right thing. They are his parents. His name should be Chambers and not Bertrand."

"You're right, but I still miss him."

"Of course you miss him. He was with us for almost one year. And don't forget you're still his grandmother."

"What about Sarah?"

"I had two grandmothers on my mother's side."

"What do you mean?" asked Nellie with a furrowed brow.

"My life wasn't always a bed of roses Nellie. Do you remember I told you my mother looked like you?"

"Yes."

"Yes Nellie. My father was French and was sent to one of the French Islands in the Caribbean to teach. There he met my mother who was also a teacher. It didn't matter that my mother was an educated woman, she was still considered nobody because she wasn't white."

"You have never said anything about this before."

"That's true."

"So what happened?"

"My mother was in the family way and since she was not married, it carried a lot of shame. Do you know what that meant Nellie? My mother's family were middle class people and she was an educated woman. Because she didn't live up to the standards of a so-called middle class family, they deserted her when she most needed them. She became a social outcast. She did not fit in with the white colonials, her people no longer wanted her and the black people were suspicious of her. My father persuaded her to leave with him for Paris, but she refused in spite of the way she was being treated. When I was two years old they finally got married, but that changed nothing. Not only did I not fit in, but I was considered a bastard."

"Oh Francois, why didn't you tell me?" she asked. "But they got married. Didn't that mean anything?"

"My mother just didn't fit in. She wasn't white and her people thought she had committed a horrible sin. She was never invited to any parties, and after a while, neither was my father. My mother swore she would never allow me to go through what she and my father suffered, so they packed me off to boarding school in England."

"Is that the reason you came here instead of going back to your island?"

"Yes and no. I didn't like England and I didn't want to go back home, especially since my parents had already passed on, so I decided I had to go somewhere where I could practise law and use what I had learnt in England. The opportunity presented itself so I settled here in Barbados."

She drew closer to him and held his hand tightly. She had no idea that this charming man she had married had also suffered the same way she did.

"You told me it was an accident," she said.

"My parent's death? I don't know, but they said my father had been drinking. He did drink a great deal. I guess it was his way of handling the situation. Well they both died on that fateful night."

"It must've been hard for you," she said squeezing his hand a little tighter.

"It certainly was. Now you see why Alastair is a man to be admired. Douglas is his son and nothing will ever change that. I wish my father had had the same kind of backbone. He was rather weak and depended on my mother's strength. Had the accident occurred when I was still a young boy, I don't know what would've happened to my life, but I had just finished law school and was able to support myself through the apprenticeship with the money from the sale of my parents' home."

"I wish you had told me Francois. But looking at you, no-one would know your mother looked like me."

"But I never forgot it Nellie. I know who I am and I am proud of who I am. Because I look the way I do, has opened many doors for me on the Rock. How little they do know!" he said staring out at the ocean.

"You were lucky. My mother had a hard life since my father refused to recognise me. Only Nora's father kept us from starving."

No more words were said. They quietly watched the ocean play before their eyes.

"Francois, I must tell you something."

"What is it Nellie?"

"Do you remember how everyone always wondered what happened to Thomas Hurley?"

"I know ......

He put his finger to her lips.

"Whatever happened must have been an accident," he said.

She tried again to say something, but he prevented her from continuing. She was now convinced her husband knew the truth surrounding Thomas Hurley's disappearance.

* * *

There was harmony in the Chambers-Bottomsley household. Sarah Bottomsley seemed to know her place and kept to it. A nip of rum which she shared each evening with John Bottomsley helped to make the situation more bearable. The two imbibed daily on the porch and watched the setting sun make its final escape beyond the horizon. His presence and common sense saved her from a fate worse than death; embarrassment.

Douglas was now two years old and had learnt to say Grandpa. John Bottomsley was as pleased as could be. The bigger he got, the lighter his skin became. The resemblance to his mother and his grandfather was frightening. He was the apple of his great grandfather's eye, and he taught him secretly to say Grandma.

"Grandma," he said one day to Sarah Bottomsley.

The tears flowed down Sarah's face. There was no more fear or hatred in her heart for the child. Sarah was a changed woman as far as Douglas was concerned.

"Nellie, we would like to come by on the weekend and bring Douglas for a visit."

"You don't have to ask Emily. You know we would be happy to see you."

The child seemed to remember Hurley. He ran after it and pulled its tail, but Hurley was now old and quite cranky, and tried to scratch him.

"Grandma," yelled the child looking at Nellie.

"It's alright," she replied.

"Did you hear what he called you?" asked Francois.

"Did he really say Grandma?" she asked.

"He certainly did."

"Say Grandma again," said Nellie.

"Grandpa," he said this time bringing tears to Francois' eyes.

"Who taught him to say that?" asked Nellie as she watched him running again after Hurley.

"Grandpa, Grandpa,"

"Leave Hurley alone," said Nellie. "He is old and tired and will scratch you."

"Do you ever wonder what happened to Thomas Hurley?" Emily asked.

Nellie's face turned ashen.

"Did I say something wrong?" Emily asked.

"I just remembered how much I hated him for sending you so far away."

"He can't do that anymore. My mother should never have married him in the first place, but I guess she was lonely."

"Perhaps," said Nellie as she looked up and found her husband looking directly at her. "And whatever happened to his sister Ginger?"

"Mama said that after he disappeared, she simply up and left the island."

"The last thing I heard was that she met a gentleman from her England and returned home."

"I hope she's happy," said Emily.

* * *

## 70

Life at Bottomsley couldn't have been better. Emily stayed at home to look after her son's upbringing while Alastair continued to manage the plantation which was still a great success. Ursy fell into the same trap as her friend Clytie. As much as she wanted to leave Bottomsley, she found it difficult to leave Douglas Chambers. There was nothing she wouldn't do for the little boy. Sarah Bottomsley carried on with her game of pretence but it was clear she did not relish the thought of sitting down to dinner with Nellie; the woman she thought had taken her place in her husband's bed and in his heart; and the woman to whom she had almost lost her daughter. Sometimes Alastair would seek the elder Bottomsley's advice when it came to matters of the plantation, but his sole interest was his great grandson, who was now four years old.

"Read to me Grandpa," Douglas would say to him. And so the great grandfather would begin.

*"Once upon a time, there were two neighbours who just couldn't get along. There was the sly old Brer Fox and his neighbour Brer Rabbit who tried to keep out of his way. Brer Fox had always hoped that one day he would catch Brer Rabbit and cook him for dinner because Brer Fox really loved rabbit stew. He kept laying traps for the poor little rabbit and one day he finally caught him."*

*"That's the end for you Brer Rabbit," said the greedy Brer Fox, as he licked his lips. "Tonight I'll put you in the pot and my family and I will have rabbit stew for dinner."*

*"Please do not kill me," begged poor Brer Rabbit. "What will happen to my children if you eat me?"*

*Brer Fox thought about his own children for a while and what would happen to them if something ever happened to him.*

*"Please Brer Fox," pleaded Brer Rabbit. "Do anything with me, but don't throw me into the briar patch."*

*Brer Fox realised how fearful Brer Rabbit was of the briar patch and he himself knew how uncomfortable and painful a briar patch could be, so instead of killing Brer Rabbit, he threw him with one big swoop into the long and sharp thorns of the briar patch. Then Brer Fox peeped inside to see what Brer Rabbit was doing.*

*"How do you feel now Brer Rabbit?" he asked. "I know you wish that I had killed you," shouted Brer Fox.*

*Brer Rabbit laughed out loud and he laughed and laughed.*

*"Thank you Brer Fox. Oh thank you for throwing me here. Oh thank you Brer Fox," he said as laughed even louder. "I was born and bred in the briar patch."*

"Did you like the story?" the old man asked Douglas.

"And what did Brer Fox have for dinner," he asked.

"Nothing," said John Bottomsley. "Brer Fox and his children went to bed that night without any dinner."

"Brer Fox was bad. I'm glad he didn't have any dinner," said the child.

Emily listened in silence as the old man told the same story her father had told her many years before. A smile crossed her lips as she ran her hand over her bulging stomach. She was going to have a second child, Douglas' brother or sister.

* * *